W9-AYK-054

More Advanced Praise for *Suspicious Circumstances*

"Sandra Ruttan's *Suspicious Circumstances* soars. It is complex, exciting, and elegant. In musical terms, it's listening to Bach. I'm in love with Lara Kelly, the smart, strong, vulnerable protagonist. Her detective lover better move fast or I'm in there. A gripping adventure, a large cast of marvelous characters, and twists that follow turns. Read it. You'll love it too."

Robert Fate, Author of *Baby Shark*

"A well executed procedural with a spark between our protagonists, an excellent feel for political machinations on a small town scale and a plot that twists and turns like a bad tempered rattlesnake."

Russel D. McLean, Crime Scene Scotland

"In a town plagued by corruption and peopled with citizens afraid to talk, cop Tymen Farraday and reporter Lara Kelly form an uneasy alliance to investigate a mysterious videotape which hints at the death of a woman. In *Suspicious Circumstances*, Sandra Ruttan has created a gritty suspense novel driven by realistic dialogue and a knowledge of the unpredictable legal system. She also explores the potential for evil in the human heart, even as her protagonists, emotionally guarded but touchingly brave, try to delve into that very depravity. *Suspicious Circumstances* is a plot with endless twists and turns, lots of unexpected heroes and villains, and enough unanswered questions to keep you reading to the very end!"

Julia Buckley, Author of *The Dark Backward*

Suspicious Circumstances grabs you by the throat on a storm-swept cliff's edge, and never lets go. Sandra Ruttan writes with a machine gun rhythm that pulls you through every unexpected twist and dark turn in her complex and richly drawn debut. Don't have plans when you sit down to read this tasty, dazzling thriller. Every page of *Suspicious Circumstances* leave you gasping—and begging for more."

Bill Cameron, Author of *Lost Dog*

"Sandra Ruttan weaves a delicious tale of cops and reporters. I learned things about both that I never expected. A real treasure."

Sharon Wildwind, Author of *Some Welcome Home*

"Sandra Ruttan has graced the world of psychological thrillers with this fast-paced, absorbing tale, fraught with corruption, murder, mistrust, a number of unconscionable villains and two exceptionally likable protagonists, all craftily entangled in a delightfully twisted plot. Sit back and be prepared to get lost in this riveting story, because you won't want to put it down until you've turned the very last page."

JB Thompson, Author of *The Mozart Murders*

"*Suspicious Circumstances* twists and turns and twists again, leaving the reader breathless and unsure which end is up. And that's just the beginning. Ruttan's deft touch intrigues and satisfies, making her a powerful new force in the mystery field."

JT Ellison, Author of *All the Pretty Girls*
Available Nov. 2007

SUSPICIOUS CIRCUMSTANCES

A NOVEL

BY
SANDRA RUTTAN

TICO PUBLISHING

PUBLISHER'S NOTE: This is a work of fiction. Names, characters, places and incidents either are the product of the author's imagination or are used fictitiously, and any resemblance to actual persons, living or dead, business establishments, events or locales is entirely coincidental.

TICO Publishing
Moreno Valley, CA
Crooksville, OH
www.ticopublishing.com

Library of Congress Control Number: 2006937994

ISBN-13: 978-0-9777688-9-9
ISBN-10: 0-9777688-9-9

Printed and bound in the United States of America.

DESIGNED BY:
Kathrine Rend - Rend Graphics
www.rendgraphics.com

Dedication

For Kevin. I dreamed. You believed.

CHAPTER 1

Pulsing light shimmered on the rock face. Thunder rumbled, lightning flashed and, for a moment, the image of the woman was clear. She scrambled along the ledge, glanced back over her shoulder and pulled herself onto the crest of the hill. Her loose, white shirt and dark hair were buoyed by the wind. Then the light faded and the black of the moonless night engulfed her.

The moan of the wind and drumming of rain softened. Electricity crackled as the woman backed away from the trees toward the ledge, her arms outstretched. Lightning shot through the sky again as she wavered on the edge, then fell out of sight as the thunder rumbled one last time before the picture turned to static.

Reporter Larimer Kelly looked down at the remote in her hand as she pressed the mute button and set the VCR to rewind. She could feel the vacant gaze of the man sitting on the chair on the other side of her desk and raised her eyes a millimeter at a time until she was looking Mr. Brodie in the eye.

"Jest like I said. One second she's there an... and then..." He raised his hands suddenly, spraying water from the hat he was holding. "Then she's gone," he added with a shrug.

Lara wiped water from her cheek and drew a deep breath. She studied the enlarged eyes, the somber, wrinkled face, the broad shoulders and coveralls that made her think of plumbers or mechanics. The bumbling, oversized hands that bore nicks and scars, suggesting manual labor. Picturing him holding a hammer wasn't hard, but a sophisticated video camera?

"How much for it?"

She quoted a price for the video and then added, "If I run a story and if it turns out to be a big one, there'll be a bonus."

"Oh, okay." He scratched his head, which was covered with thinning brown hair that looked like it hadn't been cut in some time.

"I do have some questions for you, Mr. Brodie."

The hands went up again and the misshapen hat sailed across the desk. Lara picked it up with her fingertips, and tossed it back to him.

"S-sorry about that."

"It's only water." She mopped up the spray with a napkin and tossed it in the garbage. This man had walked into her office ten minutes earlier, a complete stranger, offering to sell her a video for a story. Lara had thought of politicians and prostitutes or cops taking bribes, not a woman falling off a ledge. "You were about to say something."

"Oh." His forehead wrinkled and he raised his overgrown eyebrows. "Oh yeah. Duane. Call me Duane."

"How did you get this on video?"

He rubbed his nose with his thumb, looking at the ceiling. "My camera was on. I was taping the lightning. And took some pictures of the storm. With my Pentax."

"Do you do a lot of filming?"

"Sold some photos to the magazines for those weather people. Storm-chasers. Now I'm figurin' out how to use the camcorder. Wanna see my pictures?"

"Another time, perhaps." She bit her lip. The video was disturbing. There was a real possibility she'd just watched the last few moments of someone's life before they fell to their death, but was it newsworthy?

Or was someone playing a joke? "Why didn't you take this to the police?"

"Oh, I did. They say there ain't nobody missin'." His face resembled a pug as the skin billowed into rows of folds. "They asked if I'd been drinkin'."

"Had you?" Not that it mattered. Either the tape was a hoax or it wasn't. Whether or not the cameraman had been drinking wouldn't change that.

Duane's eyes widened. "No, Ma'am. I swear."

"Call me Lara."

"Layr-ra. Lara. Like Sara." He nodded, staring down at the floor, his pink cheeks deflating. He glanced up a second later. "The cop said... somethin' 'bout how ye can't, you know, no reason to start lookin'..."

"To launch an investigation without evidence of a crime?"

"Yep." He pointed hat and hand at her. She pressed against the back of her chair until she was sure the sodden article was staying on the other side of the desk. That line was a test. Police investigated reports of suspicious activity and then determined if there was a crime, they didn't wait until a body fell on their desk. Even in Oakridge. Still, it didn't prove he was lying.

"The police watched the video?"

Duane frowned. "No. They jest said it's likely nothin' 'cause nobody's missin'."

"Do you remember which officer you talked to?"

She frowned as he stared at the ceiling, looking like he was digging through dusty boxes in his brain, searching for the right answer. Something about this didn't add up. The twisting in her gut started again.

Duane stopped staring into space and started poking in his pockets until he produced a card, which he passed to her.

Officer Robson Walker. Nobody she'd heard of in the few months she'd been in Oakridge, so not one of the cops with a history. That didn't mean he was clean, though. Just that he didn't have a reputation. She copied the information and handed it back. "If I print a story the police might want to talk to you."

Duane nodded his apparent understanding, gave her a lop-sided smile and took the money she offered him. Using both hands to pull his hat on, he half-shrugged and waved.

He stood in the doorway and looked from left to right.

"Go left."

"Oh yeah. Thanks."

Lara picked up her pen, twirling it in her fingers as she sat staring at the doorway for a moment. Curls swept across her forehead and blocked her eyes. She tucked the strands behind her ears, took a deep breath and picked up the phone to call in her first favor.

***

It was a few hours later when the stocky form of Lara's editor filled her doorway.

"Burning the midnight oil?" he asked.

"I thought you left for the day."

"To play golf. If the staff think I'm lazy, they don't suspect I'm checking up on them."

Lara felt a shiver trickle down her spine. Hatcher's reputation wasn't a secret. He spied on his reporters, had a long-standing feud with a local police captain and used his position with the paper to schmooze with local politicians. Lara had spent three years working at the New Haven Register before she'd accepted the job offer in Oakridge and had only been at The Ledger for a few months. During her time in New Haven she'd heard stories about Ted Hatcher, mostly about his obsession with taking down Patrick Collins, the captain of the 14th Precinct, a department shadowed by rumors of scandal and corruption.

Which made the potential scope of Duane's video more interesting.

"You working on that piece for the Historical Society?"

She nodded at the television. "See for yourself."

Ted Hatcher was an imposing man, a quarterback for some college football team until he'd wrecked his knee and been benched permanently. Despite the helmet crashing he was perceptive. Lara watched him process the contents of the video. He had the same detached look as Duane, apparently indifferent to the implications for a family who might this very moment be wondering where this woman was, praying for her safe return.

When the screen went to static, he snorted. "Is that it?"

She paused, thinking of what her research had turned up so far. If Hatcher knew everything, she had a pretty good idea of what he'd say, so she held back, only telling him what Duane had said about being turned away by the police.

"The boys at the One-Four will hate you."

Lara fought to keep her chin from jutting out. She hadn't been in Oakridge long, but was already tired of being kept on the sidelines. Hatcher gave her routine assignments and feature pieces. She'd told him when they negotiated a contract that her priority was investigative journalism. Hard news. Not 101 Ways To Groom a Poodle.

"Might be a good idea to pass this on to someone with a bit more experience."

Lara felt her back stiffen as she reached for the VCR remote. "I can handle it."

Hatcher flashed her a condescending smile. "Police incompetence? Here? With this precinct? Honey, you don't even know who the players in this story are, never mind where to start."

She unclenched her jaw. "There wouldn't even be a story if it wasn't for me. It's mine."

He glared at her but she didn't flinch as she returned his gaze. The whir of the rewinding videotape slowed and the machine clicked off. The ticking of a clock was a faint whisper, as though it feared intruding on the silence as they stared each other down. Finally he snorted, then shrugged.

"Chase it down, try to work the incompetence angle, take this right up to the captain's office." Hatcher propelled himself out of the chair, and walked to the door.

"One step at a time," she said. But Hatcher was already gone.

The gleam in Hatcher's eye, the lilt in his voice when he'd mentioned Captain Collins... She locked the video and files in her safe and bit her lip, thinking again that the tape better not be a hoax.

***

Vern Fletcher sat at the far end of the bar, away from his usual spot in the center of the action. Bars always suited a double purpose for a journalist: anesthetic for the soul and gossip for the job. A little bit of alcohol was all it took to loosen most tongues, often prompting the privileged few who knew something juicy to throw caution to the wind, and he was the kind of reporter who didn't mind drinking his way to a scoop. Not if it kept his boss, Ted Hatcher, off his back.

Bar talk didn't interest him tonight, though. His mind was replaying his conversation with Teo Chan.

He'd been on his way to his car when he saw the Asian man approaching the front doors of the Oakridge Ledger, the newspaper where Vern had worked for more years than he cared to think about.

Vern felt the skin between his brows pinch together. He'd come to The Ledger with fire and zeal and traded in all his enthusiasm for jaded realism as the job swallowed his life, chewing him up and spitting him out in the process. It was like he'd been living in a fog. By the time getting a scoop didn't seem so damned important and he'd shaken the clouds off, he went home and realized the place was half empty, his wife gone.

Work had become a routine, what he did to pay the bills, bringing in enough to keep him one step ahead of his bar tab.

It was a Friday night. He'd clocked his eight hours, was more than ready to settle down on a stool and have a drink or three.

Until he set eyes on Mr. Chan.

Vern couldn't even put his finger on what it was about Mr. Chan that had attracted his attention. Something about the desperate look in his eye, the way his shoulders quivered visibly, even from across the parking lot.

Whatever it was, Vern had put the bar on hold and talked to the distraught man. Now that he knew about Mr. Chan's problem, his missing niece, Vern wondered if he'd lost the ability to smell a story from a mile off after all. He might not be as washed out as he'd thought.

If Hatcher knew what he had planned for the weekend he'd probably have a stroke. A ghost of a smile flickered across his lips and he gulped the rest of his drink down, waving off Freddie's offer of a refill. *Screw Hatcher. This lead is mine.*

***

Monday morning, at the 14th Precinct, Tymen Farraday was watching his partner tell old war stories.

Lenny Becker was holding court in the center of the detectives' desks. Becker was a seasoned cop who somehow managed to avoid developing a beer belly, despite being in his mid-forties, with thinning brown hair and sallow skin that hinted at years of hard drinking, hard living and hardly taking care of himself.

"This guy staggers over, puts his hand on my shoulder and says, 'Man, how did that happen?' I'm like, 'Let me guess. You were asleep at the wheel.' And the guy swears he's not a sheep. So Mike says..."

Farraday didn't hear the rest of the story. He looked up as his captain marched over and the men stopped laughing, straightened and backed away. A copy of the local paper landed on Farraday's desk.

Captain Patrick Collins had sandy hair, cropped short, and a trim, athletic build. Something about his dark-eyed stare suggested he knew exactly what was going on with his detectives, even if he hadn't been in the room to hear it.

Farraday scanned the headlines, wondering if the Miller trial had gone sour. It was bad enough that the county ME had been accused of mishandling the evidence recovery in the deaths of prostitutes that had been written off as suicides. Some reporter had been claiming they were murders. Now, allegations that evidence had been mishandled in the Miller case were being used as grounds to push for a dismissal. Farraday hadn't been in Oakridge long enough to handle a call that fell inside county lines and he was glad, because a lot of solid casework could get tossed if the accusations were proven.

"I don't like surprises, Farraday."

"Sir?"

Captain Collins yanked the paper open, pointing to a story at the top of the outside column. "Larimer Kelly makes it look like we're all sitting on our desks wiping icing from our tie instead of doing our jobs."

Collins glared at Becker, who dropped both tie and napkin.

"Where's the report on the Lakeview Hotel robbery?" Collins asked.

Becker pulled a file out from under his partially eaten honey-glazed. "Waiting on fingerprints and cross-checking recent employees with priors."

"Then tear yourself away from the pastry and get back to work."

Becker mumbled something unintelligible as he got off his desk and picked up the phone. From the corner of his eye Farraday could see that his partner was still watching him.

Farraday was the new detective. It wasn't that Lenny was that old, but his air of authority made it clear that in the pecking order at the 14th Precinct, Becker was at the top of the ladder. More than Farraday's clean-cut suit-and-tie polish, dark hair and youth marked the differences between them. Farraday had the feeling Becker didn't like him. Something about the way he'd look up to find Lenny staring at him through narrow slats, the hint of a snarl tugging at the corners of his mouth, always too quickly replaced by an over-enthusiastic grin that rang false.

Of course, Farraday already knew what he thought of Becker. But that wasn't the point. He had a job to do, and if he couldn't get his partner to trust him...

"Look into this," Collins said, tapping the paper with his finger. "Some hotshot pencil pusher isn't going to make my squad the local laughing stock. If this Kelly is stirring up trouble I want him shut down."

Becker turned back to his desk as Collins spun around. Collins kept his stare fixed on Lenny for a moment before he turned back to Farraday. "Can you handle this?"

Farraday put the snickers and knowing looks of the men around him out of his mind. "Yes sir." He was on his way out the door before Collins had a chance to say anything else.

***

Oakridge wasn't big by American standards, but its proximity to Hartford, as well as the pristine lakes, and affordable housing prices had turned it into a bedroom community. Now that the population was edging toward the 90,000 mark the city was expanding. With growth came road construction and business development at the end of town where the 14th Precinct was located, named not for the number of precincts in the city but for the street it was on. And just to further confuse things, the One-Four was the equivalent of a downtown precinct, the main station housing detectives working serious crimes.

As Farraday drove first from the station to the library for some background and then to The Ledger, the gleaming facades of new high rises and business developments gave way to older, established buildings that were gradually getting facelifts. The area was fondly called *Old Town* by the locals, who'd been around long enough to remember when there was little more than the Douglas family industries to offer employment to local residents who didn't want to work in the city.

Farraday hadn't been in Oakridge long, but knew the one thing this police captain wouldn't tolerate was a reporter out to upstage the police department. Larimer Kelly had pushed a button. He had to make sure it didn't happen again.

Walking through the door to The Ledger, he felt like a hundred-pound weight had been dropped on his chest.

The easy smile of the woman at the reception desk dropped from her face in half a heartbeat as she looked at him. Her dark hair was swept up in a relaxed bun, the crow's feet exaggerated by the widening of her eyes. Mid-thirties, Farraday guessed, fairly trim, attractive and clearly not someone who was fooled by appearances, despite the fact that he was more likely to be mistaken for a politician than a local police officer. There was something about the look that settled on her face that told him she knew he was a cop, despite the cut of his suit.

"I'm here to see Larimer Kelly."

She pushed the corners of her mouth up with artificial politeness as she stood behind her desk, staring at him. "Do you have an appointment?"

Stifling a sigh, he forced a smile of his own, one he hoped passed as contrite and apologetic. "No, I don't."

The woman stepped back, moving toward an open doorway. The hum of discussion emanated from the room, although it was far enough from where Farraday was that he couldn't make out the words. "I'm not sure if Larimer is available. Wait here while I check."

Farraday had enough time to consider looking for the office on his own before the receptionist reappeared. This time, the smile was authentic, although something about the look in her eye made Farraday's shoulders stiffen. "Follow me."

Within a minute, he'd been left inside an office without another word from the woman. It didn't take him long to inspect the contents of the shelves. What was missing told him more than what was present.

There was nothing of life outside of work. Awards, books, files, as one might expect. No pictures of a wife and kids, a dog.

If he couldn't get Kelly in line he could find himself doing battle with a journalist, becoming a pawn in a game, finding his own name on the front page. Again.

Reporters. He'd grown up watching his dad deal with press conferences, prepping every answer, preparing for the inevitable ambush.

And then there was Katarina.

The sound of footsteps in the hall had Farraday turning before he thought better of it. A woman stepped past the open doorway, then stopped and came back, creases lining her brow while her bright blue eyes seemed to see right through him.

"Can I help you?"

Young, with auburn curls cascading over her shoulders. 5'5" or maybe 5'6", with a bit of shape to her, and not in a bad way. No make-up, just a creamy, clear complexion. The khaki pants, hiking shoes and a t-shirt she wore betrayed her. Not a secretary, judging from the clothes, but at ease, as though she belonged there.

A journalist.

He forced a tight smile and shrugged. "I'm just waiting." Farraday's issues with the press made it hard enough to keep his head clear. He didn't need any distractions.

"Okay." She pushed a curl back from her forehead. The wrinkles on her brow vanished and there was a glint in her eye.

He looked away, remembering the risks. His presence would stir Kelly's curiosity, shedding the scent of a bigger story on the horizon. If he didn't handle this right, he could find himself in the middle of a whole new set of problems and the last thing he needed was more trouble.

Farraday glanced back at the doorway. The woman was gone.

***

"Jimmy, I need a favor." Lara burst into the windowless office that doubled for Jimmy Wilkes' darkroom, the words tumbling out.

"It must be important."

She felt the heat in her cheeks and groaned. "I forgot."

Jimmy's cynical smile was replaced by a wide grin. "It's okay. I'm finished." He was more than a photo jock. An award-winning reporter in his own right, he was one of the few remnants of the old guard that had been at The Ledger before Hatcher took over and still had a few contacts in the police department who fed him information when he needed it. Which wasn't often, given his preference to work with photos instead of arguing with their domineering editor. Modern technology could have eliminated this part of his job but Jimmy was a stickler for the old art of mixing chemicals and hand-developing prints. He'd enlarged and cropped out enough background images to end careers and secure his own. There were some things a wide-angle zoom lens could get that a digital cameral wouldn't do the trick for, not yet anyway.

"I'd be happy to have you owe me. What do you need?"

"Here." Each reporter had a tray, where they could find prints Jimmy developed for them. Lara removed a packet with her name on it and handed it to him. "Put this on my desk and come right back."

"Why should I...?" His eyes narrowed but he didn't argue. "This better be good."

About twelve years older than Lara, she couldn't remember ever seeing Jimmy in anything but jeans, usually torn, and shirts sporting the logos of rock bands. His wavy brown hair was typically awry. Good-natured. Fair. The antithesis of Hatcher.

Jimmy was the only one who'd really made her feel welcome at The Ledger.

The easy-going smile was gone when he returned.

"He's a cop?"

"Detective Farraday. New boy at the 14th Precinct."

"The one I've heard about? Just transferred in, partnering with Lenny Becker?"

Jimmy nodded. "And I'm sure I don't need to tell you about Becker's reputation."

He didn't. Becker was known for turning a blind eye for a price, for being knee-deep in all sorts of shady stuff. Porn, drugs, prostitution, whatever. Before she'd accepted the job at The Ledger she'd heard the stories. Reporters had tried to prove allegations of corruption against crooked cops and found themselves threatened with criminal charges or in an accident. Hatcher's quest to take down a dirty police captain had been likened to a hamster on an exercise wheel, going nowhere fast.

It was one of those bits of inside information that bordered on being an urban legend. The reporters had all heard the rumors, but nobody had any proof.

"I've never heard Farraday's name mentioned in connection with any of the rumors," Lara said slowly.

Jimmy shook his head. "Becker. Jones. Another guy named Oslind. Those are the cops I'd stay away from. There are others, but those are the names I keep hearing." Jimmy shrugged. "Farraday is Becker's partner."

A non-verbal 'for what it's worth' message. *Draw your own conclusions, Lara.* That's what he was saying to her.

"Word is, Farraday didn't transfer from New Haven by choice. Hung out to dry by some reporter. Absolutely no love lost between him and the press."

"That should make this more interesting. I owe you."

"Watch yourself. I don't think he's looking for a date. Now me on the other hand..."

A smile flickered across her face as she walked into the hallway. Jimmy was comfortably predictable.

But she doubted she'd be able to say the same about Tymen Farraday.

***

"Still waiting? There are chairs down the hall at reception."

Farraday had heard that tone of voice a thousand times before, from his mother. It wasn't a suggestion. He watched the woman sit down, open a folder, her eyes riveted to the notes inside, pretending he didn't exist, carrying on with her job as though some stranger wasn't standing in the middle of her office... Her office. He felt the color fade from his face before his neck started to burn.

"This is your office?"

"Last time I checked, yes." She kept her gaze down and avoided looking him in the eye.

"You're...?"

"Larimer Kelly. Detective...?"

He was used to reporters acting like they were on a crusade, appointed by God to illuminate the masses with a catchy version of the truth. What was it his old captain had always said? *Never trust a reporter. Avoid them if you can, use them if you must. But if the reporter is a woman, stay the hell away.*

The most stubborn man in the world would have been better than this. He held up his hands as if to say, 'Okay, you have me.'

"How did you know?"

There was a hint of a smile on her face. "I have my sources."

"Which is what brings me here."

"The cliff-jumper story."

"You've given my captain a migraine."

She took another file from the top drawer of her desk, staring at him as she held it up and gestured to a chair.

As he sat down, she pushed the file forward.

"Thanks," he said, reaching for it.

She pulled the folder back, waiting until he looked her in the eye. "Not so fast. I'll answer your questions if you answer mine."

Typical reporters. Never divulge a source unless you could trade them up for a better story. Farraday felt his jaw tense as her eyes clouded, as though she knew what he'd been thinking. He tried an innocent smile, but it only reached his mouth. "I don't recall a question."

"Am I to call you Detective? You know my name, which puts me at a bit of a disadvantage."

He didn't believe that for a second but his cheeks burned anyway. "Detective Farraday."

"New transfer, partnering with the shining Lenny Becker. Your captain didn't feel the need to send his top dog my way? I'm disappointed."

It didn't sound like she was a member of the Lenny Becker fan club. He guessed she'd heard more than a few stories about his partner, just as he felt certain she knew who he was before he divulged his name.

"He's busy. I'll have to do." Farraday flashed her a smile. "I'm sure you'll get over it."

She handed him the file, standing slowly, moving across the room to close the door.

Her awareness of his transfer, who he partnered with... He knew reporters used interrogation tactics but he'd never experienced it before, not like this. People you'd never met following your career, noting arrests, partners, transfers. It was all filed and stored for future use. He swallowed, wondering how many journalists could be lingering in his shadows, lying in wait.

"Should I call you Detective or Farraday?"

"Ty, Tymen, Farraday. Suit yourself, Miss Kelly."

"Lara."

"Can I ask?"

"Larimer is a family name. My mother's twisted way of making a statement about my parentage."

"Lucky you."

"It works for me."

He suppressed a smile. "Smart. I guess I shouldn't be surprised that you've managed to make an impression here so quickly."

"So you aren't just a friendly face sent here to charm info out of me?"

He snorted. "I've got better things to do."

With the curls covering her downcast eyes, it was hard to read her expression. The statement hung between them in the silence, Farraday mentally kicking himself for his choice of words. Right now, he needed her to cooperate. He couldn't afford to alienate her.

When she looked up again her lips were straight, her eyes cold. "I see."

"That wasn't what I meant, exactly."

Her left eyebrow rose. "Is your captain that upset?"

"I'm here, aren't I?"

"And I thought you might be the police department's welcome wagon."

He ignored the sarcasm. "You got lucky. It takes more than a pretty face to unnerve those guys."

From what little he'd skimmed in the file, it didn't mention much more than the article. A statement from a witness who saw a woman fall from the ledge, footprints at the scene. An alleged suicide, without a body or much more to go on. Farraday found it hard to believe there was anything serious to this report, likely nothing more than Captain Collins looking for an opportunity to prove to the rest of the department that his newest detective could handle the press after all.

Lara's phone beeped twice and she answered it. Within seconds she hung up, stood and reached for her jacket. "Shall we?"

"Sorry?"

"You want to check my sources, right?"

There was no point denying it. "Yes."

"Let's go."

"You aren't even going to argue?"

"Maybe you've disarmed me with your charm."

He responded to the wry tone with a genuine smile. "See, there was a reason they didn't send Lenny."

***

Hilly streets wove past buildings scattered along the roadside. This part of the city was old, the houses and shops plain. The real business of commerce was done in the area where Farraday worked, the other side of the city from this, the original town. This street had a Mom & Pop Convenience Store, a local grocer instead of large chain stores and a no-name hardware store in desperate need of a repairman's attention. Somehow, this neighborhood had eluded the development overtaking other areas. Branches dangled over the sidewalks; already leaves were starting to collect on the pavement, the red, orange and yellow hues slowly claiming dominance. In the stretches between the buildings bushes pressed against the road. While other cities were defined by steel, cement and man-made structures, this area was distinctly green and ungoverned.

Lara liked driving along these roads. The lush foliage and quiet streets seemed more human than the concrete jungle expanding to the west.

She hadn't even mentioned the video in the article or the fact that Duane Brodie had gone to the police first, which made the presence of a detective in her office first thing Monday morning all the more interesting. Lara tapped her fingers against the steering wheel as she drove, wondering if Hatcher's idea about this story leading all the way to corruption in the captain's office might have some merit after all.

A guess put Farraday at 5'11" and he was fit, with short, dark hair and dark eyes. His charcoal suit could have been the attire of a businessman. He sat quietly as she drove, scanning the file, but she could still feel the tension billowing off of him.

He wasn't fond of reporters.

"You resent this."

"What? Your driving?"

She glared at him. "Checking up on a journalist."

He didn't look at her. "I'd be lying if I said I was crazy about it."

"There's a videotape. A very compelling videotape that supports the statement from the witness." From the corner of her eye, she watched his jaw fall open as he took that in, obviously retracting whatever retort had been forming before he processed her words.

His brow was creased with wrinkles. "You didn't mention the video in your story."

She shrugged. "I didn't need to. Sometimes, it's a good idea not to play all of your cards. Whatever you think now, when you see the tape you'll be interested."

"What makes you so sure?"

"I bet what you've read so far is enough. There's a story here, if you aren't too stubborn to admit it."

"There's an interesting character who lives by the lake and, apparently, likes to play with video cameras. To play devil's advocate, for all I know the story here could be the failure of a mental institution to keep him locked up."

"Are you always this open-minded?"

"Only when I try very hard."

Lara suppressed a smile. "Why don't you like reporters?"

The edge crept back into his voice. "Who said I don't like them?"

She rolled her eyes at him. Lara had parked and was halfway out of the jeep, her backpack in hand. "What are you waiting for? An engraved invitation?"

His eyes narrowed as he undid his seatbelt. "It says here that she turned, with her back to the ledge, before she fell."

She nodded.

"You're sure she was alone?"

Lara stopped short of closing the door. "Why do you ask that?"

"How many jumpers jump backwards?"

"I was too busy thinking about whether or not the story was a hoax."

His dark eyes widened. "That did cross your mind?"

"Of course." She felt her back stiffen, the heat in her cheeks. "You can leave the file. It isn't far but you'll need your hands free."

She slammed the door and started walking up an unmarked trail, the rocky path winding its way through the trees. "I'm glad it didn't rain this morning."

"I guess this trail would have been pretty ugly a few days ago."

"Not as nasty as my dry-cleaning bill."

"Guess I'll be stuck with one of my own."

She glanced down at his mud-splattered pants and shrugged. "The brush is so thick the sun can't dry up all the muddy patches."

It was a moment before he spoke again. "I didn't mean to offend you."

She stopped walking and turned to face him. "Really?"

He put up both hands. "I've known some reporters who got so carried away they didn't stop to think about what they were doing until after the story came out in print, if ever. By then it was too late to undo the damage."

Her shoulders dropped as she let out a deep breath. "I've known a few reporters like that too."

He stepped forward but she didn't move. "I've also known some cops who would rather discredit a good journalist than accept getting a little egg on the face."

They were standing so close and, because she was higher on the trail, were eye to eye.

"I'm not one of those cops."

"And I'm not one of those reporters."

After a moment she turned and started walking again, neither speaking until they reached the top of the hill.

From that vantage point there was a clear view across the lake and down the side of the rock-cut to Duane Brodie's cabin. This was a small cove, one of a number visible from this spot, locally known as The Point, because the rock cuts here were higher. The lake was long and wide, bending and twisting until the thick foliage obscured the far ends from sight.

"He swears he only does it at night."

"Excuse me?" Farraday turned to stare at her.

"Videoing. Says he only works at night or in an intense storm."

Branches and debris were still scattered across the ground. The wind had vented her wrath on the area only a few days before, and today it was as though she was catching her breath. The air was still, a bit cool, but otherwise it was a pleasant fall day.

He cautiously leaned out over the edge, surveying the rocky shoreline below.

Lara moved beside him. "That seems to be where she stood before she went over." She pointed to a muddy area just to Farraday's left. He squatted, looking at the ground.

"Is this where you got the partial footprint?"

"Yes. It matches another partial from the trail. That only proves someone came up here before Saturday and stood with their back to the ledge." She omitted the fact that she'd also found shoe prints caked in the mud, wondering just how much he knew already. The article said nothing about the video and she was reasonably certain he hadn't known about it, judging from his reaction.

But then why follow up on this story at all?

"Before Saturday?"

"I was here Saturday. The spot on the trail was still damp but this one had nothing to shelter it, no shield from baking in the hot sun. Whoever made the prints did so before the heat dried the earth. And if you believe the video the print is redundant."

Farraday knelt down beside the place where the woman would have been standing. He paused and then inched forward, looking out over the edge.

"Do you have a camera?"

"In my backpack. Did you find something?"

"This is an outcropping. There's a sheltered spot here, under the rock. It looks like it might have stayed dry. See for yourself."

Lara removed the camera and wound the strap around her arm securely. She leaned out beside him, balancing on one hand.

"Steady. Can you see it?"

"Barely. How did I miss this?"

"It's not the easiest place to spot. You can't see it unless you get way out over the edge."

"It's a pretty crummy scene. Nothing can be contained, the wind and rain have washed away just about every possible trace of physical evidence." She wiggled back from the ledge, passed him her camera and nodded at her pack. "There's a first aid kit in the bag with some gloves and cotton swabs. You're going to have to hold me so I can reach this.

He set the camera in its case and grabbed the first aid kit. "I'll do it."

"I'm quite capable."

"I never said you weren't, but if this is evidence in a criminal investigation-"

"You don't know it's evidence and you wouldn't even be here if I hadn't brought you. Besides, this is for me." She was counting on his cooperation. Whatever the reason for his captain's interest, he needed her to get access to the witness and the tape. And since he was still unconvinced there was a story, never mind a crime, he couldn't just declare this a crime scene and remove her.

Not without admitting he believed her story had merit, or that he knew something before she even brought him there. And that would be a bigger story for her in the long run. It was a win-win scenario for her, lose-lose for him.

He passed her what she needed from the pack. "For you?"

"Insurance. All I need is some crooked crime scene tech planting evidence or switching samples to make me look incompetent. You can either help me or wait, but the only way you'll stop me is if you arrest me."

"Tempting." He clenched his jaw but didn't argue. "Do you do this often?"

"Not if the local cops have anything to say about it." She inched forward and Farraday reached for her waist.

Lara collected a sample and passed him the plastic bag. "Looks like blood." He handed her another bag and swab from the kit, still holding her waist with one hand until she'd pulled herself back from the edge.

"Do you think someone grabbed that ledge and cut themselves trying to hold on?"

"From what I saw on the video, the rain was coming from the opposite direction, this way." Lara gestured out over the ledge, toward the lake. "This area was shielded, so it might have stayed dry. Could even be prints. There should be a plastic garbage bag and tape in the backpack. I can cover the area to try to preserve anything that's left in case you want to follow up."

He didn't argue. Once she'd taped the bag over the rocks where the blood was he asked her the obvious question. "What about the woman?"

"Duane Brodie said he went out in his boat the next morning, never saw a body. I walked three miles in both directions and didn't find her either. Straight down you've got a rocky shoreline. You have to go seven or eight feet out to get where the shelves of rock are completely below the surface of the water. Not high enough to affect small boats and canoes but still shallow enough to kill or cripple some kids who've jumped over that far. If this woman grabbed the ledge she should have landed almost straight down. The lake isn't high enough there to pull her in."

"Then where is she? If she'd fallen out further, she might have missed the rocks, although the chances are slim. It can take days, even weeks for a body to surface, depending on water temperature and currents." He stood up, looking over the edge again. "But if she fell straight down, she should still be there. You believe this guy?"

Lara finished writing notes on the plastic bags and secured them in her backpack. She glanced at the detective. "As much as I believe anyone who shows up with unsolicited material they say the police don't want."

Farraday spun around, his eyes wide. "He went to the police?"

"The One-Four."

"My precinct? We sent him away so he came to you? Why...?"

"I'm not an idiot, Farraday. If I said that the police dismissed potential evidence of a crime, I'd need to have more than enough for a filler article to make my editor stand up to the heat."

"Still, it makes this guy seem more reliable."

"It doesn't mean he's not a crack."

He frowned. "What's giving you doubts?"

"Look," she pushed her hair out of her face as she stood up and met his gaze, "you'll find out, if you don't already know. He's got a reputation. Duane likes to be... helpful. Without the video I wouldn't have touched this. Even then..." She shrugged.

"What convinced you?"

"The footprints helped."

"And?"

"The other witness."

"I didn't see anything in the file about another witness. Background on Brodie, weather reports, a transcript of the statement and what you found here."

Lara looked out over the ledge and shook her head. "Those few seconds as she fell…I can't imagine what was going through her mind."

"What troubles me is her jumping backwards. Why? Unless you're so uncertain you can't bear to look, but wouldn't you hesitate before you got to the edge?"

"It was like there was something else she was more afraid of."

"Is this your way of avoiding the subject?"

Her eyes narrowed for a second. "You didn't miss anything. I kept the other witness statement out of that file."

"Why?"

"I didn't want anyone to know who it was." She started walking down a different path, toward Duane's home. "There's something you should see." Lara took a turn, moving west. Instead of continuing down the hill, this path was almost level. She pointed back up the rock cut.

"That's where the woman was standing. Now, if you look that way," she gestured in the other direction, "you can see where Duane was filming from. The patio doors. He had a pretty clear shot."

"Of the ledge, but not the open area at the top of the hill. The trees along this side obscure it from view."

"What are you thinking?"

"There might be more here than meets the eye or, in this case, the lens. Someone else could have been up there."

Lara opened her mouth, but hesitated. "I could see her climbing."

"Your story said she was dressed in a white shirt. What if she was being followed by someone wearing dark clothing? They'd blend right in with the trees."

She turned away, looking back up the cliff.

"If you know something you'll have to share it with the investigating officer," he told her.

"Isn't that you?"

"My captain didn't seem to think I would find a case, just a reporter causing problems."

"Lucky for you, you found both."

"No comment. I've had more than enough trouble for one day."

***

Duane's home was shadowed by the hill. From the level area where Lara had pointed out the view from the cabin a spacious path led down to the water, but the shoreline was hemmed in by trees. In order to get to Duane's they had to follow an increasingly narrow, precarious path weaving amidst the undergrowth. After dodging branches and jagged rocks, a rustic, serviceable abode came into view, a few feet from the shore. The driveway was a mix of gravel and drying mud, with several potholes scattered across the wide path.

Farraday surveyed the loose gravel drive that led up to the sagging cabin. "His car's gone."

"Duane doesn't drive a car. He has a moped in that shed." The small structure was on the far side of the clearing, tucked behind some brush.

"Did he give you a full tour?"

A wry smile flickered across her face as she knocked on the door. "Wait until you see his Bee Gees collection."

"You're joking."

"I wish I were. Any more exposure and I'll need reorientation to this century."

Through the window beside the door Farraday could see the table, covered with flyers, an empty chair pulled out, as though someone had stood up abruptly and forgot to push it in. The counter was bare except for a stack of garbage bags and two empty boxes. The floor was spotless, the fridge door shockingly white.

"Maybe he's around front."

Farraday followed her around the house to an oversized patio that reached the shore, a sturdy dock attached.

Lara walked straight to the railing and looked down. "Looks like he's out fishing."

"Where did he have his camera?" Farraday asked as he turned to look at the patio doors.

"Right here." She walked over, pointing to a spot on the other side of the glass. "Had a good view."

Farraday put himself in the camera's approximate position. "Of the ledge, but you can't see the spot underneath the outcropping where you got those samples from."

"Does that matter?"

"It would explain why he didn't say anything about it and why it wasn't on the tape." He glanced at her. "Assuming it wasn't in the video."

"I would have found those samples on my own if it had been. Why is it important if he knew about it?"

"If she held on it might prove she actually slipped or she changed her mind about jumping, for starters."

"Small consolation to any family she might have. Out with it."

He offered an innocent smile. "Am I that transparent?"

"It's more likely that I'm just that suspicious."

"I was wondering how long she held on for."

A whirring sound cut through the silence. Farraday nodded toward the dock. "Duane?"

A small aluminum boat was creeping toward shore. The lone occupant shut off the engine, the gentle bobbing of the wake nudging the boat closer. The man reached out, grabbed the weathered wood and jumped on the dock, a rope in hand that he tethered to a cleat. "Hi, Miss Kelly."

Lara introduced Farraday and explained his interest in the videotape. Duane looked like he'd been force-fed a lemon as he glanced at the detective and then started shuffling past him, heading toward the house, staring down at the dock as though he was afraid the boards were going to disappear and let him fall through the gaps.

"I gave the tape to Miss Kelly," he muttered.

Farraday kept pace with him. "That's okay. I'd just like to ask you a few questions."

"Haven't thought of nothin' else that I fergot to tell Miss Kelly."

"I'd like to hear it from you myself."

Duane's shoulders rose and fell again as he fumbled with the clasp before sliding the patio door open.

"Do these doors face west?"

"Yeah." Duane sat down in an oversized, fading chair. Farraday and Lara followed him inside, sitting on the dingy couch.

Once Duane had relayed his story Farraday made him go over it again, asking question after question. Then he stood up.

"Your camcorder was here?" He pointed to the spot on the floor beside the patio doors.

Duane scratched his head. "I guess, yeah."

Farraday glanced around the room again. "Do you have a telephone?" From the corner of his eye he could see Lara's head snap up but he didn't meet her gaze.

Duane banged his thumbs together. "Yeah. On the wall over there." He pointed over his head, turned to look and corrected the angle of his thumbs accordingly. Farraday couldn't see it from where he stood, and moved across the room to double-check.

"Why didn't you phone 9-1-1?"

Duane's mouth hung open, lips quivering. "I…I guess I should've. I don't get no calls. I didn't think of it."

Lara's eyes narrowed as she stared at Farraday and then in the direction of the phone, which was an old wall mount, the kind you rarely saw anymore. Duane had collapsed against the old chair, all his furniture looking like overused items he'd bought from a second-hand shop two decades earlier. His cheeks puffed out like a chipmunks.

"I appreciate you answering these questions for me," Farraday said, still avoiding Lara's gaze.

Duane's face brightened and he released his breath. "I like to help."

"You didn't happen to see anyone else that night, did you?"

Duane glanced at Lara, eyes wide, and then shrugged. "I didn't see nobody."

Lara, Farraday noted, had suddenly developed an interest in scrutinizing the carpet.

Farraday stared at him for a moment, watching the color creep into Duane's face. He thanked him, wondering what it was that Duane was holding back.

And what Lara Kelly knew that she wasn't telling him.

CHAPTER 2

As they walked only the rustle of leaves broke the silence. Farraday was a better investigator than Lara had given him credit for. Bringing him here had seemed like the best way to handle him, to make sure she knew what he learned.

To keep him from questioning Duane alone. Her instincts had told her it would be better to keep an eye on Farraday, and she was glad she'd listened.

He'd seemed to blunder his way through his exchanges with her, yet he'd handled Duane effectively. She was convinced now that Duane was legit. He didn't seem capable of misleading a reporter and a detective so convincingly. Still, it was a rookie mistake to make assumptions.

"What were you getting at, with the questions about the phone?" she asked.

"I wanted to know why he didn't call for help."

"Are you thinking of charging him?"

"Not without a body, I'm not."

Lara glared at him. "I didn't bring you here to trick witnesses and boost your arrest record."

"It's a fair question. Why didn't he call the police?"

"Call the station that has thrown him out on his ear so many times before?"

"Fair enough. But if not the police, what about a neighbor? He wasn't afraid to take this tape to you."

"He waited almost twenty-four hours before bringing me the video."

"Maybe he didn't call the police because he knew she was dead."

Lara's breath caught in her throat, the gravel crunching under her foot as she spun around. "What are you saying?"

"You didn't find a body. Maybe there's a reason."

"Then why bring me the tape at all?"

Farraday shrugged. "Some people like attention. It makes him look like a hero, coming forward with information about this woman's tragic suicide. And it would explain how he caught her on film in the first place."

After a moment Lara held up her hands in surrender, trying to mask her thoughts by looking contrite. "I shouldn't have jumped to conclusions."

He looked away, face clouded, unreadable. "I wouldn't want someone taking advantage of my sources either."

She half-smiled. "You're surprisingly gracious for someone who detests my profession."

Farraday exhaled audibly. "Look, we both know the drill. An unscrupulous reporter can blow an investigation by tipping off suspects and silencing witnesses. My own experience taught me not to trust anyone unless it's earned. Anyone. Reporters included. You shared your research and substantiated your story. If you don't judge me by the rumors you've heard about my precinct, I'll try not to hold my problems with the press against you. Fair enough?"

Lara took a minute to pretend she was considering what he'd said, pushing the darker possibilities to the back of her mind for the moment. The way he talked about the rumors... She was beginning to wonder if he was really here about the jumper story, or trying to find out what she knew or suspected about the corruption in the department.

Although she couldn't see how this story, even with the police turning Duane away, led to the corruption. Right now, she couldn't see how it led anywhere but maybe a slap on the wrist for the cop who'd turned Duane away. Without a body, who was going to take it seriously?

"Fair enough." She uncrossed her arms and tossed him her keys. "I believe you made some comment about my driving."

"I didn't mean it like that."

Lara backed toward the passenger door, holding her hands up. "Don't worry about it. Truth is, I want to record the photos I took and log the films Duane gave us."

Farraday had asked about other photos and Duane had willingly relinquished the films on the condition that he would get the negatives and a set of prints back. There was no guarantee the pictures would hold any answers. She hadn't thought of it, foolishly, because he said he was photographing the lightning over the lake but when Farraday had pressed him Duane admitted he did take some shots of the hill. Now that the police were interested Lara knew it was important to have every piece of evidence she could find to protect herself.

And as long as she had Jimmy develop the films she could at least keep Farraday from seeing them before she did.

She clicked the remote to unlock the jeep and had the door half open before she stopped, staring down. Farraday opened the other door. "What's wrong?"

"Didn't you leave the file here?"

"On the seat." He leaned in, looking on the floor and underneath the passenger seat. It took less than a minute to confirm it was gone. Their eyes met and they both jumped out, running up the trail.

Farraday got there first. Lara leaned over the edge beside him. The plastic had been pulled off and the ledge was glistening. Someone had dumped water all over it.

"Is there any chance of getting prints now?"

He shook his head. "There wasn't much chance to begin with. But that settles it."

"Your dry cleaning bill is going to be as bad as mine?"

He smiled wryly. "Someone doesn't want us to learn the truth."

Like Farraday's captain, for example. She was beginning to wonder how good of an actor Farraday was. "If you hadn't shown up this could have been over."

"Only two people know I'm here. Believe me, Collins does not want this to be legit."

"Wouldn't that be a reason to swipe the file?" she asked as they walked back down the trail.

"Not with this physical evidence and the story already in print. Collins knows messing with a reporter is like poking a hornet's nest. Better to leave them alone if you can."

"You aren't offended at the insinuation?"

He put his hand on her arm to stop her. "Cops pretend not to notice dirty cops, but the truth is, you need to know who you can trust. A dirty cop can hang you out to dry in a heartbeat if it suits his purpose. Don't get any ideas. That's off the record."

"Cops and reporters aren't that different, you know."

"Why do you say that?"

"In a way, we both make a living from the suffering of others. No crime, no cops and no stories people would pay to read. Tragedy sells." She felt his grip loosen and she pulled away from him, walking to the jeep.

"I do this to see justice done."

Lara folded her arms across her chest. "So do I."

"I'm sorry about your file."

"No big deal. It wasn't the master."

He glanced at her sideways, his mouth hanging open before he pulled it into a tight grin. Farraday started the engine and pulled out onto the road. "You're good."

"I'm careful. Besides, I had a feeling about this story. I know enough about Oakridge to protect myself."

"You think it was a suicide?"

She shrugged. "To be honest, I was more interested in why the cops ignored this. Take the next right."

"Where are we going?"

"My house. Right again."

Once he started down the driveway the trees thinned, revealing a cedar house with scrolled trim, bright curtains and the fading remnants of a flower garden. He parked the jeep and followed her inside.

"I'll just be a minute." Lara jogged up the stairs, leaving Farraday at the landing, just inside the living room.

The room was spacious yet cozy. The dark blue and red tones of the chairs and green quilt over the couch contrasted the gold paint on the walls. The furniture embraced the fireplace and the mantle was filled with framed photos. Farraday stepped closer, examining the faces of politicians, a few actors, some landscape shots, sunsets and wildlife.

There was a small stack of books on the couch – *Lifeless, Dying Light, Pale Immortal.* A copy of *A Field of Darkness* sat on the coffee table.

"Ever the detective." She returned, tucking a short-sleeved black t-shirt into her jeans. Her hair was mostly contained in a ponytail, which curled around her neck and hung over her right shoulder. A tabby, gray with black and white stripes, bounded down and ran across the room, rubbing against Farraday's legs.

"I would expect no less from you." He followed her to the kitchen. From the window he could see the large front lawn between her porch and the trees. Thick hedges blocked almost all sight of the road.

"What happens now?" she asked.

His pager went off. "I'm due in court."

"I didn't know you'd been here long enough to be testifying in a case already at trial." Her brow wrinkled.

"The Miller trial. I dealt with the incident at the hospital last week."

"I'll drop you off."

***

Lara let the screen door fall shut as she dropped bags and her pack on the kitchen table and pulled her hair free. Skittles, curled up in a ball on the stairs, gave her a weary glare as she walked past him.

She'd replayed the encounter in her mind, rubbing her neck, pacing her office. He'd said his life experiences taught him not to trust anyone unless it was earned. Then he seemed to do an about-face, forgetting his attitude toward reporters and his guarded displeasure, asking for her opinions.

If her editor knew a detective had followed up on this story… Thanks to Wendy's warning she'd left the office before Hatcher could track her down and cast more doubt on her judgment. He'd been clear about trying to make this a piece on police incompetence, which meant she needed to keep Farraday off Hatcher's radar until she knew what she had.

She'd searched the archives at the library, checking city papers online until she found the headline she was sure would lead to answers. She requested a hard copy from the librarian, who took the opportunity to remind Lara she could look the information up online, but when Lara wouldn't waver Nancy had said back issues should be filed, either in the binders or the archives, Nancy's term for anything in a grungy box, in an overflowing, dusty basement. Microfilm wasn't in the budget in this small branch. The boxes would be available in the morning.

Now she was home. One of the nice things about Oakridge was people could still afford a bit of land. She'd been careful with her funds during college and scholarships had kept her from using the surprising amount of money her mother had saved for her education. Still, until she knew if Oakridge was going to be home, she was renting. She had a year to decide if she wanted to buy the house, but after three years in a tiny apartment in the city she'd jumped at the chance to have some space of her own, especially when she saw the oversized fireplace and the claw-foot tub.

The tub was where she turned her attention now. She poured strawberry bubble bath under the tap. Closing the bathroom door to the hall, she stepped through the entry to her room and tossed her clothes in a pile on the trunk at the end of the bed. Leaving that door partly open, she returned to the bathroom and slipped into the tub, leaning back against the headrest.

Detective Farraday... In only a few hours he'd managed to turn everything upside down, to throw her perspective out of focus. Lara closed her eyes. Focus. Damn. She'd forgotten to give Jimmy the films. And it would have given her a chance to see them before Farraday did.

She slid under the water, thinking about the file that went missing while she was with the detective. Technically, Duane could have accessed her vehicle while they had been at the top of the hill, but how could he have known they were there? Duane had brought her the tape. Why steal the file?

Lifting her head, Lara reached back to squeeze the water from her hair and stiffened. She felt a sudden chill, despite the heat of the bath. A creaking sound, distant enough to be from downstairs, was followed by a thud and then another creak. She stood slowly and pulled her robe on. Treading softly into the bedroom, she grabbed a five-pound weight as she approached the door. A full-length mirror hung at the end of the hall on the closet door, ensuring nobody could get to her room without being seen. Half expecting to see some lunatic coming upstairs, she frowned.

The hallway was empty.

She kept her back against the wall as she made her way to the top of the stairs. There was no sign of anyone, nothing but silence. She drew a deep breath and tiptoed downstairs.

The house was empty. Her pack was undisturbed on the table. She still kept the wall behind her as her heart rate slowed. A creak drew her glance to the front entrance, where the screen door swayed from the breeze. Skittles was huddled on the patio, evidently undecided about how far to take his rebellion.

Lara set the weight down and walked outside to pick up her cat. This time, she closed the screen door carefully behind her and listened for the click of the latch before turning the lock.

***

Overwhelmed by the sense that she had slept late, Lara bolted upward and then dropped back against the pillow when she saw the time. 5:14 am.

She'd tried reading by the fire, tried harder to forget the sound of footsteps.

Houses creaked so she could discount the sound as phantom noises but she couldn't rationalize the notepad that had been moved by the phone. She always kept the pad in the cubby under the table, but it had been set out beside the phone, dropped at an angle.

As though someone had been in a hurry.

Lara sat up. Skittles was curled in a ball beside her pillow, right paws hanging in the air, purring.

She dressed, stretched and got on her treadmill. Her headache was gone but questions gnawed at her. Would Farraday be back to continue an investigation? Or would they try to discredit her? She could fight back but her days in Oakridge would be numbered. Every cop would be an enemy, every potential source reluctant to trust her.

When she was ready for work she called to check her voice mail and then phoned Wendy, The Ledger's receptionist.

"It's Lara."

"You on your way in?" Wendy never identified callers if Hatcher was around.

Lara glanced at the clock. It was just after 8 am. He was early.

"No. I'm doing some research."

"Interviews until noon? See you after lunch."

"Thanks. By the way, if Detective Farraday is looking for me, tell him where to find me."

"Sorry, did I hear you right?"

"Just don't let Hatcher know."

Wendy helped reporters skirt Hatcher when he was on the warpath. Don't use their name if they call when he's around; tell them when he'll be out of the office. Lara appreciated the warning. If she could avoid Hatcher for a little longer she could come up with another story to get him off her back and buy herself some time to sort this out.

Nancy was turning the lights on when she arrived at the library. A pleasant person with a bright smile, strawberry-blonde curls and energy. Wearing black jeans and a sweater, she barely met the minimum standards for the dress code the other librarians in the bigger libraries adhered to. She'd told Lara that was part of the reason she liked working in a satellite branch - greater flexibility and independence. Plus, no commute.

"We don't serve breakfast you know."

Lara grinned. "You should. I'd live here."

"That's why we don't. Have you seen some of the people who hang out here? I don't want to find them waiting for the doors to open. But I brought you a muffin. Everything's on the table in the room beside the computer lab."

There were some things about the look and feel of newsprint that Lara liked. She knew she could do searches online, but that didn't give the same context for the placement of a story on the printed page. Lara sorted papers until she found the front-page article and, she suspected, the reason Farraday had been transferred to Oakridge.

The article was hardly that damaging. In contrast to the usual scandals that rocked police departments it was little more than water off a duck's back. A man who'd received a green card because of the sponsorship of one of Warren Farraday's businesses was accused of murder, a murder he'd allegedly planned before he moved to America. The story ran with a picture of Farraday's father, an international businessman.

The reporter implied a source close to the Farraday family had leaked information. It was clear that the reporter, Katarina Collins, was referring to Tymen Farraday, although he was never named.

She scanned the news following the article until the date of Farraday's transfer to Oakridge. There was no mention of disciplinary action, nothing to suggest Farraday had even been put under investigation.

In fact, the silence on the topic was curious. The media continued to follow the murder case as it progressed but the Farraday name never reappeared. Either there was more there that someone had enough power to conceal, or it was a smokescreen to justify his transfer.

But why? Why not just transfer to Oakridge if he'd wanted to leave New Haven? It didn't make sense. There must be more to it than what the media was willing, or able, to tell.

Lara photocopied the articles, packed up the papers and took them back to the counter.

"That was quick," Nancy said.

"I got lucky."

"That's good, I guess."

Lara leaned over the counter and lowered her voice, relaying what she'd been looking at as Nancy pushed the box under the desk. "Can you let me know if anyone else takes an interest?"

Nancy arched an eyebrow. "What aren't you telling me?"

"Nothing. Just a hunch. And a little insurance."

"I'll file them special."

"Thanks. You're a lifesaver. I'm going to hang out a bit longer."

"Are you here?"

"Depends who's asking. If it's Hatcher, definitely not."

Lara walked back to the small room. She stashed her copies in her bag and rubbed her neck, still thinking about what she'd learned.

"Hiding from your boss?"

She jumped. Farraday was leaning against the doorway. She didn't know how long he'd been there, but didn't matter. The papers were gone. There wasn't anything out that hinted at what she'd been doing.

"Did your captain send you this time or did you miss me?"

Farraday straightened. "Both. I missed you at the office and I haven't finished my report. I believe we cut it short yesterday."

"You talked to Wendy?"

"She told me you were here." Farraday paused, hands in pockets, looking at the wall with a cynical grin. "Well, 'If you know how to read you might know where to find her,' was what she actually said."

Lara suppressed a smile. "The boss is looking for me."

"That rules out heading back there. How about that other witness?"

She paused, looked into his dark eyes and instantly regretted it. "The other witness it is."

"Your car or mine?'

"You can drive." She followed him to the door, waving to Nancy. "Thanks for the muffin." Nancy was watching them, her eyes pinched.

"Muffins? Where's mine?"

"You have to spend more time here before you get special service."

Farraday pulled the car door shut. "In only a few months you've worked out a code with The Ledger secretary and the local librarian plays lookout. Any other spies I should know about?"

She shrugged. "You're the detective. You figure it out."

"Touché." He turned the car toward the exit.

***

"We're going about a quarter of a mile past Duane's. Betty Zimmerman was my other source."

"You didn't mention her in the article." He glanced at Lara. "What did she see?"

"You should hear that from her yourself. Turn here." They crawled over the bumpy drive to an old stone house, perched on a rock cut overlooking the lake. The house had a simple elegance, plants creeping along the walls and overgrown flowerbeds pushing into the lawn. Every window was dark, each blind shut. Even on this warm day the heavy wooden door was closed.

"Can you see Duane's house from here?"

"No. It's tucked into another inlet."

Farraday knocked on the door. It creaked open slowly, revealing a wide-eyed, wrinkled face.

Betty's gaze flitted from Farraday to Lara and then to the ground. "I didn't think you'd be back."

"I told you the police might want to talk to you. Can we come in?"

"I suppose." She closed the door, the sound of metal scraping against metal indicating the chain was being unlocked before the door opened wide.

Once inside, Lara introduced Detective Farraday.

Betty remained standing, wringing her hands. "Have you found her?"

"No, Mrs. Zimmerman. Miss Kelly told me in confidence that you spoke with her. I'd like to know what you saw."

"She can tell you. I..."

"I'd like to hear it from you myself."

Betty sank down onto a chair. "Peaches went out to do her business. Usually she stays close but this time she ran off down the drive. I had half a mind to leave her out, but she's all I have now that Frank is gone. I went after her. That's when I saw the woman. She was running down the road, no coat or boots, screaming at the top of her lungs."

"What did she look like?"

"Young. Long, dark hair." Betty looked away for a moment. "She only glanced over her shoulder for a second."

"Was she just screaming or were there any words you could make out?"

Betty hesitated. "Go away, go to hell and then screams."

"Did you see anyone else?"

She drew a sharp breath and looked down at the floor. "I didn't want to be running about in a storm. It wasn't any of my business."

Lara watched as Farraday tried to get her to talk. Betty didn't really look at the woman. She hadn't seen anyone else. She just wanted to get her dog in from the rain. She didn't know anything useful.

Half a dozen questions later, Betty mashed her lips together and shook her head, refusing to say another word.

Once outside, they could hear the deadbolt slide into place, securing the door.

"What do you think?"

Farraday scratched his head. "She's her own person."

"How diplomatic," Lara said dryly. "Do you think she's credible?"

He shrugged. "There's nothing to suggest she isn't. She confirms the presence of a disturbed woman running along the road before the time the video was recorded. But she's edgy, nervous. Was she this reluctant to talk to you?"

"Why do you think I didn't identify her? There's enough evidence to indicate that this woman was here. What I don't know is where she is now."

Farraday rubbed his forehead. "My captain would like this to be wrapped up, nice and tidy, without any loose threads left to unravel."

"You mean as nice and tidy as a suicide can be without a body."

"If it was suicide why would somebody steal the file and try to destroy evidence?"

"That could have been a prank," she said as she closed the car door.

"There's a remote possibility some kid came along and saw us and thought they'd play a joke. But the file seems deliberate. Taking unmarked plastic off a cliff is one thing. Breaking into a vehicle is another. And the two things happening together?" He fastened his seatbelt. "I don't buy it."

"I've been wondering about who else could have taken it."

"Other than the person chasing her?"

Her head snapped up. "You're convinced there was someone else there?"

"She was screaming, 'Go away, go to hell.' Someone was following her."

"She could have been delusional."

"Okay. Possibly, but you said it seemed like there was something she was more frightened of than the cliffs behind her. What if she was afraid of someone who was trying to kill her?"

"If someone was chasing her they could have seen Betty."

"So why grab a file instead of dealing with Betty? The file was luck, unless one of us is being followed, which opens up a whole new set of questions. Anyone chasing this woman could have known Betty saw her, even if she wasn't named in your article."

Lara exhaled. "That might explain why Betty's keeping her door locked."

"The only way someone would have known about Betty is if they were here that night. And if they were, then there's more to this story than what you put into print."

"They could have known if they were following me."

"Before your story ever came out?" Farraday shook his head. "Only if they knew Duane had a tape and that he took it to you. And if they knew that- "

"Why not just deal with Duane? Okay, let's assume somebody got nervous when they saw my story and followed us yesterday. Why take the file? It was mostly what I put in my article."

"And enough information to question Duane's credibility." Farraday's thumb tapped against the steering wheel. "If I were the killer and I read that file I'd be wondering how your story ever made it to print."

"You think it was murder?"

"It's a hunch."

"Great." A pulsing started in Lara's temples. The drumming intensified when she saw the way Farraday's eyes narrowed as he looked at her. "Reporters aren't the only ones with reputations, you know. A cop with a hunch is like a dog with a bone."

He almost smiled. "We use that expression for a reporter on the scent of a story."

"So what happens when the cop and reporter are working together?"

"The dog's a Rottweiler?"

"You're a laugh a minute."

"I was serious."

Farraday's cell rang and, after a few brief words that failed to clue Lara in to the reason for the call, he hung up.

"A source of mine. He looked at those samples we collected yesterday."

"Results this quick?"

"If you know the right people, sometimes you can get answers fast. There's a huge difference between response times from crime labs and private labs."

"Did he learn something useful?" she asked.

"We're about to find out."

Once they arrived Farraday cautioned her. "Let me handle this. He isn't fond of reporters."

"Must be the clubhouse rules. Are you worried about me or about being alienated if your friends think you've joined the dark side?"

"I can never be turned."

He smiled and she felt her shoulders relax, forgetting the retort she was about to unleash. Farraday entered the third room on the right, closing the door behind her when she slipped inside.

Doctor Eaton had simple glasses and graying hair around his temples. He looked up from the paperwork on his desk.

"You look well. How's Trin?"

Farraday looked as though he was about to say something, but hadn't expected Dr. Eaton's question. "Fine. This is Lara."

Dr. Eaton barely glanced at her. "The blood was type O. There's enough for a DNA match if you bring me something to compare it to."

"Just one blood type?"

The doctor peered up over his glasses, which had slid down his nose. "You were hoping for more?"

Farraday shrugged. "Is there anything else you can tell us?"

"Without more evidence, no." Dr. Eaton lifted the file toward Farraday, who glanced at Lara.

"Can you keep this here?"

"Does this look like an evidence locker?"

"Somebody stole a file on the case. I'd rather keep this here, for now."

Dr. Eaton's eyes narrowed. "A reporter is more trustworthy than a police department?"

Lara felt the heat in her face but Farraday didn't flinch under the doctor's skeptical stare. "And your office is safer than the station."

"Humph." The doctor scowled but set the file down on his desk. "Do call when you need this."

Once they'd left Dr. Eaton's office Lara asked, "How did he know?"

"I told him when I dropped off the samples."

"How do you know him?"

"He used to work overseas. He's been a family friend since I was a child."

"If he already knew I was a reporter why did you warn me off?"

"He's old school. It's not proper for a young lady to be too nosey."

"They failed to mention that at my finishing school."

"Don't let it bother you. He likes you."

"Really? I couldn't tell."

"He acknowledged your presence. If you didn't make a good impression you would have been out of his office in less than thirty seconds."

"Who's Trin?" she asked, recalling the name that had caused a tiny hesitation in Farraday's response.

"My sister. What's next?"

"Let's go back to my office. You should see what started this whole thing."

Chapter 3

Farraday followed Lara inside the back entrance of The Ledger. He watched her pull the films Duane had given them from her pack, stopping at the first door on the right, one without a nameplate to identify it as an office. The Ledger was in an unusual building. He'd asked Lara about it, in passing, and she said it used to be part of a residential school, which is why there were so many small rooms instead of one large newsroom. There was only a red light outside the room Lara stopped at, which was currently off. Lara opened the door and gestured for him to follow her.

"Jimmy?"

"Right here." He came from the hallway behind them, glaring at Farraday before smiling at Lara. "How's my favorite customer?"

"In need of your professional services."

He winked at her. "The words I long to hear. What have you got?"

Farraday closed the door. Jimmy glanced at him and almost scowled. "It may not be my specialty, but I could help with the ball and chain you've been dragging around lately."

A smile flickered across Lara's face. "You'd be the first one I'd call."

He nodded. "Shoot."

She handed him the rolls. "ASAP, quick and quiet. You haven't even seen me. And we need two sets of prints."

Jimmy looked up as he wrote notes on the sleeves he'd put the films into. "What are you up to now, Lara darling?"

She held up her hands. "I don't want Hatcher on my case-"

"Not a word." Jimmy made the motion of zipping his lips with his fingers.

It hadn't been hard to pick up on the cue to stay out of the conversation. Jimmy hadn't even tried to curtail his flirting with Lara, although Farraday noticed she ignored it. He followed her out of the office, aware of the cold stare the photographer was giving him.

"I take it Jimmy doesn't usually drop your photos off on your desk."

"Huh?" She closed her office door once he was inside.

"I saw the trays. You sent him in here to check me out."

Lara shrugged. "You need to stay under Hatcher's radar. If he finds out you've been snooping around... I don't want him hounding me until there's more to go on."

"Fair enough. What did you say your editor's name was?" He watched her pull a TV and VCR out of the closet behind her desk.

"Ted Hatcher. Can you plug this in?"

Ted Hatcher. Great. He'd been so focused on this story, and on Lara Kelly, that he hadn't even thought about which paper he was dealing with. Once he'd plugged the cord in he turned to see Lara putting a video into the VCR, holding a red folder.

She sat in the chair next to him instead of sitting behind her desk. He felt her watching him from the corner of her eye as the tape started. The more he saw, the more his stomach twisted.

The cop who'd ignored the tape had made a serious mistake. Whoever it was, he'd be lucky if Captain Collins only made him the poster boy for ineptitude. No captain wanted to deal with an internal investigation, especially if it highlighted the incompetence of one of his own men.

When it was over she rewound the tape, then sat back down in her own chair as he turned to face her.

"How could any cop ignore this?"

"He never watched it."

"You spoke to him?"

She hesitated. "With deception, I admit. That's why I never used it in my story."

"Who was it?"

"Officer Robson Walker."

If she'd used it he wouldn't have been sent here to check up on her. Heads would already be rolling at the station. Mistakes like this happened, especially with rookies, but Walker had been on the force for almost four years.

Lara was covering some cop's ass while he'd been sent here to put hers in a sling.

"I have to tell Collins."

She was looking at her desk, avoiding his gaze. "I understand."

"I'm doing it for you. You'd be discredited. You wouldn't be able to get a police source inside of a hundred miles. That's, that's..."

"That's why he sent you." She looked up. "Don't look so surprised."

"Why did you talk to me then?"

She leaned back in her chair, her shoulders sagging. "Before I had enough to write this piece, Hatcher warned me I'd be a target. Oakridge is known for heavy-handed officers. The story was printed and inside of one business hour you were in my office."

"Why are you telling me this?"

Her forehead wrinkled. "Isn't it obvious? On the surface, without a body, this story was shelved. Hatcher thought I could turn this into something on local cops trying to intimidate the press and get a bigger story than negligence. 'Coercion and Corruption Plague Captain's Office.' He only cares about exposing the sins of the 14th Precinct."

"Your boss wants you to go after my captain. Why?" He needed to know how much she knew, what she suspected. If she knew about Hatcher's feud with Collins...

"There's some bad blood between them. Beyond that, I don't know and I really don't care. I didn't take this job so I could lead the latest witch-hunt. Something about this little tiff smells rotten. It isn't my job to peddle my editor's sour grapes."

Farraday had settled back against his chair, staring at her. There was more here than what met the eye and she'd stepped right into the middle of it. At least on the surface, she seemed disgusted by the idea of a petty vendetta between Hatcher and Collins.

She also didn't seem to be aware of how much danger she could be in.

"Do you think your editor is honest?"

Lara half-shrugged. "I don't think he'd fabricate a story, if that's what you mean."

But you aren't saying that you think he's always straight with people. He could see the unspoken question in her eyes. "Collins will be fair if he knows the truth."

"What makes you so certain?"

"You'll have to trust me."

"I already did. I didn't have to tell you any of this."

"Which brings me back to my original question. Why did you?"

She let out a deep breath. "I'm not playing you. I don't work that way. Okay, I'm not going to show all my cards the minute somebody walks in the door and starts asking questions, but I'm fair. Maybe I'm just naïve, but there are a lot of politics in this town. Playboy Jimmy aside, I don't know if there's another person here who'd cover my back if I needed help."

Farraday stood up. "I'll talk to Collins."

***

Farraday knew the fear of being burned again had made him edgy, guarded. Everything was filtered through his growing cynicism. He was always looking for a lilt in the voice or a shadow on a face that would give away a lie, even when he was off the job, something that had never been a problem for him before.

He'd thought he was jaded enough, ready to handle himself, until he unraveled in a matter of minutes with Lara. She hadn't taken advantage, hadn't used it to find out everything he knew without sharing any of her information. That impressed him, but the fact that she'd been in a position to extract more information than he'd planned to share had brought his own fears front and center in his mind. He wasn't as tough as he'd thought, maybe not ready for the mess he'd found himself in.

As he approached the station door he caught a glimpse of movement from the corner of his eye. An officer, Farraday's age with dark hair, fit, a bit shorter than average, yet normally self-assured on the job, was being poked in the chest by Lenny Becker. Becker's finger kept time with the movements of his mouth.

From this distance Farraday couldn't tell what was being said but he could see the red face, the angry line of Walker's mouth, the snarl curling Becker's lips.

Lenny Becker, who had a reputation for backroom deals and turning a blind eye for the right price but kept his arrest record high enough to appear clean. Lenny Becker, a man who knew how to grease wheels and stay off Internal's radar. Lenny Becker, lecturing a cop who'd made a glaring mistake that had led to a story in the paper about a missing woman...

"Farraday! I've been waiting."

He hadn't seen Captain Collins walk out of his office. Whatever was going on with Lenny and Walker would have to wait. He marched into the office and Collins closed the door behind him.

"How's it going out there, Ty?" Collins passed him a glass of water, pouring another cup from the cooler behind his desk. "Sorry to put you on this. The last thing I wanted was to send you after a reporter. This story didn't look like it had much to it, though. Kelly could be a rogue reporter, just stirring up his own trouble, or he could be a player. What do you think?"

Farraday shifted, keeping his gaze on the desk for a moment. Setting his cup down, he looked up.

"Kelly has a video Duane Brodie shot. Duane brought it here first. Officer Walker brushed him off. Walker was negligent. Kelly could have had an exclusive and, according to Kelly, Hatcher wants your head on a platter."

"In less than two days you've seen the video and gotten Kelly's take on my feud with Hatcher? How the hell did you manage that?"

"I saw the video, interviewed Duane, saw the scene of the incident, read most of the file before it was stolen..."

"Whoa. Kelly gave you access to all of this? What the hell did you find to hold over his head?"

"Kelly's been cooperative. I know, I know," he said as Collins' eyes narrowed. "Kelly isn't like any other reporter I've had to deal with."

Collins stared at him for a minute, a shadow on his face as he tapped his fingers against the desk. "What happened to this file?"

"It was stolen out of Kelly's vehicle when I was inspecting the scene. Kelly was with me the whole time. Potential evidence we'd taped off was destroyed. At the very least, there's more here than someone wants us to know. And when things don't sit right-"

"It usually means something's crooked." Collins leaned back in his chair, rubbing his forehead. Then he stiffened. "Hatcher didn't see you did he?"

"No. Kelly kept me out of his line of sight. Hatcher wants to bait you for coercion if you try to discredit this story."

"Could Kelly have an ally who took the file to persuade you the story was legit?"

"I don't think Kelly would show me all the evidence, take me to the witnesses and then play a risky game. Besides, the file was one thing. If someone had followed us they might have known where to look for it. But there was no way for anyone to know we would be taping off evidence at the scene."

"Unless Kelly planted it."

"I don't think Kelly is who you should be worried about. This old feud could explode in your face. Kelly made it clear Hatcher will hang you out to dry in a heartbeat if he gets the chance."

Collins stared at him. "It isn't like you to take the word of a reporter."

Farraday paused. "I think Kelly is okay."

"I don't know how to feel about that, exactly, but it isn't warm and fuzzy. Keep an eye on Kelly, see where this leads. If there's a body in Doe Lake we need to find it before someone else does and deal with Officer Walker. Becker can partner with Jones while you're on this."

"What about-"

Collins held up his hand. "One thing at a time."

"If someone did steal this file, there's more to this than an apparent suicide. If that person realizes Kelly has more evidence, they'll be back." Farraday stood up and reached for the doorknob. He paused, turning to look back at Collins. "Don't see a conspiracy behind every headline. Whatever's going on here, it's not about you. Hatcher might try to write it that way but Officer Walker will be on the chopping block if an ax is going to fall."

Lines of worry etched Collins face. "I like Walker."

"So do I. But that doesn't mean I trust him."

Collins frowned, his eyes narrowing. After a moment, he nodded. Farraday opened the door and walked away.

***

"The usual." Vern Fletcher slid onto the barstool, glowering at Freddie's cocky grin.

Freddie suppressed his smirk, setting the drink down. "It's a little early for you."

He glared at the bartender, who held up his hands and backed away. Vern turned his eyes down to his drink.

The past few days he'd been running in circles, getting nowhere fast. Mr. Chan's story had panned out, cementing Vern's conviction that his instincts had overridden his complacency because he smelled a lead, pure and simple. It wasn't like he cared about Chan or his missing niece.

At least, that's what he kept telling himself.

Then Larimer Kelly had stirred the pot without even knowing it. He'd spent the past two days checking her sources.

Fortunately, Chan hadn't seen the story about the alleged suicide of a young woman. There'd been no frantic calls, no tears and despair.

It was a hell of a coincidence he found out about a missing woman only a few days before Lara's story about the woman at the lake ran.

What had been missing from her article was what interested him. There had to be something more, a hunch confirmed when he'd seen her leave the office Monday with a detective on her heels.

He wasn't ready to go to her with his suspicions yet. After all, he'd wanted this story for himself and he'd given up his weekend to lay the groundwork.

Lara's article had distracted him from his original line of inquiry and he'd missed his chance to catch David Douglas, the local businessman who ran the factory Teo Chan's niece had worked for. Douglas had included a personal letter in Choy Kim's application for a visa.

Now Douglas was out of town and Vern had a list of questions and nobody to answer them.

Mr. Chan was expecting him tomorrow. Vern was going to have to find a way to get enough answers to convince him that he could handle this on his own.

He didn't want Teo Chan going to the police. Not until he knew more.

***

Lara hurried down the hallway at The Ledger, Jimmy right behind her.

"Don't you think you're being naïve?"

"Spare me the big brother routine, Jimmy."

"I'm serious! And keep your voice down. You never know when Hatcher's lurking around the building. We should take this into your office."

"There's nothing to take. You're overreacting."

"Maybe you're smitten with the dashing detective."

"You're jealous!"

"Lara," the voice growled.

"Don't be ridiculous. I'm not playing games with you or Farraday or anyone else. Well, maybe keep-away with Hatcher, but that's because I need more time."

"You trust this guy? How do you know he hasn't twisted all your information to discredit you? You know the kind of stuff they say about his partner? And those other detectives? Jones and-"

"Do they say that about Farraday?"

A pause. "No, but-"

Lara exhaled. She was barely aware of Jimmy turning and walking away as she stomped into her office. She stopped cold.

Farraday was sitting in the chair he'd occupied the day before, tapping his fingers on the arm absent-mindedly. Lara was about to ask how he got past the building security but didn't. She and Jimmy were always the first ones in so she had a feeling she wouldn't want to know.

He smiled innocently. "I'm officially on the case."

"I found something interesting." She pulled a small community paper off her desk, opened it to a marked page and passed it to him. It was nothing more than a classified ad, announcing the engagement of Robson Walker and Megan Douglas.

Who bore a striking resemblance to the woman on the video.

Farraday glanced at the paper, his eyes widening. "I guess we know where we're going this morning."

Lara followed him out of her office, wondering what he'd heard. His eyes had betrayed nothing. No amusement, no concern, no anger.

Making her wonder just how good an actor he was, since it was hard to believe he hadn't overheard the argument. She took a deep breath outside Jimmy's office, but then opened the door anyway.

The office was empty, as was her tray. "Remind me to get those photos later."

They walked out to the parking lot and she headed straight for her jeep. He didn't object to taking her vehicle, or her driving.

***

Oak Creek was barely more than a crossroads, with half a dozen stores huddled around the intersection where two busy highways met. The population sign read 620 but they hadn't passed many homes before reaching the village. She parked in front of the grocery store, looking up and down the sidewalk.

"Where do we start?"

"I'd rather not talk to the police. If I ask the cops about Walker he's sure to hear about it."

"We should have looked up the address in the phone book at my office."

"Too late now."

They walked to a nearby phone booth, Farraday scanning the local names until he found the right one. He tapped the page twice. "Oakridge Crescent."

Lara nodded back in the direction they'd come from. "We passed it coming into town, just a block before the grocery store. You'd better go alone."

"What will you do?"

"Shop for antiques." She nodded at the three competing stores filling the short street as she passed him the keys.

Farraday walked back to the jeep. He'd checked the missing persons reports. Nothing had been filed for the past few weeks in this area, and nothing state wide for the past two months matched the general description. It was as though the woman on the video had come out of thin air and disappeared into the pelting rain without a trace, like an apparition.

It didn't take him long to find the right address. The two-story Victorian home was at the end of a fresh paint job. Farraday parked on the shoulder of the road, walking on to the property. The owner was working on the lower left side of the porch, so absorbed in his task he didn't even hear Farraday approach.

"So this is where you live," he said, trying to sound casual and ignore Officer Walker's startled expression as he turned to find Farraday standing on his front lawn.

"This is unexpected." Walker set the brush down and reached for a towel.

"I'm just getting to know the area. I saw your picture in the paper. Congratulations."

"Thanks." Walker glanced at Farraday's suit. "This is strictly a social call?"

"Why wouldn't it be?"

"You aren't exactly a water cooler man. Becker says you spell life w-o-r-k."

Farraday flinched. Cops could take a read off you and peg you pretty quickly. As the new man in town, he expected some talk. He just hadn't heard any of it until now.

"I heard Collins sent you after that new reporter."

"Yeah. I guess the new guy gets the dirty work." He didn't see any reaction on Walker's face, so he took a gamble. "Duane Brodie had a video, though."

Walker's jaw hung open for a split second, but he recovered fast. "Duane Brodie is a crack. He's been in and out of the station three dozen times since I've been on the job, easily. The closest he came to a legitimate complaint was when his neighbor hit him with a golf club for picking berries on her property."

"He wants to help, though?"

"Harmless, besides squandering man hours. I'm surprised Collins is wasting your time."

Farraday shrugged. "That reporter stirred things up."

Walker offered a cynical half-smile. "I thought this was a social call."

"You brought it up."

Whatever Walker was about to say died on his lips as the screen door opened and then clapped shut. He smiled as he turned to look at the woman who'd emerged from the house. "Meg, this is Detective Tymen Farraday. Detective Farraday, my fiancé, Megan."

Farraday reached to shake her hand, noting the raven hair, the soulful brown eyes, the willowy figure.

"Can you stay for lunch? I was just about to set the table."

He shook his head. "I have a friend waiting for me."

Farraday felt Walker's eyes watching him but forced himself to try to stroll casually back to the jeep after he said goodbye. It didn't take long for him to return to the main street and locate Lara. She got in the passenger side and he filled her in as he drove.

***

"Are you sure it's her?" Lara asked.

"Of course I'm not certain. But she's slim, has long, dark hair and dark eyes."

"So do dozens of other women. It makes no sense."

"It explains why there isn't a body on the rocks," Farraday said. "And why Officer Walker wouldn't want anyone to see that video or hear Duane's story."

"Then why let Duane take the tape with him? Why not get rid of it? Why risk his career just to hide the fact that his fiancé is suicidal? And how did he even know what was on the tape, unless..."

Farraday nodded. "He was there."

"But why steal a file?"

"Maybe he didn't have time to read it and felt he had to take it with him."

"There are more questions than answers. We have no body. We have no victim, if you're right about Megan. We have a missing file, evidence tampering, a suspect and no hard evidence of anything as far as we can tell."

"Collins isn't going to like this."

Lara smiled. "For once even Hatcher might agree with him."

"The thing is, Walker suspected something the minute I set foot on his property."

"And suspicion is an indication of guilt?"

Farraday shrugged.

"I was suspicious when I saw you in my office."

"That's different. We're adversaries. Walker and I are supposed to be colleagues."

"Adversaries?" She didn't even try to keep her brows from rising.

"If you ask Jimmy."

So he had heard their argument.

"If I were your captain, your first official day on this would be your last. He's not going to be too happy about the fact that our only suspect to some minor offenses is one of his own officers."

"That's why I'm convinced there's something we're missing. Rob Walker doesn't strike me as the type to take risks without a damn good reason."

"Protecting his fiancé isn't enough? And you can forget trying to get an ID from Betty Zimmerman. She left town."

Farraday's eyebrows shot up. "For good?"

"Apparently she goes away every winter. She decided to leave a few months early. I tried to call yesterday and got her answering machine with the message." Lara watched him for a moment and then continued. "There's something else we haven't considered. If I am being followed, they know you're working with me. If you didn't tell Rob Walker and it's him-"

"I didn't lie, exactly. I expressed a lack of enthusiasm about babysitting a reporter. Walker mentioned he'd heard I was following up on your story."

"Baiting you for information?"

"That would be my guess. Are you sure you've told me everything?"

"Ty..."

He held up a hand. "Not that I doubt you. I just want to make sure we aren't overlooking something obvious."

Lara shook her head slowly. "You have the samples, you've seen the video and you spoke to Betty and Duane yourself. That just leaves the photos."

"The photos." Farraday pulled into the back parking lot at The Ledger, which bordered a grove of trees that joined up with a park, filled with walking trails. It was quieter than the front parking lot, obscured from the view of passerby, but it was where she'd told him to park. He engaged the emergency brake and passed her the keys.

***

Lara grabbed the packet of photos off her tray and started to walk back into the hallway, almost colliding with Jimmy in the process.

"The boss is looking for you." Jimmy nodded at Farraday. "You'd better not let Hatcher catch you with him."

"Say no more." They turned around and went out the back exit.

"Why don't you park out front?"

"I like using the back entrance."

"It's pretty secluded and quiet back here." He looked at her and she glared at him. "Where to now?" he asked her.

"My place," Lara said, ignoring the inference that it wasn't safe for her to park behind her place of work.

When they got to her house Farraday followed Lara into the living room, where she spread the photos out over the coffee table.

She pointed to a photo on the edge of the table. The lightning was firing into the water, illuminating the rocky ledge that framed the shot on the left side. At the top of the ledge, dark but distinguishable, a man was standing with his back to the camera. It looked like he was running on the path as he was caught in this split-second record of time.

"There's no way to know if this was taken before or after the video was shot."

Lara rubbed her forehead, trying to remember exactly what Duane had said. "I had the impression Duane took most of his shots after he turned the camcorder off."

"But he did say he'd let the video run while he snapped a few photos."

"There's no way to prove this is Rob Walker."

"It could be." Farraday picked up the photo and stared at it. "But it would never hold up in court. Still, now we know someone else was there that night. If it was Walker it explains why he didn't want to see the video."

"Maybe he thought Duane would forget about the tape. When Duane tried to persuade me to look at his photos I made up excuses."

Farraday grinned. "But you listened to the Bee Gees? Where are your priorities?"

"The records were on when I arrived. I swear, it was not by choice."

"For all we know Walker pulled her up and saved her life."

"Which would explain why he'd want this to go away. Should we drop this?"

"You already knew someone else was there that night. Why drop it now?"

She swallowed as she stared at him. Day one she'd had the upper hand. Now, every time she felt his eyes on her she felt like he could see right through her. Like he had a pretty good idea of everything she was holding back. "How'd you know?"

"A hunch, more than anything. Something about the way Duane evaded a few of my questions. Like he'd been coached, at length." He watched her. "Why didn't you want me to know?"

"It could have been a murder, and with a police officer implicated for negligence, at least..." She shrugged, feeling her cheeks burn. "Still, there was no body, so I wasn't taking it forward without more to go on. But if nobody died, the shoe print, the photos. They don't really matter."

"Shoe print?"

"I didn't tell you. But like I said about the footprints, there's no way to prove they were made by a person on The Point that night."

"We don't know that the woman was Megan and we don't know this is Walker." Farraday passed the photos to Lara. "Have you got a safe place?"

"Safer than the front seat of my jeep."

"On Monday we can take them to the lab, along with the video. Our techs might be able to get something off the film that we missed."

"I wouldn't mind a clear audio track."

"That could tell us if she was screaming at someone, like Betty Zimmerman suggested."

"You think your captain will support continuing this investigation?" It seemed like the case was disintegrating before them, which should have made Farraday happy. There would be no body, no more stories in the paper and no need to expose a negligent officer. Nothing more than a hand-slap would come of this. Captain Collins would be able to turn his attention to bigger problems, which Lara knew he had.

Farraday shrugged. "It just doesn't make sense. If she didn't die there was no crime, as far as I can tell. Walker wouldn't want to watch the video to protect Megan's identity, but why steal the file? The article was printed, he knew you had Duane's tape and the damage was done. Why not just go to Collins and come clean? Collins would have handled this quietly. Instead, if this was Walker, he risked further exposure." His brow wrinkled. "And why was Betty Zimmerman so afraid she left town?"

"You're making assumptions."

"They're valid points. There are too many loose ends here. We still have more questions than answers."

"You don't have to convince me. I agree. Will your captain?"

"That," he said as he stood up and started walking toward the door, "is a good question."

She followed him out to the jeep so that she could drop him off at his car.

Chapter 4

Farraday spent the better part of the next day sitting in court, waiting to finish testifying. One stupid incident with a guy with a temper and he had to lose hours of his life, hours he could have spent on his own casework. When it was finally over, he returned to the station.

He hadn't been at his desk for five minutes before Lenny Becker slapped his shoulder. "You been in court all day?"

"Miller's lawyers are playing every card they can think of."

"Watch yourself. Word is, the captain's on the warpath. That's my cue." Becker moved away as Collins appeared in his doorway, glaring at Farraday.

"My office. Now."

Becker smirked as he leaned back in his chair, feet comfortably on his desk, his hands entwined behind his head.

"What have you got for me?"

Farraday heard the words as he closed the door. He sank into a chair after tossing the Oak Creek paper on the desk. "Page thirteen. See for yourself."

Collins pulled the paper open, surveying the page. He looked up at Farraday. "I put you on a case not a social calendar."

"The witness who saw the woman on the road the night of the incident was Betty Zimmerman. Kelly kept Betty's name out of the file and out of the story because Betty was reluctant to talk. I spoke to her myself. She was terrified, hiding behind locked doors. Betty said the woman was screaming, 'Go away, go to hell,' and looking over her shoulder as she ran."

Collins frowned. "She was being chased?"

"Duane took a photograph that caught the image of a man coming down from the ledge around the same time as the video was shot. We suspect the photo was taken just after Duane shut the camcorder off."

"What does this have to do with Rob Walker and Megan Douglas?"

"She fits the general description of the woman on the video."

"You think Megan Douglas is the woman on the video? Do you have any idea who she is? That reporter prints Megan Douglas' name in the paper and trust me, I'll be the least of Kelly's worries."

Farraday shrugged. "Look at the facts that we have. A distraught woman running down the road, screaming, looking over her shoulder. It suggests someone was behind her. The woman who witnessed this was terrified. When I went to speak to her in the middle of the day she had the chain lock and deadbolts on."

Collins rubbed his jaw as his frown deepened. Farraday continued.

"Duane shoots the video. Around the same time he takes a picture that proves someone else was on the ledge. He brings the video to the police and is dismissed. Walker never even viewed the tape."

"Which isn't like him. His record is solid."

"Which suggests he knew what was on the video and wanted to protect his fiancé."

"She's alive?"

Farraday nodded. "Playing housewife-to-be out in Oak Creek."

"Then there's no suicide? Reporters can dish personal dirt but I'm not interested. If Megan Douglas is the woman on the video we can drop this."

"I'm not so sure."

Collins' eyes narrowed. "I need you on other things."

"I haven't forgotten. But this doesn't explain the stolen file or the destruction of potential evidence. Rob Walker was on duty. There are witnesses." Farraday raised his hand. "I checked. Discreetly, and I haven't even told Kelly. Walker didn't take that file."

Collins sighed, scratching his head. "What next?"

"Maybe we should search the lake."

"A formal search would confirm the story. Internal will be here in a heartbeat, turning Walker's life upside down." Collins tapped his fingers against his desk, frowning.

"You were hoping Kelly embellished the story."

"It wouldn't be the first time a reporter did." The phone rang and

Collins picked it up. He barely began to speak when he stopped, his head snapping up as he met Farraday's gaze. "No, don't send anyone else. I'll handle it."

He set the phone down. "There's been a break-in at Betty Zimmerman's."

***

Vern leaned back, thinking about his conversation with Teo Chan. Chan's niece, Choy Kim, had been missing for a week. It wasn't easy to persuade him to wait.

Chan had wanted to go to the police. It had taken all of Vern's finesse to keep him from pursuing a formal missing persons report, something that wasn't troubling Vern personally. He knew the police would likely write her down as just another wide-eyed girl who'd headed for the bright lights of New York City.

Vern turned at the sign for the municipal office and parked his car. He glanced at his watch as he grabbed his notebook, sprinting to the door, cursing the volume of traffic at this time of day.

"I have an appointment with Graeme Garrett," he told the receptionist.

"Your name?" she asked, sitting back down in the chair she'd looked about to abandon when he walked in.

"Vern Fletcher. From The Ledger."

"Just a minute."

He turned away, his fingers drumming the countertop, looking back to see her eyes narrow. Vern stopped tapping as she set the phone down.

"You can go through. Second-last door..."

He'd begun moving as soon as she hung up.

Graeme Garrett was the fallback man for the mayor. In the court of public opinion he was the mayor's right-hand man, but Vern knew better. Graeme had wormed his way into the post somehow, his actual contributions to the municipal government somewhat sketchy. Usually, Morrow's press secretary handled journalists when the mayor wasn't available, but occasionally Garrett stepped in when the mayor was too busy to bother with the reporters.

Why Garrett got involved was a mystery to Vern. All he knew was that every time Garrett handled the press, the reporters Vern knew usually dropped the story.

Vern had asked for the mayor, but had been told Garrett was available. Others praised Walter Morrow, a man who'd take time out of his busy schedule to throw the opening pitch at a school softball tournament.

A mayor too busy to talk about a missing girl but with enough time to roll up his sleeves for a little baseball. Only in America.

Vern raised his hand to knock on the open door but the stolid figure turned and gestured for him to come in.

"Have a seat Mr. Fletcher. How can I help you?" The dull blue eyes stared without a hint of emotion on the man's face.

Vern had seen Garrett on several occasions, but he'd never spoken to him. He'd heard stories about City Hall's cold fish. Graeme Garrett's relentless gaze had a way of making even the seasoned reporter uncomfortable. He was broad-shouldered, short, with sandy hair and a bearing that reminded Vern more of a bouncer than a politician. If Garrett's hair had been dark he could have played a mob hitman in a movie. He had that kind of look about him.

"I'm not sure if you can," Vern said carefully as he opened his notebook, watching Garrett's face from the periphery of his field of vision, looking for any change in Garrett's demeanor. "I'm trying to find a woman who apparently works for you."

"For me?" There was a small crease on the brow. "I don't know who you could mean."

"Well, she has a legitimate green card. She was working at one of the factories. When I went there I was told that she was working at the mayor's office."

"I don't recall hiring a factory worker." His tone was calm, almost hypnotically soothing, but he averted his eyes as he spoke, looking away from the reporter for the first time.

"Apparently the woman hadn't quit her job. Her supervisor was told she had been reassigned to work here."

Garrett didn't blink. "It must be a mistake."

"Perhaps you could ask the mayor and any staff here if they know Choy Kim?" Vern passed a copy of the photo Teo Chan had provided of to Garrett. He noted the way Garrett's eyes widened when he heard the name and wondered if Garrett was prejudiced or jaded enough to dismiss a missing immigrant for the same reasons the cops might.

"This is a matter for the police."

"Immigrants are sometimes reluctant to trust the local authorities. Bad experiences in their homelands..."

"America is their homeland now." Garrett stared at Vern.

"Some have trouble adjusting. My number." Vern passed his card to Garrett, who didn't even glance at it.

"Our secretary will call if we can be of any help to your inquiries. When did you say this woman went missing?"

Vern hadn't said, deliberately, but he couldn't think of a way to avoid answering. "A week ago."

"Did I not notice a story about a woman committing suicide at the lake?" A sly smile spread across Garrett's face. "Perhaps the answers to your questions are in your own office."

Smug little bastard. Vern hadn't learned anything helpful about Choy Kim but he'd acquired a new awareness of the mayor's lapdog.

He wondered how the pretentious prick had managed to elude his interest until now and promised himself that when he'd dealt with the missing girl, he'd see if there was a juicy headline he could dig up on Graeme Garrett.

***

Two squad cars were already outside Betty Zimmerman's house, as well as an old Buick. An officer was taking a statement from an older woman. Farraday followed Collins inside.

The splinters on the door jam explained how the perp had gained entry. Inside, kitchen cupboards were left open, bags of rice and pasta partially spilled on the floor, the table littered with envelopes and their contents, what looked like bills and junk mail offering pre-approved credit cards.

"Does anyone know where she is?" Collins asked.

Officer Joynt was one of those wide-eyed, fresh-faced types, with reddish-brown hair and freckles. He shrugged. "No."

Farraday entered the living room, noticing the books spilling off the shelves, on to the floor. A desk in the corner was covered with more scattered bills and letters. "The perp could have been looking for a clue about where she'd gone."

"It may be unrelated but I'm not taking any chances," Collins said. "If this is your guy, there's something he's afraid of. And it likely wasn't Megan Douglas on that video."

"Which puts us back to square one."

Farraday followed Collins outside. Officer Joynt caught up with them as they reached Collins' car.

"I just finished with Ruth Alton's statement. Are you handling this?"

"Betty Zimmerman was a witness in something else I was working on. Did Mrs. Alton have anything helpful?"

Joynt scanned his notes. "Betty asked her to water the plants and said she'd call in a few weeks. Mrs. Alton forgot to ask about fish food so she came to see if she needed to buy some. When she approached the house she found the door swinging on its hinges so she called the police and waited outside. She said Betty had seemed upset about something for the past week or so."

"Does she know if Betty has any family she might visit?" Farraday asked.

"Husband is deceased, no children. Parents are dead and Betty was an only child."

"In-laws?"

Joynt shook his head.

"Can I get a copy of what you have?"

"I'll put it on your desk. And the phone rang just after I got here. It was a security company, saying they could hook up an alarm system tomorrow."

"A little late now." Farraday glanced at Collins.

"I'll copy the message and put it with the statement." Joynt paused. "There's something else. Mrs. Alton also spoke to a reporter who'd been asking questions about Betty. She told the reporter Betty left town."

Farraday sank into the passenger seat and pulled the door shut as he glanced at Collins.

"What's your gut telling you?" Collins asked.

"Nothing good."

"I'll get Joynt to follow up on this and have him copy everything in the file to you."

"Aren't Walker and Joynt usually partnered?"

"I can't imagine any officer of mine being this sloppy," Collins said, his mouth twisting as he stared straight ahead, his face shadowed. "Walker's on a different rotation for the next few weeks, which gives Officer Joynt some time, but I doubt he'll come up with anything that you don't find first unless there are prints that match something in the system. Whoever did this is reckless. What would they have done if Mrs. Zimmerman had been home?"

"Good thing she wasn't. I'll give the story to Kelly. That will keep Hatcher happy and buy some time. Maybe if Kelly writes it like a robbery our guy will think the trail has gone cold and he won't do anything rash."

"You saw the damage to the door jam. Crow bar, most likely. If this guy finds someone standing between him and whatever he's after..."

Farraday frowned. "Let's hope we can catch up to him before somebody gets in his way."

After Collins dropped him off at his car, Farraday went home to his apartment, a rented space above the home of his landlady. He'd feared an older landlady would want to mother him but Mrs. Taylor was quiet and unobtrusive, which he appreciated. He had a private entrance and came and went as he pleased.

Everything that had happened was flooding back. The stolen file, Hatcher's plan, Walker's suspicions, Megan Douglas' resemblance to the grainy image on the video, Duane's photo, Betty Zimmerman's sudden departure...

The stolen file kept coming to the forefront of his thoughts. Who knew where they would be? Assuming it wasn't just a random theft. But why steal a file from an SUV loaded with CDs that hadn't been touched? Farraday had noted them on the drive out, so he hadn't needed to ask. No, the theft had been about the story, about the woman on the video. The tampering at the scene proved that.

Nobody had known they'd be there, not even Collins. Farraday hadn't even known Larimer Kelly would talk to him about the story, never mind take him to her sources. Duane had easy access, but why give them the video and steal a file? And the only way he had enough time was if he'd taken it while they were at the scene, then destroyed the evidence before he returned to his boat and eventually, his cabin. He couldn't have beaten them to the jeep after they left his house. How could he have known they were there?

Still, it wasn't wise to rule anyone out completely, not yet. They were followed, the site was being watched, or it was pure, dumb luck. Farraday didn't believe in extreme coincidences and he didn't believe in this kind of luck either, especially not when so many quirks kept coming up in this investigation. One small, apparent coincidence could be a fluke, a strange twist of fate. Two smelled of something contrived. Anything more... He sighed. Something was going on.

He couldn't shake the image of Lara and the file from his mind as he stared vacantly at the television. Kids running and jumping in the leaf piles, a dog running along the trimmed hedges by the side of the road. Reminding everyone fall was here and it was time to clean up your yard.

Reminding him of Lara's front yard, except the bushes at her house were higher, wilder and easier to hide in.

He'd tried to call from the courthouse but couldn't reach her all day. There was no answer at her office or at home.

Farraday jumped off the couch and barely stopped to turn the TV off, grabbed his coat and keys and slammed the door behind him.

It wasn't a long drive but it seemed to take forever. The last lingering rays of sun were behind the trees to the west, the sky not yet filled with night but not light either. A wind had picked up, the trees along the overgrown road swaying under the gentle breeze.

He kept telling himself he was being silly, that she'd likely just been hiding from Hatcher, maybe working at the library. Gravel crunched under the tires as he pulled over and cut the engine. The still night air was silent, the way you expect it to be at two in the morning, but for this early in the evening the quiet seemed unnatural, unnerving and Lara's jeep was in the driveway. Farraday reached for his keys and pulled them out.

He'd told Lara he had a hunch about this case and he had that same, unsettled feeling in the pit of his stomach now, the voice that was telling him something wasn't right. He slid out of his car.

The darkening shadows blended into the trees, making it hard to distinguish any possible unnatural forms lurking in the bushes. It didn't take him long to cross the grass, cautiously surveying the yard. He stepped up onto the porch, keeping his eyes on the open area in front of the house. Cautiously making his way to the door, he reached for his gun.

The frame was splintered, just like Betty's, the wood cracked. A crowbar by the mat looked like it had been tossed aside, the wooden door hanging open.

Farraday heard someone shout from inside the house, the sound of furniture behind pushed, followed by a thud. He yanked the screen door open and ran toward the sound of the scuffle. In the unlit room he could just see the silhouette of two forms ahead of him, wrestling over something, and that the contents of Lara's pack had been strewn across the floor.

"Stupid bitch."

The gravelly, low voice was followed by a thump. In the dim shadows, it looked like Lara had hit the intruder with something and her assailant lashed back, the thud followed by the stinging sound of skin on skin as her head snapped back from the force of the blow. The intruder grabbed her arm, for one moment locked in a tug of war.

"Lara, let go!"

Her assailant swung at her, the smack knocking her back against the wall. The dark figure plowed into Farraday and shoved him aside. He winced as his shoulder hit the wall but fought to keep his balance. The front door banged and then there was nothing but silence as he weighed his options in a split-second. It wasn't a choice, not with her injured. Farraday moved to where Lara was lying and knelt beside her.

Even in dim flicker of firelight he could see the blood. "Damn it."

Farraday holstered his gun and grabbed his cell phone.

***

The two minutes since he'd hung up the phone had crawled by. At last, Lara's eyelids fluttered, her hand reaching for her head as she tried to sit up.

"Stay still," Farraday ordered. "You've probably got a concussion."

"I'll live," she muttered, pulling herself up against the stairs. Glancing at him, she saw the concern and frustration muddled in his eyes, his frown and a glint of fear fading as he watched her move. "You didn't get him."

Farraday shook his head. He disappeared into the kitchen. "Here," he said when he returned, kneeling down and pressing a cool cloth against her forehead.

"Some day this has been. I already had a headache."

"Your head's going to hurt a lot more before long."

"Why? You planning to knock me out again?"

"Funny." He gently held her arms.

She tried to shrug him off as he helped her up. "I can walk."

"Don't argue. I'm not letting go until you're on the couch."

Lara bit back her response as his arm wound around her waist securely. "I don't mean to sound ungrateful, but what are you doing here?"

"I couldn't shake the feeling that something was wrong. When I got here I saw your door had been forced open."

"My life was quiet until I met you." She wouldn't admit it, but she was glad he was holding her. It felt like a million pins and needles were pushing into her skull, her vision fading to black and then something comparable to the static insomniacs without cable watch at 3 am. Lara was trying to sort out a tangible doubt, the genesis of a question about why someone had broken into her house, why Tymen Farraday had arrived just in time to protect her...

Farraday pulled the chair over by the couch, where he'd made her lie down. "Before my captain gets here-"

Her eyes flew open, her head jerking up. "You called your captain? What the hell for?"

"Lara, just listen. I should have told you earlier, in your office, when you leveled with me about Hatcher and his plans to go after Collins."

"Should have told me what?" She sat up. He'd left the room. She could hear the hum of the fridge as a door opened and then closed. Someone had broken into her home and assaulted her, and he was apologizing. "What aren't you telling me?"

"Lie back." Farraday returned and walked across the room. He sat on the couch beside her, pushing her back against the pillow. "Just promise me," he said, looking her straight in the eye, "that you'll give me a chance to explain."

He put an ice pack against her forehead, staring at her until she felt the tension in her face dissolve and her shoulders relax.

"You've got a nasty goose egg." Farraday disappeared again, the sound of cupboards opening followed by the tap running her only clues until he returned, a bottle of Aleve in one hand, glass of water in the other.

Lara watched him, noting the troubled look and wrinkled brow. Before she could say anything she heard an engine in the driveway. It stopped, shortly followed by quick steps on her porch and into her kitchen.

"Ty?"

"In here." Farraday stood up.

Lara noticed the sheepish look etched with guilt.

Collins sat down across from her and looked at Farraday.

"This is Larimer Kelly." Farraday didn't look at either of them, so Lara gave Captain Collins a small smile.

"Call me Lara." She watched the reality hit Collins eyes as they widened and then he glared at his detective.

Captain Patrick Collins was a handsome man in his own right. His face was broad and pleasant while Farraday's was narrow and distinctive, but Collins had the same dark, warm eyes.

"Lara." Collins nodded at her before looking at Farraday, who still stood with his back partially to them. "Whenever you're ready, Ty. And this time, don't leave anything out."

Farraday turned. "After we got back from Betty Zimmerman's I had a bad feeling. I came over here to make sure Lara was okay."

"What were you doing at Betty's?" Lara asked.

"Someone broke into her house."

Lara's hand and the ice pack fell against her stomach. "Was it a robbery?"

"Can you write it that way?"

"Are you serious?" The question died on her lips as she looked at Farraday and then his captain. They were both staring at her, Collins' eyes narrowed, his jaw set. "Why?"

"We think the break-in could be connected to the lead you've been following. Nothing appears to be missing from Betty's house. And your front door is the mirror image of the job this guy did on hers," Captain Collins said. "This guy is reckless. That makes him dangerous."

"You don't have to tell me that. He stole my flashlight."

Farraday frowned. "You're lucky that's all he did."

She felt her eyes pinch as she glared up at him. "I might have broken his nose when I hit him. That wasn't all my blood."

"Blood evidence would help. I'll take some samples."

"My pack is-"

"Empty. I have a kit in my car." He turned and left the room. Within seconds she heard the screen door snap shut.

Lara sighed, leaning back against the couch.

"That's a nasty gash. We should have someone look at it." Collins pulled out his cell phone.

"I'm fine. You already went to the scene of a break-in this afternoon. If anyone finds out you were here..." She shrugged, letting him draw his own conclusions.

He put his phone away. "You've got a point. Are you alone out here?"

"Just me and the cat."

"Then stay somewhere else. Odds are this guy will be back."

"This was him being back. He was here before, the other night."

The captain's head snapped up. "This is the first I've heard of it."

She put up her hand in an effort to stem the anger in his voice. "I didn't tell Ty. I wasn't sure."

"Do you know if he took anything?"

"Ty wouldn't let me look. This guy wore gloves so there won't be any prints."

He went into the kitchen and returned with her pack and the contents that had been scattered, the front door snapping shut again, followed by the sound of footsteps on the porch steps.

She sorted through them quickly, putting her files back together before tossing them on the coffee table and shook her head. "As far as I can tell everything's here."

Lara looked up as Farraday finished at the base of the stairs, plastic bags in hand. He dropped them down beside the files.

"It looks like we may have a sample."

"It's a start. But without something to compare it to that's not much," Collins said.

"There are the samples we have from the scene," Lara said, looking at Farraday's face. His eyes were shadowed with lines of worry, though they widened at her words.

"I thought the sample we had was from the woman."

"Well, since we're considering theories, maybe the man pried her fingers off the ledge and cut himself. Maybe the other sample wasn't from the woman." She drew a deep breath. "I can't imagine a police officer breaking into my house, assaulting me with another cop not ten feet away."

Collins exhaled. "I don't think Megan Douglas is your mystery woman. If Walker's fiancé was suicidal he could have dealt with this quietly instead of turning into a criminal."

"And we have to report this. When Hatcher finds out..."

"Good point." Collins nodded at Farraday. "I can leave. But what about you?"

"Driving by when I saw a dark figure on the porch. I investigated, found the door had been forced open, and entered the house. It all happened too quickly to call for back-up, and that part isn't a lie."

"That will work. She needs a place to stay," Collins said. "This is the perp's second attempt and she shouldn't be here alone."

"Second attempt?" Farraday glared at her. "You didn't say anything."

She shrugged. "I wasn't sure. I am now."

"Then he's right. You need to stay somewhere else until this is sorted out."

"I'm not going anywhere." She folded her arms across her chest.

"This guy has been here twice. You could have been seriously hurt. As it is, there's blood all over you."

"I'm going upstairs to change. I'll even bag my clothes for you. But I'm not leaving my home. And I can walk," she said when Farraday moved toward her.

She marched up the stairs, leaving him to face Collins alone.

"Anything else I should know about?"

Farraday sighed as he collapsed against the sofa. "You didn't ask and it isn't important."

"It isn't? Beautiful girl, knows how to work a source for a story. Sound familiar?"

"It isn't even close. You know that."

"That's what makes this worse."

Farraday felt his neck burn. "What was I supposed to do? Would you expect me to walk into your office and announce that Larimer Kelly is a man?"

"That's different."

"Are you saying I shouldn't trust her just because she's a woman? I didn't expect an attitude like that from you."

Collins sighed as he ran his hand over his hair, scratching his head. "You know this has nothing to do with being chauvinistic. I didn't expect you to keep things from me."

Farraday's jaw twisted for a moment and then he exhaled. "She's wondering why I called you."

The color faded from Collins' face. "What are you going to tell her?"

"How about the truth?"

"You trust her that much? Ty, I hope you know what you're doing."

"She could have blown Rob Walker's career apart from day one. Lara had everything she needed to turn the jumper story into a front-page exclusive on police negligence. Hatcher's pressuring her to write this as an expose on corruption and abuse of power in your office."

"So you believe."

"You doubt that?" Farraday had always admired Collins' values and sense of fairness but pig-headed judgments came to the fore when Ted Hatcher was involved. "How could she stage this break-in? There was no way she could know I was coming over to check on her."

Collins rubbed his chin mechanically. He didn't respond.

***

Lara came down the stairs wearing pajamas, a deliberate sign of her determination to stay in her own home. Collins shook his head as Lara dropped her bagged clothing down on the table.

"The department can put you up in a hotel for the weekend and sort something out until this is cleared up. We'll give you the first crack at whatever comes of the investigation."

"I already have first crack. Literally, if you count the job this guy did on my head." She gauged the size the swelling with her fingertips as she felt the goose egg growing on her scalp. "I'm not running."

"We all agree this was likely the same guy who broke into Betty's house, right?" Farraday asked.

Collins and Lara glanced at each other and both nodded.

"And we all think there's more to this story than we've learned. Correct?"

They exchanged another glance and nodded again.

"Then this guy could come after me next. How many of us can run, Uncle Con?"

Uncle Con. The words sunk in. Farraday's faith in his captain, his conviction that Collins was clean... She'd heard Collins start in on Farraday about holding out on him during this investigation.

Farraday's words. *I'll tell you everything. Just give me a chance to explain.*

"You want her to know you have her back? Then you stay here and keep an eye on her." He glanced at her before glaring at Farraday as he stood up. "Wherever you've got your evidence stashed - yes, I do know it isn't in our evidence locker - keep it there until Monday when we can secure it in my office. Who's got the blood samples?"

"Dr. Eaton."

Collins rubbed his chin. "Leave them there. I don't know what you've stepped into," he looked down at Lara, "but I want it cleaned up. If an officer from my precinct is involved, I want him behind bars."

He passed Lara's ice pack to Farraday, who took it to the kitchen. Collins leaned down toward her.

"My nephew thinks he can trust you. For now, that's enough for me." His eyes pried into hers with a forcefulness that told her Farraday's judgment was barely enough and that she was on thin ice with Collins. The tension in his expression made Farraday's attitude toward reporters seem charitable. After a moment, he unclenched his jaw. "Don't make me regret it. I protect my officers and especially my family."

Usually, a warning like that would have put Lara's back up, but her head was pounding. Between the tough words, the tension in his features and the suspicious stares, she sensed genuine concern for Farraday. It was clear that he was speaking as a father figure, not just a captain.

"Nobody knows you're related?"

Collins shook his head. Farraday returned, his eyes narrowing as he approached them, extending his hand to pass her the ice pack.

"They won't hear it from me." Lara took the pack, putting it on her forehead while he tried to steer his uncle toward the door.

"If anyone finds out, I'll know where it came from." He glared at Farraday out of the corner of his eye and muttered, "I hope you know what you're doing. And whatever you do, don't you let her out of your sight. If anything happens to one of Hatcher's reporters-"

Farraday held up his hand. "Don't worry. I'm not going anywhere," he said.

Collins nodded, letting the screen door snap shut as he walked away.

***

When Farraday returned to the living room Lara was putting the phone down.

"They're on their way," she told him.

After that, they drifted into an awkward silence, Lara sitting on the end of the couch, her face contorted into a grimace as she held the ice pack in place and absently rubbed her neck with her other hand.

Farraday never did sit down, instead holding the back of the armchair with his hands. Whatever Lara thought about Collins being his uncle, he couldn't tell.

A sharp rap at the door caught his attention and he let go of the chair, walking to the hallway. He could see the uniformed officer at the door.

Officer Rob Walker.

For what felt like minutes but must only have been a few seconds they stood staring at each other, Walker's eyes widening at first, then narrowing as his face darkened.

"Detective Farraday," he said. "We had a report-"

Farraday nodded. "There's been a break-in."

"Is this your residence?" Walker checked his notes. "It was reported the call came from..." He glanced up at Farraday. "Larimer Kelly."

"This is Miss Kelly's residence."

"And you're responding to this call?" Walker's cold stare was now matched by the puzzled look of his partner, a new recruit Farraday wasn't familiar with, who'd finally come to the front steps from the patrol car.

"Something keeping you?" Farraday asked him, opening the screen door and stepping outside.

"I, uh-"

"He was radioing in, responding to another patrol car that was on their way here," Walker said curtly. "What are you doing here?"

Farraday started to relay the story he'd run past Collins earlier. He hadn't said more than that he was driving by when Walker interrupted him again.

"You just happened to be driving by the house that Larimer Kelly lives in. Isn't that the reporter you've been checking up on the past few days?"

Farraday was glad it was dark on the porch, because he could feel his neck burning again.

"As a matter of fact, I was coming here to check on her. I'd left a message and hadn't heard back."

"Why not just say that then?"

"Because when I got here, there weren't any lights on inside. I was going to leave." It wasn't a complete lie.

"But you saw a dark figure at the door and," Walker paused, checking what he'd written down so far, "investigated. Did you see a vehicle?"

Farraday stared at him for a moment, reading the disbelief in Walker's eyes. He shook his head and forced himself to look at Walker's partner. "You should call for paramedics. Miss Kelly was struck in the head and knocked unconscious during an assault." He glanced back at Walker. "If you'd like to see the scene..."

He gestured to the door while Walker's partner looked from one to the other. Walker stared at Farraday for a moment before speaking. "Make the call."

It was a good point. He hadn't seen a vehicle, making him wonder where the intruder had come from.

Walker opened the door and went inside, Farraday following him.

***

Once the police and paramedics had left, Farraday turned the deadbolt and checked the windows and the patio doors. Only the lamp beside the couch was still on, encompassing barely more than the sitting area in light.

"I see where you get your charming disposition." When he didn't say anything, Lara asked, "Why do you call him Con?"

"I shortened Collins to the only thing I could manage when I wasn't even three. He's been Uncle Con ever since." He sank down on the sofa beside her. "I should have-"

"No." She raised her hand and shook her head, wincing from the affect of the motion on her headache. "You didn't tell him about me and he wasn't too pleased."

Farraday stretched his feet out, folding his hands behind his head. He looked at her. "That's putting it mildly. I owe you an explanation."

"No you don't."

"There's more."

"I don't want to know."

Farraday glanced at her. "Really?"

"Not like this, not because you feel you have to tell me. I've got three stories pending and you might have saved my life tonight. I can't find it in my cold reporter's heart to be angry."

His smile reached his eyes. "You know about the corruption in the department."

"I've heard rumors." She sighed as she leaned her head back against the sofa.

"My uncle brought me here to sort it out."

She felt like ice had been slipped down her spine. "You'd better watch your back."

"Right now, I'm watching yours. And his. That's why nobody knows."

"Is there anything I can do?"

Lara felt him squeeze her hand. "I appreciate your understanding."

She shrugged, feeling his hand slip away. "This is more important than my ego." Lara looked at him, noting the lines around the corners of his eyes despite the dimness of the firelight and one lone lamp.

His forehead creased with wrinkles for a moment, and then a small smile tugged at the corners of his lips. "I guess you're stuck with me. Unless you want to come to my place?"

"Gee, there's an original pick-up line. Did you get my message?"

"What message?"

"I called your cell. Megan Douglas has a sister. There's an old family property between Betty Zimmerman's house and Oak Creek, down a side road."

"That's fits the direction the woman was coming from." Farraday rested his hands on his knees, looking at the fire before turning to Lara with a fading smile. "I called your office earlier. When I didn't hear back I got worried."

"I was at the library." She tried to stifle a yawn.

"You go upstairs. I'll move the chair over by the landing."

"No way."

His jaw dropped. "You can try kicking me out but you won't succeed."

The ghost of a smile flitted across her lips, despite her efforts to keep her face straight. "I could have you charged with trespassing."

"Very funny. Collins would have a fit-"

"It's not that. One lecture from him is quite enough. But you won't get any sleep in those chairs. Besides," she removed the ice pack from her forehead and wiped the water from her brow, "you're beat. The Macy's Day Parade could take a detour through the living room and you'd miss it."

"Thanks for your ringing endorsement of my protective services."

"I just think it would be better if we stayed on the same floor. There's a bedroll. I can camp here or upstairs. You can take the bed or the couch. Your pick."

"I'm not sleeping in your bed. Or the couch. I'll sleep on the floor."

Lara retrieved a mat and sleeping bags from a closet under the stairs, returning to find he'd already moved the coffee table to make room on the floor. It didn't take him long to prepare a make-shift bed.

As she lay down on the couch she watched him pull off his jacket, toss his keys and wallet on the coffee table, unclip his gun and put it under the edge of the pillow.

Within minutes Lara watched Farraday's eyes fall shut as sleep claimed him, the glimmer of firelight outlining his tired face.

Pure, heart-stopping terror had engulfed her when she was being attacked. As she came to, she'd been fighting her terror, but the fear had abated the moment she recognized Farraday.

He'd shared a confidence with her, which made her feel like she'd proven herself. If he'd walked into her office acting like he trusted her already she wouldn't have known if he'd taken note of her character, her values, or if they mattered to him. With some, superficial trust lingers until trials come and you see if your faith holds or cracks under pressure. This was a deeper confidence that had been earned. She'd had no doubt in herself, only concern about whether it was possible to persuade the burned detective that she was honest.

After hours of pouring over newspapers at the library, she'd been left to wonder why Farraday hadn't followed his father into the family business. Now, she knew who had influenced Farraday's choice. She'd been thorough and found no hint of his connection to the captain of the 14th Precinct, suggesting Farraday's secret was as safe as it could possibly be.

Watching his face in the firelight, she hoped that, for his sake, she was right.

***

Vern Fletcher staggered to the bathroom, barely conscious of lifting his hand to switch on the light. His eyes were shadowed but not bloodshot.

The events of the previous night were running through his mind as he stared at his reflection. He'd instinctively driven to the bar after his chat with Graeme Garrett, but had stopped outside, watching regulars scuffling across the pavement, a new spring in their step as they closed the distance to the door.

Somehow, this had become his life. He used to be disgusted by seasoned reporters he'd met in his early posts, the ones who barely dried up long enough to put their stories into print.

Vern had returned to the office, spending the rest of the evening pouring over what little information he had about Choy Kim.

It didn't offer any substantial clues about what had happened to her. Just as he'd been about to pack it in, Hatcher had sauntered into his office and sat in a chair.

"Well, well, well. When was the last time I saw you burning the midnight oil?"

Vern had hastened to hide his collection of papers but he wasn't quick enough. Hatcher had extracted the photo and a scrap of paper that was clipped to it.

"This changes everything, doesn't it?" Hatcher had whistled as he scanned the note. "You're after Larimer's story."

"You think that's her?" He'd snatched the photo out of Hatcher's grasp.

Hatcher had laughed. "You think it's her. That's why you've opted for your desk over a drink tonight. What are you waiting for?"

"Maybe some concrete evidence instead of the usual crap and conjecture we print."

"You have forty-eight hours or crap won't be just something we print. Understand?"

He'd grabbed his bag and walked out the door. This was just what he didn't need: A deadline to meet or a shit-storm unlike anything Hatcher had thrown at him in the past.

Vern reached for the toothpaste. He needed to be at the factory before shift change. Glancing at his watch, he cursed under his breath, scrambling to find a fresh change of clothes that didn't need to be ironed.

***

"You should have slept in your bed," Farraday said. Lara's motions were stilted, hesitant, her face shadowed by dark smudges under her eyes.

"To be honest, I doubt I could have slept anywhere."

He stared at her as he poured syrup on his waffles. "You were pretty defiant last night. I thought you were okay."

"How okay are you supposed to be when someone assaults you in your own home?" She put up her hand. "I'm not looking for sympathy."

"You do look rough."

A sarcastic smile flitted across her face. "I guess I got banged up more than I thought. I definitely got more than I bargained for when I went ahead with this story."

"Just think of all the fun you would have missed."

"Fun? I did miss that part."

"Well, at least there's the pleasure of my company."

"Hmmph. When you're not chastising me for not listening to you, insulting my profession, criticizing my driving or subjecting me to a lecture from your uncle, you're alright."

Farraday smiled.

"We're going to the sister's today, right?"

His smile faded. "I am. You get to stay right here and rest."

"Says you? I don't think so."

Farraday put his best look of intimidation into the full length of his face, staring at her sternly. "My uncle put you under my protective services."

"I agreed to last night to keep Collins off my back." She pointed her fork at him. "And yours, I might add."

"I thought this guy knocked some sense into you."

Her eyes narrowed. "More like my head hurt too much to argue. And if you're babysitting me all day then you can't follow up on any leads."

He looked up. "I just thought I'd take a quick look at the estate and then grab a few things from home."

"If I don't get to go, neither do you."

"I'd like to see you stop me." As soon as the challenge was out, he knew he'd been baited. The smug look that crossed her face told him she had something on him. He decided to try a different tactic.

"Lara, you have a concussion and from the look of that gash you should've had a stitch or two. Not to mention how stiff you are which is obvious just watching you move. You should take a nice hot bath and spend the day off your feet. I'm sure Dr. Eaton would second that opinion."

"I had the distinct impression Dr. Eaton prefers people that are permanently off their feet." She shook her head. "Rest, yes. But if you're going, I'm going. You can argue all you want but it won't get you your keys."

"I have a spare under the body."

She shrugged, her eyes glinting with amusement. "You left your door open last night. The battery's dead."

He carried his plate to the sink and looked out the window. Farraday tried to piece together the events of the previous night. He remembered closing the door when he first arrived and then he moved the car later, in a hurry to get blood samples... Farraday turned, his hands up. "Fine. You win. We'll both go after you've had a bath. I'll do the dishes."

A broad smile filled her face. "Dishes? Having you around might not be so bad." She picked up the apron off the table and tossed it to him, leaving before he had a chance to respond.

He shook his head, tried to unravel the apron and then threw it over a chair. Lara Kelly wasn't the only one who got more than they'd bargained for with this story.

***

Vern had been outside the factory for an hour, finding mostly immigrant workers who didn't speak English. He finally found one that could get past the most basic questions and understand him. Vern couldn't place her accent or where she was from, exactly, but it didn't matter. They could communicate.

The petite woman smiled glibly and shrugged. "Yes, we know Choy. She not work here now."

"When did you last see her?"

The dark eyes scrunched together and the woman's face crinkled as she nodded. "Last week. We...wensday."

"She worked here that day?"

A nod. "Yes. She worked. Then she go to office. When I go home she got into car."

"Did you see anyone else in the car?"

More wrinkles, then a shake of her head. "Someone, yes. I not know who."

"Man? Woman?"

"Man."

"What kind of car was it?"

"White."

"Big or small?"

"All your car big here."

"Really big? Or just big?"

"Bigger dan some."

"What did your supervisor say on Thursday when Choy didn't come to work?"

She shrugged again, backing toward the other women who were waiting, the ones who didn't speak 'good' English. "She said Choy have diff'rent job now."

"Thank you."

Choy hadn't left on her own. Vern had just twenty-eight hours of Choy's movements to fill now, between the time she was last seen at the factory and the time Larimer's woman went over the ledge. He went inside. After a few minutes of talking his way past reception, he managed to find the personnel office.

"How can I help you?"

Stacy Ling had a wide smile that reminded Vern of an eager puppy, anxious to go fetch so that she would earn a pet from her master.

"Do you know this woman?" Vern passed her a photo of Choy Kim.

The first signs of confusion creased the woman's brow. "Yes. Choy used to work here."

"I spoke to you on the phone. You said she was offered a job at the mayor's office."

The smile faltered for a second and then filled her face again. "Yes, that's right."

"Are you aware that Choy's family hasn't seen her since she left here last week?"

The jaw dropped open as the smile slipped from her face. "Have they spoken to someone at the mayor's office?"

"No, but I have. I was told there must be a mistake, that nobody by the name of Choy Kim was working there and that nobody had been hired in the last month." A city alderman who owed him a favor had confirmed Garrett's statement, much to Vern's annoyance.

Stacy Ling shook her head vigorously. "No. That isn't right. He picked her himself."

"Who picked her?"

"He works for the mayor. That's all I know."

What the hell is going on here? Vern flipped his notepad to a fresh page. "Can you describe him for me?"

***

They drove to the Douglas estate in silence. It had been on the tip of Farraday's tongue to ask whether or not she trusted him to give her a full report but then he thought about how he would feel if he'd been injured and was expected to stay behind. A lesser person would have moved on to something they were certain would pan out and out of harm's way. Instead, Lara seemed more determined to know what had happened to this woman and why. He glanced at her.

"I'm up to this," she said, sticking her chin out a little and sitting up straight.

"I don't blame you. After all this, there better be a big story in it for you."

Her brow creased. "Sad, isn't it? I have to hope something terrible happened so that I have something people would want to read. No one would run a story like, 'Cliff Jumper Found Alive: She decided not to jump'. Who cares? We have this perverse fascination with pain and suffering and a sick desire to look into the morbid details of every death and every sin."

"It's a part of life."

"Sure, but what about people liking their jobs, falling in love and still holding hands when the kids are gone?"

"That's my parents." He turned down a long, windy driveway, navigating around the bumps and through the dense foliage crowding the road. "Reporters hounded my dad, plying him with leading questions, trying to twist things into a scandal. I never understood why anyone would want to make a living from deception and trickery."

"Makes us sound almost criminal, doesn't it?"

Farraday braked suddenly as the road dipped. He was trying to avoid the tracks in the mud, which had formed deep grooves in the dirt that pulled at the wheels of the jeep, but he couldn't avoid the grooves and the potholes.

Lara braced her arm against the dash. "This road is terrible."

"I thought the Douglas family was wealthy."

Farraday felt Lara's eyes on him and then he realized what he said. "I did a little research of my own. Mr. Douglas is a prominent businessman. He has ties to the old police chief."

"Our photogenic mayor, Walter Morrow? Interesting."

"I didn't tell you before because I really thought you should rest. How did you find out about the sister?"

"Luck or fate, whatever you want to call it. I came across a story about Mrs. Douglas drowning."

Farraday stopped the jeep and stared at her. "She drowned?"

Lara nodded. "Fifteen years ago. They found her body in an inlet, death ruled accidental. No explanation about what happened. The only thing useful was the mention of her two daughters."

Farraday tapped his fingers on the steering wheel, clenched his jaw.

"What is it?"

"Where did she drown?"

"They found her in an inlet near the old marina."

"Down from Duane's?"

"Yes, that's the one." She nodded. "It's an interesting coincidence."

"And it may be a real clue."

"To what, exactly?"

"Well, we haven't really searched for a body," Farraday said.

"No, but..."

"There are some pretty strong undercurrents. Fishermen have reported having things go under and finding them floating on the other side of the lake."

"What's that got to do with this case?"

"You told me Duane stays in the general area where he filmed the video. This woman could have surfaced miles away."

They reached a once-proud house that stood two stories tall, with a wide wraparound porch that had columns supporting an upper level, where glass doors opened onto a balcony. It wasn't hard to imagine this as a majestic home, but now the weathered wood was in desperate need of paint and even the balustrade visibly sagged in some places. The windows looked dusty, the curtains faded, like things had been left untended for years.

Farraday surveyed the house for any sign of movement or indication of life, and Lara followed him around back, where he tried knocking on the other door. Still no answer. "I guess there's no point hanging around here."

"What now?"

He turned to look at Lara. "The old marina."

***

When they reached the marina Farraday put the jeep into park, slowly extracting the keys.

"Ready?"

She nodded, still saying nothing. He reached for her pack.

"Let me. Don't," he said as she started to speak. "We're here, you won. Just know when to quit, alright?"

She offered a thin smile and let go. "How did you hear about the undertow?" she asked as they walked over the rocky shoreline.

"An old cop-shop story, actually. That's why there are boundary markers for swimming at all the beaches."

"I thought it was for lifeguard zones." They were at the water, the shore spreading in both directions. "Any insight into which way to go now, Detective?"

He was silent for a moment, then shrugged. "My guess is left, but only because it looks like the shoreline narrows to the right and we might not be able to follow it far. We could split up anyway or take our chances. Personally, with the possibility that we're being watched, I'd rather stay together."

"Left it is." She followed him, up and down over the rocks, balancing on loose stones and navigating scattered deadwood and debris.

Farraday reached for her hand as she sunk a boot-depth into the mud, exactly when the first drops of rain started to pelt them. "We can turn back."

"Maybe we should have taken a boat."

She pulled herself up onto a shelf of rock blocking their way. It was about three or four feet tall. Lara felt her back spasm as the pain shot through her, but she managed to get her feet up underneath her body. She stood up and stiffened again.

"Are you okay?" he asked after a moment.

"Yeah," she said, her voice low and thick, like it was choked with emotion. "You were right."

He jumped up beside her and looked at the shore. Amidst the rocks and deadwood it was easy to discern the battered form lying face down in the mud, a spray of dark hair haloing the still head. The white shirt was tattered, her knees still in the water.

Farraday hopped down, reaching back to help Lara. She slid down as gently as she could, wincing at the jolt of pain that surged through her back as she almost fell against him, barely steadying herself at the last second.

He pulled out his cell phone. "Go ahead and get some shots of the scene. I don't want to risk anything being washed away if it really starts to pour before the crime scene guys get here."

***

It wasn't long before Farraday was caught up in a sea of activity. Crime scene personnel descended on the area, taking more photos, samples and eventually turning the victim. Farraday glanced at Lara, swallowing hard.

"Do we have an ID?" he asked the ME.

"Nothing on the body."

"She looks just like Megan Douglas."

"Right. The Douglas sisters." Dr. Lessard rubbed his temples. "My son went to school with the twin hellions. Megan and Susan.

"You won't get much off this body, at least in terms of trace evidence. She's been in the water too long. Decomposition suggests she's been in the water seven or eight days. Skin is loose but the nails haven't separated. Body surfaced recently. The birds haven't picked at her much."

"Thanks."

For some reason, Lara heard that exchange perfectly. It was like those moments when you're half-asleep, but it's a sleep that heightens the sense of hearing and you're more keenly aware of any sound than usual. After the ME and Farraday finished talking, the rest of the conversation faded, becoming an unintelligible hum. She lost track of time, feeling the shooting pain coursing through her back, into her neck, pounding at her temples, wishing she'd brought some painkillers with her. She closed her eyes and leaned her head against the large rock beside her.

The next thing she remembered was Farraday nudging her. She lifted her face up.

"We can go."

"You're done?"

He nodded. This time, he helped her over the rocks and held her arm as they walked back to her jeep, and she didn't argue. When they reached the marina she heard a sharp intake of breath and looked up to see someone walking toward them.

The woman was a bit taller than Lara, with golden hair, dark eyes. Despite being bundled in a coat appropriate for a chilly fall day she was obviously fit. Against the dismal gray sky this woman resonated with a warm glow that wasn't artificially created with make-up.

She reminded Lara of the girls in high school that had made her feel three inches tall or, alternatively, like a bumbling oaf. Stylish. Graceful. Elegant. The kind of woman that made Lara feel like an awkward kid.

Farraday handed Lara her keys and strode right up to the woman, grabbed her arm and pulled her out of the way of the other police personnel starting to return from the crime scene.

"What the hell are you doing here?"

"I came to see you." The woman wrenched her arm free from his hold. "You didn't come home last night."

"I don't have to explain myself to you." Farraday's back was rigid, his jaw clenched. "You have no business being here."

"Here as in your house or your crime scene?"

"Don't even think about it, Katarina. You aren't a reporter anymore."

Lara's eyes widened at that. She didn't like herself much for listening but they were so close she couldn't avoid it.

"I don't care about your case. I'm here to see you. You haven't returned my calls."

"Not now. I'm working. You're going to have to wait."

"Just ten minutes. I came to see you and I'm not leaving."

"Typical. That's the way it's always been, hasn't it? You have to be the center of attention, have everyone drop everything when it suits you. Just show up and get mad because I'm not home or I'm busy with a case. Grow up."

He turned away and she grabbed his arm. "How long are you going to play the victim? We need to talk. Whether you like it or not-"

"There's nothing to talk about." He pulled his arm free and walked away, not looking back.

Lara watched the woman clench her fists, turn and look back one last time. She stared at Lara, eyes narrow, mouth drawn in a tight line, before she turned again and walked away.

***

Lara wiped the water from her eyes, leaning back against the incline of the tub. Her stomach protested the fact that she'd missed lunch; frankly, she'd lost her appetite viewing the body at the lake. Farraday had left her at The Ledger, going to the station to wrap up a few details. It gave her enough time to finish the clip about the break-in at Betty's, get Jimmy to rush the photos and put together an exclusive on the recovery of a body. She'd been catching up on her messages when Farraday called to say he was on his way.

Then Hatcher had stormed into her office.

"Ducking out again?" He'd stared at her as she tried to put her jacket on. "What happened to you?"

"Minor concussion. I'll live." Clearly, the police report about the break-in and assault hadn't interested him, or he hadn't heard about it.

Neither of which seemed likely.

"Are you making any progress with the negligence angle?"

"I've been a little busy." She hadn't needed to say more: Jimmy had walked in with her copy. Hatcher had intercepted it and given her an approving glance.

"So you have. Now we really do have a case for police incompetence. Solid lead, good photo. This paves the way for follow-up."

"Does that mean I'm off the hook?"

"I do like my reporters to check in every once in a while. But it looks like you've been working hard. Take the weekend off."

"Gee, thanks. As though I wasn't off already."

He'd patted her shoulder and she'd winced as the pain shot through her. "Sorry. I can be generous. Take Monday too. Don't worry about checking in. I'll trust you to put in the time while you chase this down. I want to see you take this story all the way."

"Yeah, yeah, thanks," she'd muttered, holding up her hand as a goodbye as she'd walked out the doorway, not daring to look back.

They'd made one stop. She gave Duane some extra money, since the story had panned out, and they persuaded him to leave town and not come back until he checked with them first. Just in case there was a reason Betty was running, a reason that might still put Duane in danger.

Farraday insisted on ordering dinner so she had time for a bath. She'd been soaking for almost an hour. Her body had absorbed almost all the heat and she pulled the plug to let the cool water out. She got dressed and stepped out into the hallway. Still combing her tousled hair, she heard voices from downstairs.

"It's a positive ID. ME's preliminary report will be in Monday."

"Couldn't we put a rush on it?"

"I told them to go slow, to be thorough. Besides, you're supposed to be off this weekend and nobody else is touching this."

"Shouldn't I be at the autopsy?" Farraday asked.

"If you get called in, go. I did get Lara clearance at the ME's office, but only under your supervision. Still, all things considered, I'd prefer you stay here with her. Lessard will give you the information you need without you being there."

"I'll likely be working straight through until this case is finished. I can't see Lara taking a day off."

"What were you thinking, letting her out today?"

"It was that or I was held hostage. Don't ask. Betty Zimmerman was keeping her doors locked during the day. Whatever she knew or guessed at, she didn't feel safe. Considering how much Lara does know, she's going to have to live with me shadowing her until we close this."

"Sure there isn't more to it than that?"

Lara didn't know how Farraday felt about the inference, but she felt her own cheeks burn.

"She's the only thing standing between Hatcher and Walker's job. If something happens to her Hatcher will bring in a reporter who uses his rulebook. We don't need that."

There was silence for a moment. "Did you talk to Katarina?"

"You told her where I was?"

"That's not an answer, Ty."

Lara descended the stairs then, effectively ending that line of discussion.

"Any news?"

"Your victim is Susan Douglas. You realize," Collins looked her in the eye, "you'll have to turn that tape over to us now."

Lara nodded.

"Does Hatcher know anything?"

She held his gaze unflinchingly. "He knows some of it. I went with enough to take front page, but not enough to put your department in the hot seat. He wants me to push it that way in my follow-through, though."

There was an awkward silence while they all absorbed that. Lara sat down on the couch, watching Collins.

"What's next?" Collins finally asked.

"We need to find out who broke in here," she said. She felt Farraday's gaze on her from where he stood, but didn't meet it.

"Find out what happened to Susan Douglas and we should find the person who broke in."

"Unless it wasn't someone involved with her death," Lara said.

Farraday exchanged a glance with Collins and sat down on the edge of the other chair before he spoke. "Who do you think it was?"

"Another reporter."

Looking down, she could imagine the incredulous glances exchanged. When there was still silence after a few moments, she lifted her head.

Farraday was staring at her. "What makes you think that?"

"You drove to The Ledger in your car. You parked out front. We left from the back, in my jeep. Only someone who knew my vehicle could have followed us."

"Okay," he said slowly. "I'm with you so far."

"That means not a cop, but a reporter. Or the man in the photograph. Someone who knew the location of the scene and was keeping an eye on it."

"So what you're saying," Collins leaned forward, "is that Hatcher might have someone watching you."

She nodded. "To see if I was playing ball or to make it seem like there was more to this story. Maybe Hatcher thought if he spooked me, I'd panic."

"Then he might not have expected anything to come of the alleged suicide. Finding a body might be enough to keep him off your back," Farraday suggested.

"Or it was the man in the photo covering his tracks and Hatcher has nothing to do with it." Collins rubbed his chin.

She shrugged, feeling the pull on her shoulders, already the soothing effects of the bath wearing off. "It could help to know for sure. Hatcher wasn't that interested in how I got injured. Normally, if someone broke in and assaulted one of his reporters, he'd want to milk that in the press. He'd never let a story pass without a damn good reason."

"Work every angle, but Susan Douglas is your priority." Collins stood to leave. "Are you in the office this weekend?"

Lara shook her head. "I'm off until Tuesday."

"Then that gives you time to work without Hatcher breathing down your neck."

"Who says I'm working?" she asked.

Farraday and his uncle laughed and she smiled.

"Just be careful," Collins said as he turned to leave.

She nodded. His gaze had still lingered on her at times but his eyes had crinkled at the corners at her comment about work. She guessed Collins was getting over the shock of having Farraday hold out on him.

Farraday returned with a tray of food. He'd built a fire while Lara was upstairs and the orange glow flickered off the walls, warming the room. Lara could still hear the rain pelting down and thunder boomed as the lights flickered. She saw a shimmer of lightning from the window and the lights went out.

"Good thing I made the fire first."

"There are candles and matches in the drawer by the fridge."

"The fire's enough for now," he said.

They ate in silence, listening to the crackle of thunder. When they finished Farraday poured two glasses of wine before he divulged his thoughts.

"You're worried we'll think you sold us out. If it's a reporter, that is."

Lara stared into her flute, watching the reflection of the flames shimmer on the glass. She nodded.

"It's not your fault if Hatcher plays dirty. Besides, since I'm keeping an eye on you, it would be nearly impossible for you to pull a fast one."

"What worries me is the idea that I even would. His attitude toward me has improved, but I don't think your uncle likes this."

"My uncle has his own set of bad experiences. He'll get over it."

She wasn't so sure about that, but didn't argue. "Where do we go from here?"

"Where would you go with this story?"

"I need an ME's report to be conclusive. What do we know? A woman is dead. There was someone else on The Point the night she died but we don't know who it was. The victim is related by impending marriage to the cop who dismissed Duane. Is that a coincidence? No one reported Susan Douglas missing. Why?"

"Why indeed. That's a damn good question."

"Then that's where we'll start tomorrow." Lara lifted her glass, making a pledge. "We'll find out everything we can about Susan."

Chapter 5

Vern unwrapped his Egg McMuffin, leaning back in his car.

It had been so long since he'd monitored anyone he'd forgotten the creature comforts that sustained him on surveillance. He'd been tempted to go home and get a CD player but he didn't want to risk it.

Vern wrapped his hands around the coffee cup. It was cool this morning, a reminder that winter wasn't far away. The kind of crisp fall day that made you dig in the back of your closet for a warmer jacket or a thick sweater, something he hadn't realized until he'd already left home.

The front door opened. A man stepped out and reached down to pick up the paper. His eyes studied the words on the page, his jaw clenched then his lips moved, his face going white before turning a dangerous shade of purple. Vern snapped pictures as his target reacted to what he saw.

He tried to remember if they'd been working on a piece about the mayor as the scowling man disappeared and the door slammed shut.

For the next thirty minutes Vern checked his watch every thirty seconds. Time moved slower than molasses that had just been taken out of a cold room. The only sign of life he noted was an older woman walking along the sidewalk, then going up to the house across the street from Garrett's. The door opened and a man who looked to be about the same age as the woman invited her in.

He rummaged through the wrappers and napkins scattered on the floor in the back, found an empty bag and started picking up trash, which was why he heard the vehicle before he saw it. Heard it slowing down just as the dark form registered in his peripheral vision and he lifted his head.

The Land Rover had pulled up in front of Garrett's house, the engine humming. Nobody got out, but as Vern looked through his camera and snapped a few photos he could just see the driver punching numbers and then lifting the phone to his ear. The dark-haired man leaned his arm on the door, the window obviously down. The man turned and looked at the pavement, although Vern couldn't tell why, and the movement still didn't give him a clear look at the face. There were other forms in the vehicle, in the back seat. Then the driver took the phone away from his ear, twisting around so that all Vern could see was the back of his head.

Garrett's front door opened and he appeared. The burning red shade his face had turned when he'd seen the newspaper and swore earlier was now gone, though the jaw was still set, mouth drawn in a hard line. Graeme Garrett jogged down the steps and got in the front passenger side of the vehicle, then the Land Rover's taillights went on, the driver did a meager shoulder-check, and pulled out onto the road.

Vern started his car and followed from a comfortable distance. He couldn't ID any of the other people in the vehicle, and even with the zoom lens on his camera couldn't get a good enough shot to make out more than the most non-descriptive 'male, dark hair' generalizations.

First, they went to the Lakeview Hotel. It was a barely-operating hotel with access to Doe Lake, the kind of place that you'd stay in if the Super 8 was full and you were adventurous enough to try something that triple A didn't list in their hotel directory. Not that he had much reason to go by the old hotel that was turning gray with age and in desperate need of some color to make it look like less of the almost-forgotten relic it was, but Vern realized now that he'd seldom seen more than half a dozen cars in the parking lot at any time.

Graeme Garrett was the only one who got out of the vehicle at the hotel, and he wasn't gone for long. When he returned to the vehicle, he was having a heated exchange with another man.

Walter Morrow.

The man with the wide smile, the photogenic face. His hair was a bit darker than Garrett's, he was a few inches taller, and he was a better fit for his three-piece suit. Morrow looked more like a politician than Garrett ever would.

Suddenly Morrow grabbed Garrett's arm and it looked like he twisted it hard. Garrett spun around, raising his fist, and then froze. They stood like that for a moment, nothing but the sound of Vern's heart thudding echoing in his ears as he paused, camera in his hands. Morrow glared at Garrett and let go of him while Garrett slowly lowered his free arm. Garrett's back was partially to Vern now, so he couldn't see his face, but it looked like he responded to Morrow before he turned and walked back to the vehicle, head down.

Morrow watched Garrett climb into the vehicle and shut the door.

The Land Rover pulled away, Morrow still standing outside the hotel. Vern put the camera down on the front seat, turned the keys in the ignition and shoulder-checked. A car drove by just then, your classic working girl in the front seat, peroxide blonde with some dark roots showing, thick make-up, big hoop earrings, a slinky dress only partially concealed by a short fake leather jacket that wasn't done up in front.

Vern didn't get a good look at the driver, just enough to tell it was a scruffy guy with wiry blond hair that shot out in all directions, what looked like the tip of a tattoo on his neck. Something about the ink was familiar. The only other thing he noted was that the woman was clearly taller than the man.

As Vern pulled out onto the road, doing a u-turn to follow the Land Rover, he saw the car parked in front of the hotel, Walter Morrow escorting the woman inside.

The driver was still in the vehicle.

Vern drove down the road, hoping he wasn't too far back to catch up with the Land Rover. Within a minute he'd caught up enough to see them make another turn. They followed the long, windy road through the trees at a slow pace, since the weekend traffic was largely comprised of seasonal tourists out to snap photos of the fall colors. Finally, the Land Rover pulled off the road, stopping at the Doe Lake Motel.

The Doe Lake Motel was actually a series of cabins that spread along an opening between the rock cuts, a gentle slope leading down to the lake at the far end of the main building, with trees bordering the cabins to the back. It originally consisted of one main building, which was in worse shape than the cabins were.

In its day, the motel had been the lesser choice for those who couldn't afford the Lakeview Hotel. It had been closed for years, but here was Graeme Garrett, going inside the main building.

The others followed him, but Vern had been forced to stay out on the road, relying on his camera to spy from a safe distance, so he couldn't add much to the limited descriptions he already had of the other occupants. The Land Rover was parked on an angle, so even the ones who got out on the side Vern could see clearly had their backs to him.

They were men, dark hair, average height...

Not a whole hell of a lot to go on.

Vern set the camera down and grabbed his notepad, jotting down descriptions of everyone he'd seen. That was when he felt it, that creepy 'I'm being watched' feeling that made the hairs on the back of his neck stand up on end.

He looked up slowly, and saw the other vehicle. The Doe Lake Motel was on a well-treed road, and he'd remained on the one end, just at the edge of the clearing that marked the motel property. The car was on the other end of the clearing, maybe a hundred feet away.

It hadn't been there when he'd pulled up. Vern was certain of that.

But even at this distance to the naked eye, he didn't need a second look to tell him who the driver was.

Dan Van Biers.

Ledger reporter who'd been chasing down stories on the drug scene in Oakridge, and writing about the deaths of two prostitutes who'd allegedly overdosed. Dan had included enough speculation in his work to cast doubt on that, but because the women had been found outside the city, the county had been handling their post mortems.

Dan's stories had also included more than enough to raise questions about the reliability of so much as a death certificate signed by the county ME.

Vern decided to leave. Whatever Dan was doing there, with two of them hanging around the chances of being seen were too great.

Besides, he had more than enough to go on. He turned his car around and drove to a nearby convenience store to get a newspaper and try to find out what had produced such a strong reaction from Graeme Garrett.

***

Farraday drew a deep breath and squared his shoulders. He stepped out and sprinted across the lawn to the freshly painted porch.

Walker opened the door. "Twice in one week."

"I need to speak to Megan."

Walker straightened, folding his arms across his chest. "What's this about?"

"Please, just get Megan."

After a minute, Walker gestured for him to come in and disappeared down the hallway, leaving Farraday to sit on the edge of a straight-backed chair. This was hard enough when you didn't know the people affected. With a cop involved, who was also a colleague, he didn't know what to expect.

They walked in and sat on the couch, Walker's arm winding around Megan's shoulders protectively.

"Detective Farraday, right?" She looked from her fiancé to Farraday questioningly. "You wanted to speak with me?"

Farraday nodded, leaning forward. "Can I ask when you last saw your sister?"

"Two weeks, I guess. At our engagement party."

"She lives at the estate on Elm Road?"

Megan shook her head. "Nobody's lived there for years. There's a key under the porch on the left side; look for yourself. My father built a new house on the other side of the property and I own the old house now. What are you asking about Susan for? Is she in trouble again?"

Again. Walker was avoiding Farraday's gaze. "I'm afraid I have some bad news. We found a body yesterday, down by the old marina on Doe Lake."

Walker's head snapped up. "Are you saying…?"

Farraday nodded. "We've had a positive ID from dental records. It's Susan."

The color drained from Megan's face as she turned to Walker. "It can't be. He must be wrong."

"Meg..."

"You said she'd be okay." There was a high-pitched note of hysteria in her words, followed by a low, thick whisper. "You promised. You said-"

Walker stood, pulling Megan to her feet. "Come on. Upstairs."

She cast one furtive glance at Farraday but didn't argue.

After a few minutes he got up and went to the door, trying to decide whether or not to leave when he heard footsteps coming down the stairs.

He expected venom in Walker's eyes when he returned. Instead, Walker sank onto the steps slowly, his shoulders sagging as he sat down. "I don't envy you."

"You don't seem surprised."

"Susan was always... trouble. You didn't grow up here so you wouldn't know, but when she was a teenager she was sent away."

"Where to?"

"A private facility. A residential place, where she could be kept under watch."

"She was dangerous?"

"To herself, mostly. Reckless. She crashed a car in a drag race on Lakeshore Drive, killing Kyle Joynt. Yes, Officer Joynt's brother. When she sobered up she lost it. Literally."

"What did Megan mean when she said you promised Susan would be okay?"

"Oh," he shook his head dismissively, "she was a mess at the engagement party. In my opinion, she was itching for a fix. Susan always did need something to take the edge off. I put up with her as part of this family but that's it. I didn't want Megan getting pulled into Susan's problems." His shoulders drooped. "Maybe that was selfish."

Farraday shook his head. "I can understand that. Do you know where Mr. Douglas is?"

"He's away on business," Walker mumbled. He stood up, scratched his head before going to a small table and removing an address book. He wrote down the numbers and gave Farraday the sheet of paper. "Should I call him?"

"We'll track him down. You know I may need to ask her some more questions."

"I know."

He opened the door, pausing. Walker looked lost, standing in the hallway, hands in his pockets, vacuously studying the floor.

"It was Susan on that video."

Walker's head snapped up again as he gaped at Farraday.

Farraday turned and walked out of the house.

***

Vern was still smiling as he thought about Lara's story. He'd received a message from Hatcher, telling him not to worry about the deadline.

Lara had bought him more time, but she'd raised more questions. Why had Graeme Garrett reacted so strongly to the story about the body being found at the old marina?

After Vern left the motel and got a newspaper, he went to the library, looking up everything he could find on the mayor's right-hand man.

Graeme Garrett had been in law enforcement, making the move to city hall years ago. There were no references to a family in any of the articles. He'd never been implicated in any scandal, explaining why he may have stayed off Vern's radar.

Whatever the papers said, it was what they didn't say that Vern couldn't get out of his mind. Vern had no doubt about what four-letter words escaped Garrett's mouth as his face colored when he saw the newspaper that morning. Whatever had bothered him was somewhere in Lara's story but Vern couldn't see it.

When Vern had asked about Choy Kim, Garrett had dismissed her as Lara's jumper. Garrett couldn't do that now. The woman was Caucasian.

Garrett had winced when he'd seen Choy's photograph. Garrett had lied about not knowing the young woman, or about her alleged job at city hall.

Garrett also owned a white Lexus.

A coincidence, perhaps, but Vern's mind was starting to generate some interesting possibilities.

***

"We located David Douglas." Farraday sank into the armchair, stretching his legs out.

"Does that mean the name can be released?" Lara asked, cupping her mug of tea in her hands. "There's more."

"Thanks," Farraday said as Skittles jumped up on his legs, purring. "Guess I've become part of the furniture."

Lara smiled, going to the kitchen for a cup.

"Yes, you could run her name tomorrow. Did you learn anything?"

She recounted what Farraday had already heard about Susan's youth, as well as a number of things Walker hadn't said. Megan had been a passenger in the car Susan had crashed but according to the story The Ledger ran, she'd passed out before the accident from excessive alcohol consumption. Both girls had gone away for the summer following the incident. Susan hadn't returned in the fall. Although she hadn't confirmed it, local suspicion had been that the girls had been sent to a reform school, Susan remaining there until she was almost eighteen.

"Walker told me some of this. He failed to mention Megan went away or that she was in the car that night."

Lara shrugged. "He wants to protect her."

"Megan did something hundreds of teenagers do. The difference is, she got caught. The consequences were steep. At her age, with her connections, it isn't surprising she wasn't charged. Not in this city." Farraday rubbed his jaw. "Walker seemed genuinely shocked that it was Susan on that video. I don't think he knew."

"Then it couldn't have been him at the scene that night."

"And he has a solid alibi for the theft of the file and the break-in here. He could know more but be caught up in this somehow. I hope not, for his sake."

"And the department's."

His phone rang. After a series of one-word answers he closed his cell. "The ME's office. They've got something."

***

"No scrapings from the nail beds, but see here and here?" Dr. Lessard held the hand up for inspection. "Broken nails. This one is partially torn."

"Indicating a struggle," Farraday said.

"There are also scrapes and scratches on her hands, like something sharp was ripped from her grasp."

"Like rock?"

"It could have been. That's not all. Six of her ribs were broken, the abdomen and chest were bruised, her pelvis was shattered and she had facial fractures. Both legs were broken, as well as her right arm. These were all recent injuries, occurring just prior to her death. The extent of the fractures and bruising suggests she impacted something with force, like being thrown against a wall or hit by a car."

"Or falling from a cliff onto a rock ledge a few dozen feet below?"

"That's possible. Even without the pulmonary edema fluid the amount of water in the lungs certifies drowning, but death was inevitable at the point of impact. One of the ribs pierced an artery. She was bleeding out. Internal hemorrhaging. Body is a complete mess. We're still waiting for toxicology results."

"Could she...? Would she have been able to move?" Lara asked.

"Not likely. Any movement would have been excruciating."

"Is that all?" Farraday asked. "This seems to confirm what we already suspected."

"Tisk tisk, Detective." Lessard wagged a finger. "I called you down for this." He looked as though he was about to pull the sheet back completely, but glanced at Lara as she sat down, her face wrapped in her hands. Lessard crossed his arms instead.

"Just tell us. There are some things we don't need to see."

Lessard shrugged. "She had a baby."

Lara lifted her head slowly. "That's a crime?"

The medical examiner glared at her. "Recently. Based on the medical evidence I'd say, within twenty-four hours of death. I'd lean toward less than twelve and as little as six, but there's no way I can guarantee that without more evidence. Being in the water for a week didn't help."

"Is there any way to be more specific?" Farraday asked.

"Short of finding a record of birth, it's unlikely. There is something else I can tell you, though. There was rupturing to her uterus that hadn't been corrected. Without a hysterectomy she could have bled to death within hours."

"Why is this important?"

"No doctor in the country that has a license and wants to keep it would have let this woman out of the hospital. This is incomprehensible medical malpractice." Lessard paused. "And she was dressed. Street clothes, not a hospital gown. As you know, since you found her. Dark pants, a white shirt. There was something else recovered. I sent it to the lab for testing."

"What was it?

"Based on my experience? I'd say heroin. A bag of it, stuffed inside the pocket of the pants she was wearing."

Farraday whistled. "Do you think she was using?"

"Well, there's no evidence of track marks, but she could have been snorting or smoking the stuff. Hopefully when the lab work comes back, I can tell you more."

"Thanks. You've been a big help."

"Worth interrupting your plans on a Saturday night for? You shouldn't bring your dates to the morgue, Farraday."

Lara followed Farraday out of the room without comment. Once in the corridor, she took a few deep breaths.

"Your first autopsy?"

"Was it that obvious? I thought I hid it well. You?"

"It never gets any easier."

"So she grabbed the ledge, scraping her hands as she struggled to hold on."

"Maybe our guy pried her hands off, making her fall."

Lara winced. "Her ribs broke and bones fractured on impact. But that doesn't explain how she got in the water."

"Unless her attacker went down to the shore and pushed her in."

"I guess I don't have to ask where we're going now."

***

Lara sank onto the couch, barely noticing the dim embers left from the earlier fire. Farraday paused long enough to throw another log on and stoke the coals, coaxing flames strong enough to embrace the thick wood he'd added. It was the last thing she remembered before the room went dark.

She woke suddenly, sunlight pouring in the window. Her jeans clung to her legs uncomfortably. *Why am I...?* Then she recalled the events of the night before.

Lara walked down the stairs. Farraday was still asleep on the couch. Glancing at her watch, she retreated to the bathroom. She never slept this late, but she was seldom checking medical records and interviewing hospital staff at 2 am.

They'd turned up with precisely what Lessard hinted at: Nothing. No doctor would handle a delivery in such an incompetent manner. They were beginning to suspect that no doctor had even attended the birth of Susan Douglas' child. Instead of eliminating possibilities during this investigation, every fact seemed to raise more questions and complications. Why hadn't Walker or Megan mentioned Susan's pregnancy? Who was the baby's father? Shouldn't he have reported her missing when she disappeared?

Lara stiffened, turned the taps off and grabbed a towel. She was still tucking her shirt in as she jogged downstairs, the stiffness from her injuries having mostly subsided. "What time did you say David Douglas' plane was coming in?"

A foggy eye opened slowly and closed again. The tension returned to Farraday's face. "Just after noon."

"Then you need to get ready. We don't have much time."

He sat up, the sleeping bag falling to the floor, and went upstairs without another word.

***

"I still don't understand why you wanted to be here."

Lara found it hard to pull her thoughts together cohesively enough to explain. "Call it a hunch, okay? What time is it?"

"12:20. The plane should land any minute."

She stretched up on her toes, surveying the crowd filling the terminal.

"What are you looking for?" Farraday scanned the area, unable to find anything of significance. "What do you expect to find?"

"It's what I don't expect to find."

"We came all this way to look for something you don't expect to find?" He glared at her. "It's a good thing this isn't our first day working together."

Lara's look contained enough venom to stop an elephant cold. "I don't see the grief-stricken daughter waiting for dear old Dad."

Farraday took another look around. "Okay," he said slowly. "But what does that tell us? How does it help us with this case?"

Before she could respond they saw David Douglas. He had short, sandy hair, broad shoulders, a curl to his lips that wasn't welcoming. A throng of associates in three-piece suits shielded him as he walked through the lobby. There was no emotion, no evidence of the reason his trip had been cut short. They watched as the group stopped to speak to someone.

"Satisfied?" Farraday asked.

"Yes. Can you see who they're talking to?"

Farraday shook his head, but then his eyes narrowed. The group of men was moving again, dispersing to allow the person they'd met to walk beside David Douglas.

"I've seen his face in the newspaper before. Can you place him?"

She shook here head, standing on her toes as the men disappeared out the door. "He is familiar, though."

***

They turned to walk away. The person who had been observing them lowered the newspaper that had shielded his face.

***

"Why do you think it's important Megan wasn't there to meet her dad?" Farraday pulled out onto the highway, merging into the flow of weekend traffic.

"Call it a reporter's hunch, but I think something's going on in this family, something they don't want the rest of the world to know."

"It could be they just had enough scrutiny over Angela Douglas' death and the mishaps of the girls."

"Possibly. But why send both of your beloved children to a reform school voluntarily? Why keep one of them there for almost two years? Megan didn't know where Susan was staying. Isn't that odd?"

"It's uncommon for twins, granted, but we have nothing implicating the family and no connection between a lousy childhood and Susan's death, not to mention the missing baby."

"Do you remember when we drove out to the old estate?" Lara asked. "There were tracks in the mud."

Farraday glanced at her. "I didn't even think about that, but at the time we thought it was the main road."

"Didn't Megan say the house hadn't been lived in for years?"

"That doesn't mean the road isn't used, but it's worth taking another look."

***

Lara surveyed the house while Farraday searched for the key Megan had mentioned. From the exterior there were no clues that answered any of her lingering questions. It looked like a beautiful home, let go, haunted by faded lace curtains stretching across the weathered windows.

"Fall has always been my favorite time of year."

"What?"

Lara flushed. "Did you find it?"

He straightened, holding up the key. The lock slid open smoothly, as though it had been used that morning. Inside, the entry was large and airy, affording them both enough room to survey the layout of the interior.

A winding cherry staircase rose up before them, railings encompassing the open corridors above. The two-story design of the entry added to the feeling of openness and luxury. To the left, etched glass doors were open, showing the spacious living area. Practically new furniture filled the room, covered in plastic that was coated in dust, which was making Lara sneeze. Judging from the rooms, she guessed nothing was taken when the family moved out. She could envision how this house had once been immaculate, polished, a place used for entertaining the social elite.

The dining area was a good size, though not as big as the living room.

Lara looked closely at the floor, looked in the rooms on both sides of the hallway, and then examined the stairs. She straightened, noticing Farraday's puzzled look.

"It's nice flooring, but not that interesting."

"Look here and here," she said, rolling her eyes. "Don't you see?"

"All I can see is dust. There must be an inch coating the floor."

"Now look over there, by the stairs. What don't you see?"

He moved and bent down, looking where she pointed. Farraday surveyed the area closely and then looked up the staircase.

"It's almost clean down the center."

Lara nodded, exchanging a glance with him. "As though something was dragged down the steps."

They moved without a word, carefully studying each step, but when they reached the top landing, all they could conclude was that the stairs had been wiped or swept recently.

At the top they had to decide which way to go. One of the doors, to a room on the side of the house that faced the backyard instead of the driveway, was open.

"It's as good a place to start as any," Farraday said.

Lara wondered if this house spooked him as much as it did her. It didn't seem right, building another house and leaving all their beautiful belongings behind to collect dust. "Didn't Megan say nobody had lived here since they moved?"

"That's what I understood."

"Why leave all that furniture behind?"

"Most rich people I know are too cheap for that."

"Ironic, isn't it?"

"Do you smell that?"

"I wish I couldn't." Lara could see the poster bed covered with tangled sheets and bile and knew they had solved one riddle.

This was the place where Susan Douglas had given birth.

***

Lara left the estate while Farraday looked for evidence. After being so visible at the crime scene at the lake they were concerned people would start to notice her presence. Instead, she drove to the address Farraday had written down for her to pick up some things he needed.

Her hand froze as she reached for the door of his apartment and realized it was open. She was paralyzed for a moment, thinking of the person who had broken into her home and assaulted her, but the wood wasn't splintered. There was no evidence the door had been forced. Cautiously patting the door with her fingertips, it opened enough to dispel her fear and replace it with tension.

They stood still, studying each other for a moment before Lara entered.

"Who are you?"

"The one with a key," Lara replied coolly, holding it up in her fingers. She pulled out Farraday's list and took a bag from the hall closet.

"You aren't wondering who I am."

"I know who you are."

"Really? What has Tymen told you?"

"Nothing." Lara returned from the bedroom where she'd collected Farraday's clothes. She pulled the zipper shut, figuring whatever she didn't have Farraday could live without for one more day, and walked toward the door.

The woman stepped in front of her. "How do you know who I am?"

"I did my internship at the Herald."

"You're a reporter? I don't believe it. Tymen hates reporters."

Lara shrugged. "Ask Captain Collins if you don't believe me."

The dark eyes narrowed, her gaze lingering on Lara's face. "You were at the lake, at the crime scene Farraday was working."

Lara nodded.

The woman's eyes widened. She took a deep breath, the suspicion fading from her face, replaced with a look of shock. "You're Larimer Kelly."

Lara saw Katarina glance at the gash on her forehead.

"Someone assaulted me the night before last." She left it at that.

"Can you tell me what you're doing here?"

"It's not what you think. Farraday's at another crime scene-"

"And he needs clean clothes? He hasn't slept here in days. Ty trusted you enough to give you the keys to his place." Katarina turned, looking down at the driveway. "And his car. It hasn't taken you long to gain his confidence."

"It hasn't been easy, thanks to you."

Katarina's eyes narrowed. "I know I hurt him, but not talking to me isn't going to help." She looked at Lara, her forehead dimpling, dark eyes glistening with unshed tears. "Could you talk to him for me?"

Lara felt her breath catch in her throat. "You must be joking. I'm not getting involved in your problems. Besides, Farraday tolerates me because he has to. I'm not sure I could help even if I wanted to."

"He'd never let you set foot in his home if he didn't have some level of respect for you."

"You're here."

The ghost of a smile faded as quickly as it had formed. "But, as you pointed out, I'm not the one with a key."

Lara bit her lip, refusing to be baited. "I have to go."

"Will you tell him I want to see him?"

Mashing her lips together in a tight line, Lara gripped the bag, turned and left before Katarina could say anything else.

***

Katarina listened as the car door closed and the engine started. Wondering why Ty would be put on a case like this, forced to work with a reporter.

Larimer Kelly had a kind of fresh-faced sincerity working for her. She didn't seem like the type to be cunning and manipulative. Still...

Katarina stood up. For the first time in a long time she felt a surge of energy, a drive to do more than chase after Ty and try to make amends. She'd made a mistake and it had cost him. It had cost her too, and she was beginning to realize how much, that she might never regain his trust.

But she could keep an eye on Larimer Kelly and try to find out what was going on.

***

Lara and Farraday were in her living room, catching up on what he'd learned at the crime scene.

"They found everything they needed to confirm what we thought, even the placenta. Someone definitely gave birth there recently."

"The pieces are starting to come together."

"We still don't have a baby," Farraday said.

"Or a motive for her death."

"Or a reason why neither Walker nor Megan thought to mention Susan's pregnancy."

"Maybe they didn't know."

Farraday frowned. "They'd just seen her at their engagement party. How could they not know?"

"She might not have been full term."

"Remind me to ask if there's any way to find out. How did you manage?"

"I didn't get everything." Lara nodded to the bag she'd packed at his apartment.

Farraday picked up chopsticks and sat on the floor, leaning against the couch. "I'll survive. What happened?"

"Katarina Collins was at your place. I didn't even think to ask how she got inside."

Farraday looked at his plate, poking at his rice, concealing his thoughts behind a mask of stone. Lara watched him from the corner of her eye.

Eventually, he tossed his chopsticks down. "What did she say?"

"Not much she didn't say already, at the marina."

Farraday looked up but remained silent.

She took the plunge. "Look, I don't know the whole story. I know about the article but I don't have all the facts so I'm not going to pretend to understand how you feel. But I can see that this is bothering you. Her pain is her problem, but you need to find a way to get past this."

Farraday pushed his plate aside, reaching for his glass. "Do you believe in forgiveness?"

"God's forgiveness? Or man's?"

"Person to person. Do you think we have to forgive everything?"

Lara sighed, pushing her own plate away. She took a sip of wine and then raised her hands. "Yes. I guess I do."

"Really? I don't think most people would agree."

"Maybe I don't define forgiveness the way they do. I think that you have to find a way to let things go so that you aren't holding them over people or living under how you feel about them. For a time in my own life I was angry. I held that against everyone, but living with the anger meant I was still giving power to the people who'd hurt me. It was like they were still hurting me. I had to stop being angry to let the pain go." She leaned back, staring at the ceiling. "It doesn't mean that it never hurts. It just doesn't control me."

They sat in silence for a while, until he finally spoke.

"Did you go back to these people and work things out with them?"

"Sometimes. I had to learn to let my mother make her own mistakes and live with the consequences. I also learned that I didn't have to accept those bad choices affecting my life."

There was another long silence. Only the crackle of the fire filled the dark quiet that engulfed the room.

After a few minutes, Lara took a deep breath. "What I think isn't important. Do you believe in forgiveness?"

He nodded slowly. "Yes."

"She was curious about what I was doing there and why you weren't sleeping at home. I didn't want to mislead her but I didn't-"

Her explanation was halted by a sharp knock at the door. Farraday went to the kitchen. Lara stood up to turn on the halogen lamp in the corner of the living room.

She turned to see Collins march into the room, Farraday not far behind him. She didn't need a second glance to know that something was wrong. "What is it?"

"Someone broke into Duane's house."

Lara exchanged a glance with Farraday. "At least he's safe."

Collins glared at her. "It might have helped if I'd known that."

Farraday sat down. "We went to see him after we found Susan's body and persuaded him to go away."

"How did you manage that?" Collins collapsed against the chair.

"There was a storm-chaser convention on in Canada. It wasn't hard to convince him that this would be a good opportunity to sell photos."

Collins shook his head, ironing out the wrinkles across his forehead with his hands. "I cursed his little hobby when this story broke. I guess I should just be thankful we don't have another murder."

***

The next two days were like a hellish dream that wouldn't end. Lara had become the talk of the office. Her colleagues were beginning to resent her and even Jimmy warned her that Hatcher would get suspicious if she kept turning out exclusives at this pace.

Farraday was also under increasing scrutiny as the case expanded.

Internal had launched an investigation into the videotape and Walker's alleged negligence.

From his desk, Farraday could see the weight of stress in Collins' weary stare.

He jerked his head to motion for Farraday to come into the office.

"How are you holding up?"

"I should be asking you that," Collins replied. "You look exhausted."

Farraday sank into a chair. "Any news?"

Collins shook his head. "I don't think there's anything more we can do today. Why don't you go?"

Farraday nodded absently. It was Tuesday night. He'd interviewed potential suspects, re-interviewed Megan Douglas, followed up on the original ME's report, confirmed with that Susan had no drugs or painkillers in her system when she died and now he was arranging an interview with the elusive David Douglas, all while still trying to keep an eye on Lara.

"I'm worried, Uncle Con." All his thoughts had come into focus then, slowing and sorting to allow him to zero in on the undercurrents that had been tugging at him all day. "Betty's house, then Lara's and now Duane's."

"I know. Don't worry about checking in here. Stay as close to Lara as she'll let you. Hatcher might have had someone swipe a file but I'd like to think intimidating witnesses in a potential murder case is out of his league."

Farraday laughed.

"What's so funny?"

"Even you think an unscrupulous editor has a line he won't cross."

***

Lara had spent her afternoon at the library, digging through old archives. She'd promised Farraday she'd stay somewhere public. He wanted her to be surrounded by people she could trust. *Without a thought to the fact that he knows as much as I do.*

A few weeks ago she couldn't have imagined sharing her research with a detective as the case unfolded, though she'd prepared for that possibility. She never promised her sources anonymity, usually eliciting some verbal agreement to cooperate with the police if necessary, which had helped with this investigation.

Today had been grueling, rifling through boxes of papers she'd had to hunt for in the basement because Nancy was unusually busy, but all she wanted was to go home and tell Farraday what she'd found. Lugging boxes hadn't helped her back, which seemed fine until she jerked it the wrong way.

Since Farraday's job required dealing with autopsies and toxicology he was bringing the gritty facts to the table. For her part, she'd learned enough about the Douglas family to answer some of her lingering questions and raise several new ones.

She set the lid back on the box, jolted by the sudden awareness of movement beside her.

"I didn't mean to scare you."

"I was just lost in thought." She took a deep breath. "I didn't know you hung out here."

"Every reporter who works for Hatcher hides from him here sooner or later."

Lara leaned back, studying Vern Fletcher. They'd barely exchanged the odd pleasantry since she'd started working at The Ledger. "Come to offer me some advice?"

He frowned. "Why? You need some?"

"Everyone else at work seems to think so."

The left side of his mouth formed a half-smile. He shook his head. "They're wasting their breath."

"Then to what do I owe the pleasure?"

"I thought I should make the effort, since I saw you here on my way out."

Her arms folded across her chest as she stared at him. "I didn't know you had such a low opinion of me."

He matched her smile. "On the contrary, you're the one to watch. Not because you've snagged these headlines lately, but because you're good. You've got talent, heart, enough smarts to stay out of Hatcher's way."

"If we're done with the ego-stroking, I've got somewhere I need to be." She pushed her chair back but he stopped her, setting his hand down on top of hers.

"Do you know how David Douglas connects to the mayor's office?"

The skin between her brows pinched. "I've heard rumors. Why?"

"The mayor's office is interested in your story. You're shaking the family tree."

He was halfway out the door before she got the words out. "How do you know?"

Vern's step faltered and he turned back to look at her. "I know a lot of things, but you don't want to keep Detective Farraday waiting."

He'd turned on his heel and walked away. Lara's hands trembled as she picked up the box and put it back in the storage closet Nancy had told her to use.

She was heading toward the door when Nancy stopped her.

"What's going on? You've been swamped."

"Since the closure of the 4th Street branch we've turned into a zoo." Nancy had lowered her voice. "You know those articles you talked to me about? Someone has been asking for those issues."

"Someone you know?"

"Graeme Garrett."

Lara felt her face wrinkling with her question. "Graeme Garrett?" She shook her head.

Nancy's eyes popped wide open. "Now that's a surprise. The public relations fellow for Walter Morrow. Right-hand man to the mayor."

Lara looked up to see Farraday pushing the door open, looking worse than she felt. "Thanks Nancy. I owe you again."

***

Lara listened while Farraday recalled the events of his day. At last his voice trailed off and he looked at her. "What about you? Any luck?"

"Just old-fashioned elbow grease and hard work." She ran it down.

David Douglas had inherited the family businesses, mainly handling international business trips with their overseas operations, leaving the factories in Oakridge under the supervision of others. He avoided the press and was known to be ruthless on the few occasions he did step in to deal with local operations. He was influential because his businesses employed a lot of residents, but nobody ever referred to him as liked or even respected.

The Douglas family had come from old money, long established in the area. The only boy with three stunning older sisters, David grew up in their shadow, with enormous pressure to succeed as the only male heir to the family name and business. When he turned twelve the family dynamics changed forever. His mother's body was found with the beaten body of his oldest sister, who had endured serious injuries but survived. Both women had been raped but the police did nothing more than complete a standard checklist, the investigation never gaining momentum. No suspects were ever named.

David was never far from the spotlight following the attack. Photos and reports on the other siblings ceased, with no mention even of marriages or children in the local paper.

Five years later, David was questioned about a rape. Mr. Douglas ensured his son had a lawyer during questioning and the case eventually faded away. No charges were ever filed.

"Are you ready for this? The rape victim was Elizabeth Johnson. She married Frank Zimmerman and over the years became known as Betty."

Farraday stared at her for a moment. "Let me get this straight. Susan's father was the only identified suspect in the rape of Betty Zimmerman, our missing witness." He rubbed his jaw. "If I was attacked like Betty was, the one person it would be hard not to fear would be the person who raped me and got away with it."

"Assuming she knows who it was."

"It makes sense. She was locking her door in the daytime. She witnessed the daughter of her suspected rapist being chased and was too frightened to phone the police. She was afraid of someone."

"When are you interviewing David Douglas?"

"First thing tomorrow."

***

Security at the Douglas Estate exceeded what Farraday's parents had at home. He'd been screened at the driveway and had to hold up ID to a remote access camera before hearing a click and watching the gates swing back slowly. At the front entrance a man re-checked his ID before silently leading him inside.

The room he'd been left in was small and serviceable. Farraday could see through an open doorway into the office, a stately desk set against a backdrop of glass panels that looked out onto the fields between this estate house and the original one, the river dividing the two properties. The hard-backed chairs in the room where Farraday waited were replaced in the office by leather seats in a custom Italian design.

After waiting for twenty minutes he got up and looked out the window. The room was narrow and uninviting, with only a small opening permitting natural light to enter. He could clearly see the old house.

"Ahem." Farraday turned to see David Douglas. His light brown hair didn't detract from the chill of his icy blue eyes. The corners of his mouth seemed ready to twist into a scowl. It certainly couldn't be put down to the overpriced suit or the clean-cut appearance, but something about the way the man carried himself reminded Farraday of low-brow thugs for hire on TV shows about the mafia.

"Mr. Douglas." Farraday extended his hand. "I'm Detective Farraday."

Douglas looked at the hand for a split second, shook it quickly and pulled his own hand back. He sat down.

"You have a surprising career for a Farraday. Your father has a solid reputation in the international business community."

The tone, the intonations and the nuances of the face all told Farraday more than the words did. It was power positioning. Douglas was letting him know he'd done some research. His voice resonated with scathing criticism of his decision to pursue law enforcement, inferring that

Farraday didn't live up to his father's standards, that he lacked the skills to be successful in business himself.

This one statement told Farraday more about the man than he could have gotten from the most carefully prepared line of questioning. It told him something of the values of the man and the resources he had.

"I'm sorry to have to speak to you under the circumstances. I understand you were out of the country when you received word."

There was barely a perceptible nod, a way of making Farraday keep his eyes on the subject, preventing him from jotting anything in his open notebook.

"Were you at Megan's engagement party?"

The cold eyes darkened, the rigid brow wrinkling with the abrupt change. "Yes."

"Did you speak to Susan that night?"

"Of course."

"How did she seem?"

"Fine."

"Not depressed, anxious?"

"I said she was fine."

"Do you know where she was living?"

"Here."

"Here?"

"Yes. She had rooms upstairs."

"Megan said-"

"Megan wanted Susan to be more independent. Susan wanted to be with her family."

"So it was her choice to live here?"

"Of course." The words could have chilled warm beer left sitting in the midday sun on a beach in the Caribbean.

"Can I ask why Susan went away during high school?"

"It's none of your concern."

"When did you leave on your business trip?"

"That hardly matters."

"Did you see Susan between the engagement party and the night she died?"

"No, I didn't see her again before she killed herself."

Have I ever had a clear-cut suicide where the parents accepted that immediately without looking for another explanation? Farraday knew the answer. "When did you leave for Japan?"

"Nineteenth of September. Right after I put flowers on my wife's grave, if you must know." David stood, walking to the window. He pointed to a spot Farraday hadn't noticed before. Farraday could see a tombstone and an open plot beside it, presumably for Susan.

The only way to approach David Douglas seemed to be to try to keep him off balance, ask the unexpected. The words weren't helpful. Only the tone and facial expressions told Farraday how carefully the answers had been prepared.

"How far along was she in her pregnancy?"

"Are you a tabloid reporter or a detective?" The words were just a forum for venting his scorn, the strength of his antipathy masking his lack of anguish. "She wasn't pregnant."

"Our pathologist was able to establish that Susan gave birth only hours before her death."

Douglas remained silent, his body rigid, his face blank. Farraday knew the interview was coming to an end. Still, he had to ask the new question that had arisen in his mind.

"I thought your wife died September thirteenth."

"Sorry? Yes, why?" Douglas blinked.

"You said you put flowers on her grave on the nineteenth before you left."

"That was our wedding anniversary."

"I see. How is it you lived in the same house for a week and didn't see Susan?"

"We both led busy lives." Douglas pushed the words out between clenched teeth.

"Can you tell me why no one reported Susan missing?"

"She came and went as she pleased. She didn't live by a schedule."

"Can I see her rooms?"

"Certainly."

His quick compliance caught Farraday by surprise. When he stepped into Susan's room he understood. It was pristine, not a picture or poster to be seen, bed stripped and left bare, a message to him, clearly stating that there was nothing here to be found. Farraday noted two boxes by the door, both closed and sealed. All that remained of Susan's life was about to be put away forever.

Douglas led him to the entry and opened the door. "I expect your report on Susan's suicide should be concluded shortly. Thank you for your attention to this matter."

The heartless, calculated way those words came out made Farraday feel like someone had dropped a handful of snow down the back of his shirt.

"This is a homicide investigation. I'll keep you informed."

Farraday turned and walked away, leaving Douglas standing in the entrance.

***

Lara had been confined to her office all morning. It wasn't long before the door creaked open and then swung wide when Jimmy saw she was there.

He turned and shut the door behind him. "Out with it."

"Out with what?"

"Don't play innocent with me. What the hell happened to you?"

She'd evaded his questioning glances for days, only talking to him in the hallway where he couldn't ask about her injuries or her decision to work with Detective Farraday.

Lara sighed, looking into the usually playful eyes now filled with concern. "Someone broke into my house. Farraday chased them off but we don't know who it was."

"What was he doing at your house?" Concern was replaced with a dark look as Jimmy scowled.

"There was an incident and he came to check up on me. Thank God for that, or who knows what would have happened. Look, you know I have to cooperate with him on this. And he's given me a lot of information to work with."

"Are you sure it was a hunch and not a set-up?"

"Jimmy..."

He stood, turning away from her for a moment before he looked back at her. "You know what they say about the One-Four."

"Farraday hasn't been here long enough to be part of that. My gut tells me I can trust him."

"That doesn't mean I have to like you having a cop from a dirty precinct as the only one watching your back."

Lara was unable to muster a response before Jimmy opened the door and walked away, leaving his words echoing in her mind, mixing with her own lingering doubts.

She went back to her research. It wasn't long before she was reading profiles of David and Angela Douglas. Angela had been the public face of the family locally, smoothing over Douglas' standoffishness, according to some columnists.

A photo of the family, taken when the girls were ten, prior to Angela's death, showed Douglas seated, his wife standing beside him, hands on his shoulders. She had a wonderful smile the other three lacked. Douglas' face sported an upward twist of the mouth but the chilly eyes drew her focus. This was highlighted by the fact that Susan and Megan, one on each side of their parents, were pushed out to the edge of the shot, barely still in the frame, neither smiling. David, Megan and Susan failed to resonate the cheery warmth that emanated from the pale face and sparkling blue eyes of Angela Douglas.

Angela didn't swim or sail or like being on the water, according to an article on a charity event. A simple appearance at a beach fundraiser for swim camps had drawn attention.

Lara found little about Susan's social life. A newspaper photo from a fundraiser for Mayor Morrow's last campaign had a series of snapshots from the event, most staged with the usual plastered grins and sunny dispositions, but some casual shots captured conversations and attendees performing their social obligations.

One shot showed Susan Douglas scowling as she pulled away, overshadowed by the man who had his hand firmly on his arm, his practiced smile faltering.

Susan Douglas and Walter Morrow. Lara's chin rested on her hand as she thought about what Vern had said, about how David Douglas connected to the mayor's office.

Her thoughts were interrupted by a knock at the door. "Come in," she said, turning. She froze when the door opened and then reached to shut the screen off.

Megan Douglas entered after a split-second pause. Her brown eyes widened, framed by long, dark lashes and she hesitated before speaking. "Are you Larimer Kelly?"

Lara nodded, gestured to a chair and got up to close the door. "Please, call me Lara. Is there anything I can get for you, Ms. Douglas?"

"No, thank you." Megan sat down.

Lara's mind was racing, wondering about the reason for Megan's visit. "I'm very sorry about Susan. I... I can't imagine how you must feel."

Megan nodded, her lips pursed, her gaze on the desk. Then she looked straight into Lara's eyes. "I appreciate how sensitive you've been in your articles."

"I was concerned you would find them intrusive."

"Everyone loves a good scandal, and we're supposed to be an important local family. I read *People* myself." She offered a wan smile. "But I came to ask you for a favor."

Lara swallowed. "I can't make any promises."

"I want to know how you got the videotape."

Lara felt her forehead crease. "Mr. Brodie brought it to me. If he hadn't I doubt I would have been involved in this story."

"If the police... If Rob...?" Megan drew a deep breath.

It took a moment for Lara to realize what Megan was really asking her. "Oh no, Ms. Douglas. Duane didn't take the video to anyone for almost twenty-four hours. It was already too late. There was nothing your fiancé could have done."

Her head bowed. All Lara could see for a moment was the raven hair. When Megan looked up she was composed. "Please. Call me Megan."

There was silence for a moment.

"Are you working with Detective Farraday?"

Lara nodded.

"He seems... like he really cares. Do you think Susan was murdered?"

Lara paused, her lips parted. "Yes, I do." There was no change in Megan's expression. Lara watched her closely but she seemed to take that answer without the slightest hint of surprise. "Can you tell me if Susan was using drugs?"

Megan shook her head immediately, emphatically. It was the strongest reaction she'd produced since she'd walked into Lara's office. "No. She was clean."

"Okay. Can I ask you a question? It's personal."

Megan nodded.

"When was Susan's baby due?"

Megan's face was almost translucent. "She was pregnant? Couldn't the, uh, the people who look-" She swallowed hard. "Couldn't they tell?"

"She'd given birth not long before her death. Without the baby we don't have enough evidence to be conclusive."

Megan's eyes filled with tears, her shoulders sagging. "I, uh, just thought she was gaining a little weight. Susan was dressing in loose clothing. I was just glad she wasn't using anymore. She looked healthy."

"You're certain she wasn't using?"

Megan nodded. "She'd been clean for over a year."

"Do you have any idea who she was involved with?"

"Could that help you?"

"Whatever happened to Susan, it was deliberate. If there was someone she was close to, that she might have confided in, they might be able to give us an idea of who would have wanted to hurt her. At this point, any information would help."

Megan took a deep breath and sat up straight. "There are some things you should know."

***

"He was going to find out sooner or later that this wasn't a suicide," Farraday said.

Graeme Garrett scowled. "And you wanted to see how he took the news."

"Maybe I felt cheated by the fact that her room had already been stripped clean."

"A natural reaction by some parents when they lose a child. It wasn't the crime scene. What did you hope to find?"

"A journal, evidence of sexual activity, indications of where she was spending her time, phone numbers of colleagues, friends..." Farraday glared at Garrett. "Shall I go on?"

Garrett turned to look at Captain Collins. "Mr. Douglas' family is established in this community. Some people," he glanced at Farraday, "might not appreciate that. Is Mr. Douglas a suspect?"

"I don't care where you work or who signs your paychecks," Collins said. "That's none of your business. You've been afforded this courtesy but we aren't disclosing the status of the investigation at this point."

Graeme Garrett picked up his briefcase and walked out, slamming the door behind him.

"That went well."

Collins frowned. "That could have been a disaster. You rattled the cage of one of the most powerful men in this community, a man with allies who have influential positions. David Douglas is not someone you want to have as an enemy. Do you have any reason to suspect him?"

"I find it suspicious that he lived in the same house as Susan and apparently didn't know she was pregnant. They shared the same roof but didn't see each other for a week."

"Megan Douglas never mentioned her sister was pregnant either."

"True. But David Douglas has a history."

"A history of not knowing what's going on in his family? That can be said of most men."

"A history of brushes with the law, enough to add up to reasonable suspicion."

Collins' mouth hung open for a second as he stared at Farraday. "You better have something good to support a statement like that outside this office."

"How about being questioned in the assault and rape of Elizabeth Johnson, a.k.a. Betty Zimmerman? What about the circumstances of his mother's death? She'd been raped. The cops never did more than complete a limited checklist, going through the motions. His oldest sister was also raped but she never gave a statement to the police. That family had the power to demand answers and they let the police drop it. The incompetence of that investigation makes Rob Walker's mistake look like a tiny blunder."

"Or complicity in the cover-up of a murder."

"He has an alibi for the night of September fourteenth."

"That doesn't mean he didn't know about it. What I want to know is how Rob Walker stays in his future father-in-law's good graces. I've had a few run-ins with Douglas. He isn't too fond of the police."

Farraday paused, then shrugged. "Maybe he's complicit. Or he isn't in Douglas' good graces. One thing I don't understand is why send Graeme Garrett here instead of a lawyer?"

Collins' grin had a sour twist to it. "It was a message. David Douglas just told us he has an open line to the mayor's office. And he's not afraid to use it." Collins stared at his desk for a moment before he looked into the eyes of his nephew. "This just got a whole lot messier. You'd better watch your back."

***

"You didn't mention that Choy Kim wasn't the first girl from your factory that Graeme Garrett took to work for him."

Vern Fletcher stared at Stacy Ling, the personnel staff he'd gotten information from before. She stared back, cowering like a kicked puppy.

"You didn't ask about them. You only asked about Choy."

"I'm asking now."

Stacy shrugged meekly. "He gets them jobs. That's all I know."

"They have jobs here."

"Jobs with more money."

"Doing what?"

"I don't ask. They agree to go. I couldn't stop them if I wanted to."

"How many? I want names and dates."

Stacy Ling's shoulders sagged as she stared up at him, her hopeful look fading quickly. She bit her lip as she reached for the binder on the edge of her desk.

When Vern left the factory, he walked to his car and started to open the door. A hand pushed it shut, prompting Vern to look up.

Dan Van Biers. Usually the kind of guy who didn't attract much attention, one who blended into the furniture, young, average-looking, average height. Brown hair, not a scrawny guy but not bulky either. Not even someone who got into arguments with Hatcher.

"Are you after my story?"

Vern laughed. "You don't mince words, do you?"

"I'm serious. Snooping around the motel on the weekend. I've been working a long time on these drug stories and the dead prostitutes-"

"Whoa. Back up. First, I'm not interested in your story. I'm chasing my own lead."

"Yeah?" Dan glared at him, his jaw tense, even his fists clenched.

"You better not be or I swear, I'll burn you. Bad enough I've got Lara Kelly's story bumping mine off the front page."

Vern shook his head. "Look, kid, you've got nothing to worry about with me. I'm chasing down a report about a missing Asian girl. Someone Graeme Garrett ties to. It's got nothing to do with your prostitutes or your drug angle."

Dan frowned. "Garrett's involved? Then it might. I haven't seen a story about this."

"That's because I haven't written one yet, and the family hasn't reported it to the police. For now, they're keeping quiet and I expect you to do the same. Consider it good faith, my way of saying you can keep your drugs and hookers and whatever else."

Vern grabbed the door again, pulling it open, climbing into the seat. As he reached to close the door, Dan put his hand on it and stopped him.

"Maybe," Dan paused, looking over his shoulders in both directions before he continued speaking, "I can help you."

For a moment, Vern sat, half turned in the driver's seat, looking up at the younger man. The anger had dissipated, being replaced with a seriousness that was matched by tension. The way Dan looked around to make sure nobody was listening...

"Okay," Vern said. "Not here, though." He grabbed a business card from the glove box and wrote down an address before he passed it to Dan. "I'll see you there in half an hour."

Dan nodded and let go of the door. Vern shut it and pulled his seat belt on, glancing in the side mirror to see Dan briskly walking back to his own vehicle.

***

Lara sat in silence, still digesting what Megan had said. There were gaps, but a hazy image of the victim in this story was surfacing, edges of the picture starting to come into focus.

It didn't take long for her to find what she was looking for, using the clues Megan had provided. She made notes, sent pages to print and backed herself up with a lengthy email with attachments. As she locked her files away her door opened again.

There was no hesitation in the gait of the man who entered now. He strode right up to her desk, his icy blue eyes boring into hers. She resisted the urge to sit down under that pressuring scrutiny and felt her back straighten involuntarily.

"Can I help you?"

"You live up to your reputation." The tone was cold, so she wasn't taking this as a compliment. Lara felt his eyes on her but avoided meeting them completely. There was something about the piercing gaze of this imposing man that made her feel he could peel back skin and bone and read her mind. She suspected it came in handy in the business world he lived in when he wanted his influence felt.

Lara said nothing. There was a deliberate softening and the broad frame of David Douglas sank into a chair across from her.

She counted to five slowly and sat down, keeping her back straight. Lara knew that body language denoted weakness and an opponent like this would read even subtle changes others might miss. "I'm not sure what reputation it is that you're referring to."

"Smart and shrewd. Normally, I'd send someone else to do this, but I wanted to see for myself."

"See what?"

"If you're someone who knows how to take the advantages life offers and exploit them for their own gain."

Lara tried not to frown. "I prefer to rely on skill and decency."

Was that a glint of amusement in the lift of his cheeks? Every nuance of his stony mask seemed to be manipulated for a purpose, his face firm and unyielding. He pushed his lips up and down and narrowed his brow all a little too deliberately.

"And you possess those qualities as well. Your professors speak highly of you. Full scholarship, multiple awards. You're eager, ambitious, looking to make a name for yourself. I could use a person like you."

Lara tried to keep the shadow from flickering across her face. "For what?"

"On my staff. With an international business, I need someone who can read a client, gauge reactions and write without the appearance of illiteracy that dominates the average graduate our schools produce these days. You have the skills. It's an opportunity to travel the world and establish yourself in the business community."

He was poised, slick, oozing with confidence.

"I can offer you a six-figure salary with a lucrative signing bonus. Say, an October 1 starting date?"

"Mr. Douglas, I..."

"Call me David."

She ignored his order. "I made a commitment when I took this position. I have a contract."

His face went cold, turning a stony gray. It was expressionless now, just a hard, unreadable rock. "Contracts can be broken."

He stood and was at the door almost before Lara realized he was moving. He opened it, turned and stared at her, waiting until she blinked before he spoke.

"Some young people overrate their own importance, the prospects they'll have. You could lose your job, be in an unexpected accident. It's good to take an opportunity when you get one. You might not get another chance."

"I'll bear that in mind, Mr. Douglas."

She watched him disappear out the door and fell against her chair. As she drew in a deep breath the phone rang.

"Lar-" she began, before she heard the voice on the other end of the line. "I'll be right there."

***

Lara paced silently, crossing and uncrossing her arms.

The door opened and Farraday smelled pizza. The scent of food reminded him of how hungry he was and he noticed it even caused Lara to slow her step. Collins walked into the living room, glanced at Lara and then looked at his nephew, his brow creased.

Farraday shook his head as he walked out of the room, returning with plates, napkins and soda.

Collins set the pizza down and shrugged off his coat. He sat in the big armchair, leaving Farraday and Lara the sofa. "I sent the video and photographs to a different lab, one that can't be connected to us from our office. They identified traces of movement that wasn't from the trees, but they can only say that the photo is of a man, approximately 170-210 pounds, with short, dark hair."

"Susan was clean when she died," said Farraday, "without even painkillers present in her system. Lessard found a partial bite mark on her left hand."

"Enough for a match?" Collins asked.

"Lessard thinks so. He said not to hang our whole case on it."

"He didn't mention that before," Lara glanced at Farraday, her eyes pinched.

"Lessard never highlights details unless he's sure he can use them. At least, not before his final report comes out." Collins took a slice of deluxe, relaxing back into his chair again. "What about you, Lara? Making any headway?"

"Well, let's see. Susan spent her time away at a draconian reform school called Raddison. Angela Douglas didn't swim. She had a life-long fear of the water and wouldn't even go out on a boat, making her death suspicious. I also found out where Douglas' oldest sister is."

Farraday nodded. "Sounds like you made a lot of progress. We can follow up on all of that tomorrow." He observed the tension in Lara's face, the pinch in her shoulders, her rigid back. "I interviewed David Douglas today. He's already flexing his muscle with the mayor to try to control this investigation."

A bitter smile flickered on Lara's face. "He offered me a job."

"He what?"

"He promised me a lot of money if I'd work for him. Then he suggested this was a once-in-a-lifetime opportunity and that my career would end or I'd be in an accident and never get another chance."

"When was he there?" Collins asked.

"Just before Ty called."

"Which means there was enough time for Graeme Garrett to leave the station and call him." Collins drummed his fingers against the arms of the chair. "He would normally take his time, sort this out through middle-men if he could. He's worried about something."

"He's a calculating viper. If he didn't kill Susan, he knows who did."

"We're getting ahead of ourselves," Farraday said quietly.

Lara threw up her hands. "I know. It's just... he really got to me. And after everything I'd just heard about him-"

"Who were you talking to?" Collins put his plate down, the remaining half-slice apparently forgotten.

"Megan Douglas. She came to my office."

Farraday dropped his plate on the coffee table as he sprang to his feet and reached for his coat.

"Where are you going?" Lara demanded.

"To see Rob Walker. If Douglas finds out Megan talked to you..."

Lara collapsed against the couch as Farraday left. "What if Rob Walker's in on this?"

Collins glanced at her, his mouth twisted in thought. "Then we'll have a serious problem."

Chapter 6

Farraday tried to ignore the lingering questions about Rob Walker as he drove. He could imagine Susan Douglas running down this road, in desperation, fear, excruciating pain, with someone chasing her. This was where it had all begun, at least for them, with a semi-amateur photo jock playing with a camcorder on the night of a fall storm.

The resurgence of Indian summer had turned the rain of the last few days into pure humidity, seeping into every crevice and corner of the city. It was the kind of heat that weighed on you, that you carried. Even at this time of night it charged the air with an unnatural energy that couldn't be ignored. It got under your skin.

Farraday barely noticed the dark sedan parked in front but when he got to the door he could hear tense voices inside. He rapped quickly, and then heard movement in the hall.

The door opened. Walker's eyes went wide. "Th-this isn't-"

"I won't be long." There was no resistance as Farraday pushed the door open and walked into the main room. Megan's back was rigid and her skin taut and flushed, her fists clenched.

David Douglas jaw was clenched so tight it was quivering. "Do you have news for us, Detective?" He let the words come out slowly, oozing with contempt. "Perhaps more seamy questions about Susan's life to satisfy your curiosity?"

"Not at all." He lied smoothly, another skill he'd had to acquire on the job. "I have paperwork for Megan to sign, just formalities."

He sat down, opening his briefcase, deliberately sorting every piece of paper he had one by one.

Douglas stood slowly, glaring at Farraday. "I'll come back later."

He didn't look at Megan or Rob Walker as he walked out. Farraday saw Rob flinch as the door slammed shut. Once Douglas was gone Rob sank down beside Megan, who clasped his hand.

"Papers? At this hour?"

"A complete lie." Farraday said as the sound of a car faded in the distance. "I'm worried about Megan."

"Why?" Walker leaned forward, staring at him. "What's going on?"

"Did you know Susan had been living with her dad?" Farraday watched the color drain from Megan's face.

"I-I can't believe she'd stay there."

"Who knows you went to see Larimer Kelly today?"

"You went where?" Walker's jaw dropped as he turned to look at her. "Why?"

Megan stood up slowly. "He doesn't approve of Rob, you know. Thinks it's my way of rebelling. Dad hates the police. I never really understood that, until I thought about Mother." She turned around, rubbing her arms hypnotically. Then she stood still. "Did he kill Susan?"

"I don't know."

"But you think he might hurt me."

"He has something to hide and after you left The Ledger, he went there. If he finds out you talked to Lara, it might not be safe for you to stay here." He saw Walker glance at Megan and nod his agreement. Farraday took a deep breath. "I have a plan."

***

Collins opened his eyes to see his nephew sink down onto the couch slowly. "It's late. And Lara needs a TV or the internet. What kind of reporter doesn't have the internet?"

Farraday smiled. "One who keeps missing her appointments with the company. They need to put a cable in, and she's been a bit busy." He remembered her explanation for using the computers at the library, although she often still used archived newspapers as well. The smile faded. "David Douglas was there when I arrived. I waited while Walker and Megan packed."

"They're gone?"

"Someplace safe. I told Walker you'd handle it."

Collins nodded. He tipped his head toward the stairs. "I practically had to drag her upstairs and put her under house arrest. Can't you persuade her to take a vacation?"

"You're welcome to try offering her the hotel break-in story as compensation, but I wouldn't hold my breath if I were you. She's determined to see this through."

Collins stood up. "Then let's hope he's not our killer. If he is, I doubt that was an empty threat he made."

***

As Farraday drove to the highway he felt Lara's eyes on him and turned.

She pushed a Bruce Cockburn CD into the player. "Aren't the guys at work wondering what you're doing?"

Farraday shrugged. "I don't know. I've hardly been at the station."

"What's Lenny up to these days?"

"This dragged out long enough that he's on vacation."

"You make it sound tedious."

"You know what I mean." He flashed a smile at her. "It still feels like we have more questions than answers and David Douglas doesn't want us finding out any more than we already know. I had a bad feeling about this investigation."

"That's because you had to work with me."

Farraday suppressed a smile. "I plead the Fifth."

When they finally arrived at the residential school where Susan had spent more than two years of her life, they had to present ID to a guard to be let past the towering brick walls. From the outside, they seemed harmless enough. Inside, a barbed-wire fence added an extra layer of insurance, so that nobody could climb to freedom.

A woman waited on the steps, wearing a gray skirt and sweater, a simple white blouse underneath. Her once-blonde hair was pulled back into a tight bun but her face was full and relaxed, denoting a calm disposition.

"Jane Eyre meets the 21st century," Lara muttered.

"Doesn't look like they employ a relational philosophy of youth reform."

Lara's eyebrows arched slightly, the corners of her mouth curling up just a touch. "No, I guess not."

***

"Our guests are afforded comfort while learning to live with structure in their lives," Maureen Norris explained as she led the way through the main hall. "We have dormitories upstairs for the young ladies and school rooms, two dining rooms and a gymnasium."

"Is this facility strictly for girls?" Lara asked. "I thought I read something about male students."

Ms. Norris paused, casting an unreadable glance at her. "We have a separate facility for boys." The words were clipped, curt, impersonal. Something about the way she said it made Lara almost feel guilty for asking.

Ms. Norris led them outside, to a large stone terrace, and pointed across the field. Between the twin buildings there were three rows of fencing, complete with barbed wire at the top. There appeared to be a distance of several feet between the fences, likely making it impossible for members of the opposite sex to exchange names, never mind anything else.

"We're specifically interested in what you can tell us about Susan Douglas," Farraday said. "Why did she come here?"

"Her father sent her. He felt it was for her own safety."

"Did she have visitors during that time?"

"No."

Farraday glanced at Lara. "No visitors at all?"

"We don't encourage visitors, Detective. They detract from the goals of reform that the guardians of these children have sent them here to acquire."

But you didn't exactly answer the question, Lara thought.

"I'd like to see her file."

"That information is confidential," she said with a thin smile.

"Not when I have a warrant," Farraday said, handing her the document. Collins had called for it the night before. "You can either comply or I can call in a local unit and we can comb through your facility room by room until we're certain we have all the information we need."

The smile vanished. Farraday couldn't quite make out what Ms. Norris was thinking but superficial information was a waste of his time. It may not help solve the case but until he knew otherwise he had to hope that Susan's one-time residence would yield some clues about her life and, possibly, her death.

"Ms. Douglas has been murdered. I'm certain you understand we're trying to ensure there is adequate reform for the person who took her life," Lara said.

"Yes, of course." Ms. Norris opened a door and led them into an office, giving Farraday another sharp glance as she did so.

She lifted a file off the large, basic wooden desk and paused. "I'll show you what it is you need to know." Her shoulders sagged as she left the room, following the corridor until they came to a wide, wooden staircase that sloped gently to a side door. They didn't speak as they walked across the field toward the trees.

It wasn't long before there was a gap in the trees and Farraday could see where they were heading.

"Right over there." Ms. Norris pointed to a small tombstone on the far left side of the graveyard. Farraday strode over to the marker.

"Baby Douglas?"

"Susan's child."

Farraday spun around. "She had a child here? How did the child die?"

"There's a report in the file. This is a copy I prepared for you. You can take it with you."

It was clear from her detached tone and rigid frame that she was finished with them. She handed Farraday the papers and turned.

"You realize we need to exhume this body," Lara said.

Ms. Norris paused, looked back, gave them a brusque nod and marched away.

***

Sunlight warmed his face and Vern blinked. He sat up, groaned and reached for a kink in his back.

The pictures of four young women stared up at him from the coffee table, asking the same question over and over. Vern rubbed his temples, forcing his feet to hold his weight as he shuffled to the bathroom.

Before Choy Kim disappeared, four women made that same trip to Stacy Ling's office. Each had accepted the job willingly.

And none had ever been seen again.

They were orphans or immigrants whose families were overseas, making it easy for them to disappear. They'd willingly moved out of their tiny boarding rooms because accommodations came with the job, with all loose ends tied up neatly behind them. Nobody had reported them missing because no one expected to hear from them again.

Until now.

Five women who'd received green cards through sponsorship by David Douglas had been selected by Graeme Garrett personally for mysterious jobs and just disappeared.

Then Dan Van Biers had told him about Morrow, Garret, Douglas and all the rumors that they were connected to drugs, prostitution and a hush-hush porn business.

All of which made his angle that much more interesting. Asian women going missing... It didn't take a genius to start coming up with some possible explanations.

When Vern was ready he tracked down his target for the morning, on his way to a meeting at St. Christopher Secondary School. Dan had given him the tip, telling him that's where he'd find Walter Morrow.

Although Morrow had no formal relationship with the school, which made Vern wonder what he was really doing there.

"Mayor," he said, extending a hand. "Vern Fletcher."

The plaster grin faltered. "From The Ledger?"

"That's right. I just wanted to commend you."

"On what?" Morrow quickened his pace.

"Hiring immigrants. You've helped young girls like Karen Li with skills secure promising work experience. I'm certain these young girls are a valuable asset to City Hall."

"Ms. Li has moved on. We're fortunate to offer hard-working immigrants an opportunity, but they soon take the next step up the ladder."

"Then that explains why you've hired Ms. Kim."

"Who?" Morrow asked. All around them school kids sauntered up the steps, backpacks in tow, on their way to class.

"Choy Kim. The girl you hired this month."

"We haven't hired anyone recently."

"Really? She was picked up by Graeme Garrett."

Morrow coughed and then reached up to straighten his tie, using the mechanical gesture as a way to buy time to compose his expression. "I must be mistaken. Perhaps you should check with Mr. Garrett. I'm afraid I've been rather busy lately, you know, charity functions..." He let his words trail off, replacing them with another artificial smile.

Vern smiled back. "I understand. Really, I just wanted to say I felt it was a commendable practice, helping new Americans gain valuable work experience."

He shook Morrow's hand, trying not to read too much into Morrow's expression, or the feeling of eyes boring holes into his skull as he walked away.

***

Farraday and Lara sat on one lone bench in silence, listening to the scuffling of leaves that suggested squirrels were moving through the wooded area surrounding the graveyard, stocking up on their winter food supply. Some golden leaves fluttered to the earth, buoyed by the gentle breeze.

Neither said much. Lara presumed Farraday, like her, was thinking about the child who'd been buried here, forgotten, just another dirty family secret in a long list.

Her reverie was broken by the sound of trucks arriving, Farraday taking a deep breath before he forced himself up off the bench, going to give them instructions.

She had to move to get out of their way and sat perched on a rock while Farraday watched as the tiny coffin was raised from the earth. There wasn't much else in the file and every answer seemed to raise more questions. She looked up to see Farraday brushing off his hands, moving toward her.

"Find anything helpful?"

"It's as useful as I would expect of any information she's willing to hand us when she gets a warrant," Lara said, her voice laced with sarcasm. "The ME's report says the baby had a rare, genetic disorder and was stillborn."

"Does it say who the father was?"

"We should be so lucky. No name, even for the child. Come on. You should know by now that we have to work for every scrap of info we can get on this case."

"It would be nice to have a break," he said.

"This is a dismal place to be buried." She straightened the papers without looking at Farraday, mindful of the eyes still close by, tidying up from the exhumation.

"I can't say I find any graveyard cheery."

"Do you think anyone even comes to visit? They don't like guests at the school, but what about the cemetery?" Lara asked as she looked out at the dozen headstones scattered across the opening shadowed by looming trees.

"I guess that depends on whether they've reached Raddison's goals of self-discipline," Farraday said. "Sorry. Maybe we should see if there's any way to find out."

It wasn't long before they had photocopies of the logged entries dating back to the time Susan lived at Raddison.

"She was telling the truth," Lara mused, studying the records in detail as they drove back to Oakridge. "Nobody came to see Susan Douglas."

"Nobody who signed in. Money can buy plenty of things, including concealed access."

"True." Lara paused, her eyes narrowing with concentration as she went back to the first page. "Here we go. Not secret visits, just misdirected access."

"What did you find?"

"Here, here and here. Various dates, after Megan left and the baby died. Our doting Daddy signed in to see Baby Douglas."

Farraday's lip curled. "What did Megan tell you about her time at Raddison?"

"She wasn't fond of the place but she said it helped her sister straighten out, although she admitted Susan went back to using after she left."

"Did Megan say why she was here?"

"Apparently, Douglas thought she could help Susan transition into life here. Susan had been depressed, suicidal and had called the police to report that she'd been raped. David had Susan packed up and sent to Raddison before she could make a statement."

"You failed to mention that before."

She blinked. "You ran off before we covered everything. I meant to tell you." He'd told her about sending Walker and Megan away on the drive. "Do you think Rob Walker is involved?"

Farraday twisted his jaw thoughtfully, considering that. "Douglas didn't even acknowledge Walker's presence when we spoke yesterday or when he left the house last night. Walker seemed genuinely afraid of him."

"I had this impression from Megan, like she'd pulled her way through by keeping her eyes forward, not really seeing what was around her. Like she had ideas of problems but no actual experience with them, as though her whole life had been second-hand."

"If things were as bad as we guess, it's a wonder she wasn't in therapy."

"Maybe she was. Hey," Lara snapped her fingers, "she said Susan had been clean for a year. How many die-hard junkies who go back to using after months in Raddison can kick the habit on their own?"

"Do you think she went to a rehab clinic?"

"After that place? No, more like AA for society drug addicts."

"Is that how it's listed in the phone book?"

Lara glared at him. "I wish I'd asked Megan but I didn't want to put her off and I thought she'd be around for future chats."

Farraday shrugged. "I can't watch everyone."

"Nobody's making you stay." She crossed her arms.

"I can leave you with Walker and Megan if you prefer," he countered.

"Skittles is used to you. That makes you the lesser of two evils."

Farraday laughed. "Then I guess we're stuck with each other."

***

"You again?" Lessard didn't look particularly happy to see Farraday walk through the door, Lara behind him. "I'm behind on my preliminary findings. What now?"

"An exhumation," Lara said, passing him a copy she'd made of the ME's report they'd been given.

Lessard tilted his head, surveying the papers. "What more do you need?"

"Anything you can tell us," Farraday said.

"We'd like genetic typing to identify the parents."

"Let me see. You dug up an unnamed baby from a private graveyard and you don't know who the parents are? I'd like to see the legal precedent for that."

"Susan Douglas was the mother. We want to know who the father was."

"This says the child appeared to be delivered full term, weighing 6 pounds 8 ounces. Cause of death was a rare genetic disorder, resulting in the child being stillborn. Hmm."

"What are you thinking?" Farraday asked.

"I'd like to know how they came to that conclusion when there is no evidence of blood work being done in these reports," he said as he flipped through the pages.

Farraday glanced at Lara. "How soon will you be able to take a look?"

"First thing tomorrow," Lessard said with a sigh. "Now get out. I'm busy."

Chapter 7

Lara seemed to be deep in thought. Farraday finally decided to break the silence and offered her some information he was sure she would follow up on.

"My family spends summers in this area. I've always loved coming here."

"Uh-huh."

"If I'd volunteered that much personal information when we first met you would have had your next ten questions ready for me."

She shrugged. "Everyone loves coming here."

"Except you?"

"I didn't come here on family vacations."

Farraday thought about that, recalling what she'd told him about her home. "This is where you lived?"

"Don't remind me."

"My family still has a house here."

"You know, I forget you're wealthy. Your parents were okay with you being a cop?" She knew the answer but it was better to have Farraday tell her himself. That way, it wasn't another piece of information she had to worry about holding back.

"Mom understands."

"And your dad?"

"He thinks he failed with his children." His father had staged a subtle resistance to Farraday's career choice, introducing him to business and political contacts, hinting at foreign posts like the ones he'd held when Farraday was young.

The main street came into focus as they made their way to the north side of town. "Left at the next intersection."

It wasn't hard to find the simple home of Eileen Parsons. What it lacked in stature it made up for in charm, complete with a white picket fence. Lara noted the berry bushes and wildflowers fading now as fall took hold.

Farraday knocked at the door, which was opened almost immediately by a graceful woman, about the same age as Betty. Her blue eyes shone, her expression pleasant.

"Can I help you?"

"Eileen Parsons?" Farraday asked.

"Yes," she said.

"I'm Detective Farraday from Oakridge, Connecticut. This is Lara Kelly."

"Farraday? I know that name."

"My parents own a house on the bay. Warren and Evelyn Farraday."

"Yes, I know them." Eileen's face brightened with a warm smile. "A lovely family."

"Mrs. Parsons, we were wondering if we could speak to you."

"What is this about?" Eileen asked as she studied Farraday's ID.

She invited them in and led them to the sitting room, furnished tastefully with priceless antiques. As Lara turned to sit down she noticed a series of pictures on the wall. In the far corner there was a large picture of David and Angela Douglas. It was the first picture she'd seen of just the two of them. There was no point of contact between them, just a formal shot with each smiling into the camera on their wedding day.

"Mrs. Parsons, we have some difficult questions to ask you," Farraday began.

Eileen Parsons looked at Farraday, then at Lara. She nodded.

"Are you in contact with your family?"

"Oh yes. Margaret, Jeanette and I are quite close."

"What about your brother?"

The blue eyes cooled a few degrees. "He isn't in touch with anyone."

"Do you ever see your nieces, Susan and Megan?" Lara asked.

She shook her head. "No. David wouldn't allow it."

"Why is that, Mrs. Parsons?" Farraday asked.

"He just wouldn't." Her face clouded. "Has something happened?"

"You're not aware Susan died?"

"Susan? My word, what is she? Barely more than a teenager. I didn't know."

"I'm sorry to have to tell you this. Susan was murdered."

Eileen was silent, her fingers pulling on the pendant around her neck. Lara found her eyes drifting back to the portrait of David and Angela. Something about it was nagging at her, beyond the distance between newlyweds. Megan's dark eyes, the raven hair... There was nothing of her features in Angela's face and little of David Douglas in Megan's allure.

Lara looked up to see Eileen watching her. "She was Papa's choice. David barely knew her a month before the wedding."

"When were they married?"

"September 19, 1979. Not long after David turned eighteen."

"Do you have a picture of your sisters?"

Eileen nodded, leaving the room. Farraday glanced at Lara as they listened to Eileen climb the stairs. "What are you thinking?"

"Practically an arranged marriage, right before college. How common is that?"

"Why is it important?"

"If you have grandchildren on the way you want them raised in a proper family."

"They didn't even know each other." Farraday frowned. "How could they be expecting?"

"They weren't. Susan and Megan were born December 16, 1979."

Eileen returned and passed Lara a portrait of the three sisters, obviously taken in their teen years. They were stunning, pleasant young women, closely resembling each other. It was hard to tell them apart.

"Margaret is in the red dress. Jeanette is in the center."

"Thank you." Lara passed the picture back, ensuring Farraday had a chance to glance at it quickly. She'd confirmed her suspicion. Blue eyes were a Douglas family trait. Megan and Susan had gotten their dark eyes and raven hair from someone else.

Farraday excused himself to take a call on his cell and Lara moved to his chair, closer to Mrs. Parsons.

"I can't imagine how difficult it must have been to lose your mother."

There was a tinge of sadness and a hard edge to Eileen's eyes as she stared off, nodding absently. "We were a loving, happy family, except for David. Even as a boy he was different, strange. Did he kill Susan?"

Lara pushed her heart down out of her throat. "To be honest, we don't know. Did you know Susan had a baby several years ago, when she was in reform school?"

Eileen turned and looked right into Lara's eyes now, her face edged with pain, but also strength and resolve. She shook her head.

Lara took a deep breath. "Mrs. Parsons, this is a difficult thing to ask. Do you know who attacked you?"

"Of course. It was David, and our cousin, Walter. We were never allowed to see Walter much. My father's sister thought David was a bad influence and she put as much distance between our families as she could."

Eileen sighed. "I should have spoken up then. David was never right. He... He actually enjoyed hurting: people, animals, whatever. Never smiled, even as a child, and he got into fights at school. He once squeezed a snake until it died. Then he put the skin and guts into the teacher's desk." She sighed. "Papa couldn't admit he was raising a monster."

"Mrs. Parsons, if David attacked you, what happened to your mother?"

Eileen Parsons wiped a single tear from her eye. "Mama found them. Saw what they did to me. She threatened to send David away and tell Walter's mother. They turned on her and when they were done, she wasn't moving. David told me if I ever said a word he'd kill me. My sisters and I, we took the money Papa offered us and went away."

"This cousin, was this his idea?"

Eileen shook her head. "No, it was all David. He knew how to manipulate Walter, how to talk him into anything." She took a deep breath. "I haven't seen Walter since the day my mother died and haven't seen David since his wedding. Angela came once with the girls, but never again."

Lara nodded. She reached over and gently squeezed Eileen's hand. "I can't imagine how difficult this must be for you."

Eileen clasped her hand down as Lara started to withdraw hers. She leaned toward her, tears trickling down her cheeks. "If he killed Susan, it's my fault."

"No," Lara said, shaking her head. "It's his fault. He made his own choices. Even if you'd testified, David was a minor at the time. He wouldn't have stayed in jail. Nothing you did then could have changed things for Susan now."

Lara looked up. Farraday was holding back, watching from the hallway. She stood up, giving a tiny shake of her head, hoping he'd take the hint.

They walked to the door in silence, Eileen Parsons putting her emotions aside to do her duty and see them out. As Farraday turned to thank her, she clasped his hand.

"I hope you find out what happened and that you put this wicked person away."

"I intend to."

Eileen nodded. "Thank you."

The door closed behind them, the sound of the latch clicking into place the only thing that invaded their silence.

***

"What if I'd had questions for her?"

"Did you?"

"That's not the point."

Lara blew out a deep breath. "I don't think there's more she can tell us than this."

She'd told him what Eileen had said already, as soon as they got in the vehicle. He stared out the window now, at the house where David's sister lived, and then turned the keys in the ignition.

"There isn't a statute of limitations on murder," Lara said. "Can't we do something about the death of David's mother?"

Farraday exhaled. "It isn't hopeful. I'm not saying we shouldn't look into it, but he was only twelve when he committed those crimes. It would be hard to get this before a grand jury, even harder to get a conviction. Depending on the judge, he might not even serve any time."

"What about Susan's rape?"

He glanced at her. "We don't know she was raped."

"I mean the baby, the one sitting in Lessard's lab." She swallowed hard, trying to push the image of that tiny coffin from her thoughts. "Can we do anything about that?"

"You said she reported it to the police, right?"

Lara nodded. "That's what Megan said."

"Then if DNA proves the child was David's, we might be able to do something. The statute of limitations is extended to twenty years if the victim notified authorities within five years and the identity of the assailant is established through DNA evidence."

Lara shook her head. "This guy has literally gotten away with murder, not to mention assault, rape and who knows what else, for three decades. No wonder he makes my skin crawl."

***

Lara was quiet for the rest of the drive, staring out the window. Farraday didn't push her to talk.

He pulled into a parking spot at the ME's office and they went inside. Lessard was the one who'd called while they were at Eileen Parsons, relaying that apparently no expense had been spared in the burial process, and he'd already found something.

Lessard was waiting for them in his office.

"Bread stick?" he offered Lara as he opened the fridge beside his desk. "Or perhaps you'd prefer pizza."

"No thanks."

Lessard shrugged and put the food away, leading them into the other room. "Alpha thalassemias," he said, handing Farraday a new file.

"I'm not even going to try," Farraday said. "What is it?"

"A rare, genetic disorder."

"So the original findings were correct?" Lara asked.

Lessard nodded. "Except there was no way for the ME to know that because no autopsy was ever performed."

Farraday looked up from the papers in his hand. "We had a copy of an ME's report."

"I made some calls. The person who signed that alleged report wasn't an ME. Office staff identified the name as that of a janitor who worked graveyard shift in the office for three months and then quit in late December 1995."

"Paid off," Lara suggested, glancing at Farraday.

He nodded. "Or blackmailed. Either way, another cover-up."

"So what caused this disorder?" Lara asked.

"The million dollar question. It's extremely rare. In fact, I've never seen a case before. A gene in the globin chain is missing and..."

Farraday glared at him and he stopped.

"Never mind. It's enough for you to know that this happens when the parents are closely related. Siblings, half-siblings and first cousins are most likely. I have confirmed that Susan was the mother. You need to look in the family tree to find the father."

Farraday's skin turned the color of ash and Lara felt her face pale.

Lessard frowned. "You did say you wanted to learn the identity of the child's father."

"We suspect Susan's father was also the child's father," Farraday said quietly. "David Douglas has a history of raping family members."

"And what better way to keep Susan from talking than to send her to Raddison. That girl didn't stand a chance."

"We need to look up those records and see if we can prove Susan reported this." Farraday turned to Lessard. "Thanks."

"Not so fast," Lessard said. "One more thing. This baby wasn't stillborn. He was born alive. Even with the disease this child could have lived a few years."

"Are you saying this baby was murdered?"

"Strangled. The bones in his neck were crushed."

***

"I spent my afternoon and half the evening doing grunt work, trying not to raise suspicions," Collins said as he sat down in the chair in Lara's living room. "This had better be good."

He opened his notebook. "May 15, 1995 a call was made from the Douglas residence. The caller was identified as Susan Douglas. She said she wanted to report a rape."

"Did she actually make a statement?" Lara asked.

Collins shook his head. "The case was handled by a well-known, up-and-coming detective who made a visit to the family home and let the girl off with a warning for making a prank call."

Farraday groaned. "Lenny Becker."

Collins leaned back, glancing from Lara to Farraday. "So how does this help us?"

"We exhumed a body at Raddison," Farraday said, rubbing his forehead.

"And I'm just hearing about this now?"

"You were in court yesterday. The child was Susan Douglas'. Born seven months after that report was made."

"Okay," Collins said slowly. "She was raped as a teenager and two months into the pregnancy tried to file a police report, accusing her father of raping her. He had her sent away, the report went nowhere. She had a child, who died."

Lara shook her head. "Was murdered."

He held up a hand. "Save that for later. What does the rape then have to do with her murder now?"

"She'd given birth again, recently. What if it was another rape?"

"Susan tried to report it before. Why wouldn't she try again?"

Lara shook her head. "Daddy dearest made sure she never got to make a statement. She's had problems and has a reputation as a drug user. It would be her word against a very formidable, respected businessman with powerful connections."

"Not if the DNA from the child proved David Douglas was the father," Farraday countered.

"But you don't have the child. You don't even know if this child is alive or dead. What you have are suspicions. We need physical evidence to corroborate this."

"We have the body of the child born at Raddison," Lara said. "Lessard confirmed the father was a close blood relative of Susan Douglas. The child had some extremely rare genetic condition that occurs with inbreeding."

Collins winced. "How does that help you with this case?"

"It may be the only thing we can hold over David Douglas with certainty. If we order a DNA test we can prove parentage. With Susan's age at the time of conception it's statutory rape. Even without her statement in court we can present a strong case against the father of her child."

"Against a man who is a prominent member of this community, with an unblemished record for bringing economic advantages to the region... We need more."

"How about a history of raping women in his family?" Farraday offered. "And murder."

"You two," Collins rubbed his head slowly as though warding off a migraine, "had better tell me everything."

***

"Thank you for coming." Lara stood as Alyssa Martin approached her. Mrs. Martin came from an established local family and had the misfortune of inheriting a socialite problem. She was in her thirties, married to a prominent attorney, had three children and was reluctant to meet with Lara. Mrs. Martin glanced around hastily before sitting down.

"I didn't want you on my doorstep. What do you want?"

"Your husband doesn't know your history?"

"His family doesn't and that's the way it's going to stay. It's none of your business."

"Agreed." Lara held up her hands to indicate she had no interest in Alyssa's secrets. "I'm only interested in what you can tell me about Susan Douglas."

"Why do you think I haven't contacted the police? Anything Susan shared with me as her sponsor was confidential."

"I know where the lines are drawn."

"Then you know this is a waste of my time." She stood abruptly.

Lara stood too. "Can you look inside your heart and honestly tell me that keeping Susan's secrets matters now? What if she was the one sitting here and it was your murder we were investigating?"

"I can't be known for sharing things," she said.

"Only foolish reporters burn sources. I have to keep my word and the confidence of the people who talk to me," Lara said. She preferred consent to take her information to the authorities, if necessary, but she was prepared to settle for just knowing whatever Alyssa could share. "I just want to find out who hurt Susan."

"For me the high was about unwinding, having fun. For her, it was escape. Now that she was trying to sort out her life she felt that she had to return to the family home."

"And you disagreed with her decision?"

"There are some things that are unforgivable," Alyssa said, turning to stare at Lara, as though she was deciding if the reporter understood. "Have you been to Raddison?"

Lara nodded. "We know about the baby."

"It wasn't him this time. But he knew about it."

"Do you know who it was?"

Alyssa crossed her arms, avoiding Lara's questioning gaze. "She wasn't due for a few more weeks. Susan was happy about the baby. She'd bought a house and hired painters to decorate, said she wanted things to be different this time."

"She told you about her other child's murder?"

"All she said was that the child never had a chance. Why do you think she went back to using? Susan was desperate to find a way to numb that pain." Alyssa sighed, rubbing her forehead. "I never wanted to know who the father was and she never tried to tell me."

Lara watched Alyssa turn to walk away, feeling cheated. 'If not David, then who?'

Alyssa stopped and turned back.

"She said everything started with Kyle."

"Her personal problems? I thought they went back to the death of her mother."

"She never elaborated, Miss Kelly. I'm just telling you what she told me. She said... She said if Kyle hadn't died she wouldn't be pregnant now."

Lara watched the rigid form walk across the grass, not even making the pretense of being out for a walk in the park as she headed straight for her car.

***

Vern squeezed his fists tightly, channeling all the rage into his fingertips that he could. He hoped it was enough to siphon the anger away from his heart, which had gone into overdrive when he'd found the letter.

Sleep had left him early, earlier than usual for a Saturday morning. He was still no further along in piecing together what had happened to the five women or how Garrett was involved. As a single male with no history of involvement, no evidence of dating or even taking companions to political events, it wasn't hard to guess what Garret's interest might be. But Vern couldn't substantiate it.

The only thing he knew for certain was that Garrett had lied to him. The more he looked into Garrett's past, however, the more links he saw outside the mayor's office, to David Douglas, who had instructed Stacy Ling personally to assist Garrett in finding the right candidates for his 'jobs', a fact Ling had been reluctant to provide.

He was on his way to the kitchen when he saw it. A single white envelope lying on the floor, where the mail fell when the postman dropped it through the slot in the door.

Vern had shivered when he saw it.

He'd hesitated for a second before opening it. The note had been simple, to the point, his instincts dead on. "You wouldn't want her to go missing. Stop looking." He'd turned the note to find a printed photo, Julie's face smiling, evident even behind the latte she lifted to her lips, a date and time stamp in the corner testifying to the fact that the photo was less than 24 hours old.

His heart had flipped and then his stomach had lurched. Julie. His ex-wife.

Losing her once had been almost unbearable. To lose her again, like this...

Vern unclenched his fists and took a deep breath. There were ways around threats, and after all his years in journalism he'd heard his share of stories. One came to mind and he grabbed a bag quickly, taking what he needed as well as the letter as he walked out the door.

Chapter 8

Lara reached behind her coat, extracting a tape recorder. "It's all here. Highly inadmissible, but enough to let you form your own conclusions."

"Do you use that in all your interviews?"

"People don't think about how things will look in print. If you're going to quote a source you have to back it up." She stared out the window. "It felt good sitting there on that bench, feeling the warm sun, the smell of autumn in the air. I almost forgot you were watching me."

"It's not as though you're under lock and key."

"No. It's just a little reminder that there's a potential danger. Things have been quiet though. Maybe this guy realized he was taking unnecessary risks."

"It's possible. But I don't want to take any chances."

"We're no closer to solving this case," she said.

"David Douglas looks like a solid suspect. We know he's lied to us and the fact that he offered you that job suggests he's afraid of what you might find."

"Does he have an alibi?"

Farraday snorted. "A man like him can fabricate an alibi in a heartbeat. We're waiting on further tests to decide if we have enough to proceed with statutory rape charges."

"You can think it's hard to not know your dad but it could have been a lot worse. It could have been David Douglas."

Farraday glanced at Lara. There was a blue tinge under her eyes and her cheeks were sunken. He couldn't remember the last time they had a day off. It was beginning to feel like they had been running full speed, only to discover they were on an exercise wheel like a rat in a cage. Farraday had a rule for when a case started to feel like this.

He braked, making a sudden turn.

"Where are we going?"

"Your house. You're packing a bag."

"I'm not going into hiding."

He glanced at her. "We're going away. Just for a break."

"You aren't trying to get rid of me?"

"I know better than to waste my time." Since he'd been to his place that morning he had everything he needed in the car. When they got to her house he verbally listed off the things she needed to pack.

"Not until you tell me where we're going." She crossed her arms, sat down on the couch and glared at Farraday. He stared back with indomitable resolve, eyes unblinking. She didn't move.

"Then I'll pack your things myself." He turned toward the stairs.

"Fine." Lara leapt from the chair. She shot him a fiery look, her mouth open to say something else, but she closed it and stomped up the stairs.

"I'll feed Skittles," Farraday called in a conciliatory tone, smiling as he went into the kitchen.

***

"I don't know why you didn't just tell me," Lara repeated. The Farraday family had spent money tastefully, finishing with detail and purpose. The house was elegant but not lavish and the design fit the more basic requirements of a well-equipped cottage instead of serving as a medium for displaying wealth.

"If I told you, would you have agreed?"

"I still don't know why you thought we should come here." Lara heard the edge going out of her voice as she sank into the leather sofa, feeling the heat from the fire Farraday had just started. He brushed his hands off as he turned toward her.

Farraday was wearing jeans and a sweater instead of the typical dress shirt and pants that he wore for work. It was the first time she'd seen him dress casually.

"Never mind," she murmured. "I get it."

"Don't get too comfortable. I want to give you the tour."

"Tease." She got to her feet.

They were in the main room, which opened up onto a large deck overlooking the lake. Tranquil water reflected the orange and gold tones of the leaves of the trees that embraced it, shimmering softly in the warm autumn sun.

Farraday led Lara back to the entry, this time crossing the hall. "The kitchen," he said, gesturing left. "And the dining room." This time he nodded to the right. He barely gave Lara time to look before he grabbed their bags and started up the staircase.

At the top of the stairs he nodded to the first door. "My parent's room." The next door opened to a bathroom and a door across the hall opened to reveal a spare room, which Farraday said his mother was planning to redecorate. All the furniture had been covered in plastic. At the end of the hall there were two more rooms opposite each other. "My room," Farraday nodded left, "and Trin's room. I'll put your things there."

The poster bed was beside a fireplace, complete with a handmade quilt with a Celtic border. Wine-colored drapes hung to the floor, shielding the large window. Without touch, Lara couldn't be certain of the fabric. It appeared lush and thick. When she turned back to the door that she noticed the large picture on the wall. She assumed it was Ireland, knowing the family had lived there, a scene of rolling green hills and ancient abbeys forgotten in the fields.

Farraday was watching her from the door. "Ready?"

"For what?" Lara asked. He didn't answer. Instead, he led her back downstairs.

***

"And that's where I lost Sea Wars with Trin." Farraday nodded to a spot a few feet off the beach. "You can't see the rock that's close to the surface from here. Trin pushed me back. I tried to stop myself and broke my arm."

"Ouch." Lara was soaking up the stories of summer vacations with the Farraday family. "Did you get even?"

"She felt bad. She spent her allowance buying me ice cream and Marvel comic books. And the first crime novel I ever read. The Hardy Boys."

Lara laughed. "My first crime novel was probably Trixie Belden."

She noticed a subtle change in Farraday, a wistfulness that was shadowing everything he said since he'd first mentioned his sister.

"You miss her."

Farraday nodded. "I know I have to forgive her. It hurts too much to be angry."

Lara followed him back into the main room, wondering why he was angry with his sister. As Farraday went to stock the fire she noticed a small picture on a bookshelf in the corner. Farraday and Trin on one of those summer vacations, arms around each other, laughing, Trin with her blonde hair and delicate face, Farraday with his strong features, even as a boy. Lara looked at Trin, into the eyes of the sister Farraday was so fond of and felt a twinge of familiarity. She'd seen those eyes before, only not this carefree but with weight and pain.

Trin. Not short for Trinity or Trina, like she'd thought. Lara felt her face flush, grateful Farraday's back was to her. She wondered if this made his hurt harder or easier to bear. A lover could eventually be exorcised. But family... Now she realized Farraday's hurt was linked to how much he loved his sister. She'd thought it was a different kind of love, a relationship reduced to smoldering embers that Katarina hoped to rekindle.

Katarina had found Farraday at a crime scene because her uncle, Farraday's captain, had told her where he was.

And Lara had filtered everything through her assumptions and missed the obvious.

Looking at the photo, Lara thought she finally understood how hard this must be, for both of them.

She caught a glimpse of movement from the corner of her eye and glanced at Farraday as she put the picture back on the shelf. "You should call her."

He didn't say anything for a moment. Then he nodded and left the room.

***

Lara went upstairs to change. Farraday had shown her the hot tub off the back deck and he'd started it up on their way back inside after their walk. She had a feeling, after the long hours, the bumps, bruises and the strain of the past few weeks, that a hot tub was reason enough to forgive Farraday for dragging her away in the middle of an investigation.

She couldn't resist the urge to peek into his room. It was smaller than Trin's, with only a single bed against the far wall. The drapes and bedding were dark blue. Five framed ink drawings were hanging on the near wall and when Lara looked closely she could see Farraday's unrefined youthful signature in the bottom right corner.

Lara hadn't been in the hot tub for more than a few minutes when Farraday slid in beside her. She looked at him, her questions unspoken.

"I tried her home and her cell. Her message said she's on personal leave."

Lara scrambled to recall any mention of family problems. "Is... Are you...?"

"She's just taking personal time. I managed to get in touch with one of her colleagues. They didn't know where to reach her or when she's expected back." Farraday's dark eyes clouded and his jaw twisted. "Maybe I was too hard on her."

Lara touched his arm. "I think she knows she did something wrong. Not just to you, but to your whole family."

"She wanted to be a detective. Dad blocked her application and made sure she didn't get in. She was furious. Trin knew there was only one thing he would hate more. Journalism was her rebellion and she decided to write under our mother's maiden name to hurt Dad."

"And the story, the one that-"

"There were things that were true but there were things that were misleading. My dad helped people get work visas but he chose people carefully. The murder wasn't related to how he got into the country. That man was qualified."

He paused, his mouth twisting. Lara suspected he was reflecting on what had happened, weighing what he was willing to say now. She could guess what had happened. "But Trin needed a source for her story so she inferred she got the information from you."

"It wasn't just that. Trin wasn't even working for the newspaper anymore. She resigned and went away. For months, all we got were occasional letters, and then she popped up with the articles she did. Freelance, unsolicited." Farraday turned and looked into Lara's eyes. "That was what hurt the most. She was becoming someone I didn't know, someone I couldn't understand or respect."

For a moment, he said nothing as he looked at her. She didn't know what to say back.

"You remind me of who she was. Her values, her tenacity and strength. I felt like she'd lost that."

Lara felt the intensity of his gaze. It was like some tangible connection held her focus, locked her in an exchange with him, unable to look away and unable to look into her own thoughts for fear he would see what she was thinking and feeling. She felt certain Farraday was about to reach out to her. All this time she'd kept his unresolved relationship in the forefront of her mind and never suspected Katarina was his sister.

It had also been important that they preserve the working relationship they had built, making it necessary to stay focused, and she was reluctant to jeopardize that now. She'd managed to avoid this confusion when she thought he was still emotionally involved with someone else but now that she knew he wasn't...

She turned away, looking out at the lake and drinking in the fall colors, the leaves swaying in the soft breeze.

***

"I know it's cruel but I traded places with Max."

"The mangy, musty stuffed dog?" Lara nodded and they both started to laugh.

The black night sky enveloped the house. They were working on their second bottle of wine and Lara was definitely feeling relaxed. It felt wonderful to be able to unwind. They'd sat for hours exchanging stories about their most embarrassing moments. She couldn't help noticing the crinkles around his eyes and the deep, hearty laugh.

"I never played the game again," Lara said. "I guess I just wasn't cut out to be part of the in crowd. What about you?"

"Me?" His face straightened, but his eyes gleamed mischievously. "I can honestly say I never played spin the bottle."

"See what you missed, growing up overseas?" Lara looked up, observing the mantle clock for the first time and groaned. "Please tell me that clock is wrong."

She needed only to look at her own watch to confirm that it was past midnight. "So much for getting to bed early."

Farraday stood and pulled Lara up with his hands. "I'll make you a fire upstairs."

She opened her mouth to protest, but remained silent. Lara didn't feel the need to fight with him. She still didn't want to think about how things had begun to change, from the first awkward, distrustful exchanges to laughing and talking and losing track of time, but with the peaceful fog of several glasses of wine that couldn't all be absorbed by her dinner she felt it best to say nothing at all and try not to think about Tymen Farraday.

***

Lara felt sleep slipping away, her mind clicking into gear, getting ahead of her body, which unenthusiastically clung to the covers. She squeezed her eyelids shut, willing herself to slip back into the restful hold of a deep sleep, but it was gone. Lara opened her eyes and looked at her watch. It was 9 am.

She got up and dressed. Stepping into the hallway, she noticed Farraday's door was open. Glancing in, she could tell the golden morning sun hadn't disturbed him.

Lara went downstairs, wondering what to do. There was no TV or radio, no way to get news or be easily entertained and she felt restless, her body fired with energy she needed to burn.

He'd spent part of the afternoon showing her the beachfront but she'd observed that the property included a few miles of woods to the east side. She took her camera out, trying to recall how long it had been since she'd just gone for a walk and taken photos for fun. Since the night Duane Brodie had walked into her office her life had been almost completely consumed by this investigation.

Initially, when Farraday had insisted they take the rest of the weekend off she'd been furious. It wasn't until they got here and she started to feel the tension slipping away that she realized the critical discernment he'd shown. She failed to see when things were spinning out of control and, despite knowing the best way to refocus was to take a break, she could never pull herself away.

Farraday's priority was supposed to be investigating the corruption in the department, but he didn't seem bothered by the fact that he had to put that case on hold while he pursued Susan's death. Instead of pushing for a resolution, he appeared to be waiting for the opportunities to present themselves. It was a smart plan, one she wasn't sure she'd have the patience for. It was a fundamental difference between them. He seemed to have an ability to resist pressure while an investigation unfolded, refraining from rushing ahead of the case.

Lara noticed something in the woods, a little to her left. She was still within sight of the main house, but there was a small cabin there, a building Farraday hadn't pointed out on their tour. As she got closer she noticed what looked like a rough path through the woods, winding back to the main road. She walked toward the small porch on the side of the isolated structure.

***

Farraday felt the warm sun prodding him. He kept his eyes shut, listening for evidence that the day had begun but heard nothing.

He rolled onto his back and opened his eyes. It had been a great impulse to come here and get away. This had been the most consistent dwelling of his life, the thread that remained constant when they had moved from country to country. He didn't begrudge the opportunity to see the world but he appreciated the anchor that the summerhouse represented for him, the one place he could truly always come home to.

There was his parents place in New Haven but that had never really been his home. After the conflict started with Dad and Trin it was never the same.

And it was such a stupid argument between two stubborn people unwilling to give an inch. Other families had serious things to fight over and they'd let a dispute over career choices turn into a rift and hurt everyone in the process.

Farraday glanced at his watch, surprised that Lara wasn't up yet. He grinned as he recalled their crazy childhood stories from the night before, remembering how the smile on her face had lit up her eyes, which sparkled like crystals when she laughed.

He'd always kept the family summerhouse as a refuge, the one place he'd never taken a girl he'd dated, not that there had been many. There was too much of his life here to conceal and anyone who spent time here with him would see him exposed. He'd felt that yesterday, looking into Lara's eyes, unable to pull away.

He checked his watch again and pushed the covers back and got up.

Still hearing no sound from her room, he dressed and stepped into the hallway, observing immediately that the other door was wide open. It only took a quick glance to confirm that Lara was gone.

He sprinted down the stairs. The house was still, with the quiet that is acquired in the peaceful hours of night and hasn't yet been dispelled by the activities of the day. He saw no sign of her from the patio doors, the stillness outside almost taunting him. Farraday went to the main door to check the car.

It was still there, evidently undisturbed. Now he felt his heart pounding, his mind spinning with questions.

A sudden noise, like a crack followed by a crash and a cry pierced the silence. Farraday was running before he even realized where he was going. The door to the old cook's cabin hung open. He leapt up onto the front step and ran inside.

Lara was pulling herself up off the floor. She glanced at him with evident self-annoyance, her cheeks flushed.

"What happened?"

"I went through a floorboard," she muttered, stepping gingerly on her right ankle. "It looks like it's rotted out. I should have been more careful."

Farraday reached for her arm. "What were you thinking, going off alone?"

"I was taking some pictures. I never left sight of the house."

He froze, certain his panic and fear were displayed on his face.

Lara's face, which had first held the fluster of embarrassment and then the edge of defensiveness, softened now. "I'm sorry. I was just curious. What is this place?"

"An old cook's cabin, used when my grandparents lived here."

"I didn't realize this property had been in your family for so long."

"For over a hundred years. Trin and I used to play in here when we were kids. It hasn't been used since we were teenagers."

Lara swallowed. She doubted that. She'd found a bottle of water with an unbroken seal and a bag of Doritos on the floor. They had the misplaced look of things that someone in a hurry had forgotten to take. They hadn't expired and one window was open, the curtain fluttering in the breeze.

If someone had been there, they hadn't done anything and they were gone now. Knowing of the possibility would only add to Farraday's fear, not to mention his sense of violation at the thought of someone sneaking onto his family's property, watching them.

And it could be just as simple as local kids, hanging out. The summer home wasn't used much, it wouldn't be surprising if local kids were taking advantage of the old cabin.

"Hey!" She fought to hold back the tears as he examined her ankle. "I'm really sorry. I should've known better."

He straightened, reaching under her knees as he stood, lifting her up. "I really couldn't have imagined this when Uncle Con sent me to follow up on your jumper story."

Lara smiled back sheepishly, accepting the statement as his forgiveness.

"I guess you just got out of making beds."

She opened her mouth to argue and then realized that she couldn't. "And I guess this counts out another hour in the hot tub."

"Then it will be brunch by the fireplace with ice for your foot," he said, and then smiled. "At least now you can't run off on me."

***

The rest of the morning was spent matching wits over cribbage and absorbing the stillness of the warm autumn day. As the sun began to move closer to the water they both grew quiet, the inevitable return to the pressures of this case surfacing in their minds. It was an unspoken reality, something neither felt the need to discuss because they completely understood how the other felt.

"Why is this your favorite time of year?" he asked as they began the drive back.

"In the summer I had no escape from my mother. School gave me a feeling of security. All the other girls I know talked about spring and summer weddings. Why pay for studio photographs when you could have the calm, crisp scent of fall and stand against the golden leaves? Nothing could be more beautiful."

Farraday glanced at her. "I never thought of you as a romantic."

She shrugged. "Most honest men want women to be romantic and idealistic. Isn't that what makes it possible for them to find wives that overlook their faults?"

The corner of his mouth turned up and he shook his head. "And I thought I was going to hear the 'men feel threatened by smart women' speech. Is that why you aren't involved with anyone?"

"Who says I'm not?"

"Guys have been calling day and night since I've been at your place. Unless you're just pretending not to be involved with Jimmy."

Lara's eyebrows rose. "Jimmy is a good friend. Most of the reporters won't give me the time of day, especially with the stories I've scooped lately."

"Funny. The guys at work are quite content to let me take the hot seat on this one. You're avoiding my question."

She glanced at him, tucking her auburn curls behind her ear. "You really want to know? I don't think I'm a good judge of character."

His mouth opened and then he looked at her face. "You're shrewd, discerning, haven't jumped to rash conclusions."

"That's the job. I'm not invested in anyone being guilty or innocent." She paused, smiling cynically. "Well, I guess I might be a little invested in seeing David Douglas go to jail. But with the relationships, it's the personal dynamics. I don't trust myself."

"For me, it's the other way around."

"What do you mean?"

"I don't trust the other person. I can't be confident about how they feel. How well do we really know anyone? If I hadn't been shadowing you day and night I'd still be pretty suspicious about your motives. But I think you're being too hard on yourself."

"My mother doesn't have a good track record when it comes to relationships. The police were at our place sorting things out more than once when I was growing up. I always criticized her for staying with abusive men but it isn't just poor, uneducated women who make bad decisions. One of the boys I dated in high school was arrested last year for beating his wife and son. I always thought he was a nice guy. What does that say about my judgment?"

"Teenagers don't have the self-control, aptitude and experience to make good decisions. There's too much pressure here on kids just to be involved. I hear parents saying it's a learning experience, but nobody stops to think that you can learn this vicariously, instead of taking the regrets and heartache forward and letting it cloud your relationships in the future."

"You'll get no argument from me." Lara's somber expression gave way to a lighter tone. "Your turn."

"A good investigator knows not to give up their secrets if the subject still has information they're seeking. You should know you trade detail for detail."

"You can't be serious."

He just shrugged and smiled. "Maybe there's nothing to tell."

"Unbelievable. I tell you something I've never told anyone." She crossed her arms. "And that's when you decide to remind me you're a cop?"

"You did miss your calling. Look out Hollywood, here comes Lara."

She tried to look annoyed but his chuckle was her undoing. Lara threw up her hands. "Count yourself lucky," she said. "I can't find it in my cold reporter's heart to be angry."

Farraday's cell rang, sparing him from further interrogation. "Can you get that?"

She reached to the back seat, pulling the cell from his coat pocket. Since it was on the third ring she didn't even glance at the call display before she flipped it open.

"Hello."

"Have I dialed the right number?" a woman asked. "928-2727?"

"Yes. Can I help you?"

"I was hoping to speak to Tymen."

"He's not available at the moment. He's driving," Lara floundered, wondering just who was on the line. "Can I give him a message?"

Lara listened to the voice on the other end of the line and then nodded, verbally affirming she would relay the information, the uncertainty gone from her voice as she ended the call. Setting the phone in the console between them she met Farraday's puzzled glance with obvious amusement.

"You haven't been home in days," she chastised him. "Call your mother."

Before he could respond the cell rang again.

"Oh please," he said, his voice a mix of amusement and resignation. "Let me guess. My dad wants to talk to you now."

Lara grinned, flipping the phone open. Her smile faded.

"We're on our way. Likely another twenty or thirty minutes." She closed the cell, glancing soberly at her sparring partner. "Collins is at your place. Someone broke in."

Tymen let out a deep sigh. "I guess the weekend really is over."

***

"Where the hell have you two been?" Collins demanded. He glanced at Lara's foot and scowled. "What happened?"

"Just a ridiculous accident," she said, hobbling to a chair. "I'll live."

"I came here looking for you." Collins sounded like a parent about to embark on a lengthy lecture. "When I couldn't find you at Lara's I got worried."

Farraday sighed. "I am an adult. I do forget to check in for curfew."

"Funny." Collins crossed his arms. "And call your mother. There are three messages on my machine and now she's calling my office."

Both Lara and Farraday laughed. Collins' face was starting to turn a deep shade of red when Farraday finally put up his hand. "I guess I should have told you. We went to the summerhouse. It was an impulse but I thought we both needed a day off, a real break."

Lara was watching Farraday's uncle closely so she noted a glint of suspicion in his eye when Farraday told him where they'd been. He didn't say anything but she felt certain she knew what he thought about the two of them going away together.

"As much as any day off can be when you're still under guard," she said.

Collins' cheeks returned to their normal shade. "I can't tell if they took anything."

It looked like the intruder had actively sought out every piece of paper they could find and strewn it across the room. Lara did notice some CDs scattered by the stereo but they also seemed showy, placed in a way to attract attention to their disruption but with no evidence of theft.

"No, everything seems to be here," Farraday said, picking up some of the CDs, collecting some of the papers, tidying a few pillows on the couch. With just those few motions, the place no longer looked like a home that had been invaded. Without the damage to the door from being pried open it would be hard to tell that anyone had broken in and searched the place.

"What do you want to do about the damage to the doorframe? No police report, no insurance claim."

"I'd rather keep this off the radar. It won't be hard to fix this."

"We're all satisfied this is tied to the Douglas case?" Lara asked.

"Seems reasonable to me," Farraday said. "This clearly wasn't theft."

"You said you went to my place first," Lara said to Collins.

He nodded. "Your place is fine. At least, it was a few hours ago."

"Maybe they've decided Lara doesn't have what they're looking for," Farraday said.

"Or maybe the appearance of a search was just to throw us off because they were really coming after you."

"Anything's possible," Collins said. "We can't afford to rule anything out." He turned to Farraday. "I need you in the office first thing in the morning. We're bringing David Douglas in."

"Really?"

"The DA feels we have a solid case on the statutory rape charge. You get to take first shot at him tomorrow. I'll give you the relevant details for a story," he told Lara. She nodded her thanks and watched the door close behind him.

***

Farraday lost an argument about seeing a doctor and had to settle for a promise that Lara would use her old crutches for a couple days. He'd gone upstairs for a shower.

He came down to find her on the floor, the door near the bottom of the stairs open. "I thought this was a closet," he said, looking into the dusty room. The floor was strewn with unpacked boxes, a camping pack and the old crutches Lara said she had.

"That's pretty much how I've been using it. I meant to get this stuff upstairs weeks ago."

"And this seemed like the time?"

"It can be stacked in the corner until I'm back on my feet. Don't worry: I don't expect you to do this for me. Since you're practically living here and I'm stuck on the main floor for a few days we could use this bathroom." She looked up at him. "The phone is in the kitchen."

He frowned, looking at her with a puzzled expression.

"Your mother. If she keeps calling your boss you'll be in serious trouble."

***

Lara had just finished clearing out the bathroom and was about to pull herself up off the floor when the phone rang again.

Farraday intercepted the call. She turned, brushing her hands off, watching his brow crinkle as he glanced at her with uncertainty. He extended the phone without comment and walked away.

"Hello?"

"Lara."

She frowned, trying to place the familiar voice. "Who's this?"

"Vern Fletcher."

Lara pushed herself up off the floor, using the wall to balance so she didn't have to put any weight on her foot. "What can I do for you?"

"Be careful. What I told you the other day, they're asking questions about you."

She sighed, hopping on one foot to the chair that was closest, trying to remember what he'd said. "Who?'

Silence.

"Vern," Lara began, a no-nonsense tone in her voice.

"Look, this is about more than you know."

"Then why don't you fill me in?" She kept herself from blowing out a deep breath, but cryptic phone calls with veiled warnings annoyed her. For a minute, she thought he was just going to hang up.

"The problems with the cops, drugs, child porn... It's like you found yourself in a landmine in the desert and you're worried about not having sunscreen."

"If you know so much, why-"

"Just look deeper."

The line clicked and went dead.

***

The next day was a mental whirlwind for Lara, confined to the four walls of her office after Farraday made Jimmy promise to check in on her regularly.

Collins, true to his word, sent her all the information she needed to put out a convincing report on David Douglas' arrest. She called his attorney, who declined to comment on the charges, and had already finished the first draft of the story when Ted Hatcher walked in.

"Another accident. You should really be more careful. But I'd love it if it was police brutality, something we could use on the front page."

He sat down across from her. She felt him watch her as she continued with her work, trying to act like there was nothing unusual about him coming in, closing the door and planting himself in her office without even asking a question.

"What's on your mind?" Lara asked as she finally looked at him.

"Oh, I just wanted to see how you are. Making sure everybody's treating you okay."

Lara suppressed a sarcastic smile. She'd endured a few of Hatcher's pep talks. His overbearing brute persona had been dominant lately, but she knew he could play nice.

The thing she didn't know was which was the real Hatcher.

"Everything's good."

"Really? You should probably take some time off. Banged up and bruised, now a hurt foot." He nodded at her crutches. "That's the kind of stuff sick days are for."

"And here I am, thinking my editor would rather have me working."

Hatcher gave her one of his smiles, the kind that makes your stomach feel queasy. "The work seems to come easy to you."

"What does that mean?"

He leaned back in the chair, his eyes fixed on her. "How does a fledgling reporter move to a new city and put out so many exclusives? You've ruffled so many feathers that not even your colleagues want to talk to you."

Lara would have had to be deaf to miss the skepticism seeping through each word. "They wouldn't speak to me before. This is nothing new."

"Some might wonder what kind of games," he drew out that word, "you have to play to get such impressive leads."

When she didn't respond he put his hand on his chest, eyes wide with affected innocence. "Now me, I try not to jump to conclusions and just hope all my reporters will level with me before they're tempted to cross any lines that can't be uncrossed."

"If you feel our working philosophies are incompatible I have an offer from the Banner."

"Oh, I don't think you've crossed the line," he said, a little too quickly. "Dan Van Biers has been feeding me nothing but conspiracy theories on his dead hookers, so if what you give me gets that off the front page, I'm happy. But you should make sure someone can back you up. I know the gals feel threatened by a stunning little looker like yourself and the guys are all dogs. If you need someone to talk to, my door is always open."

"Thanks," Lara said, failing to suppress the dry edge that snuck into the word. She turned back to her work although she was aware that he was still watching her.

Hatcher stood and walked to the door. "Just remember, there's a way things are meant to be. Not even a cop you put out for is going to save your ass before he covers his own. And there's only so much help a sympathetic editor can give you."

He disappeared, leaving her to steam silently.

Jimmy poked his head in a moment later. "Is it safe?"

"That pig." She spat the word.

"Don't let him get to you. I've let everyone know you're taking the heat over this story."

"That isn't even stretching the truth. Someone broke into Farraday's place." She stared at him for a moment, letting her anger subside long enough to remember what she wanted to ask Jimmy. "What can you tell me about Vern Fletcher?"

His eyebrows shot up as he closed the door. "Why?"

"Call it professional curiosity."

"Lara..." Jimmy stared at her for a moment before he sat down, holding a package. "Vern was a top-notch reporter. He was fielding offers from national papers before you were in high school."

"What happened? Did he burn out?"

Jimmy snorted and shook his head. "He'd probably have rebounded from that by now. No. It was his kid. His little girl died slowly. Cancer."

Lara's eyes widened. "I didn't even know he was married."

"Divorced. Vern tried working away the pain and then when she died he got so far into the bottle he couldn't see what was going on around him. By the time he sobered up..."

"His wife was gone," Lara murmured.

"He's a decent guy. Vern wouldn't shaft you."

Lara glanced at Jimmy. "Right now I find it hard to trust anybody."

He frowned and she could guess at the unspoken retort to her comment that he was choking back. "This came for you." He set the large brown envelope on her desk.

"You didn't have to bring this down."

"You should stay off your foot. Besides, I was curious."

Lara picked up the package gingerly and then tore it open. "No return address. I'm sure whoever sent it didn't leave fingerprints." She froze, only her eyes moving to scan the documents. Lara flipped a few pages, her brow wrinkled.

"Is it about the case?" Jimmy asked.

"It's a report from that accident, the one Kyle Joynt was killed in. Whoever sent this highlighted one thing and circled it. See?" She held up the page.

Jimmy got up and moved beside her to look at the papers. "Signing officer is G. Garrett."

Now Lara's whole face pinched questioningly, her head clearing from the rage Hatcher had stirred in her. "G. Garrett?"

"PR guru and errand boy to the Mayor." Jimmy shrugged. "Graeme Garrett."

"Why would he be signing a police report from ten years ago?"

"Didn't you know? He was a cop." Jimmy's eyebrows rose. "I remember this now. He was a rookie, a nobody, barely on the job. Only a few years older than Megan and Susan were at the time. Suddenly he was Walter Morrow's right hand man at City Hall. Not much of a front-runner in his own right but a hell of a hound dog to have keeping watch on your playing field. Like a politician's bouncer."

"He turned up at the police station after David Douglas was first questioned, throwing his weight around."

Jimmy's face darkened again. He handed the report back to Lara and started to walk away. "You know, I never thought I'd say this, but I'm glad you have a cop watching your back." He paused at the door. "I'm just not sure it's enough to have nobody but you watching his."

He walked out, leaving Lara still flustered by Hatcher's insinuations and curious about the source of the anonymous report.

***

"Detective Farraday." The magnanimous tone resonated off the walls of the interrogation room, booming out from behind the simple table he was seated at. David Douglas' back was to Farraday as well as to the observation window, making it hard for onlookers to gauge his facial reactions.

A man with dark hair, a bit taller than David, and muscular sat at the end of the table. The kind of person who seemed to have a lot of energy on reserve, not someone settled comfortably in his chair, content to sit back and watch. Dark eyes that reminded Farraday of a hawk.

Farraday crossed the room. "Thanks for coming in."

"Really, Detective." There was something accusing and amused in the tone, as though David knew he'd been given no choice but that he believed he was still in control of the situation. "I thought you might dispense with the usual formalities and invite me to your home instead. Or is this where you sleep at night, hiding behind the presence of your fellow officers?"

Farraday ignored the insinuation, the probing about his vulnerability and the inferred knowledge that he wasn't sleeping at home. He also kept his eyes from rising to look in the two-way mirror at the back and remained standing, leaning into the corner.

David leaned forward. "Are you one of those fabled cops who lives and breathes and even dies for the job?"

He can say a lot without saying anything at all. Farraday cleared his throat. "Do you know why we're here?"

"For the record, my client is here of his own free will-"

David held up his hand, silencing his lawyer, who scowled at his client, but didn't argue. The man leaned back in his chair, watching.

Shifting his body to look at Farraday head on, David smiled. The kind of smile that told Farraday the man had glacier water running through his veins.

"As a scapegoat for your incompetence. You think I hurt my daughter."

"I don't think that. I know. You see, no matter how many cops you buy off or how many tracks you try to cover, things have a way of coming to the surface. It wasn't hard to find the real reason you sent Susan away. I still have questions about why you sent Megan, but that's not important right now."

"Did you see Megan on the weekend?"

"Why would I?" Farraday opened the file, a standard tactic for redirecting the suspect's interest. What does the report say? What does he have inside? Does he know more than I think he does? That's what a file was to a suspect: A source of endless questions that could expose their own self-doubt and guilt. David was too cool to let it register on his face, not even glancing at the papers that apparently drew Farraday's interest.

"Do you know what alpha thalassemias is?" Farraday asked, still not looking up.

David eventually drew Farraday's gaze off the page when he refused to answer. Then he smirked. "It's Greek or Latin or some other antiquated language."

"How insightful. It's also the name of a rare genetic disease."

"That's sad. Are you canvassing for donations to find a cure?"

"That wouldn't be necessary if people were educated. This disease is the result of inbreeding between close family members."

David's face was a perfect wall now, unmoving, unreadable, the mask of unaffectedness. "How vile. But then, with your profession, you would have more experience with the seamy deeds of lesser beings."

Farraday grabbed the chair, brought it to the corner of the table and sat down. "Oh, I may have awareness of some things. But you have the experience."

He let those words sink in, the cold blue eyes staring back relentlessly. Farraday sensed David was simmering just below the surface, trying to hold his temper in check. His mask of control was slipping, his left cheek twitching, the drumming of his fingers stopping cold at Farraday's words.

"It was the disease your first grandchild had."

"I don't have grandchildren." The words were forced, his teeth clenched.

"Susan had a son when she was at Raddison."

"How do you know that?" The sharp lines of anger crept into David's face, a subtle note of panic in his voice.

"We exhumed the body."

David jumped to his feet and took a swing at Farraday, who blocked his punch just in time. The lawyer grabbed David from behind, pulling him back as the door opened. David shrugged off his lawyer and straightened when he saw Collins, tugged at his tie and tried to regain the look of control and composure he'd brought into the room.

"I demand that you deal with this insubordinate excuse for an officer." David's teeth were clenched, his cold stare now focused on Collins. "I want another detective."

"That's not how it works," Collins said, closing the door. "Detective Farraday is working this case and he is handling the charges against you. Just be thankful assaulting a police officer isn't one of them. Yet."

"What charges? I didn't kill Susan."

"But you did father her child." Farraday's eyes were fixed on David's profile.

David's head spun. "That's sick. No wonder you don't uphold the family line. You can't get your head out of the gutter."

"We have a medical examiner's report confirming Susan's baby was fathered by an extremely close relative. Either a brother, father or half-brother had to be responsible for her pregnancy. Susan had no brother or half-brother..." Collins let his inference sink in.

David froze for a moment before a smile slid across his face. "So this is your way of baiting me for dirt? I can confess to assaulting my own daughter, or I can admit to an affair by which I had another child and hand him over to you as a suspect? I didn't think it was the job of the police to look for smut for lowbrow reporters. That little bitch you spend so much time with must know all the right moves to keep you going back for more, dishing dirt for her to build her career on while you satisfy your own perversion."

Collins stepped between Farraday and David, his hand up to stop Farraday from responding.

"You're under arrest for the statutory rape of Susan Douglas," Collins said. "Anything you say can and will be used against you in a court of law. You have the right to an attorney..."

"Can they do this?" David was seething, yelling at his lawyer.

"Just relax," the man said as he pulled out a cell phone. "I'll handle everything."

Collins pulled David's arms behind his body and cuffed him.

***

A few hours later Collins called Farraday to his office. "What have we got?"

"It isn't good," Farraday said dismally. "There isn't enough to prove beyond reasonable doubt that David murdered his grandson. It's hard enough proving parentage, and you're bluffing. We don't have conclusive DNA yet that says David was the child's father."

"He's one sick, slimy bastard. He'll take any card he can and play it if it suits his purpose."

Farraday didn't say anything. He didn't trust himself. Just thought of Douglas' inferences about Lara...

"What about Susan?" Collins asked, "Do you think he's guilty?"

"I don't know. He can obviously lose control when provoked. But we have a source who insisted he wasn't the father of this child. She won't go on the record, though."

"He knew you weren't sleeping at home. He practically admitted he had someone break into your place."

"Then maybe I can sleep soundly tonight for a change."

Collins shook his head. "He made bail."

"Already? Unbelievable."

"The DA called. His lawyers want the charges dismissed."

Farraday laughed bitterly, shaking his head. "I bet they do. On what grounds?"

"We'll find out tomorrow morning. Everyone is coming here for a little chat. Make sure you bring your best poker face. We don't want you facing a harassment charge that will cloud the investigation, or your career.

"I doubt I could damage my career more," Farraday said, moving to the door. "If David Douglas gets off I'll have a very powerful enemy."

"You won't be the only one."

***

When Lara and Farraday got to her house, he sat down, tugging his tie loose as he put his feet up on the coffee table.

"How was life at the office?"

Lara scowled. "Hatcher cornered me and I couldn't run."

"What did he want?"

"To let me know what people might be saying about what… services I have to provide to get such impressive connections with the local police force."

Farraday winced. "How'd you handle that?"

"I suggested that if we didn't see eye to eye I could work elsewhere."

"What did he say?"

"He assured me that he would never think such a thing about me."

"Sell-out," he said with a small smile.

"Yes, well, I don't exactly have family money to fall back on. I'd rather not be between jobs right now."

"I heard David Douglas was hiring."

"That's not funny," she said, throwing a pillow at him. "You must be happy, having that man behind bars where he belongs."

It was his turn to scowl. "He made bail."

"Really? Unbelievable."

"Ah, you've echoed my sentiments. We have a meeting scheduled to discuss his lawyer's desire to have the charges dropped."

"On what grounds?"

Farraday shrugged. "I'll let you know as soon as I do."

"Just when it seemed like we might be tying up some of the loose threads. I was beginning to think we were making real progress."

"Not yet," Farraday said. "We're not there yet."

***

Vern leaned back in his chair, his eyes scanning the story on David Douglas' arrest. Larimer had another exclusive. He could kiss her.

Not that he needed incentive for that. She was attractive in a down-to-earth way. Not polished and glamorous, but still good-looking. And smart, as her work demonstrated.

She'd given him the clue he needed. Garrett may have taken the girls officially, but why would he do that for himself? Sure, he was a slimy bastard who made Vern feel nauseous, but he was smart. He wouldn't make careless mistakes.

Vern had been following Garrett long enough to know he was connected to David Douglas. Garrett's presence at the airport had raised questions in his mind, but he couldn't find an explanation. If there was one thing Walter Morrow's PR man was good at it was keeping his own life out of the spotlight.

Almost every journalist in Oakridge had heard rumors about Morrow and Douglas being connected through some questionable businesses. They weren't really rumors, but more rumors of rumors, something anyone with an iota of common sense wouldn't stand behind if pressed.

And David Douglas was one of Morrow's biggest financial backers every time he was up for reelection.

Vern rubbed his hand over his jaw, considering the new possibilities this information raised. He already knew Garrett was connected to the girls. These young women had, for a brief time, worked at City Hall and then disappeared. He could find no trace of them after their abrupt departures and no evidence of their future employment. And Choy Kim had left the factory in the usual way, but never made it to City Hall.

He knew Garrett was connected to David Douglas.

And now he knew David Douglas was a sick man.

Vern leaned back, considering his options, wondering if it was time for Mr. Chan to report his niece missing.

He just didn't want to play his ace until he was certain he couldn't be trumped.

CHAPTER 9

Walter Morrow, Graeme Garrett, David Douglas, the DA and Michael McClure, the lawyer who'd accompanied Douglas the day before, were all seated when Captain Collins and Farraday arrived. Once the formalities were observed the attorney said he wanted the charges against Douglas dismissed.

Michael McClure continued. "My client is prepared to make a statement. David?"

David cleared his throat. He wore reading glasses, a V-neck sweater instead of a business suit, shirt and tie, appearing to have aged ten years overnight. Not the powerful businessman, but a mild-mannered grandfather-figure. He took a piece of paper from his pocket and began reading.

"Regrettably, the police are aware that my recently-deceased daughter, Susan, had a child ten years ago. This happened when she was residing at a rehabilitation school. I was trying to help her overcome her drug and alcohol abuse, which was the reason she was sent there. I realize now that I should have informed the police of this incident myself.

"Unfortunately, my attempt to protect my daughter has caused a misunderstanding. It is true that Susan had a child. It is also, unfortunately, true I was the child's father. But I am not guilty of statutory rape.

"This is a tragic error. Susan was a very disturbed girl who grew increasingly self-destructive after the death of her mother. She used Rohypnol, which is now more commonly known as a date-rape drug, to incapacitate me and assaulted me. Her drug problems contributed to some serious, wild behavior.

"I was unaware of this incident at the time and pursued no blood testing or charges with the police. The headmaster at Raddison informed me of her pregnancy and only then did I learn what she had done."

Farraday listened with detachment and assessed the faces at the table. There were nods of support for David, as well as grave looks of concern for the hopeless state of a single parent raising a strung-out, drug-addicted teenager who committed such horrific acts.

Graeme Garrett had winced and blanched visibly when David stated

Susan had given birth to a child ten years ago. Farraday had also noticed the face of Walter Morrow pale with this statement, his eyes widening as he exchanged a glance with Garrett.

Farraday viewed Morrow as an ally of the Douglas family but he was beginning to wonder about the rumors he'd heard about their shady business dealings. He was also beginning to wonder about the reason for Garrett's interest in this case.

"Well, this is truly a regrettable position to be in," Walter Morrow said after David folded his statement and put it back in his pocket. "I feel we have unnecessarily intruded upon a private grief, one that has no business in the public domain. I don't feel that the public's best interests are served with a costly trial that will do nothing more than exacerbate a family tragedy and discredit a respected member of our community."

"From the standpoint of available evidence there's a compelling case here. If we choose not to proceed with the charges we could be sending a message to this constituency that justice is swayed by power and influence and affluent members of society are afforded a different standard of accountability," said Sam Greavy, the DA.

Walter Morrow stared at Greavy for a moment, then glanced sharply at the attorney.

Farraday almost smiled.

"Then we look forward to seeing you in a courtroom, Mr. Greavy." Michael McClure stood and walked out, followed by the meek version of David Douglas. The remaining people watched them depart in silence.

Walter Morrow and Graeme Garrett stood up. Morrow tapped his fist lightly on the table, still looking at Sam Greavy. "I hope you know what you're doing," he said. He turned to Collins. "And I hope you know what you've gotten yourself into."

Garrett followed Morrow out of the room silently.

Greavy stood up. "Nice article in The Ledger this morning, don't you think?" he said, picking up his briefcase and walking out of the room.

Collins and Farraday sat in silence. They had won this round, but barely.

"Thank Lara for the story," Collins said at last. He stood up, Farraday following him back to the main room.

"She's going to love this," Farraday said as he walked to his desk and picked up the phone. It took less than a minute for him to give her the abbreviated version.

"What?"

Farraday held the phone back from his ear, wincing.

"Is it safe?" he asked after the ringing in his ears stopped.

"I can't believe him. He's so sick that he would hide behind his own daughter."

"It's going to come down to which one the jury believes. Susan's reputation isn't going to help. If it hadn't been for your story the charges might have been dropped. Greavy didn't seem too happy to be in a corner."

Lara was silent for a moment. "It's a shame there isn't someone who had access to the house, someone that could shed some light on what it was like to live there. Maybe we should talk to Megan."

"She didn't tell us about any of this before. Do you think she knows?"

"There's only one way to find out."

***

Farraday had hidden Walker and Megan, not in police protection, not in a secluded hideaway, but in the guesthouse at his parent's estate. Dogs were kept on the acreage and they had ample security. It was Farraday's way of hiding them in plain sight, in a place he could justify visiting for other reasons not related to the case. They were safely concealed behind the thick trees and the stone walls that marked the property lines.

The guesthouse was attached to the main home, an apartment above the garage similar to the apartment Farraday had rented. He'd told Lara he had to find a new place to live soon. His landlady was upset about the break-in, saying that having a detective there was supposed to make her feel safer and it wasn't reassuring to know that his home could be robbed.

Farraday pushed a control that opened the end door of the garage and drove inside. Lara could see Walker's car in the space beside them, concealed from prying eyes. She managed to get out and follow Farraday using her crutches. There was a set of stairs along the back of the garage, leading up to a back entrance to the guest suite.

"This is brilliant," she said. "You can get in and out without being seen. Does anyone else know they're here?"

Farraday shook his head, pausing to knock on the door. "Not even my uncle."

Lara heard the latch slide and Farraday was inside the door before she saw Walker standing on the landing. His eyes narrowed as he looked at her. They'd phoned ahead to tell them they were coming, but this was her first time seeing Rob Walker face to face since the night she'd been attacked.

"Hi," she said. Walker nodded at her and they followed Farraday down the short hall that opened up to a spacious living area, equipped with a kitchen, dining area, the couches surrounding an enormous fireplace that filled the better part of one wall. Lara could only imagine what it would look like with all the blinds open, the sunlight streaming in the high windows. For now it was clear that the windows had to stay shut and the blinds closed, the normal state when the suite wasn't being used.

Once everyone was seated Megan spoke.

"I hope that had nothing to do with this case," she said, nodding at Lara's foot.

Lara smiled sheepishly. "Not really."

"I just want to clear a few things from the beginning," Walker said, leaning forward to look at Lara.

"This conversation is off the record, as far as the press is concerned."

Walker nodded at that, his shoulders relaxed as he leaned back.

"What did you want to talk to me about? Did you learn something?" Megan asked.

Farraday relayed what they knew. When Farraday finished there was silence in the room. Walker looked ill. Megan's face had lengthened, her skin almost a pasty white.

"Did you just want to tell me this?" Megan asked slowly. It was Lara who answered.

"We want justice for Susan. It's important that we know everything you can tell us now so that we don't proceed with charges if there's another explanation. Are we wrong?"

Megan's gaze was on the floor and when she looked up a few tears spilled. She got up, rubbing her arms as she walked slowly around the room.

"I-I've spent my whole life hiding from this." Her voice was low. She drew herself up, turned and faced them. "It wasn't Susan that was responsible for the car accident the night Kyle died. I was driving."

"Megan," Walker whispered hoarsely.

She put up her hand to stop him from saying more. "I know I should have told you. Susan and Kyle spiked my drink. I was tripping badly. When Susan saw us careening toward the tree she pulled on the wheel. We spun around, impacting on the rear passenger side. That's why Kyle was the one who was killed."

"But Susan took the blame?" Lara asked.

"She didn't take it. She was given it. Dad was there before the police were. He had a long chat with Graeme Garrett before he wrote the report that said Susan was driving."

"And the drugs?" Lara asked.

"Where do you think she got them?" She held up her hand. "No, I don't actually know how he imports them and what happens with them or where they're kept. I just know. Susan always had a ready supply."

"What was your dad's interest in the drugs? He doesn't strike me as a user," said Farraday.

Megan shook her head. "Just the money."

"And the accident? Did you make a statement that night?" Farraday asked.

"Yes. We both did. We both told the truth. The report was a lie. I overheard Dad arguing with Susan later. She," Megan drew a deep breath, "accused him of raping her. Two days later we were sent to Raddison."

"Did you know Susan was pregnant?"

"If I'd known I would have stayed for her. I guess that's why she never told me. He..." She shook her head. "I used to think he didn't love me, that something was wrong with me. I guess I should be grateful."

"Would you be prepared to testify, if necessary?" Farraday asked.

Megan nodded, sitting down again, collapsing into the support of the couch. Walker put his arm around her and pulled her close.

After a minute Lara told Megan, "We couldn't have made it this far without your help."

Megan's face was still pale, but she managed a faint smile. "It's the least I can do for Susan now."

As Lara followed Farraday to the door Megan spoke again.

"There is something else I remember," she said. "It's never made much sense to me, but it might to you."

"Anything could be helpful," Farraday said.

"Walter Morrow came to our house after the accident. He was still with the police then, but it was just before the election. He was saying something about owing Officer Garrett, how this could ruin things. I... I didn't understand what our accident had to do with their business, but that's what he said. Then he asked what Garrett wanted from Dad. I didn't hear what Dad said, but Mr. Morrow said he'd do his part and it helped that David would let him use his kid. It never made any sense to me. Does that mean anything to you?"

"Not yet." Farraday shook his head. "But it might help us when we know more."

Walker crossed the room, reaching them just as Farraday was holding the door.

He looked at Lara. "I... I know you could have gone after me the minute you saw that video, but you didn't. Why?"

"Without even knowing Duane I wasn't sure about his credibility. I wasn't trying to hurt a cop just because I could. If I thought you'd deliberately concealed a crime it would have been different, but we all make honest mistakes."

Walker nodded. "I can see how you might think I covered this up, how it could look like I was involved."

Farraday started to speak but Walker held his hand up.

"It was a crazy night. Lenny was throwing his weight around, as usual, harassing us. It was getting to Sean, my partner, so I stepped aside and asked Lenny if he could knock it off. That's when Duane came in."

"I thought he talked to you," Lara said, puzzled.

"Not right away. I only heard part of what he said to Sean. Sean took the video and then Lenny stepped in and smacked Sean on the back, saying something about hand-delivery of his personal entertainment." Walker winced as he glanced at Lara. "Sorry. Lenny told Duane that he should know by now that we don't run around on false leads without evidence of a crime."

Lara looked at Farraday, her eyes wide. "But-"

"Sean started telling me what Duane said was on the video and then Lenny yelled at Sean, telling him to drop it. I asked Duane if he'd been drinking and he said no. I gave him my card and started to tell him that we'd take a look around the area and check it out when Lenny marched back over, stuffed the video in Duane's hands and practically pushed him out the door. Collins came over then and said we had a call. Sean tried to tell him what happened."

"So you were in the wrong place at the wrong time," Farraday said.

"And I was engaged to the wrong person." He glanced at Lara. "But you never jumped to conclusions or printed speculation. I...I appreciate it." He reached out and shook Farraday's hand first, then Lara's.

Walker shut the door behind them. Farraday pulled out his cell phone and dialed Collins' number, quickly relaying what they'd learned from Megan and what Walker had said about why he didn't watch the video.

"What did he say?" Lara asked when Farraday closed the cell and put it away.

"It's easy enough to confirm his story. He's going to look into it and take care of the investigation if Rob's version holds up."

"Do you doubt him?" She was following him down a different set of stairs, moving slowly because of the crutches.

"I believe him. Collins just has to do things by the book." Farraday watched her navigate the final steps. "Are you ready for this?"

"No." She felt her stomach twisting tighter with each stair she descended. "These crutches hurt."

"Why don't you leave them? Take a break for a few hours."

He opened the door at the bottom, leading into a small corridor. Lara followed to the main entry, where they left their coats and her crutches.

It was an elegant house, with a wooden staircase curling up to the second level, accentuating the high ceiling. Superficially, it reminded Lara of the old Douglas estate, the grand old house exuding wealth, but she felt different here.

Where the Douglas house had been a show of money the Farraday house was a home. Instead of lavish paintings lining the stairway, curios with trinkets from travels abroad graced the walls. A case in the hallway contained rare bears and there were even family photos that resonated with joy and affection, something the Douglas home lacked completely.

"Hey, you did the same thing at my house," Lara said defensively when she noticed Farraday watching her as she looked around.

"The old Bay Bridge," he said, snapping his fingers.

"What about it?" Lara turned, surprised.

"The picture in your bedroom. It's the old Bay Bridge. It was so familiar but I couldn't place it until now."

"When were you in my bedroom?" she asked.

"I-"

"Don't worry. It's a bad habit I have, leaving that door open." She smiled and he put his arm around her waist to help her keep her weight off her foot.

He led her to a room on the east side of the house, at the opposite end from the garage. A beautiful bay window opened up to a view of the garden. Lara had noticed the patio doors just outside the room before they entered. At the far end she could see through the open door to an office, high shelves lining the walls with books and pictures, the corner of the desk visible from where they stood.

This main room could have doubled as a library. On the inside walls, where the fireplaces didn't protrude, cherry shelves were filled floor to ceiling with bound books. It was an enormous room, elegantly furnished but also clearly lived in and appreciated. Lara had been so busy eyeing the books that Farraday had to nudge her to get her to move forward.

It was then that she noticed the couple sitting on the couch closest to the fireplace. Mr. Farraday was at the end, reading. He was an older version of his son, with dark hair that showed no signs of fading with age. His wife was leaning against him, her lighter hair curling gently around her face. Farraday's parents looked young. Without any movement from either of them she could see that they were both healthy, vibrant and their choice to sit close together in a spacious room told her more about their marriage than anything Farraday had ever said.

They looked up simultaneously. Lara sat on the nearest couch, across from Farraday's parents, and they both stood. Farraday and his dad were close to the same height, making his Mom seem even shorter than she was. While Farraday's dad patted his back, his mom clung to him, just for a moment.

Lara had worried that her career could be an obstacle between her and the Farraday's, but she saw no evidence of that as Farraday introduced her.

"Lara, my parents, Evelyn and Warren Farraday."

"I'm Warren," Farraday's dad said, the same glint in his eye that Farraday had when he teased her. "I know good reporters never jump to conclusions."

"Thanks," Lara said dryly. "I wasn't sure how to ask."

Evelyn stepped forward, clasping Lara's hand in her own.

"I'm glad we get to meet you." Her eyes resonated with warmth and genuine pleasure. "We've heard so much about you."

"What has Collins been saying?" Lara asked as Farraday sat down beside her.

"Oh, not just Patrick. Trin said she met you, and even Ty told us a little."

Lara thought it best to say nothing, suppressing the impulse to sneak a look at Farraday. Even without openly watching him she sensed his back stiffen.

"Where are you from?" Warren Farraday asked, his eyes on her face.

"I grew up in the Baysville area."

"Really? We have a summerhouse there. We should really go out again, before the bad weather sets in."

"Which reminds me. The old cook's cabin needs some work," Farraday said.

"That cabin hasn't been used in years," Evelyn said. "What made you think of that?"

"Some of the floorboards have started to rot out. That's where Lara hurt her foot."

"I'm sorry," Evelyn frowned. "We shouldn't have neglected it."

"I wasn't aware you were planning to go to the house." Warren's face held the first hint of a shadow since they had come in.

"It was an impulse," Farraday said. "We both needed a break."

"How is it that you started working together?" Evelyn asked.

When Farraday didn't answer right away, she looked at Lara. "He doesn't tell us about his job. At least, he doesn't tell us any more than we pry out of him."

"It's hard to explain what you do to people who don't work in the field," Lara said. "But with history of law enforcement in your family you must have some idea of what Ty does."

"Oh, I understand the essence of the job. It's the nature of his cases that he isn't willing to share. I was surprised he told us he was working with you. Trin had mentioned it, but it's not like Ty to volunteer information. Usually I have to pry and occasionally interrogate him. I haven't even heard the name of his new partner."

There were two threads underlying her words. One was light, a teasing tone, hinting at years of trying to guess her son's secrets. Lara felt certain that Evelyn respected that need for privacy. The humor seemed to thinly veil the other thread, the concern, knowing he faced danger in his career and not knowing enough to prepare for the feared phone call, the news that something had happened to him. Lara felt torn between keeping Farraday's confidences, trying to find answers to the things she'd only been able to guess at about him and an impulse to reassure the woman she'd developed an immediate liking for.

"How about going riding?" Warren asked Farraday, who looked at Lara.

"Do you mind?"

"I'll be fine."

As soon as the door clicked shut Evelyn moved to the armchair beside Lara.

"Ty must miss Finola."

"Finola?"

"His horse. He's had her since she was a foal. A purebred Arabian."

"Arabian's are beautiful." This was the first she'd heard about Farraday's love of horses. She realized how much she didn't know about him, how much he hadn't shared.

"Do you ride?" Evelyn asked.

"I've never had the chance to ride more than the carousel but I always wanted to learn."

"Then you must come back when your foot is better. We have another mare, Brea, who's very gentle."

"That's a kind offer," Lara said, feeling the heat in her cheeks. She didn't know how to respond. Once this case was over...

"How did you meet Ty?" Evelyn asked. It wasn't exactly the same question that she'd asked before, but it led in the same direction: Farraday's work.

"I wrote an article that Collins wanted him to check on."

Evelyn's eyes narrowed. "Do the police usually check up on your work?"

"No. I'm sure if Ty knew what he was in for, he would have begged for someone else to get the job."

"You two seem to get along."

"It's not that," Lara said. "At least, not anymore. He wasn't thrilled about working with a reporter, any more than I wanted the police checking up on me. It's this case."

Evelyn didn't speak for a moment. She tucked her feet up under her body and looked directly at Lara. "I've been worried about him. When he wasn't at home for so many days..."

"He's hardly been back to his place since he started staying at my house." Lara saw the look on Evelyn's face as those words sunk in. "He didn't tell you."

Evelyn shook her head.

"It's this case," Lara repeated, wondering how to explain. "I'm sure Ty wouldn't want you to worry and I don't want you to think... Someone broke into my jeep and stole evidence and then they broke into my house and assaulted me. Collins tried to persuade me to accept police protection."

"But you refused."

Lara sighed. "Whoever broke into my house knew Ty was working on this case already. Neither of us could have just walked away. The next day we found Susan's body. He's been sleeping on my couch ever since."

Evelyn nodded slowly.

"I'm not sure that should make you feel better," Lara said.

"I know Ty works murder cases. I know it's dangerous to be a detective. There are risks in everything in life. Sometimes, I feel when he doesn't tell me, it's because he's protecting me and that makes me scared. I guess at some point every parent has to accept that they are no longer the protector but the protected." Evelyn's eyes clouded, although that didn't affect the renewed warmth of her smile. "Ty has always put the family ahead of himself. Even now he's trying to take care of us, to make sure we don't worry about him when he's putting his life on the line for others."

There was almost an unspoken understanding between the two women, an agreement the secrets they shared would stay between them. Lara no longer felt hesitant about asking Farraday's mother questions and Evelyn appeared eager to have a chance to talk endlessly about her son to a willing listener.

***

Farraday found them on the couch, looking at family photos. He quickly assessed from the stack of albums on the table that Lara had seen everything from his baby photos until junior high.

He didn't say a word, sinking down into the armchair and watching the two of them as his mom closed the book and set it down. They'd been laughing when he walked in, his mom looking amused but unapologetic.

"See? I told you I'd be fine," Lara said, her eyes sparkling as she smiled. He didn't get a chance to respond. They were interrupted with the news that dinner was ready. After they'd eaten Evelyn and, to a lesser extent Warren, pleaded with them to stay overnight.

"Our bags are still in the car," Farraday reminded Lara. They'd been forgotten in the midst of the break-in, Douglas' arrest and everything else going on. "What do you think?"

"It is getting late. We could start out early in the morning."

"What do we have tomorrow?"

"Short of Lessard coming up with any more evidence we're back to looking for Betty Zimmerman. The more we learn, the more certain I am that she knows who was following Susan that night."

"That's the missing piece. Whoever it was made sure she fell onto the rocks."

"And pushed her into the water."

Farraday frowned. "It's unfortunate Susan was buried on her family property. It might have been helpful to see who was there."

"Jimmy stood sentry and took photos of everyone coming and going. He should have them ready tomorrow."

"I thought I told Jimmy to keep an eye on you."

"Nobody's going to attack me in the newsroom and you don't see me going to the One-Four and asking the boys to chaperone you."

"That's different."

"Not really."

"You're incredibly stubborn."

"I only seem stubborn when you know you're wrong."

"She reminds me of Trin."

Lara and Farraday both stopped at Warren's comment. Lara felt her cheeks burn. Farraday stood up.

"I'll get our bags."

Warren followed Farraday into the hall without a word. Evelyn's wide smile reached her eyes but she didn't say a thing. She picked up the tray on the coffee table and left the room, leaving Lara alone, wondering what Farraday's parents really thought of her.

***

Farraday was up at what seemed like the first light of dawn. With fall quickly taking hold that wasn't as early as he'd hoped for. Lara's room was empty. He took his bag downstairs and set it beside hers, heading to the dining room.

"You didn't really think we'd let you leave without breakfast," Warren said when he walked in. "Your mother wouldn't hear of it."

Lara was seated at the table, looking rested. Her hair seemed thicker than usual, curls cascading around her face and down her back.

"And you caved in to their pressure?"

He sat down at his place. Fried potatoes, turkey bacon, sautéed mushrooms and toast.

Lara scrutinized the contents of his plate but didn't say anything. Evelyn picked up the paper, tapping the front page after she scanned it.

"This must be what's keeping these two so busy."

Warren and Evelyn skimmed the article together, then turned to the inside page, reading in silence. Farraday glanced at Lara, who remained silent. Evelyn and Warren looked up simultaneously.

"Now I understand why you don't like talking about work," she told Farraday as he reached for the paper, her voice filled with disgust.

Farraday skimmed the story and glanced at Lara. "You didn't write this."

Her head tilted as she lifted one shoulder. "There are some lies I don't want to be associated with, on any level."

The article relayed the details of David Douglas' defense, his claim that he was the one who'd been sexually assaulted by his daughter. Lara didn't believe it, and she didn't feel she needed the headline, so she'd given the story to another reporter.

Warren looked from Lara to Farraday, his eyebrows arched, approval in his expression. He seemed to respect that Lara's personal values had come ahead of the front page and her portfolio.

"Who's Vern Fletcher?" Farraday asked as he looked at the byline.

"Your typical cynical, jaded reporter," she replied, looking up then. "Why?"

He passed her the paper. She skimmed the article on the missing girl, reported to the police just this week, despite the fact that she'd been missing since before Susan's death.

Lara arched an eyebrow but said nothing more, making a mental note to re-read the story later. The rest of breakfast passed without further reference to the case or Lara's articles. Farraday didn't offer any apologies when he finished eating.

"Thanks for letting us stay. And thanks again for giving Megan and Rob the guest suite. I really appreciate it."

"Nobody was using it," Warren said, helping Lara from her seat while Evelyn walked out with her son.

***

Evelyn squeezed Farraday's arm as soon as they were in the hall. "I know you won't let anything happen to her. Just make sure nothing happens to you either, okay?"

He smiled as he put his arm around her. "I'll be careful."

"And you have to bring her back to go riding."

"Lara rides?"

"No, but she's always wanted to."

"I'll try to persuade her to tolerate me a little longer when this case wraps up."

***

Warren helped Lara up and then stepped back, looking directly at her while he spoke.

"I understand you persuaded Tymen to talk to his sister."

She nodded, guessing Ty must have told him when they'd gone riding.

"I appreciate that. It's good to know Tymen has someone looking out for him."

"Collins keeps an eye on him."

Warren's eyes narrowed. "My son has always been close to Patrick. But Patrick isn't on the streets. David Douglas is an unscrupulous man, likely guilty of more than you could even guess at. You've both made a dangerous enemy."

"Hopefully we won't have to worry about him much longer."

"Hopefully," Warren echoed, but the words were hollow, spoken without conviction. He helped her to the door.

Lara didn't say anything. She felt the skepticism from Warren Farraday weigh in her mind like a premonition of things to come, yet unseen but already unfolding.

***

"What did you think?" Farraday asked as he pulled out onto the road.

"They're both really nice," Lara said.

He glanced at her. "That's all you're going to say?"

She shrugged, changing the CD to Rubyhorse. "Your mom's easy to talk to, very warm and open."

"It's always been hard on her that I'm not as forthcoming as she'd like," Farraday said. "I could tell she was thrilled to be able to ask you questions about me."

"You aren't the only thing she's interested in. She's very curious about this case."

"I don't know why this case should be any different from any other."

"It's your first big case since your transfer. Your family has been going through a difficult time and you moved away. They're worried about you because they don't know how you are. Not physically, but here." She tapped her chest. "They couldn't reach you for days on end, your sister said you wouldn't talk to her. They're concerned that what happened changed you, that in your heart you'll never be the same."

Farraday was silent for a moment. He finally glanced at her. "I didn't think about that. I guess you're right. I should have let them know I was okay."

"I doubt it helped when they heard you were working with a reporter."

Farraday sighed. "I don't think either of them are anxious about that now."

"You say that like they've found something new to worry about."

"Can't you guess?"

"Good journalists work on facts, not speculation," Lara said firmly. "And you aren't the closed book your mother thinks you are. You just pretend to torment her."

Farraday's smile faded. "You might be right," was all he said.

***

They snuck in the back door at The Ledger. Lara remembered to check for a processing light before pushing Jimmy's door open.

"Nice of you to limp by," Jimmy said, leaning back in his chair.

Lara sat down, returning Jimmy's grin. Farraday remained standing.

"What have you got for us?" he asked Jimmy.

"Not many big surprises. Megan and Rob are MIA," Jimmy opened a file he'd pulled from a locked drawer at the bottom of his desk, "but then I suspect you already knew that."

He pushed the folder to the edge of the desk, carefully turning print by print. "See, a lot of people you'd expect. Angela's family, some local businessmen, even a few associates from overseas. These men," Jimmy tapped a photo, and then pointed at another, "are from Germany. They arrived the day before the funeral."

Lara analyzed each photo carefully, looking for anything that stood out. On the second-last photo she saw a face that didn't have an obvious explanation. "Is this Graeme Garrett?"

Jimmy nodded.

"That's not surprising," Farraday said. "Walter Morrow has him monitoring this investigation, keeping tabs on our case against David Douglas. He knows the family."

"Actually, it is a little unusual," Jimmy said, his mouth twisting. "There's nothing to manage at this funeral, not even police presence. Security was tight. It would have been impossible to get on that property without being caught. And Morrow seldom sends Garrett in if he's taking care of the situation himself. He likes to have his guard dog watching the office when he's out and about, practicing his smile for the cameras."

"That's right." Lara flipped back a few photos. "That's Walter Morrow, talking to David Douglas."

"They both came to hear Douglas contest the charges we filed," Farraday countered.

"Look, all I can tell you is what I've heard and seen over the years. I can count on one hand the number of photos I have of the two of them together."

"What are these?" Lara asked, peeking into an envelop behind the last picture.

"Just people milling and chatting. Nobody there that you haven't already seen."

Lara pulled them out, started flipping through the prints and paused, going back to one she'd skimmed.

She studied the photo silently for a moment and then set it down on the table. It showed the gravesite after the service was over, a few men walking away caught in the wide angle. It was the person beside the plot of earth where Susan's casket lay that was interesting, a shadowy figure under the tree, staring down into the open earth.

Farraday picked up the photo. "I guess his reasons were personal."

"And he wasn't alone," Lara said, pulling another photo out and setting it down beside the first one.

"Walter Morrow." Farraday whistled. "I thought he was a friend of Douglas'. I didn't realize he had an interest in Susan."

Lara froze for a split-second before her hand went to her mouth. "With all the other things that happened I completely forgot. There was a picture of them together at a political fundraiser from last year. Susan didn't look happy."

Farraday looked across the desk. "Any chance you can enlarge these?"

"I'll see what I can do."

***

"Hello stranger," Nancy said as Lara stumbled through the front door of the library on her crutches. "What happened?"

"Just a silly accident. I'm down to a few hours with the crutches each day, so it's not so bad."

"I was beginning to think you'd forgotten about us here."

"I've been pretty busy."

"Oh, I know. And he does seem intriguing. Then there are all those articles. What I don't understand is what Susan Douglas' death has to do with the mayor's office."

"What makes you think it does?" Lara couldn't help wondering how Nancy would have picked up on that when she and Farraday were just starting to piece together a connection themselves.

Nancy shrugged. "That Garrett fellow has been in here three more times, looking for information. He's been after information about you, Vern Fletcher and Detective Farraday. Then he came back to look up stuff on the Douglas family."

"I guess he's keeping you busy," Lara said, wondering why he'd need background on Douglas and not wanting to admit anything to Nancy about the case.

"Humph. I'll settle for the local potheads over him any day." Nancy lowered her voice. "Garrett gives me the creeps. He has a way of looking at me that makes my skin crawl."

"I know what you mean. David Douglas showed up in my office the other day. Talking to him made me feel like I needed to be scrubbed clean."

"I guess the apple doesn't fall far from the tree."

Lara paused. "What do you mean?"

"You are new here. I forget, since you seem to know so much about what's going on. There's always been talk about David Douglas, since he was a kid."

"I know about that. Since his mother was killed."

Nancy lowered her voice, moving a little closer. "Nobody who does business with the Douglas family would dare mention it in public. And since a lot of local people rely on his plants and exporting companies and the growth generated from his local employment base, well, I don't need to spell it out."

Nancy looked around before continuing. "Word was, he raped Cynthia Garrett. She was a friend of one of his sisters. She was only fifteen when she had Graeme."

Lara felt as though her heart had jumped up in her throat for a second. David was the youngest and he'd been twelve when his mother had died. "Is-is there any way to confirm that?"

Nancy shrugged. "Cynthia Garrett died several years ago."

She processed that as Nancy walked away. Garrett could actually be a suspect. If he really was David Douglas' illegitimate child, he could have killed Susan to get a better share of the family fortune.

But why wait so long to come after his inheritance if it was true?

Assuming he knew about his parentage. And if he didn't, there was no motive.

Unless Douglas wasn't the father of Susan's first baby and he was trying to protect Graeme. Susan could have found out the truth about Graeme, maybe after she'd gotten pregnant, and lied to get even with her dad.

She thought of the photo Jimmy had taken, Graeme Garrett looking genuinely distraught, standing beside Susan's grave. Had they had a personal relationship?

This rumor had opened up a floodgate of new possibilities and Lara rubbed her forehead. Graeme could be a Douglas and not know it. He might not be a Douglas at all. He could know and hate David Douglas. But why wait so long to take action? Even if the rumor was true it didn't explain Susan's pregnancy now.

Lara started digging into the archives, trying to find answers to new questions.

***

Farraday knocked on the door to Dr. Eaton's office. The doctor looked up and gestured for Farraday to come inside and shut the door.

"I thought about what you said when you were here before. I ran a few more tests and I found something," Dr. Eaton said.

"What did I say that got you thinking?" Farraday scarcely remembered that day in the lab, so much had happened since then.

"You wondered if there was more than one blood type present at the scene."

"I thought you established it was Susan Douglas' blood, and that was the only type present."

"Not so. The samples were so small I ran a trace amount and came back with one blood type, which matched Susan Douglas. I decided to run all of the blood samples you brought in. It didn't seem likely, because there was no indication anyone else had been injured, making it reasonable to conclude there was only one person's blood present. Reasonable and wrong."

"You found a second blood type."

Eaton nodded. "That's not all. There are clear genetic indicators here and here," he tapped on a DNA sequence print-out, "that indicate this blood comes from a close relative. Most likely a sibling or cousin."

"What about her father?"

"It's possible. Susan was type O. The second type is A. Without having the mother's blood sample, all I can establish is that they're related."

"I thought A was the dominant blood type."

"So you do listen," Eaton said. "A is dominant but if both parents have the AO genotype they can have a child that has type O blood."

"With different blood types, what made you suspect they were related?" Farraday wasn't going to complain. And given the problems at some crime labs, access to private testing was a blessing. Quick and efficient.

"David Douglas is the main suspect in Susan's death. I thought it prudent to run tests on both blood samples."

"Douglas could have been responsible. He was out of the country when we found Susan, but he didn't leave until after Susan died, so this could be helpful. Can you have this checked against the samples Lessard has from Susan's baby?"

Eaton nodded. "If you make arrangements. Where's your friend?"

"At the library. Thanks. This may be enough to close the case."

"Another crime solved under a microscope." Eaton mumbled the words with customary grumpiness. "I expect my name in the paper."

"I do have some connections. You never know, a photo might be in order," Farraday said, ignoring Dr. Eaton's glare as he turned to open the door.

***

"Here you go." Farraday handed Lara a penny.

"Huh?"

"You haven't said two words all evening. What are you thinking about?"

She tossed the coin back. "I charge a quarter."

"Ouch. Hope that's one train making a run instead of a full station."

"What's gotten into you? You're practically giddy."

"We have another piece of evidence that may seal this shut." Farraday stretched out, his feet on the coffee table. "Dr. Eaton pulled a second blood type from the samples we collected at the scene. He's confirmed the blood came from a close relative of Susan's."

"Did you know Cynthia Garrett and Angela Douglas died the same day?"

"Did she drown?"

"No. She was found hanging in her home by her son."

"Graeme."

"The one and only."

"Suicide?" Farraday asked.

"No autopsy, so no evidence that the hanging was used to conceal a crime."

"Who signed off on that?"

"Nobody I've heard of before," Lara said. "Maier."

"Remind me to ask about him."

"I did hear some interesting rumors. With Cynthia Garrett dead, it's hard to get a handle on Graeme's life. There's no mention of a father at home and there aren't any other relatives listed. It isn't going to be easy to find out how he was involved with Susan Douglas."

"Short of asking him directly."

"Assuming he doesn't mind telling us about his personal life."

"What about Betty?"

Lara shook her head. "Nothing at her condo in Florida. I called in some favors but it was pointless. Maybe it's time to have another chat with Ruth Alton."

Farraday nodded. "First thing tomorrow," he said.

***

Farraday went to speak to Ruth Alton, leaving Lara at the library. She'd spent the better part of the night considering how to get the physical evidence she needed. Graeme Garrett's birth certificate left the father's name blank. If she wanted to confirm Graeme's parentage she was going to have to find another way.

She looked up. Graeme stood at the counter, hounding Nancy for information. Nancy was holding the phone, signing for a delivery and had a customer already waiting to check books out. Her sour expression and reddened cheeks made it clear that her patience was wearing thin.

Lara managed to limp to the counter. She was beside Graeme before he turned and noticed her. She smiled.

"I couldn't help overhear. It's been crazy in here since the city closed down the other community library. I can show you where those files are."

He stared at her for a moment. "Fine."

Graeme Garrett followed her silently. She could see why Nancy didn't like him and had to admit there was more than a little resemblance to David Douglas. Graeme wasn't as tall or as dominating in stature but he made up for those deficiencies with a stare that could rival an arctic breeze emanating from his eyes.

She brought down the folder in question, reached to hand it to him and dropped it just as he was about to grasp the end. He lunged for it and she reached forward, lost her crutch and grabbed onto his hand, digging her nails into his flesh as she fell down hard.

"Damn it! You little bitch, you cut me." He grabbed her arms and dragged her up off the floor.

"Is there a problem?"

Lara didn't know whether she wanted to kiss Farraday or crawl under a rock. Graeme let her go.

"I'm sorry," she said, not looking at Graeme or Farraday. She hobbled to the bathroom without looking back.

Farraday wasn't sure what he'd just walked in on, but he'd felt his muscles tense when he saw Garrett grab Lara. "Is there a problem, Mr. Garrett?"

"She cut me." The words were spit out in anger, Garrett's face still flushed.

"I'm sure it was an accident. There's a first aid kit over there." Farraday nodded to the near wall. "Do you need any assistance?"

"No thanks. I've had more than enough help for one day."

Farraday waited for Lara outside the bathroom by the checkout counter. She came out, still avoiding his gaze.

"Do I want to know what that was about?" Nancy asked her.

"Consider it payback for the hard time he's been giving you."

"Then I owe you." Nancy said as she reached for the ringing phone.

***

"I'm not buying it," Farraday told her as he followed her outside the library.

"Buying what?"

"That your incident with Garrett was just payback for him being a jerk. What on earth were you up to?"

"I was helping him find some articles he was looking for."

Farraday stared at her for a moment and she did her best to keep her face from betraying the truth she was holding back.

He finally smiled. "You should have seen the look on his face when you walked away."

"Staggered is more like it. Did you talk to Ruth?"

"She finally broke down and told me Betty is staying in Falconbridge."

"That's not exactly down south, is it?"

"No, it isn't."

Falconbridge was only a half hour drive southeast of Oakridge and it wasn't hard to find the address of the motel Ruth had provided. Lara negotiated the stairs, wondering if her foot was ever going to heal, catching up with Farraday outside room #313.

Farraday knocked on the door. They heard movement in the room, then silence. Farraday looked at Lara, who knocked again.

"Betty?" she called.

"Is that you Ruth?"

The door slid open and Betty froze. She had the wide-eyed look of terror, like a deer caught in the headlights. She stood paralyzed, not even having the presence of mind to retreat.

"Can we come in?" Farraday asked. "It would be best not to talk in the hall."

A couple glanced over their shoulders as they walked by. Betty opened the door and gestured to a few chairs by the bed.

"What are you doing here?"

"For starters," Farraday said as he sat down, "your home was broken into. We do have a report we need you to sign."

Betty nodded. "Ruth told me. I'll take care of it when I can."

"Your sudden departure was a surprise," Lara said. "We've been worried."

"You said you wouldn't need to talk to me again."

Betty was wringing her hands as she spoke, checking the clock repeatedly. She looked anywhere but at the two people who sat across from her, sitting gingerly on the edge of the bed. Lara noticed the closet was partially open and there were no clothes hanging inside. Two small cases were on the floor by the bed.

"You can't spent the rest of your life running," Lara said.

Betty looked down for a moment before speaking. "It's not safe at home. You both know that, or you wouldn't have sent Duane away."

Lara arched an eyebrow, wondering how Betty knew that. "The only reason it wouldn't be safe is if you saw more than you told us."

Betty's head spun around sharply, her mouth open. "I told you what I saw," she said, her throat tight, the words sounding forced.

"Mrs. Zimmerman, I'm not going to pretend this is easy. David Douglas is a dangerous man. We're trying to keep him from hurting anyone else. If you don't help us we might not be able to convict him. Is that what you want? Another victim who is denied justice?"

"The police have known about David Douglas since before you were born." Betty frowned. "Him and his cousin have been up to no good since they were boys, and Walter Morrow being the mayor. The police knowing didn't do any good then and it won't help now."

Walter Morrow was David Douglas' cousin? Lara glanced at Farraday. That could change everything. That photo, his meeting with David about using his kid... Even the DNA results they had back at that point were preliminary. They'd confirmed a close relationship, but nothing more specific.

"We're building a case. We spoke to Eileen. David's been charged with raping Susan when she was a teenager."

Betty winced. "He's a sick man. In my day one didn't know of such things and those who did most certainly didn't speak of them the way people do now. There's no justice, not here. You should know there's nothing you can do about that. His money has always cleaned up his messes. They took my children away when they were born. Him a father and him just married a few months, putting on a show for everyone." She looked down at her lap. "But they were born of evil."

"It wasn't their fault. Or yours," Lara said.

"Maybe not, but there's nothing I can do to help that girl now." Betty's face was hard, her eyes void of compassion. Nothing else that Lara or Farraday said was even acknowledged with a response.

***

Lara held her head with her hand as they drove back to Oakridge silently. Betty wouldn't talk, and there was nothing they could do to persuade her.

"You know, I heard years ago people used to think kids up for adoption were defective, but wow. I can't believe anyone would blame the child..." She lapsed into another long silence, Farraday saying nothing until they were almost at The Ledger.

"Do you want to come with me to talk to Ruth again?" he asked.

"No. Why don't you drop me off here? I'll ask Jimmy to drive me home. If he can't, I'll call."

She went to Jimmy's office, relieved to find him reading a magazine.

"Just the man I need. Have you got half an hour?"

"I'm all yours," Jimmy said without asking what she wanted.

"Get your keys."

Her errand completed, Jimmy dropped her off at home. Both vehicles were already in the driveway, which meant Farraday was already there.

"Any luck with Ruth?" she asked as she came in the door, shaking her shoe off her foot.

Farraday was grabbing plates from the cupboard, the smell of pizza filtering out from the living room. "She's gone."

"On her way to get Betty. I noticed Betty's suitcases had been packed before we got there."

"If we're going to make a case we'll have to do it without Betty."

"Do you think we should tell Megan?"

"I guess she has a right to know. But we both know it's not that simple."

They ate in silence, Skittles jogging in, rubbing against Farraday's legs.

"Traitor," Lara muttered as Skittles jumped up on Farraday's lap, purring. "I almost forgot. The enlargements from Jimmy."

She hopped to the table, retrieving the folder from her pack. "They definitely had more than professional reasons for being there."

"I'd say this looks more like personal business. Morrow and Garrett were both affected by Susan's death. If not by grief, then concern or fear. If Walter Morrow is David's cousin it makes him a viable suspect in her murder."

Lara nodded. She felt guilty for holding out on Farraday about the DNA samples and the real reason Garrett might have been upset, if Susan was his sister. But as a cop Farraday was bound by protocols she could ignore. If Garrett's DNA cleared him, Farraday would never need to know about what she'd done. And if her suspicions were right about Garrett then they'd have grounds to bring him in for questioning without getting Farraday into trouble.

There had always been something unwholesome about Walter Morrow and his persona, according to Jimmy. Then there was the conversation David had with Walter that Megan overheard, about David letting him use his kid...

Before they approached the mayor it would be best if they knew the truth about Graeme. With charges already filed against David Douglas they could face serious repercussions if it was established that someone else, someone like Walter Morrow, had fathered Susan's first child.

Or the child could be Graeme's.

Would David Douglas lie to protect his cousin? Did he think his story was plausible enough to get him off without significant damage to his reputation? Morrow might not survive an election after a scandal like this, but people relied on Douglas' businesses for jobs. They would forget, just like all the other sins from before.

Before they risked questioning the mayor they needed to know more. And until she heard back from the lab she had to keep this to herself.

CHAPTER 10

It was midday when Lara hurried out of the library, glancing at her watch. She groaned. Somehow, the morning had gotten away from her, with research on other articles piling up. She was supposed to pick up Farraday for lunch, and she was late.

He'd grudgingly allowed her to take her vehicle to work and drop him off. It was a small step toward regaining some of her independence. And a reminder that eventually, life would get back to normal. He'd move on to a new case, and out of her house.

She pulled the keys out of her pocket and looked up, stopping abruptly. The blonde had a few inches on Lara. Even from behind there was no doubt in her mind about the identity of the person looking at Lara's windshield.

Bolting forward, Lara almost ran into the back of a Civic that was backing out of a parking spot, using her hands to stop herself from falling forward when she stopped abruptly. The driver glared at her and she backed away, hands trembling as she tried to catch her breath.

One look at her jeep was all it took to confirm that Trin Farraday was gone. She scanned the parking lot as she moved toward her vehicle: Nothing. When she got to her jeep, Lara could see what Trin had been looking at. A business card was stuck under the windshield wiper. As Lara reached for it she caught site of Trin, getting into a car that was parked on the road.

Lara glanced at the sentence scrawled on the back and then yanked her door open. She didn't even fasten the seatbelt before she started driving, cutting off a minivan and a station wagon as she weaved through the lot and out to the road where she'd seen Trin.

It didn't matter that she was a few vehicles back. The message had been brief, to the point, though almost unreadable. *Meet me at the old estate.* Written on one of Farraday's cards, in a rushed scrawl that looked like it had been rained on, since the card was misshapen and the ink smudged.

Lara tugged her seatbelt on, starting to catch her breath as she leaned back, *Just A Dream* on the stereo. When she stopped at a red light, still two cars back from Trin, she pulled her bag open and rummaged through the contents until she located her cell phone.

The hands-free headset in place, she listened to the phone ring as she resumed driving.

"You're late."

"I know. I'm on my way."

"Where are you now?"

"Just passing the turnoff to the marina," she said as she watched a police car turn down that road. She'd had to brake while they turned, so she accelerated now to fill the growing gap between her and Trin's car.

"What are you doing out there?"

"You said..." Her phone beeped, warning her the battery was low. She glanced down at the console, wondering where she'd put the car charger. "Where are you?"

"At the station." He'd started off with a mocking tone of annoyance, which was now replaced by real concern. "What's going on?"

"There was a business card on my windshield. One of yours. It said to meet you at the old estate."

"Lara, I would have phoned! You thought I'd left it?"

"Not exactly," she said, her jaw clenching as she forced out the words, turning down the driveway to the old Douglas home. "Look, I'm following your sister out here-"

"Trin? What the hell is going on?"

It was hard not to let the rare panic in his voice unsettle her. "I don't know. I'll..."

The beeps were followed by the silence of dead air. She pulled the headset off and tossed it on the seat beside her, wincing as her front tire dropped into a pothole, jolting her forward. Gripping the steering wheel tightly with both hands, Lara managed to navigate the remaining bumps and ruts in the road and still fill the distance. She pulled up in front of the house just as Trin was getting out of her car.

Her arrival seemed to catch Trin off-guard. For a moment, Farraday's sister stood gaping at her, pausing with her door open. It wasn't until Lara jumped out of her vehicle, wincing and regretting the move instantly as she felt the force of her weight on her sore foot, that Trin closed her car door and walked over.

"What are you doing here?" Trin asked.

"As though you don't know. I got your message."

Trin held up her hand. "I don't know what you're talking about. I didn't leave-"

"On my windshield. On your brother's card."

Trin's dark eyes widened as she glanced at Lara's jeep, as though she expected the card to still be stuck under the wiper. "That wasn't from Ty?"

All the anger and frustration that had built up in Lara on the drive over evaporated. "No. I just talked to him."

"Well, I didn't leave it. I just came out here to talk to him."

Lara felt her eyes narrow again. "Then why not go to the station? What were you doing nosing around my vehicle?" She didn't wait for Trin to answer, walking a few feet past her, looking at the house. The front door was open.

"Stay here," she said, taking another step forward.

Trin stopped her by grabbing her arm. "I don't have to listen to you."

Lara pulled herself free from Trin's grip. "I think someone's been in there, and I'm not going to be responsible for explaining to Farraday what you're doing in a crime scene. I just want to make sure nothing's missing."

"Don't you think you should call my brother or my uncle?"

"My phone's dead. Just stay there."

She tuned out whatever it was Trin started to say, the leaves crunching underfoot, helping to drown out the sound of the words.

***

Farraday barely paused to knock on the open door to his uncle's office. "I need your car."

Collins looked up. "Sign one out. It doesn't look good if I'm loaning you my personal vehicle."

"No time." Farraday put his hands down on Collins' desk. "Lara's on her way out to the old estate. And so is Trin."

"Trin?" Creases filled Collins' brow. "What's she doing out there?" He got up and followed Farraday out of his office, pulling the door shut behind him.

"Don't ask me. Lara said something about a message on her windshield, on one of my cards, and seeing Trin drive away. Then her phone went dead." Farraday stared at his uncle as they pulled the car doors shut and Collins started the ignition. "And isn't the real question what's Trin doing here, in Oakridge?"

Collins' cheeks darkened, but he didn't say anything.

"She's been here this whole time? Con-"

"I don't know what she's been doing. But she asked to stay with me for a while."

"And you didn't tell me."

"You two haven't exactly been speaking."

"Have you talked to her about-"

"Look, you two have stuff to sort out. You leave me out of it."

Farraday leaned back, cursing silently as they hit another red light.

***

The old house was still, nothing more than the soft breeze from outside making the curtains over the window by the door flutter. Lara felt like an intruder, disrupting the stillness, and tried to walk softly up the stairs so that she wouldn't break the silence.

As she entered the bedroom, the emptiness of the house suddenly chilled her to the bone, the hair on the back of her neck prickling as she felt first, then heard, the sound of something scuffling across the floor behind her.

Putting her hands behind her back, as though she was going to hook her fingers on her belt loops, she turned, one hand fumbling to start her recorder.

She fought to stay calm as she looked up into the frost-filled eyes of the man she felt certain – but couldn't prove – had killed Susan Douglas.

"You don't seem surprised."

She shrugged, staying silent.

"I knew you were trouble."

"That's why you broke into my house?"

Graeme Garrett leered at her. "I thought we could have some fun. Your friend got in the way."

Lara could feel her heart racing, but she kept telling herself to relax. If she could just keep him talking, the longer she was up here, the better her chances...

I should have told Farraday to meet us here.

"He wasn't there the first time."

The icy eyes narrowed. "I was only there once."

Sunlight glinted off the knife blade as he set it down on the dresser by the door, then removed a length of wire from his pocket and finally handcuffs.

"Don't worry," he said with a grin that made her stomach lurch. "I know you dropped him off this morning. By the time he even thinks about looking for you, we'll be finished."

Lara swallowed hard. She might only have one chance to distract him, to find a way to attract Trin's attention, but for that she needed to get to the other side of the house.

There were the cops that had gone down the road to the old marina. A 9-1-1 call could put help here in time.

She had to believe that.

Graeme Garrett didn't strike her as the type of person who needed validation, but getting him to talk would be the only way to stall him, to get his focus off of her.

To undermine his control.

"I wanted to ask you something."

"I bet." He walked away from the door as he took off his jacket and tossed it on the bed.

Lara felt a wave of nausea wash over her as she realized what he had planned for her, what Susan must have endured before her death. She felt her stomach lurch again and fought to keep her repulsion from showing on her face. There was nothing visible in the room that she could use to distract him, or defend herself with. As long as he stayed between her and his toys, those were out of the question.

"You can tell me one thing."

"I don't owe you anything, bitch. You've caused me enough trouble already."

"Why Susan?"

A vacant sheen coated his eyes as his jaw unclenched. "I loved her."

"So you killed her?"

"It wasn't that simple. She was going to leave. I couldn't let her do that."

"What are you talking about? She bought a place." Lara thought back to what she'd been able to confirm from Alyssa Martin's story. Susan was preparing to move into a house, she'd hired decorators, everything. "She was staying here, with the baby."

"They told me..." As his voice drifted off he turned away from her, staring vacantly out the window.

She bolted for the open door, but wasn't quick enough. Her coat pulled back and she relaxed her arms, the momentum pushing her forward as he momentarily lost his grip on her. Then his hand clenched her arm. Her hands clung to the doorway as she screamed for help and tried to kick Garrett off.

He let go of her arm and grabbed one leg, twisting her body until she couldn't hold on. As she landed on her back he lunged forward and she punched him on the nose, clawing his face. He slapped her and grabbed her legs, dragging her back into the room, pulling her up off the floor only to throw her down against the bed frame, her shoulders impacting with the wood as she slid down.

Then he was pulling her up by her arms. Her shirt must have been caught on the bed because she heard the fabric tear, felt the air on her skin. Once her one foot was on the ground she kicked him as hard as she could with the other, wincing with pain as her injured ankle twisted from the impact. He barely flinched but slapped her again and she fell back, her head smashing against something hard and solid behind her. She heard the crash as something shattered but felt nothing except her body falling against the hardwood.

***

Collins slammed on the brakes and was putting the car in park as Farraday jumped from the vehicle, racing toward the door, which hung open. There were two vehicles outside but nobody in sight.

There was a sickening quiet in the house. Farraday tried to tell himself that it didn't mean anything but he was filled with the fear that, in this case, he'd always been one step behind and that it would cost him now, in the end. He climbed the stairs, keeping his eyes on the upper corridor.

On instinct, he turned toward the room where Susan Douglas had given birth hours before her own death, his fingers tightening on the grip of his gun.

Fear was replaced with relief as he stared into his sister's eyes. Garrett was lying on the floor at her feet, groaning and bleeding. Shards of glass and blood coated the hardwood around his head, the base of the vase Trin had used still in her hand.

Farraday took it from her, set it on the floor, and then squeezed her arm.

Collins stepped into the room and cuffed Garrett as Farraday turned, his gaze falling on the other crumpled heap on the floor. He crossed the room with only two steps and pulled Lara up into his arms, feeling her fall against him.

Lara's tears and blood mingled on his shoulder as he held her, Collins pulling out his cell phone and calling for an ambulance.

***

When Farraday walked into Lara's living room he stopped short. It didn't seem right somehow, seeing his sister curled up on the end of the couch, mug of tea in her hands, firelight shimmering off her blonde hair.

Of course, Lara had insisted Trin feel welcome there. She'd even said she'd feel better if Farraday wasn't alone, all things considered.

But it seemed wrong, being there without Lara.

He sank down into the armchair slowly. Between giving statements and filing a report, talking to doctors and the few minutes he'd found to stand by Lara's hospital bed, watching her sleep, Trin had admitted she'd been following Lara ever since the day she'd seen her at Farraday's apartment. She'd even been watching from the old cook's cabin when they'd been at the summerhouse.

"I had to leave in a hurry when Lara started heading in that direction," Trin had admitted. "Good thing she didn't know about the other lane, where I'd parked."

His sister had been spying on them and he didn't even have the energy to be upset. Now that they were finally alone, he had to break the silence.

"Trin, I-"

"It's okay, Ty."

"No," he leaned forward, shaking his head as he rested his elbows on his knees, "It isn't. I took Dad's side when he didn't want you to join the police department, and I was wrong to do it. You were mad at me, you made me mad at you."

"Look, it wasn't you that tried to block my application. You just didn't want me put through some of what you've seen other cops go through." She exhaled as she set her mug down on the coffee table. "You don't have anything to apologize for."

"Besides being a jerk?"

The start of a smile pushed at her lips. "Thing is, I understand. I look back at myself over this past year and I don't even know who I am anymore. Stupid, petty arguments with Dad, and I took it out on you."

"You didn't exactly accuse me of wrongdoing in that investigation, Trin."

"No, but the inference was enough, wasn't it? There was an internal inquiry. Sure, it was kept quiet, out of the press, but you were transferred. And at any point I could have stood up and said I was writing under my mother's maiden name. I was my own 'inside source' into the Farraday world. Instead, I let you take the fall." She paused. "And I wasn't even working for the newspaper anymore."

"I knew that. You disappeared for months. Mom was worried."

Trin looked away for a moment, her expression somber. "I know." She drew a deep breath as she turned to look at him. "I went and finished my basic recruit training."

Somehow, she'd worked her way around Dad's interference and completed her training to be a cop.

"Do-"

She nodded. "I told them. I've been working for months now."

He frowned. "With what? How could you be here all this time if you're on the job?"

Trin leaned back against the couch. "Internal. Not formally," she said as he was about to respond to that. "Just using my connection to you as an excuse to be here, to watch the department. Uncle Con's been trying to get them to take a look at the allegations of corruption here for years."

Farraday rubbed his forehead, thinking of the tension between their father and their uncle. He could just imagine... "What happens now?" he asked her.

"I'm going through everything there is on Becker, for one thing. Plus a few other detectives. Oslind and Jones. And assisting on the drug investigation, if you need it." She reached for her drink. "Whatever Uncle Con needs, but that's not the point. I hurt you and I could have ruined your career. I-"

"Look, it worked out, Trin. No stain on my jacket. And Uncle Con wanted me here, anyway. It gave me a reason to make the move."

She froze, staring at him for a moment before she leaned back against the sofa. "You mean you took advantage of the story?"

He shrugged. "I guess. Yeah."

For a moment she stared at him, her face blank. Then she shook her head, her eyes twinkling. "And moving here hasn't been all bad," she said as he stood up. "You've never taken anyone to the summerhouse before. I guess working with a reporter has its advantages."

"There's a stack of blankets right there." He pointed at the pile on the small table near the foot of the stairs. "Good night, Trin," he said as he walked up the stairs.

Chapter 11

Lara walked into her office, dropped her coat on a chair, turned her computer on and sat down. She scanned her messages and, one by one, tossed all but five of them out.

"Well, well. Look who's here." Ted Hatcher sauntered into the room, glaring at her as he gripped the back of a chair with his hands, leaning his weight into the backrest. "What are you working on now?"

"I got a tip about the local youth drug scene," she said as she tapped the notes in front of her. "Apparently, a few homemade teen sex films are going around. I'd like to chase them down, see if there's-"

"Or you could sit at that desk and wrap up the features that you haven't worked on in the last month."

"Why? This story could be huge, especially if there's something to this report of a tape. " She picked up the message. "Apparently, kids talking about being involved in an underage porn and prostitution ring."

"Chasing up homemade videos hasn't gotten you into enough trouble already?"

"It's a solid lead, confirmed by two sources, and a note from Dan Van Biers. He thinks it might tie in with the angle he's been working on the murdered prostitutes," she said as she skimmed that message. Why he thought that made no sense to her, but if Dan wanted to talk to her, she was interested in hearing what he had to say. He'd essentially ignored her since day one, but she could tell he had talent, and she had nothing against him.

"You are ambitious," Hatcher said, almost sneering.

"I just want to do my job," Lara said, feeling her chin jut out.

"First, Dan's prostitutes overdosed. He can go write fiction if he wants to peddle conspiracy theories. Second, you're not following this up. You're in the office."

"What's your problem?"

"Believe it or not, I'm thinking of you. The doctor phoned and insisted that you take it easy for a few weeks. I may not like having a prima donna on staff, but even I have to admit that your front page bylines are good for the paper." Hatcher glared at her. "Just stay out of trouble for a few days, and then you can find a new lead. I'm giving this to Van Biers."

"He just had a huge story, about the dead prostitute, found just inside county lines. It ties in with the other stories he's been writing about."

Hatcher straightened up. "Don't worry, he's quite capable. You could even learn a thing or two from him."

Lara clenched her teeth as Hatcher walked out and then she picked up a thesaurus and whipped it at the place her editor had stood. Jimmy ducked just in time, peeking back around the doorway after a few seconds.

"Is it safe?"

"What an ass," Lara said as she stood up and started pacing.

Jimmy shut the door and grinned. "Desk duty, huh?"

"This is ridiculous! I have a lead on a major story. I knew I should have gone to the library with Farraday's sister." Lara stopped cold as she saw Jimmy's solemn face studying her.

"Let it go, Lara."

"Are you serious? You agree with him?"

He put up his hands. "I just don't think you can fight him. He knows he can't keep you under lock and key. You've made a name for yourself. If he's standing up to you on this then he won't back down, but he'll relent soon enough."

"I would think he'd be happy to have a reporter who wasn't eager to jump ship."

"That's part of the problem. Hatcher's used to up-and-comers bailing out at the first chance." He looked down at her wastebasket. "You aren't even taking your calls. Hatcher has to deal with you being more important than he is and he doesn't like it."

"That alone is reason enough to stay. I can be a thorn in his side." Lara looked at Jimmy, her eyes narrowing. "Not that I'm not happy to see you, but is there a special reason you came by?"

Jimmy shrugged, avoiding her eyes while trying to look casual. "Oh, you know, just wanted to see how you are."

"You're checking up on me." Lara threw her hands up and shook her head.

"Sue me for caring, but I thought I was your friend."

"I know." Lara sighed, sinking into her chair. "But I don't want any special treatment. I just want to get back to my life."

Jimmy nodded. "I understand that, Lara. But life is more than your job. I would think you'd know that, especially now." He darted out the door, giving her no chance to respond.

Lara rubbed her temples with her fingertips and then reached for the Tylenol.

***

"Hey partner," Lenny Becker said. "No wonder you ditched me after my vacation. Even I forgot she was a reporter when I got a look at her."

There were snickers as Farraday sat down at his desk, refusing to look Lenny in the eye.

"Yeah, no wonder you haven't been here much lately," Oslind said, his eyes fixed on Farraday. Oslind was a big man with a slick smile and a sinister look in his eyes. He was known for being lewd and difficult, and Farraday didn't like him. "You working this case from every, shall we say, angle?"

There were jeers at that as Farraday's head snapped up, glaring at Oslind, his hands clenching into fists.

"Farraday was working a difficult case." Lenny stood and held up his hand. "And our boy Farraday doesn't cross the lines. Isn't that right?"

Lenny slapped Farraday on the back, fixing him with a stare that, on the surface was friendly and consoling, but underneath held some hint of doubt that left Farraday feeling uneasy, wondering what, if anything, Lenny suspected.

Collins marched into the squad room then, paused for a second and looked at Lenny and Farraday. "My office," he said. He turned and went straight into his office.

Farraday glanced at Lenny. "I guess things are back to normal."

Lenny grinned. "Ah, the morning ritual is complete. Coffee, cancer sticks and having the captain whip my ass at the start of the shift. I've missed this."

"Really?" Farraday muttered. "Then your vacation was too long."

***

"Farraday can bring you up to speed. I doubt I need to tell either of you that the department considers this to be an extremely important case. I've even heard from the Deputy Chief about this. Garrett was a former cop and worked for the Mayor's office. Now he's facing charges for the murder of Susan Douglas, and for assaulting Larimer Kelly. The pressure is on us to close this case quick and clean."

Someone knocked quickly and didn't wait for the okay to open the door. Detective Jones appeared. "I need Becker. There's been another break-in at the Lakeview Hotel, and this time we've got a body."

Captain Collins sighed, looking at Lenny and Farraday silently for a moment. Lenny just shrugged. "The Lakeview Hotel case is mine," he said. "Farraday can handle this one."

Collins paused for a second, then nodded. "See how it plays out. Just remember," he interjected as Becker stood to leave, "this should have been a straight-forward case but it's been dragging on for weeks. I want to see everything you have on my desk by the end of the day."

Becker nodded and walked out, shutting the door behind him. Collins waved to a chair. "You might as well make yourself comfortable."

"You mean there's more?" Farraday sat down, his forehead pinched. "Why did you want me on this with Lenny?"

"I thought you could use this as a chance to see if Lenny would try to handle the evidence. How's Lara?"

"She's back at work."

"You say that like it's a bad thing."

Farraday shrugged. "I'm just glad we don't have to worry about Graeme Garrett now. As long as he's behind bars-"

Collins' eyes clouded. "I hate to tell you this, but he made bail."

***

Following Graeme Garrett had led Vern to a number of interesting discoveries. He had connections with cops, a high school principal and an assortment of shady characters, as well as occasional meetings with Walter Morrow, the mayor, and David Douglas, although those had declined since Douglas had been arrested. Vern guessed Douglas' lawyer, who was also Garrett's lawyer, had told David to behave and play nice.

And more than half the time, these meetings happened at the Lakeview Hotel.

Vern had been following some of the other familiar faces, starting to put names to them. There had been a few visits to the Doe Lake Motel as well. Not by David or Walter or even Michael McClure, the lawyer, but by the cops and thugs they met with.

He couldn't see how they connected, or what they had to do with the disappearance of Choy Kim, but he had that same feeling in his gut, the one he'd had when he first saw Mr. Chan.

The one that told him he was on to something.

Then Dan Van Biers had started to fill in the gaps. Telling him which cops to take a hard look at.

He followed the detectives to the Lakeview Hotel and decided to take a look around. After all, it was a place of business and there were other people around, although not many. It was a quiet time of year and the chipped and peeling sign out front stating they were open for business should have had the word barely added to it.

Vern wasn't really following the targets anymore, just checking things out.

Still trying to make sense of what it was about a run-down hotel that had people like the mayor and the most prominent businessman in the city meeting there.

Which was when they surprised him. They'd gone in the front doors, so he walked around the building, following the patio, and was about to walk out behind the hotel when he heard voices. Vern reached into his pocket and turned his recorder on.

"Look, I'm not saying that you have to like it, but it had to be done," a male voice said. "There's no point causing a fuss about it now."

"You're saying I don't have a choice?" another male voice responded. "I've done my share of looking the other way, but this..."

"This is necessary."

"It's a kid, dammit."

"A kid that can be linked to someone who's been a good friend to us over the years."

"Maybe it's time to think about who we call a friend. He wants us burning bodies to cover his crimes. Exactly what do we wear a badge for?"

"To keep a lid on things. This kid was trouble. He got what was coming to him. You know what his sheet looks like. It's not like he was innocent."

"Maybe I'm just having trouble with what you're making me guilty of."

"Then get over it, or you'll have a different kind of trouble, a permanent kind of trouble. This isn't a debate. He has your DNA, your fingerprints, and can have your name implicated in any crime with enough physical evidence to send you away. You think about that and then tell me you've got issues with this."

"The captain thinks there was a body."

"It's been handled."

"Just what are these robb...?"

"Drop it. Consider yourself warned. Don't make me tell you again."

Vern couldn't tell who was saying what, at first, but he risked a glance around the side of the building.

Which was exactly when a soccer ball impacted the wall right beside his head and a freckle-faced kid with curly red hair and enormous black glasses came running up from the field.

"Sorry."

Vern hadn't waited for the apology, but had turned and started walking as fast as he could, back to his car. Behind him, he heard the scuffle of feet, someone swear and then what he assumed was the kid starting to cry.

There was always that breathless bit at the beginning, as the sound caught up to the scream.

He pulled his keys from his pocket as he ran, thankful for remote car accessories, which he used to unlock and start his car. As soon as he slammed the door shut and relocked the doors they reached his vehicle, but they were too late to stop him. They reached for the passenger side door and he pushed the gas pedal to the floor and sped away.

***

Trin snapped her cell phone shut and propped her chin up with her hand. A few calls to some well-placed political contacts was all it had taken to get enough rumor on David Douglas and Oakridge's not-so-shiny mayor to raise some interesting possibilities.

Some kids, outside the city limits, had run their car into a pole. The police had searched their vehicle and found drugs. High-caliber, unlike anything you could pick up on the street.

Unfortunately for the kids, their parents had been away for the weekend, and they were in custody long enough to start sweating. Her source said a cop had told him they'd established the drugs hadn't come from anywhere local, not any known supply within a 300-mile radius. One of the kids, a boy known to him only as Hare, had started to talk. The drugs came from a local businessman who imported them from overseas, a businessman he did some filming for.

That was where it ended. An Oakridge lawyer named Michael McClure had stepped in and put a stop to all questions, managed to raise enough questions about improper procedure and, after some back-room discussions her source's source hadn't been privy to, the charges were amended and the kids released.

The drugs were nothing more than something that took up space in an evidence locker, the catalyst to an investigation that went nowhere.

This had only happened a few months ago. The only reason it could even be connected to David Douglas was through the lawyer.

It did nothing to help Farraday's case or his investigation into Susan's murder.

She stood, stuffing her papers into her bag. Then she looked up.

The man was familiar. He was standing, turning his head from the left to the right repeatedly, as though he was looking for someone, his cell phone glued to his ear. Then he lowered his hand, clicked it off, scowling, looking around the library again, this time panning the room slowly, scrutinizing faces.

Until his gaze met hers.

Vern Fletcher. During the time she'd been following Lara she'd seen him snooping around occasionally, keeping a comfortable distance.

It was beginning to look like he'd seen her, too. He strode across the room with purpose and grabbed her arm, dragging her back into a corner.

"You're Katarina Collins."

She felt her back stiffen. "So?"

He scoffed at her. "So? That means you're Trin Farraday."

Trin pulled her arm free. "Look-"

Vern let go of her and held up his hand. "You know who I am right? Reporter at The Ledger? I'm not interested in you. I'm trying to find Lara."

"She's at the office."

"Damn." He ran his fingers over his hair and then wiped his brow with his palm. Which was when she really noticed the cold sweat, she'd been so distracted by the force of his hand on her arm and his questions. "I need to see her. But not at work. I can't go there."

Trin shrugged. "What do you want me to do about it?"

"Look, I've got information. Stuff she should know about."

"Sounds to me like you should be talking to my brother."

Vern shook his head. "A cop? After tonight I'm out of here, for good. Before someone with a badge makes it permanent."

He grabbed her wrist with her other hand and stared her straight in the eye.

There was something about his expression that told her he was serious. "She should be home tonight."

He let go of her arm, offered a weak smile and, after one furtive glance around the library, walked away.

CHAPTER 12

The Land Rover pulled up behind a van and cut the headlights. Graeme Garrett got out of the front passenger side, the sliding door of the van opening as he approached.

It was a starless night, the kind where the darkness swallowed everything. It wasn't until he was inside the van, sitting down on a jump seat on the driver's side of the vehicle, that he realized the form on the floor was a person.

One of the others climbed in, pulling the door shut, and passed Garrett a flashlight. He turned it on and whistled.

"He heard a bunch of stuff he shouldn't have. No choice now."

Garrett looked down at the pale face, the gagged mouth and bound hands. Vern Fletcher looked away.

He took the gun Oslind offered him. "I'm going to enjoy this."

The others laughed as the engine spat and then caught, and they drove away. It didn't take long for them to reach the old marina.

"You sure this is such a good idea?" Garrett asked as he got out of the vehicle.

"Y'aren't goin' soft on us now, are ya?" Oslind asked while the other men walked around to the back, the doors opening.

"No, it's just this place. Susan. Seems a bit obvious."

"We didn't have anything to do with Susan."

His words were hissed, forceful. The sound of gravel crunching underfoot grew louder, then stopped as the men dragged Vern Fletcher down on the beach.

"You're sure?" Garrett asked Oslind. "Not about doing this, but here?"

Oslind nodded. "Orders from the top. Said it would make it seem tied to Susan and since it isn't, it would throw them off."

Why not just take out a boat and weigh him down? It seemed like the smart thing to do. Better to have Vern disappear than another investigation that could lead back to them. Fletcher wasn't the only problem. Farraday and Kelly were turning out to be a pain in the ass.

He planned to deal with them personally. Soon.

"You know what he can do," Oslind said as the others turned Vern around. Vern was standing in the water, hands bound behind his back. Oslind continued. "He can plant evidence, clear up the whole thing. That gun in your hand will tie this to another case that will turn into a dead end."

Garrett lifted the weapon and Vern looked up then. It was too dark for Garrett to tell what the reporter was thinking. He pulled the trigger once, then twice. Vern's body jerked back with the impact of each bullet. He fell to his knees after the second one, swaying.

Garrett squeezed the trigger one more time but all he heard was a click. He tried again.

Nothing.

Vern fell. He didn't move, nothing but the gentle lapping of the water making a sound.

"Job done, but next time, fully load it," he said as he turned around.

And swallowed.

"See, it might've made sense to weigh Vern down and take him out in a boat," Oslind said, as though he knew exactly what Garrett had been thinking before he shot Vern. Oslind kept his gun pointed at Garrett as he walked over to the water, beside Vern's body. He wrapped Vern's fingers around the gun, his own hands concealed in dark gloves. "But it would've made it a bit harder to do this."

The shot rang out and Garrett felt the bullet slam into his chest as the gun fired again, and then the world went dark.

***

The law offices of Blackstone and McClure were downtown, on one side of the park, etched with black glass and steel framing.

Farraday approached the receptionist and asked to speak to Michael McClure. The woman smiled as she assured him that, without an appointment, that wouldn't be possible until later in the week. He pulled out his identification.

"We can do this quietly, or I can come back every day and let your clients wonder why the police need to talk to your boss," Farraday said, staring at her long enough to convey how serious he was. He'd been up half the night at the crime scene, dealing with the murders of Graeme Garrett and Vern Fletcher, and he wasn't in the mood for games. She picked up the phone.

Within a minute Farraday was in the lawyer's office. He had barely sat down in the oversized leather chair by the desk before Michael McClure entered.

McClure was a tall man, muscular, with dark hair. He moved with purpose and energy when he wasn't being kept on a leash by clients like David Douglas.

"Detective Farraday," McClure said as he down. "What can I do for you?"

"Has no one informed you of the death of one of your clients?"

McClure's shoulders rose. "You mean this business with Garrett?"

"I understand you handled his release."

McClure nodded, his face as unmoving as a brick wall. "As his lawyer, I was responsible for handling the arrangements. It was quite normal."

"I'm establishing a timeline for Mr. Garrett's whereabouts before his death. At this point, you are the last known person to see Mr. Garrett alive. What time did you handle his bail?"

"It was unusually late. The judge didn't have time to hear us until after 3 pm. By the time the paperwork was filed, I'd say it was at least 4:30 before we left the courthouse."

"You left together?"

McClure nodded. "We went to dinner to discuss his options."

"Where did you go?"

"Callandre's, on 5th Street."

Farraday wrote this down, familiar with the chic restaurant that did a healthy trade with businessmen from the area. "Did you see or talk to anyone else during dinner?"

McClure seemed to consider that, though his eyes appeared blank instead of thoughtful. "The waiter. I don't believe I had ever seen him before, though, and I don't recall his name. I'm sure you'll be talking to the staff there. Do you know when, exactly, Mr. Garrett died?"

"I can't comment on that, Mr. McClure. I'll speak to the staff at Callandre's, though a description of the waiter would help. What time did you leave?"

"Just before 7, if I recall correctly. Mr. Garrett called a cab, and I walked home."

"You walked?" Farraday raised an eyebrow.

"I live in a condo downtown, just a few blocks away."

"And did you see or hear from Mr. Garrett at any time after you left?"

McClure shook his head. He gave Farraday a brief description of the waiter: About 5'10", brown hair, blue eyes, young. Farraday noticed the soft drumming of fingertips against McClure's desk while he rattled off the vague features he could remember.

McClure shrugged. "I thought this was fairly straightforward. Mr. Fletcher and Mr. Garrett had a confrontation and shot each other."

Farraday forced a thin smile. "As a defense attorney, surely you can think of a dozen holes that could be poked into that conclusion.

A smirk was McClure's only response.

"I'll be in touch."

Farraday walked out of the office, considering the unusually defensive tone the lawyer had been unable to subdue, and the fact that when he'd announced his departure, McClure appeared to start breathing again.

***

Farraday paused outside Callandre's, observing the busy restaurant before he went inside. He hadn't thought he would need to deal with lunch rush approaching 2 pm but the restaurant was still doing a brisk business with the downtown crowd.

"Table for one, sir? Or are you meeting a party?" The hostess was a young woman, with long, silky black hair and a wide smile.

Farraday stepped close, lowering his voice. "I'm here to speak to the manager."

The smile wavered. "That's not possible right now. Could you come back after lunch?"

"I'm afraid I need to insist." He showed her his ID. "Could you tell him Detective Farraday would like to speak to him in private?"

The girl paused and then turned, presumably to find the manager. She hadn't gotten far when a man approached her, glaring at her. Farraday saw her point in his direction and then the man looked at him, stepping forward briskly.

"I'm Ian Vincent," he said. "Right this way."

Farraday offered the hostess a small, apologetic smile, and followed Vincent down the hall. It wasn't long before Farraday was sitting in a small room, just off the kitchen.

"What is this about?"

"I'm investigating the murder of Graeme Garrett. I understand he was here for dinner last night."

Farraday paused. Ian Vincent had dark brown hair and appeared to enjoy sampling the restaurant's cuisine.

"So?"

"Can you confirm that Mr. Garrett was here that night?"

Ian Vincent's eyes darkened, but he nodded. "He dined with Mr. McClure."

"Was there any anyone that you observed interacting with him?"

Ian Vincent shifted his gaze.

"I've spoken to Mr. McClure already," Farraday said.

Vincent's shoulder's sagged a little. "Then you know that Walter Morrow joined them briefly and there was an exchange between them and their waiter."

"What time did the mayor join them?"

"Around 5:30. I believe he left after an hour or so. We are very busy during dinner."

"And what about this incident with the waiter?"

"I... The waiter seemed to know Mr. McClure and Mr. Garrett. There was an argument, and the mayor asked me to remove him."

"What was the waiter's name?"

His face reddened. "It was his first night and it turns out he'd given me a false name."

"You didn't check his resume?"

"He had a referral from a prominent client." Vincent shrugged.

"Who was the client that referred him?"

Ian Vincent flushed deep red. "Well, it was actually another employee who told me he'd been referred..."

Farraday confirmed the description he'd received from McClure. He spoke to a few other employees who had worked that night before he left, wondering why McClure had lied to him when it would be so easy to confirm the truth of what had happened during Graeme Garrett's last supper.

***

Farraday tried Lara's cell and got her voicemail. He cut the call without leaving a message and returned to Garrett's house, hoping to find Graeme's neighbors at home. His cell phone rang.

"I've got someone going through Garrett's belongings." Collins relayed the information and Farraday assured him he'd check up on that shortly.

He walked up to the house across the street and knocked.

The heavy wooden door creaked open slowly, a thin, gruff voice demanded to know what he wanted. He held up his badge.

"My name is Detective Farraday. I was wondering if I could ask you a few questions about your neighbor from across the street."

"Dead now, isn't he? What more is there to know?"

"I was wondering if you saw him Thursday night."

"I never talked to him in my life!" Farraday could see the sagging skin on the old man's face as he relaxed his hold on the door and stepped forward to look across the street. He wasn't a big man, appearing thin to Farraday's quick assessment, but his eyes were sharp and intense.

"I'm sorry, mister..." Farraday let the word hang deliberately, inviting the man to offer his name.

"Ainesworth," he said brusquely. "Peter Ainesworth."

"Mr. Ainesworth, I wasn't asking if you had spoken with him. I was wondering if, by chance, you'd seen him from your window and could tell me what time he came home, or if he had any visitors."

The man looked at Farraday with a pucker between his brow and a deepening frown. "Farraday? Isn't that the name I've seen in the papers recently?"

"Yes, I guess so." Whenever he thought of his name in the paper, he still thought of the article his sister had printed. "I'm investigating the murder of Graeme Garrett now."

"Humph." Mr. Ainsworth practically spat the word. "He got what he deserved. Just bury him and move on, I say."

"That isn't up to me. I really would appreciate anything you could tell me."

"Well, I was home that night. Usually I play poker at Dick Farnsworth's place, two blocks over, but he came down with the flu. Likely an excuse, you know. He's been chasing Estelle Waters, and him not widowed two months. But some men just can't handle being on their own, need a woman to take care of them." He stared at Farraday for a moment and then seemed to recall the original point. "I remember he came in a taxi. Thought it was odd, usually he's driving his flashy car. He walked up to the front door and went in."

"Do you know what time that was?"

"Well, the news had just finished. Deb Halliston was coming over, since I wasn't going out. She likes chamomile, hot. I made the tea, brought it in and then saw the cab. It hadn't barely gone down the road when Deb rang the bell."

"I see. Was that the six o'clock news?"

He nodded. "Watch it every day, channel 7. The full hour."

"So it was likely just past 7:00 when you saw Mr. Garrett come home?"

"I guess so."

"Thank you very much, Mr. Ainesworth. I appreciate you taking the time."

Mr. Ainesworth moved as though he was going to close the door, then stopped and spoke again. "You know, I wasn't watching the window all night, but there was something else I saw. Can't say for certain if it will help you or not, and I'm not trying to kick up a fuss where none is needed. I was just helping Deb with her jacket and when I opened the door there was a dark truck sitting there. It was running, real quiet though, didn't even hear it until the door was open. Deb wanted to borrow a book I'd told her about. I went to get it, and when I came back I heard the doors shut, and it went racing through here, running the light."

"It ran the light at that intersection?" Farraday asked, pointing.

Mr. Ainesworth nodded. "There was honking and squealing tires. I remember now, Deb saying how murder charges obviously hadn't changed him. She lives three houses over, mind, so she knows all about him. Told her it was one thing to take the man out of a place of sin, but quite another to take the sin out of the man."

Farraday tried to suppress his smile. "Do you have any idea what kind of truck it was?"

"It wasn't a truck, not like we drove in my day. It had four doors; that I can say for certain. Dark color. One of them stylish things people drive these days. An SUV."

"And what time was this?"

"Past ten, ten-thirty."

Farraday reached out and shook Mr. Ainesworth's hand. "Thanks again."

"All right then. You talk to Deb. She'll tell you herself, if it helps."

***

Deb Halliston insisted that Farraday come inside and hear her story over a cup of tea.

"Did Mr. Garrett ever have visitors?"

"Like lady friends?" She shook her head, giving him a funny look, like she somehow didn't think that Garrett was quite right. "No. There was a young fellow staying there over the past few weeks. You know, earrings and tattoos and the works. It seemed odd to me."

"Have you seen him since Mr. Garrett's murder?"

The lines on her forehead multiplied instantly. "You know, I don't think I have." She gave Farraday a generic description and also offered him an intriguing detail. When Peter had gone to retrieve the book, she'd noticed two men coming out of Garrett's house with him.

"Do you think you could identify them?"

Her lips pursed as she considered that and then nodded. "Likely. I got a good look at the driver. But the other one seemed familiar somehow, like it was a person whose name I should know." She'd seen the black SUV before and it wasn't "coming to mind what it said, but it has one of those fancy license plates somebody makes special." Deb said she always wondered why someone would pay more money to draw attention to their car like that.

"But then, don't all those foolish youngsters nowadays? Everybody's trying to make it seem like they're more important than they are. Never did understand that. Just make the most of the time you have and stop fussing about it, that's what I say."

Farraday agreed and thanked her, heading back out to his car. It was almost 6 o'clock, and he still had one more stop to make.

***

Farraday had received the call around 3 am. Two bodies had been found in the water, at the old marina.

Two bodies. Two guns. One easy theory he could jump to.

Except it didn't explain the tire tracks in the mud or the other footprints. Sloppy. Still, it was a convenient cover story for the press.

Technically, Farraday was still investigating Susan Douglas' murder. It had been a long day, and now he had one final stop that he had to make.

The address was for a dingy motel room, the kind the department used when it needed to stash someone. Collins hadn't wanted anyone to know about this, not with the amount of profile Graeme Garrett's murder was getting already.

Walker and Megan had returned after her dad had been arrested. Collins had cleared up the issue with the videotape, and decided the one person he'd trust with this assignment would be the one who had the most to prove.

"Coffee and donuts." Rob Walker grinned. "To what do I owe the pleasure?"

"I couldn't find a water cooler," Farraday said, remembering what Walker had said to him just a few weeks earlier about his inability to socialize. Walker laughed.

"Captain Collins tells me you got the job of picking through Garrett's things. How's that going?" Garrett's belongings had been boxed and moved to the hotel room. It looked like this would be Walker's office for some time to come.

"If it wasn't for the tedious detailing of clothes, furniture, x-rated videos and political magazines, it would be interesting," Walker muttered. "I try to break it up with digesting the extensive record of Graeme's emails over the past ten years."

"He kept everything since he turned in his badge?" Farraday asked. Walker nodded.

"That's probably the best place to start. Forget folding clothes. You know what we're looking for. Anything about Susan's murder, or his connections to David Douglas or Walter Morrow, anything that suggests criminal activity." Trin had told him about her research, the night before. The fact that Garrett's lawyer – David Douglas' lawyer – had been involved with those kids made him wonder. "If there's a trail to the underground drug trade, or a connection to our department, I want to see it. Or anything that would indicate a motive for his murder, in case it had nothing to do with his plans to expose his associates."

Walker nodded. "You can count on me."

"Thanks. And, in case anyone from our precinct is asking, I'm working on this alone."

"I've got your cell number. Not a word to anyone but you or Captain Collins. What about Lara?"

Farraday paused. "Let me try to handle her." He saw the look in Walker's eye.

"Better you than me," was all Walker said.

***

Farraday found Lara in the kitchen when he got to the house. "Where's Trin?"

"Lying down. She didn't get back to sleep after you were called out."

"How was the office?"

She didn't need to say anything. The way her eyes sagged at the corners, the dark smudges standing out starkly against her pale skin, the hard line of her mouth drawn a bit too tight, as though if she let her guard down even just a bit she'd start to cry.

"Everyone was upset today, because..." Lara drew a deep breath and then shrugged. "Collins called about the Lakeview Hotel story, so I had something to pull together. I'll get used to being back to routine, just like you're going to have to get used to working with Lenny again."

Farraday turned to get a bottle of water from the fridge. "I'm worried."

"About working with Lenny?"

"About you."

"Me? I'm fine, given a clean bill of health by the doctor and a big one to pay. I'm back at work. At least, as much as Hatcher will let me be," she said, her mouth twisting.

"What does that mean?"

"I had a lead on a story. Hatcher ordered me to drop it. Do you know there are three recent overdose deaths related to the drug trade that we know about so far? Dan Van Biers thinks-"

"For once, I agree with Hatcher," Farraday said, leaning against the kitchen counter.

Lara's eyes narrowed as she looked up at him. "Hatcher just wants to pretend he's in control and keep me off the street for a few days."

"Sounds like a good idea to me."

She stared at him. "If it wasn't..."

Farraday held up his hand. "I'm not disputing your skills, just the timing. Let somebody else take this story while you work on other things. There's nothing wrong with knowing when you need to put yourself ahead of your career."

"I don't see you passing Garrett's case on to someone else. I've taken time off to heal from my injuries and I'm ready to be back at work."

"And you still have a lot to deal with. Garrett shattered your sense of security. He invaded your home and your life. You've been stuck with me shadowing you for weeks and just when we think things are going back to normal we've got two more murders. And we both know what Garr-"

"It didn't happen."

He could see the warning look in her eyes but didn't stop. "That doesn't-"

She put up her hand. "I'm going to go check on your sister."

Farraday watched her stomp out of the room.

He turned to the cupboard to look for something for his growing headache.

***

The next day the door to Lara's office creaked open. Lara looked up to see a young girl. She was tall, very thin, with unruly black hair that cascaded down her back. Lara smiled at her. "Can I help you?"

"Are you, uh, Miss Kelly?" the girl asked. She watched the hallway with skittish glances, jumping at every sound and movement.

"Call me Lara." She gestured for the girl to come in and sit down. Lara got up and closed the door. "What can I do for you?"

"My name is Kaitlin Parks," she said. "I read about how you found out about that woman who had been killed. I thought you might be able to help me."

"What do you think I can help you with?"

"There's a boy I know, Allan. He's gone missing."

"How long has it been since you've seen him?"

"Six days."

"Have you talked to his parents?"

She shook her head. "They're away on vacation."

"Do you know who he was staying with while they're away?"

"Nobody. He's fifteen. His parents left him on his own."

"How old are you?"

"Thirteen."

Thirteen. Wow. Lara frowned. "Have you been to his house?"

"Yes. There's nobody there. He hasn't been at school."

Lara studied the solemn face before her, wondering if this girl was really serious, or just trying to track down a boy who was avoiding her.

It's likely nothing more than a boy taking advantage of his parents being away, hanging out with a 6 pack and some friends, skipping school and enjoying his freedom.

"Okay Kaitlin. What's Allan's last name?"

"Hare. Allan Hare."

"Can you show me where Allan lives?" Lara asked. At least it would get her out of the office.

"Okay." Kaitlin practically leapt from the chair. "It's close."

The Hare residence was, in fact, only four blocks away. Lara had been a little skeptical at first, but when Kaitlin mentioned the address, she agreed to leave her jeep behind. It was the kind of fall day that hints of winter's imminent arrival, but still nice enough for a short walk. Lara wondered if maybe now she would get a chance to just stroll at the park and enjoy the last splash of color before the autumn winds blew the leaves away.

The walk to the Hare home was a sprint, with Kaitlin setting a quick pace. She didn't slow until they were across the street from the house.

"There." She pointed to a white bi-level. The house itself was older but well kept, with bay windows in the front. The yard was outlined with trimmed hedges and a cast-iron gate at the front walk.

Lara pushed the gate open, wincing at the loud creak of the hinges.

Kaitlin shrugged. "It's been like that as long as I've known Allan."

"How long have you been friends with him?"

"Three years. Now that I'm thirteen, I'm old enough to be his girl." Kaitlin had a smug look on her face, like this was a profound accomplishment, and Lara found herself wondering about the general sensibilities of young girls who just want to be old enough to have a boyfriend. Had Kaitlin really been chasing this boy since she was ten years old?

Lara walked up the front steps to ring the bell, studying the lines in the etched glass doors. She wasn't sure if they were French or not, but she knew they were expensive. This was an older part of town, one that hadn't decayed over time, and the yard was enormous. The Hare family was undoubtedly financially comfortable.

Still, Lara had to wonder about parents who went away and left their fifteen-year-old son at home to fend for himself. She rang the bell a second time and leaned over the rail a little to try to see in the window. Unable to catch a glimpse of anything helpful, she turned to descend the half-dozen steps to where Kaitlin stood on the walk.

"What school do you go to?" Lara asked as she walked around the house, peeking in the lower windows but seeing no evidence of movement or disarray in the basement.

"St. Christopher," Kaitlin said.

"Is that where Allan goes?"

Kaitlin shook her head. "He goes to Oakridge High."

"Then how do you know him? Those schools are on opposite sides of the city."

Kaitlin shrugged sheepishly, avoiding Lara's gaze. "We hang out together."

"Where."

"Just... around."

"Since you were ten?"

Kaitlin nodded. There was something in the darting glances, the inability to hold her gaze, the bizarre inconsistencies of avoidance and assertiveness that left Lara wondering about Kaitlin Parks. There was an elusive quality that Lara couldn't put her finger on, but it was nagging at the back of her mind like a warning, hinting of something so obvious that she should be able to see it.

Lara walked up the back stairs. The back porch had been recently painted. It was unspoiled, white, with barely a speck of dirt visible until she looked at the stairs.

There were black scuffmarks along the steps in the middle, and a little nick in the wood, as though something had been dropped onto the stair and then dragged.

Lara bent down to take a closer look. She wasn't sure what to make of the scuffing, but as she studied the stairs, she noticed the marks trailed off again, about three steps from the bottom. Whatever it was, somebody had attempted to carry it down, had dropped it and dragged it for half a dozen steps, then picked it up again. She took a closer look at the railing and saw what she was almost certain was dried blood.

She dropped her pack and started collecting samples, then pulled out her camera and took pictures. It was then, as she was setting the camera back into the bag, that she looked up and saw Kaitlin staring at her, her face wild and white and her eyes bulging.

"What did you find," Kaitlin asked, her voice quivering. Lara held up her hands.

"I'm not sure it's anything. But I want to make sure we find your friend, and that means I have to examine everything. I'd rather take photos now and not need them, than not be able to find Allan and have to come back after it's rained. Do you understand?"

Kaitlin's eyes recessed and she swallowed hard before nodding.

Lara went up the stairs, taking care to disturb as little as possible, scrutinizing every inch of wood. She found nothing more along the stairs, but when she reached the deck her heart sank.

The back door had been pried open and there were more scuffmarks. There was also a large stain on the door and deck.

Lara snapped some more pictures, grabbed a quick sample, and then descending the steps, just in time to keep Kaitlin from coming up.

"Did you find something else?" she asked.

"It's going to take some time. I want to phone a friend of mine to see if he can check on some things, and I'm going to call a cab to take you home."

Lara put her hand on Kaitlin's shoulder and ushered her to the front of the house. While they waited, Lara took Kaitlin's phone number and address, and gave the girl one of her cards.

"I can't make you any promises," Lara said as Kaitlin got into the taxi. "But I will call you and let you know if I've found anything."

Kaitlin nodded and Lara turned, waiting until the taxi was down the street to pull her cell phone out and make a call.

***

Farraday sighed. He'd been working on a list of possible sport utility vehicles that had been seen outside Garrett's home the night of his murder. The personalized license plate helped, but even with narrowing the make and model to the last three years he had a possible list of 160 vehicles registered locally.

He sighed as he received the final printout, wondering if there was another way to shorten this list, or to draw a suspect to the top without calling every number. He printed out a list of all of the models he'd narrowed it down to, and decided to go back to Fulton Avenue, where Graeme Garrett had lived, and see if he could elicit any more help. He was fortunate enough to find Peter Ainesworth in his front yard, raking leaves.

"Never in all my years have I needed someone to do my yard work," he said proudly as he saw Farraday get out of his car. "It's good for the body and the soul."

Farraday smiled. "And good for keeping an eye on Deb Halliston." He could see Deb kneeling at her flowerbeds, presumably cleaning them up before winter.

Peter Ainesworth winked and then nodded toward the folder in his hand. "Is that more about Garrett?"

Farraday nodded. "Actually, some different kinds of vehicle models, to try to find the one that was here last Thursday night. Would you mind taking a look?"

Peter Ainesworth took the file and skimmed through the pages, going back to the picture of the Land Rover. "It looked a lot like this," he said.

"And you say it went in that direction?" Farraday pointed to the close intersection, just to be certain he was right.

"Damn foolish thing, blazing through there. You'd think Garrett would know better, lobbying for red light cameras and all that crap and then letting his friends speed through the intersection." Peter Ainesworth went back to his raking.

Red light cameras...

"Thanks again," Farraday said, returning to his car, wondering if Garrett had just given him the clue he needed. When he got back to the station, it didn't take long for Farraday to enter a search on tickets issued by the camera at the intersection on the night in question. In all, four tickets were issued to SUV's, but only one had a personalized license plate.

Farraday went to Collins' office, only to find the door open and the chair empty. "Has anyone seen the captain?" he asked.

"No. He went out and he didn't say where he was going."

"Damn," Lenny Becker said, materializing beside Farraday. "You having fun cleaning up this case without me?"

"This is tedious. You lucked out. I heard there wasn't a body at the hotel after all."

"Funny story, that one," Lenny said, but without a smile. "Turned out to be some stoned hobo. The rookie who called it in thought he was dead because he was lying on a sheet of plastic that was covered with blood. We get out there, ready to write this up and no sooner does Lessard get down to take a closer look than the guy sits up and pukes all over him. That would have been something for *America's Funniest Home Videos.*"

Farraday smiled at the thought of Lessard's reaction, the string of four-letter words he knew Lessard could let fly under such circumstances.

The poor rookie had probably gotten an earful he wouldn't forget any time soon, and he'd be hoping he didn't make another call to the ME's office in the near future.

Farraday went back to his desk. He'd narrowed his list down to one likely suspect. Looking at the registry again, he felt certain the pieces were coming together, that the dominoes might be about to fall. Someone killed Garrett to keep him quiet. Finding his murderer might shed light on the illegal activities that he'd been involved in and help solve Susan's murder.

But now that he had something to take this case forward, he felt he had to talk to Collins first. If it were anyone else, he would proceed with questioning, but this... This suspect would need a subtle approach and an ironclad case to take down.

***

"Lara?"

"Right here," Lara said, looking down over the railing. "Is it just you?"

He nodded. "For now. I'm surprised you phoned me."

Lara felt her cheeks heat up. "Farraday wants me to stay in the office and write nice stories about little old ladies and their bridge clubs."

Collins laughed. "Did he confuse you with a docile reporter that I haven't met yet?"

She smiled sardonically. "I see where he gets his limited sense of humor."

"From Warren," Collins said with a smile. "What is it you've found?"

Lara gave him a quick run-down on the arrival of a young girl in her office, and her subsequent discoveries. "I'll be the first to say that I can think of a dozen reasons that would explain what I've found, and most of them aren't criminal. But I don't want to interfere with an investigation if there's more to this."

She gestured for him to come up the stairs.

"This is more than just a little pool of blood. It's fairly fresh too, and somewhat preserved from being under the covered part of the porch." Collins' eyes took on a sober look. "Looks like you might be two for two, Lara."

Lara felt lightheaded at the thought. A teenager. What next?

She swallowed. "I hope you're wrong."

***

When Collins didn't return to the office within an hour, Farraday called Walker to see if he was making any headway. On the third ring, Walker answered.

"Just wondered how it's going with those computer files," Farraday asked.

"Just a second." Walker was silent for a moment, and then spoke, keeping his voice low. "I've been pulled off of the data retrieval for a while."

"By whom?" Farraday tried to keep the annoyance he felt out of his voice. He couldn't afford to lose the assistance of the only other cop who knew about the true nature of the case, about the suspected drug trafficking and corruption in the police department that connected to Walter Morrow and David Douglas.

"Captain Collins. He has me checking up on something, but it won't get in the way. It isn't major. I'll stay on it for you."

The phone went dead, leaving Farraday to wonder why Collins would pull Walker off the murder investigation, especially without warning him.

***

Collins entered his office, not even scanning the squad room in his haste, so he didn't notice Farraday on his heel, coming in behind him and letting the door clap shut as he rapped his knuckles on the desk.

"Why did you pull Walker off the data recovery?"

Collins arched an eyebrow. "It was necessary. That's all you need to know."

"Are you going to tell me who's going to follow up on the computer files, or is that something I have to handle myself now? First Lenny gets pulled off, and he doesn't even have a murder to work anymore, and now Walker. I-"

"Stop right there. I need Walker to look into something. Right now, you and Walker are the only ones I don't have to second-guess around here, and this is something that I would have put you on if you weren't too busy with the Garrett murder. What progress have you made?"

Farraday felt his neck burn.

"Some of Garrett's neighbors were, uh, spending time together and both saw a vehicle parked outside after 10 pm. One recalled the fact that it had a personalized license plate and that the color was black or dark blue. The woman remembered seeing two men get in the vehicle with Graeme, and they both said the vehicle was speeding. Thanks to Garrett's own campaign for safer streets, the intersection they went through had a trial red-light camera. We had four possible vehicles."

"Had?"

"Only one fits the time, description and has a personalized license plate."

"Sounds solid. Are you bringing someone in?"

"You mean, I should just go down to City Hall and pick up the mayor?"

Collins blanched. "Are you telling me the vehicle is registered to Walter Morrow?"

Farraday nodded. "The one and only."

Collins was silent for a moment. "We need to have a solid case before we accuse the mayor. He probably wasn't even in the vehicle. I highly doubt he's guilty of shooting Garrett himself; people like him always keep themselves insulated. And, without a more definite time of death, we can't be certain that the men in the vehicle were responsible for the murder."

"That's true. Dr. Lessard put the time of death at likely between two and four am, but this was much earlier. Ideally, I would try to track Garrett's movements and see if I can disprove a statement from Walter Morrow to implicate him or his people. I'd like to see if Walker finds any hard evidence about the drug trade, and the connections to this precinct. If we have some solid evidence we might be able to get someone to roll."

Collins nodded thoughtfully. "So that leaves you needing Walker's information before you can approach Morrow."

"I could handle this other thing so that Walker can keep going through the files."

"No. Do your best to come up with another angle. If you've exhausted all your other leads in the next few days, we'll plan a chat with the mayor."

Farraday nodded, walking out the door without further comment.

***

Lara removed her shoes and coat, dropped her bag in the closet and was about to walk straight upstairs when Farraday touched her arm.

"What are you doing here?"

"I do live here," Farraday said. "At least, for the moment."

She forced a smile. "I guess I didn't expect you so early," she said, glancing at the clock. It was just past 5 pm.

"What's wrong?" he asked her.

"What makes you think something's wrong?"

"You weren't startled because I was here early; you were startled because you were so deep in thought you didn't even see me. What's on your mind?"

"Right now, the smell of whatever you have cooking. My stomach is rumbling."

She moved to the stove, pulling off a lid and inspecting the contents. Using a spoon to sample the sauce, she moved over to the sink to rinse it off. As she turned, Farraday put his hands down against the counter on either side of her and glared at her.

"Do you know where liars go, Miss Kelly?"

"Into politics. This does smell good. What is it?"

"Don't let me interrupt you," Trin said, arching an eyebrow as she glanced at Lara. Farraday moved away and Trin winked, leaving Lara unsure if she should be relieved she'd gotten off the hook, or embarrassed at Trin's insinuations.

CHAPTER 13

"Walker."

"You're a new one," a gruff voice asserted. "It's Lessard. I need to see you immediately."

"I'm on my way."

It didn't take long for Walker to get to the ME's lab.

Dr. Lessard was eating a piece of cold pizza. "Breakfast. Want a slice?"

Walker ignored him. "Did you find something?"

"You think this is a social call?" He pulled out a file and removed a report. "I confirmed the blood is human, type O, HIV-positive and the quantity found at the scene hints at a murder."

"Hints? We don't open murder investigations on hints."

"Keep your shirt on, Walker. There was a large volume of blood retrieved. It's outlined in the report. From the lack of spatter and the nature of the pooling, it appears your victim was stabbed or shot, moved and set down on the porch and then picked up in an effort to transport him."

"There wasn't much blood on the stairs."

The ME shrugged. "Perhaps his killers set him down to wrap his body in a sheet or plastic. It's been known to happen, Officer."

Walker glared at Lessard. "I know that. You said the victim was HIV-positive. Did you find any evidence of drugs?"

"Well done," Lessard nodded. "Heroin."

"Anything else I should know?"

Lessard shook his head. "But in case you're wondering, you likely have enough for a warrant on the house."

***

"Son of a bitch." Detective Jones pushed the words out through clenched teeth as he stared at the newspaper.

Lenny Becker glanced at him quickly as he drove. "Typo in your personal ad?"

"That damn reporter leaked the hotel story."

"What? How the hell would anyone get the info?"

"Well, it wasn't from me." Jones said, glaring at Becker.

"Hey, don't look at me. I've got no love for the press," Becker said dismissively. "Somebody else must be the source. Who's the reporter?"

"Larimer Kelly."

Becker whistled. "Her name keeps coming up, doesn't it?"

"Maybe it's time to shut her up."

"It might be wise to steer clear of that girl. She blew the lid off the Douglas murder."

"She's going to find herself on the other side of one of those news stories if the boss has anything to say about it."

***

Lara stepped out of her jeep and turned to lock the door. Farraday had some background research to do for his case and they'd agreed to meet up. She turned and jumped, then took a deep breath as she recognized the detective standing behind her.

"Well, well. Miss Kelly. We haven't had the pleasure." The voice had a hostile edge to it, the eyes had no hint of warmth and Lara could hear her heartbeat accelerating. She reached behind her waist, pretending to tuck in her shirt.

"Detective Becker. Is there something I can do for you?"

He stepped forward and seemed to get taller, glowering down at her. "You could promise to be a good little girl and stick to classifieds and feature pieces and be thankful for each pleasant day that you have to enjoy living."

They stood still, staring at each other for a moment.

"Stirring up trouble could get you hurt. You should know that."

"Are you threatening me, Detective Becker?"

"Me?" He leaned closer, giving her a wry smile as he shook his head. "*I* would never think of doing such a thing. But it would be wise for you to take my advice." He looked her up and down as she backed into the jeep door. "I can think of other things you could be doing."

She swallowed hard, about to speak, but didn't get the chance.

"Lenny. Keeping busy?"

Becker turned away from Lara, who watched the hard edge of his face smooth into a casual grin. "How's your case going?"

"You know how it is. One step forward, three steps back."

"We have a suspect. Some young punk with a list of arrests as long as your arm."

"No charges?"

"Kid gets off every time."

"That should make the captain happy," Farraday said sarcastically.

"Yeah, I'm sure. I better run. Jones is keeping a tight leash on me."

Farraday nodded. He watched Becker walk away and then turned to Lara.

"What was that about?"

"I'm not really sure." Lara paused. "You failed to mention that you aren't working with Becker on this case." She stared at him for a moment and then shook her head. "I don't believe this. You're working alone."

Farraday didn't say anything for a moment. "Walker is working the case with me, but we're not on the street together."

"You're tracking a murderer, working a very high-profile case that could implicate people who've shown they'll do anything to avoid exposure and you've been lecturing me. You have some nerve."

"It didn't start this way. Becker was supposed to be working with me."

"After the earful I just got, I'm glad he isn't." Lara's cell phone rang. The call lasted only a few seconds and when she hung up she told him, "I have to go."

She got into her jeep, reached for the door, but Farraday was holding it. "You're angry."

"Yes," Lara said levelly. "But not for the reason you think."

He moved out of the way. She glanced in her rearview mirror once. He stood watching her as she drove away.

***

"What's going on?" Lara asked, sidestepping the stains on the floor as she walked into the back entrance of the Hare household.

The inside was tastefully designed with wood trim and muted colors. Lara scarcely noticed anything else, moving against the wall to make room for the crime scene techs as they arrived.

"Search warrant," Collins said. "There was enough evidence from the blood to get a judge to give us access."

Walker appeared and filled her in on what he'd learned from Lessard.

"HIV-positive?" she asked.

"You wore gloves, right?" Walker asked.

Lara nodded. "I'm always careful. It's not that. The girl who brought me... she said she was his girlfriend."

Collins shook his head. "Then suggest she get tested, but you can't tell her why. Medical information is privileged."

"Isn't that privilege waived if the victim is dead?"

"Depends on what judge you get lately."

"Do we know if we have a murder?" Lara asked.

"Volume of blood would strongly suggest the victim is dead. We found the goldmine in the hallway," Walker said. "Spatter patterns suggest stabbing or a vicious beating." Someone down the hall called him and he walked away.

"Guess you'll be able to take another headline," Collins told Lara.

"Right now, I don't know if I want it." She lowered her voice. "I need to talk to you."

Collins followed her outside. "Don't tell me David Douglas came to your office and threatened you again."

"He didn't threaten me, but one of your officers did. Lenny Becker tracked me down this morning." She pulled out her recorder and played the conversation for him, watching his lip curl into a sneer as he listened.

"He's careful enough to say that he would never hurt you himself. What do you want to do?"

"I want you to hold on to this. And keep it quiet."

Collins looked away for a moment, hands in his pocket. She couldn't tell exactly what he was thinking.

He turned back, face blank. "Alright. We'll keep this quiet. For now."

***

Farraday hung up after trying Walker's cell again, and walked into the office. He'd barely taken three steps toward his desk before a receptionist approached him.

"Can you handle this?"

"I'm on the Douglas case. You'll have to find somebody else."

"Do you see anybody else around?"

Farraday opened his mouth to speak but never got the chance.

"You'll have to take it," she said, pushing the note into his hand. He sighed as he read it, scratching his head.

When he got to the crime scene, Farraday swallowed. Things were still quiet at the smoldering cabin on the old motel property, with only the first responding officer present on the scene.

He showed his ID and asked when the ME would get there. The officer's face lengthened. "Soon," he said.

Farraday observed his pale green shade and forgave him for the lack of information. He approached the body that was visible just inside the door of the cabin's shell, which stood charred and was still smoking in some places. It was unusually quiet for a suspected arson-homicide. He'd beaten the fire trucks.

Farraday turned. "How did this call come in?"

"My partner and I were on patrol and saw the smoke. We phoned it in."

He looked at the squad car, the bent form of another officer hanging out the passenger side door.

Farraday turned to study the body, which was curled in the fetal position, and tried to choke back the bile rising in his throat, fighting his own repulsion at the sight of the blackened flesh, the stench threatening his lunch.

Lessard, the crime scene staff and a fire crew arrived, trying to sort out their respective roles. The scene was a mess because the cops who'd arrived first had used fire extinguishers, apparently afraid that the blaze might spread, and for some reason that Farraday had missed, the fire chief had come out personally to lecture the uniformed officers involved. He decided to avoid that conversation.

As he went to talk to Lessard, he noticed a small group of kids had gathered near the old main building of the former Doe Lake Motel. Most of the kids were smoking, chatting casually, watching the scene with interest, and there were a few girls huddled together, whispering as they glanced at the firemen. One girl in particular caught Farraday's attention.

She was staring at the cabin, a wild look of fear and fury on her face. Her dark hair shadowed her pale face, and for one brief second her eyes met Farraday's and he saw a desperate look, not the casual indifference of the other spectators.

One of the firemen stopped to speak to him for a moment and when he turned back to the spectators, the girl was gone.

***

Collins looked Farraday up and down. "Sitting too close to the fire?"

"Didn't you hear?" Detective Oslind asked as he walked by. "Farraday got his first human barbecue."

Collins sighed. "Care to fill me in?" he said, gesturing to his open door.

"Don't glare at me. It's not my fault," Farraday said once the door was closed. He sat down.

"You're working the Garrett case."

"Nobody else was here and somebody had to take this call."

"What have you got?"

"Two officers on patrol saw a fire at the old Doe Lake Motel, the one that's closed down. One of the cabins burned down to a shell, with a male victim inside."

"Some kid fooling around who started a fire by accident?"

"That would be too easy. There was no identification on the victim. Tech's found external incendiary devices used to start the fire. The victim was either caught inside by accident, or on purpose."

"Well, you'll have to work it now, unless I can find a convincing reason to transfer the case. Walker won't be able to move on the Garrett data as quickly as we'd hoped, so this is something that can keep you busy while we wait."

Farraday frowned, wondering what had happened to solving this case quickly, taking advantage of the possible link to corruption in the department.

"Can I give you some advice, Ty?"

Farraday felt his forehead pinch but nodded automatically.

"We both know that working as a cop involves a certain amount of risk. I worry about every officer under me every day, just a little. And with you I know there's always a chance…" Collins looked up. "I also know that I would never hold you back from a case just because it was dangerous. You are a cop; this is what you do. I would do everything I could to protect you, but the job is part of who you are."

"I know that. You always understood that."

"Your dad doesn't."

"Uncle Con…"

Collins held up his hand. "Do you think you could put your nephew or your son in this position?"

"Look, Trin made her own choices and I-"

"This isn't about your sister."

"Then what are you getting at?"

"Lara." Collins pointed a finger at him. "Your whole life you've been surrounded by strong women: your mother, your sister, both of your grandmothers before they passed away. You have to accept that Lara is willing to put herself on the line to make sure her stories are solid. Her job has risks but doing it well, doing it right, seems to be important to her. If you try to hold her back she won't be the person I-"

Farraday jumped to his feet. "You wanted her off the Douglas case yourself."

"And you didn't try to persuade her to drop that, when she was in real danger. Why argue with her over work now?"

"I... I just think she should take some time." The words were hollow, and he knew it. "She's been through a lot."

"Lara isn't the only one, and you're trying to solve the murder of the man who assaulted her."

"Which is a pretty damn good reason she should take some time, don't you think?"

"It doesn't matter what I think. Lara's going to do what she wants, whether I like it or not. And if you fight her on it, you'll lose."

Farraday yanked the door open, stomped out and slammed the door behind him.

***

Farraday was relieved when he got the call from Dr. Lessard, hoping there would be something new, something to focus on besides paperwork. He'd been trying to establish solid links between the vehicle Graeme had been seen getting into and any regular drivers but the red-light ticket was the only violation he could find.

Trying to identify the weapons involved, particularly looking for guns reported lost or stolen within a month of the murder, hadn't turned up anything.

Today, none of this lack of progress mattered. He didn't even realize he was whistling until he walked into Dr. Lessard's lab and Lessard stopped eating, even as he raised his fork, his usually pinched face widening.

"Well, well," Lessard said, "is a shake and bake corpse all it takes to make you happy?"

Farraday stopped whistling, but flashed a smile at Lessard. "Given the factors at the scene, shouldn't we call this one 'country fried'?"

"Your friend here was likely the reason for the fire. He was dead before it started."

The pathologist rambled on about the lack of carbon monoxide in the lungs in detail until his face beamed with evidence of the approaching climax.

"He was stabbed."

"Where?"

"Not at the scene of the fire."

Farraday groaned. "Where on his body?"

"Six stab wounds in the chest. This young fellow didn't stand a chance."

"Is young just in relation to you, or do you have something to base that on?"

Lessard glared at him. "Well, the fire wasn't hot enough to turn him into a pile of ashes, which gave me enough to work with. Based on the wear and tear of the bones I've examined, I'd say he's between twelve and twenty-two years of age. I like to leave a wide margin of error in my preliminary exams, but my gut tells me he's in his mid-teens.

"See." he said, nodding to a pile of blackened belongings. "The clothes. Not useless, since he was curled up in a ball. Stylish jeans and a sweater with enough of a logo left to tell me it was from some nefarious band that sells noise pollution."

"So this is why you read the fashion magazines and Rolling Stone," Farraday said.

Lessard stared at him, his lips curling downwards. "No. I read them because I'm a symbol of popular culture. It looks like a knife with a five-inch blade.

"And, to be as thorough as always, I have come up with a list of factors that should help you put a name to the face." He paused. "Or maybe a name that will help you find the real face. This one is a little discolored."

"You have the humor of a Brit, you know."

"Funny that I'm French, isn't it?"

"Maybe your personality is trying to compensate for your bloodline." Farraday knew Lessard went the extra mile for detectives he liked to spar with, and he couldn't relax like this at the station but there was something about the stark reminder of your own mortality that an ME's examination room evoked, something that made him feel the need to take himself less seriously. He'd heard some cops say it was the subconscious awareness that it could be your body on the table one day but Farraday suspected it had more to do with the gruff disposition of the ME and his ability to take Lessard at face value, never worrying about the pathologist having ulterior motives, withholding information, trying to throw a case.

"There's a reason you made detective young," Lessard said, shaking his head. "To think, the first time I met you I thought you were stuffy."

Farraday ignored that. "The factors you were going to give me..."

"Ah, yes. There was a tattoo on the left arm, as yet I haven't been able to identify it, but I plan to take another peek for you. He also had two earrings in the left ear. Type O blood, HIV-positive, and heroin in his system." Dr. Lessard paused. "This is similar to something else I was working on, some blood that was missing a body. Same base factors. Enough blood found at that scene to certify death, and it was Type O, HIV-positive, and had heroin in the system. Not enough to overdose on."

"Do you think you could do a comparison, let me know if you come up with a match? Did you find enough blood to identify it as the crime scene?"

"Not initially, but that Walker fellow was back with more, and that time they did have the crime scene under their thumbs. That's where I was before I came to see you yesterday."

Farraday paused. "You don't mean Rob Walker, do you?"

"That's the one. Unless there are two of them running around working cases. Common enough name."

"Was Captain Collins at the scene?"

"Yes. Now you look almost as sullen as you usually do."

Farraday's frown deepened. "Have you gotten any more test results back yet on Susan Douglas?"

Lessard nodded and filled him in. Basically, it filled in a few holes, but didn't do anything to help them move the investigation forward.

"When can I get a report on that?"

"I'll finish it tonight, or first thing tomorrow."

"Thanks. How soon before you can confirm if there's a link between my victim and theirs?"

"I'll put a rush on it. Collins got approval for some things to go through private labs, so it won't take long. I'll call you as soon as I have anything."

"Thanks," Farraday said as he left, wondering what the hell was going on.

***

The conservative school clothes clashing with the wildness Lara sensed in Kaitlin. She couldn't put her finger on it, but there was something about the face that made her certain this girl was a hell raiser.

Kaitlin's hopeful look had evaporated when Lara looked her in the eye. "You haven't found him?" There was still the lilt of a question in those words, a lingering trace of hope.

Lara shook her head, leaning back against her desk. "No, we haven't."

The girl's lip quivered, but she held herself together. "Are you, do you...? What happens now?"

Lara sat down on the chair beside her, looking her in the eyes. "Kaitlin, how involved were you with Allan?"

"I told you, he's my boyfriend."

Lara swallowed. "Have you been intimate?"

Kaitlin's face went chalky white for a second before turning red.

"You should see a doctor and make sure you get a physical. Even if you used protection, you should make sure everything's okay."

"I didn't come to you because I needed a mother!" Kaitlin stood up and backed away from Lara, moving toward the door.

"And I don't want to be your mother, but I have reasons for saying this. Allan's drug use could have resulted in infections and diseases that he could have given to you."

Kaitlin spun around, her lip quivering. "You know? How do you know about the drugs?"

Lara wasn't sure exactly what she was seeing in Kaitlin's expression. The girl's face twisted with emotion as she fought for control. Lara had a split-second to measure how much honesty she felt the girl was ready to take.

"Look, Kaitlin, you asked me to look for your missing friend. You asked for my help. It's hard for me to do that if you're not being honest with me." She paused. "I'm not here to judge you. I'm just trying to give you the help you asked for."

"Then all you have to do is find Allan and leave us alone!"

"No. I have to know what I'm getting into. If you really want me to find Allan, you have to be prepared to tell me where to go to look for him. I need to know everything. Where you hung out, where he scored his drugs. I either let the police take charge of this and they'll come and question you, or you level with me. There's no middle ground here."

She watched Kaitlin, her hands covering her face, her head dropped, the long hair cascading down.

When the girl finally looked up she sighed. "Okay. You win. I'll tell you what you want to know."

***

Farraday sat down on the hard chair in the motel room. Walker rubbed his eyes.

"This is torture. You can only stare at a computer screen for so long."

"Anything interesting?" Farraday's burn victim wasn't far from mind. Collins had kept him out of the loop... Farraday wouldn't be working on the fire victim if Collins didn't think he could handle another case, which made him wonder what it was about Walker's case that Collins didn't want him involved with.

His eyes suddenly focused on Walker's expectant look. "Sorry. Can you repeat that? My mind was elsewhere."

"No problem. I heard you got a tough case, not like this investigation isn't enough."

Farraday leaned back and scratched his head. "I've hit a wall with Garrett's murder and Collins is holding me back until we know if there's something here we can use."

Walker shook his head. "All of the business documents so far are legit. He had an unquenchable interest in seamy adult entertainment. Almost half of these discs are porn and another third are standard office documents. I have ten or eleven blank discs, and another thirty that I haven't gone through. I'm labeling them all, and each of them is being catalogued, whether there's one file, none or a dozen."

"I'm sure you're being thorough."

"So what about this other case? Any leads? Do you have an ID on the victim?"

"Not yet." Farraday decided to take a gamble. "What about this other thing you're looking into? Anything interesting?"

"It's been great to get a chance to get on the street and test myself. Not that I haven't enjoyed this. It's a relief to get out of uniform."

"Are you thinking of taking your exams?"

"I already have. I just about blew my move up over Duane Brodie's video."

"How's Megan?"

"She's okay. It hasn't been easy, losing her sister, her dad's arrest. We're going to a counselor, more as a precaution. Just to make sure she works through it." Walker was quiet for a moment before he nodded at Farraday. "Lara looks like she's doing alright, all things considered."

Farraday paused. "I didn't know you'd seen Lara."

Walker looked back at the computer. "Yeah, I've run into her a few times." He cleared his throat. "She seems to be doing well."

Farraday was about to respond when his cell phone rang. When he finished the call, he said he had to go.

"Hopefully, I'll be through with this early next week," Walker said.

Farraday nodded and walked away.

***

"We have a match," Lessard said. "Your burn victim is the same person who died at Rob Walker's crime scene."

"That was quick."

"Somebody had a head start on the tests. I finally have an assistant that pays attention. Plus, with those cases in the county and all the news stories alleging lab screw-ups and incompetence, we're being pushed to turn stuff around fast. No excuses, no messes, no shortage of money or staff for the moment. Violent crimes get top priority."

"With Walker's evidence and mine, we'd have an ID and potentially a list of suspects to start looking at."

Lessard put the file on the counter. "Are you going to tell them, or should I?"

***

When Lara got to the Doe Lake Motel, she was surprised to find Walker and Collins, already there.

"I got a call," she said. "Lessard wanted to see me here."

They both nodded. "Same here."

"Quite a coincidence. My source on the missing boy says that a group of teens use this old motel sight as a hang-out. She called it 'Dope Lane'. They get high and then come off the stuff in the cabins."

"And we wonder why people go to the press instead of the police," Walker muttered. "I could just see some teenager wanting to tell me where they score their drugs."

Lara smiled. "I threatened to send you after her to get her to spill it."

"Did you persuade her to get an HIV test?" Collins asked.

She shrugged. "I did everything I could without telling her why. But it brought up the issue of the drugs and she was terrified that I'd found out what they'd been up to."

They turned as another vehicle pulled into the driveway. Dr. Lessard got out of his car and walked over to where they stood.

"You have something?" Walker asked.

"Your body. Farraday's corpse, done Cajun-style."

Lara's head snapped up involuntarily as she felt her eyes widen. She stared at Collins. "What do you mean, Farraday's?"

"He was the only one in the station when the call came in. He had to take it."

"Am I calling Walker or Farraday on this one?" Lessard asked.

Collins was silent for a moment before he finally answered, "I haven't decided."

Lessard turned but Lara stopped him.

"Since you're here, maybe you could fill us in on any other clues we could look for that would match the factors of the case. Now that we know we have a body, I'm wondering if we can establish any plausible link between the drug use and the Hare kid's murder."

Lessard grunted. "All I can tell you is that he used heroin, an exceptionally pure cut, and he was likely a shooter, if that's how he contracted the HIV. Or he could have slept around, could have been assaulted by somebody infected, or could have been born with the disease. I don't connect the dots between the facts of the case and the reasons for the murder."

Lara shook her head. "I'm not asking you to support inferences. I'm wondering if there is any specific evidence we could look for that would substantiate a connection."

"From a physical standpoint, not at this point. I haven't finished my final report on Hare's death. Now if you don't mind," Lessard said, "I get dizzy when I'm away from my chemicals too long."

Walker laughed and Lara found an involuntary smile tugging at her lips. This would be in the paper tomorrow and her name would be on the story, which pushed the smile off her face. She sighed. She'd have to deal with Farraday later.

"What exactly are you thinking?" Walker asked. "Do you think Hare might have known something about the drug trade, and been killed because of it?"

"One of his buddies could have had a grudge and killed him," Collins said.

"For all we know, it could have been a random attack. But look at the facts. He was attacked at home, he was brought here to Dope Lane and he was put into a cabin. The cabin was set on fire."

Collins nodded. "It's too much of a coincidence. This was the deliberate murder of a teenager."

"A fifteen-year-old with a rap sheet as long as your arm," Walker said. "Allan Hare was busy racking up charges and dismissals. There isn't a single arrest that's stuck until trial or even resulted in a plea."

"What kind of charges are we talking about?" Lara asked.

"Trespassing charges, stemming from confrontations with girlfriends that turned into altercations with unhappy fathers. One of those turned into an assault charge, which was also dropped. There were also break and enter charges at Oakridge High School, and a vandalism charge at St. Christopher Secondary School."

"So there aren't any drug-related charges," Collins concluded.

Walker shook his head. "The most serious charge is for assault on Bruce Parks September 24th."

"Bruce Parks?" Lara asked.

Walker nodded his head, elaborating. "Apparently, Allan was involved with Bruce Parks' daughter. The girl's parents refused to let her see him anymore. Allan confronted her dad and it got physical."

"Have you talked to him yet?" Lara asked.

Walker shook his head. "The charges were dropped four days later, without explanation. He looked like he might take the fall on that one too. From what I've been able to piece together so far, it seems like he was the kind of spoiled rich kid who needed a wake-up call from community service or juvenile detention to keep him from becoming a serious problem."

"I wonder why he dropped the charges," Lara said.

Walker shrugged. "There's no explanation. I was going to talk to him myself."

"I remember hearing about that incident," Collins said. "He made a scene and demanded that they lock Hare up for the night. From what I heard, Allan Hare's father and Bruce Parks had to be pulled off each other in the lobby of the police station."

"And then he just dropped the charges?" Walker asked. "That doesn't make sense."

"We're going to have to track down the kids on the drug scene here, as well as question Mr. Parks and follow up on all the charges against Hare," Lara said. "I-"

"You will write what you have about the body and the scene, but stay away from the drug trade," Collins said. "If this is the break I've been looking for, I want to make sure nobody gets in the way of an arrest."

"You don't have to worry about me." Lara said. "I'm not going to jeopardize this investigation."

Collins drew a breath. "I know that. I know. But I mean it. I want you staying out of this. I'll give you everything there is to put out. Just let Walker follow this now."

"I brought this to you. You can't cut me out. I can't just hand my source over and expect her to talk to you."

"Lara, we have no idea what the scope is. This could be nothing more than an altercation between some guys when they were high that got out of hand and somebody wasn't prepared to let Allan Hare walk away from it. It might go nowhere."

She stared back at him. "And that's why you shouldn't take me out of the loop. You might hinder an investigation that's about nothing more than a jealous girlfriend, or an angry father avenging his daughter's innocence. There are a lot of potential angles to look at. You can't cut me out on a hope and a hunch."

Collins turned away from them. His back was rigid and his hands were pushed down in his pockets, his neck stiff. Lara couldn't see his face, so she didn't have any idea what he was thinking. He finally turned back.

"There may be a way to handle this. But I want you," he said, pointing at Lara, "to stick to ex-girlfriends and angry fathers. Walker will handle the drug scene." He looked at Walker who affirmed that with a nod and then turned back to Lara. "Do we have a deal?"

She held up her hands in surrender. “For now.”

“Okay. This goes no further than the three of us until I give the word.” He walked away briskly, not looking back.

Chapter 14

ara spent the rest of the afternoon chasing down dead-ends from the trail of broken hearts Allan Hare had left behind,

The list of lovelorn girls she'd worked through was filled with variations on a theme, teenagers who had already acquired more relationship experience by the age of thirteen than she had in her twenty-plus years. So misguided, so dependent on a relationship that they weren't able to just enjoy being young.

She thought of that look she'd seen in Kaitlin's eyes, the look of a dozen girls she'd known in high school who felt their self-worth was tied to the approval of a man.

Rob Walker was going to follow up on the vandalism charges, and for now, she had to wait.

One of the things that bothered her about Allan's death was where they'd found his body. Why dump him where druggies were known to hang out?

The only thing that made sense to her at this point was that Kaitlin had found out Allan had exposed her to HIV. She'd gone to his house, confronted him and stabbed him.

That's where the theory faltered. There was no way the stringy thirteen-year-old could have moved his body without help.

Who would she call? A friend? Her father? And her father could have done it himself, knifed the boy and then deliberately left him at Dope Lane in the hopes that the police would make a dent in the drug trafficking.

If Bruce Parks knew Allan Hare was still seeing Kaitlin…

Lara was still considering the possibilities in her mind when Hatcher had stopped by to lecture her for not spending enough time in the office. She said she wasn't feeling well and walked out.

Which wasn't exactly a lie, since Hatcher made her sick.

***

Farraday spent the morning searching Vern Fletcher's apartment. It was a shell of a home, with not much there to even suggest a personality, never mind a life or a motive for murder. He'd turned up nothing.

After that, he'd searched the other properties Garrett owned, by the lake. They were serviceable cabins that were as spartan as Fletcher's apartment. Each had a bed, a couple of chairs, basic supplies, but nothing more. Not even fishing poles. Farraday couldn't figure out what Garrett did with the cabins, and combing through the buildings himself did nothing to move his case forward.

The investigation into Susan Douglas' murder was also at a standstill. Legal wrangling over DNA tests and waiting for results on what they did have were keeping him from making a formal arrest. He still believed David Douglas was guilty, given the fact that they knew whoever had been there that night was a blood relation.

But he lacked the evidence to prove it. A search of the grounds where the old Douglas estate was located hadn't turned up the body of Susan's baby either.

Now, he had the murders of Vern Fletcher and Graeme Garrett on his plate, as well as the burned body from Doe Lake Motel, and he felt like each investigation was going nowhere.

***

The next day began early for Lara, again. She found herself waiting at a small playground near the Parks' home, waiting for Kaitlin. She hadn't een able to reach her the night before and wanted to break the news to her before she saw it in the paper.

She looked up to see Kaitlin coming across the street, already wearing her school clothes, her dark hair blowing across her face.

Kaitlin looked at Lara. She stopped, staring at Lara's face, her lips parting with an unasked question.

Lara opened her mouth to speak, then drew a deep breath. "I'm very sorry Kaitlin. I know you cared about Allan, and I didn't want you to hear it from someone else."

Kaitlin nodded, her face turning a deathly white shade as all the color faded. Lara stepped forward and reached for her, afraid she might pass out, but Kaitlin held up her hand.

"I'll be okay. Is there anything else?"

"The police are involved now. I can manage them for you, but you have to be straight with me."

Kaitlin nodded, deflated and defeated. "I'll do whatever I can."

"Your parents should understand if you need to take the day off," Lara said, keeping pace with Kaitlin as she started to leave. The young girl stopped and turned.

She shook her head, backing away from Lara before she spun around and ran down the street.

***

Walker led Farraday around to the back of the Hare household, relaying bits and pieces of the investigation. After Walker indicated he'd told him everything Farraday straightened up and looked Walker in the eye.

"How did this case come in?"

"Collins called me."

Farraday didn't comment on that, though he noted Walker had evaded the question. "You said that Hare died from stab wounds."

Walker nodded. "There was a kitchen knife missing from a set. We haven't been able to confirm if it was missing previously, but judging from how meticulous this house is, it's reasonable to think he was killed with a knife from his own home."

"So he was attacked here, killed with a weapon of opportunity, not something that necessarily indicates a premeditated crime. Why dump his body at the Doe Lake Motel and set fire to the cabin?"

"Good chance it's drug-related. Allan Hare had heroin in his system and the Doe Lake Motel is known as Dope Lane for being frequented by teenage users."

"So this could be as simple as a fight gone wrong with another druggie, or as complicated as some involvement in the supply."

"Or it could be a vindictive father who didn't like his daughter's boyfriend. But I think the Motel is the next place to take a look at."

"Dope Lane it is," Farraday said.

***

Bruce Parks was the president of an investment firm and he fit the part. He had the aura of intelligence, the distinguished look of success, and a game face that left Lara certain he was one hell of a poker player. There wasn't a detectable trace of awareness of who she was or why she'd ask to speak to him; he was completely unreadable.

"Thank you for agreeing to speak with me, Mr. Parks." She sat in the proffered chair feeling the supple leather as she sank into the rich, wine-colored seat. It was a beautiful office, with ornate wood trim and bookshelves of leather-bound volumes, rare paintings showcased on the walls.

Bruce Parks sat down on the other side of his desk and studied her in much the same way she imagined he studied his business reports. There was a calculated interest, evident from his attentiveness, but no emotion. He turned his hands up for a second and waited.

"I work for The Ledger and-" Lara said. He interrupted her.

"Ah, Larimer Kelly. I didn't make the connection when my secretary said your name was Lara." He nodded, as though he had just fit her into a piece of his puzzle and the picture was becoming clearer. "I associate your name with front page news, not the business section."

"I'm afraid it isn't business that brings me here." Lara paused, watching his face closely.

"Oh? I'm not aware of any developments that would make my company the subject of your headlines." His eyes were level, his gaze unflinching.

"I'm afraid it has to do with your daughter."

There was an immediate shadow that darkened his face, the casual deportment with which he carried himself suddenly losing ground to a rigid stance. His jaw tensed, his eyes narrowed, his shoulders rose and stiffened.

"I take it you haven't had a chance to see this morning's paper."

She waited until he shook his head. "Do you know Kaitlin had an... involvement with a boy named Allan Hare?"

His skin started to turn red as lines creased downward from the corners of his mouth. "She was forbidden to see him. He was a bad influence."

"Can you tell me why you dropped the charges against Allan for assaulting you?"

"It was a personal matter. All I wanted was for that boy to stay away from my daughter. We took out restraining orders against him, and were satisfied that he would leave Katie alone." His voice was both curt and quiet, making it hard for Lara to tell what he was thinking. "I fail to see why that concerns you."

"Allan Hare has been murdered," Lara said.

His face seemed to contort with expressions of shock, surprise, a degree of satisfaction and indifference all rolled into one. "When you live the kind of lifestyle that boy indulged in, it's no surprise if you end up stabbed in an alley or beaten to death on the street."

Lara felt the red flag go up. He was just a little too close to the actual manner of death for her liking. It hadn't been her experience to find someone guessing at the manner of death if they didn't know. They usually asked.

"What lifestyle was that, Mr. Parks?"

"Well, I'm certain you're looking into it. Drugs, booze. He may have come from old money but he was little more than a street thug."

"How is it you learned of his relationship with your daughter?"

"My wife found out she'd stolen money so we grounded Katie. The boy turned up at our house and we phoned the police."

"Was this the night of September 24th?"

"I see you've done your homework. Of course, if there is any way I can help with the investigation, I will, but I don't see what this boy's death has to do with my family. Unless you're asserting that one of us had something to do with his murder."

"It isn't my job to identify suspects. I'm just trying to ensure my background information is correct and I am also concerned for your daughter. Teenagers often have difficulty listening to their parents.

Kaitlin may take the news of his death rather hard."

There was a change in his eyes, something elusive that Lara couldn't easily identify. He then swallowed and nodded, and spoke. "Of course, Miss Kelly. I shall have my wife remove Katie from school and speak with her." He lifted his phone and asked his secretary to call his wife immediately. As he waited, he looked at Lara. "Can I be of further assistance?"

She shook her head. "I'll be in touch if there's anything else I think of."

Lara stood up and turned to leave, stopping to study a framed picture and newspaper article on the wall. Bruce Parks and David Douglas were shaking hands, smiling at the camera. Lara felt Bruce Parks' eyes watching her. She noted Mr. Parks remained silent and glanced at the desk. He was holding the phone to his shoulder, waiting for her to leave. She smiled a flimsy apology and left.

***

Farraday gave Walker a few minutes to look around the burned-out cabin before he shared his theory.

"My guess is whoever killed Allan Hare wanted to make a statement. They dropped his body in this cabin and used jars of gas with fabric fuses to start the fire from each corner."

Walker nodded. "Simple."

"But effective. If it wasn't for the officers who spotted the smoke, there would have been considerably less left by the time we got here. They used a few extinguishers to stop the fire, which is how they found the body."

"They didn't call the fire department?"

"Yes, but the nearest station was already on a call, and there was a delay in estimated response time. The officers were concerned about trying to stop the spread of the fire to the woods. I doubt they thought much about it at all, just thinking that they may as well get their hands dirty. The smell of burning flesh slowed them down, though."

"I've heard burned bodies are nasty to deal with."

Farraday nodded. His stomach lurched just thinking about it. "Hare was no saint. He had angry fathers phoning the police on him, more ex-girlfriends than I can count and he was HIV positive. This could be as simple as any ex-girlfriend who learned they were infected coming after him for revenge."

Walker nodded. "I agree. But what about dumping the body here and setting fire to the cabin?"

"Could be where they hung out."

"Then isn't it likely they were both in on the drug scene? I mean, since we know Hare was at least a user and because of the rumors about the motel?"

Farraday turned. "When I was here, there was a group of teenagers watching us. There were about a dozen teenage boys standing around the main building, wearing winter caps and no coats. There were also a few girls here."

"We should talk to those kids."

"You think they're going to be eager to chat with the police? To begin with, this is private property and they're trespassing. We suspect them of committing illegal acts on the premises. We'll have to take them all to the station to get them to talk."

"Or we could let Lara talk to them," Walker said. Farraday stared at him, and Walker flinched. "She does have a way of getting people to talk to her without feeling threatened."

"I don't think it's a good idea."

"Surveillance then? We could catalogue the kids and follow up with interviews at home or school."

"If we can identify them." Farraday sighed. "I guess we'll be busy tonight. You may as well go home and spend some time with Megan." He looked at his watch. "We'll meet here at six o'clock."

***

Farraday stopped at The Ledger parking lot and snuck into Lara's office but it was empty.

He wasn't surprised, but he was disappointed. They hadn't talked much since their argument and with Trin at the house it was hard to catch Lara alone. He was beginning to wonder if that was part of the reason Lara hadn't objected to Trin staying there. Not just for him to spend time with his sister, but as a buffer between them, so he couldn't really talk to her about what had happened. Which also left them unable to talk openly, the way they had before. They'd gone from open distrust to sharing confidences, and now back to reasonably polite formality. He knew he was partially to blame for that, for trying to persuade her to take it easy.

Farraday walked around behind her desk and picked up her phone, dialing her cell.

After four rings the call went to voice mail. He left a quick message, saying he was in her office hoping to track her down and then he hung up, wondering if he should look for Jimmy to see if he knew where Lara was.

The door opened and a giant figure thundered into the office. The imposing man stopped when he saw Farraday and then he sneered.

"What are you doing at my reporter's desk?" he demanded.

"Looking for Lara. Do you know where she is?" Ted Hatcher's reputation preceded him and he lived up to the negative image of the overbearing dictator Collins had described him as.

"If you were any kind of investigator you should be able to find her without my help, Detective Farraday."

"Oh, I will. Don't worry." Farraday moved as if he was intending to leave, but Hatcher stepped in front of him.

"What the hell are you up to?"

"Lara is a friend, and I need to speak with her. It's none of your business."

"It is when you're feeding her front-page headlines and pulling her out on the street when I've assigned her desk duty."

Farraday felt his spine straighten. He stared back at Ted Hatcher's angry face. "If you're referring to the Lakeview Hotel story-"

"I'm not. Your little games might work on lesser minds that you can manipulate, but I'm not a fool. You're the lead investigator on the Hare homicide."

He felt his eyes narrow, wondering what Hatcher was getting at.

"That's the trouble with women. You come along and she's so busy chasing after you she loses her credibility. Stay the hell away from her."

Lara stepped into the office and stopped. Farraday watched her jaw set as Hatcher turned.

"Where the hell have you been?" he demanded.

"The library," she snapped back. "Doing research."

She folded her arms across her chest. "Is there a problem here?" she demanded, looking at Hatcher.

"If you keep ignoring my instructions there will be," he said. Farraday could see his face was dark, his hands balled up into fists.

"I'm doing my job." Lara glared at him. "If you have a problem with that, then you deal with it or I'm done."

Hatcher blanched. "You aren't serious."

"Yes I am," Lara said, pointing a finger at him. "You have no right to meddle in my life or make unfounded accusations, or insinuate that there is anything improper in my relationship with Detective Farraday."

"So you do have a relationship."

"Who I chose to spend time with is my business. I hear another word from you about this and my resignation will be on your desk."

Ted Hatcher snorted. "You just remember the lines you've crossed with me, Miss Kelly. I won't forget this."

Lara moved aside as Hatcher stormed by, slamming the door behind him. She looked up at Farraday. They stared at each other in silence for a moment before she spoke. "What are you doing here?"

"You've had the privilege of a tongue-lashing from my boss, so I thought it was my turn," he said, shrugging as he sat down in one of the chairs. She didn't return the thin smile.

"He had no right to speak to you like that."

"But then I would have missed seeing you put him in his place. I should consider myself lucky that I haven't been on the receiving end of your full temper."

Lara smiled but the expression faded quickly. “Are you here to lecture me?”

“Why would I be?” Farraday asked.

She paused. “You really don’t know?”

“No.”

She retrieved a paper from her desk and sat down beside him as she handed it to him.

He skimmed the headlines, and then zeroed in on the byline. The paper dropped to his lap. “Well, now I know what Hatcher was talking about.”

“What do you mean?”

“He accused me of feeding you another story.”

Lara’s eyes widened. Farraday took a few minutes to skim the article before he tossed the paper onto her desk. He leaned forward and took her hands, his elbows propped up on his legs as he looked up to her.

“Walker and I are working the case together,” he told her. “Is this why he’s choosing his words carefully? Was he your source?”

Lara shook her head. “I was their source.”

Farraday frowned. “How did you get this?”

“Allan Hare’s girlfriend came to me. I swear, I didn’t think it was anything, until I found the damage outside the house. I called Collins right away.”

“And he called Walker.” Farraday bit his lip, recalling his uncle’s warning, about how he was holding Lara back…

“I wondered how Walker knew about the drugs at the motel. He said he’d received some tips.”

Lara shrugged. “He didn’t lie, really.”

“Can you get away for a few hours?”

“Sure. Why?”

“Walker and I are doing surveillance tonight.”

“Dope Lane?”

"Don't get any ideas."

She held up her hands and mouthed the words, "Who me?" to him as she stood up to clear her desk for the day.

***

Farraday was barely five minutes early for meeting Walker. The passenger door opened. Walker passed him a box and slid into the passenger seat, holding a tray.

"Tea and donuts," Walker said, passing Farraday a tray.

Farraday took the drinks and set them in the cup holders. "Thanks."

"Did I miss anything?"

Farraday shook his head. "No. Nothing yet. I can tell there's activity in the main building, but only from irregular shadows and flickering lights." Farraday nodded toward the building as the lights went on and off again. They weren't as bright as room lights, but they couldn't be missed either.

"Flashlights?" Walker suggested.

"It's as good a guess as any," Farraday said. "Lara told me."

Walker sipped his drink and kept his focus straight ahead, fixed on the main building. He turned. "Told you what?"

"That she received the tip from Hare's girlfriend and when she found evidence at the scene she called Collins."

"At least I don't have to worry about putting my foot in my mouth anymore," Walker said, leaning back into the seat. "How long is your sister staying here?"

"I'm not sure. She has another friend working at The Ledger and went out with him tonight." Farraday shrugged. "Right now, I think she's trying to decide what she wants to do."

There was movement at the main house and Farraday focused the camera. He recognized some of the kids from when he'd been there examining the body, glad that it looked like this wouldn't be a complete waste of their time.

***

Dan Van Biers was the kind of person it was easy to underestimate. Trin had done that herself, when she'd first met him.

From external appearances, he was average height, average appearance. Dark hair. She was almost as tall as he was.

He'd always been the one leaning up against a wall with a drink in hand, alone, one of those people that seemed to watch life more than live it. He'd been in his final year of school when she started her studies and for a long time he'd been a subject of curiosity to her, nothing more, until she decided to break the ice. One of the other journalism post-grad students was having a party and that time, when she'd seen Van Biers settled in a corner, she'd gone to talk to him.

They'd been friends ever since, although over the past year she hadn't stayed in touch with him. He hadn't held that against her when she'd first called, a few weeks ago, to say she was in Oakridge.

Dan hadn't even pressured her for an explanation at first, but eventually she'd told him everything.

When he'd called and asked her to meet him for dinner, she'd thought he was just being sociable, but after they'd eaten he'd ordered wine. Once they each had a glass in hand he'd leaned back in his chair.

"I've been working on a story," Dan told her.

There was something in his voice that told her this wasn't just casual conversation or an update on his career. Dan had a reason for talking to her about this, whatever it was. She set her glass down and listened.

***

After soaking in a hot bath and building a fire, Lara's plans for a relaxing evening started to fall apart. It wasn't long before she realized she was glancing at the clock every ten minutes or so. Then she got up for water, then cocoa, then a snack.

She'd been looking forward to reading but now she found it hard to focus so she put the book down, switched off the light and curled up on the couch, closing her eyes.

Sleep had almost claimed her until she heard a sudden bang. She sat up with a start, wondering if Trin was back.

Lara got up and walked into the kitchen, peering out the window. She didn't see a car.

It was a black night. There weren't any streetlights on her road. She wasn't sure if it was just the oppressive darkness playing tricks on her, but she decided to check the house, just to make sure whatever had woken her was nothing more than the cat or her imagination.

Once at the top of the stairs, she cautiously pushed open the doors. Skittles was curled up in a ball on the mattress in the room Trin was using. Her room was empty, as was the bathroom.

Lara walked back downstairs, telling herself she was being hypersensitive, when she gasped. She felt herself being pulled from behind by strong arms that locked her in their hold, a hand clamping down over her mouth. Within seconds she was face down on the couch, her hand pinned under a knee, her head being pulled back by the hair with one hand, her mouth still clamped with the other.

"You little bitch. You just couldn't leave it alone. Who the hell tipped you off about the hotel story? Huh? Who'd you get to feed you the info? You gonna tell me, or do I have to beat it out of you?"

Lara bit into the flesh of the hand hard, refusing to let go, even as the hand was pulled away from her. He let go of her hair and moved up a little, giving her a chance to pull her hands free. She bent her knees and found the couch with her feet, pushing herself up into her attacker.

She didn't stand much of a chance, even facing the steely eyes that were the only part of the face not concealed by the balaclava. He was easily 50 pounds heavier, and muscular.

Lara lunged and landed almost on her knees by the fireplace. She grabbed the first thing her hands found, which was her poker. The man was inching toward her.

He made a few false starts, but she was ready. Her attacker lunged forward and she swung the poker with all her force, slashing his left arm open just below the shoulder. He swore and used the split second when the poker slid off the flesh to grab her arms, prying the tool from her hands and wrenching her arms almost out of their sockets, dragging her toward the stairs.

Lara tried to hook her feet on the coffee table but it was too light to anchor her. She managed to wrap her foot around the leg of the armchair, wrenching hard against his pull. He yanked on her arms and she cried out with the pain, losing her hold.

She heard movement on the porch. There was a rap at the door and she screamed. Her attacker released her arms, her body falling in a heap on the floor. His foot connected with her jaw, but without enough force to do serious damage. Her body went limp as he let go, and she tried to keep her eyes focused as she forced herself up and grabbed his shirt.

He turned to push her off, dragging her across to the patio doors just as the front door burst open. She reached for the balaclava, but lost the tenuous hold she had on him with her aching left hand and saw nothing more than the dark, coarse hair disappear into the black night as she fell again.

Lara felt gentle hands helping her up, even though she winced as he touched the fresh bruises on her arms.

"What are you doing here?" she asked.

"I came to see Trin," Collins answered, helping her to the couch.

"She's out. With a friend," Lara murmured. It was like a blanket of black had covered her brain. She felt the warm trickle of blood in her mouth from the kick to her face, barely aware of the hands guiding her to the couch. Lara didn't know how long she was out of it, just that it seemed like several minutes before she opened her eyes and was able to focus enough to see Collins' face.

"I'm happy to see you," she said when she came to.

"I'll bet." Collins went to the bathroom and returned with a first aid kit. "The Douglas case again?"

Lara was fighting against blacking out again, a hundred thousand points of light flashed through her mind as she tried to focus. "No. He said the hotel story."

"Are you sure?"

She nodded. "He wanted my source on that story."

Collins swallowed, looking at her as though trying to assess if she was lucid enough to be sure. "I didn't see enough to be certain, but he didn't look like Becker."

Lara shook her head. “It wasn’t Becker. I would know his voice. I don’t know who it was.” She winced as he wrapped her left wrist tightly.

“You’re going to be sore in the morning.”

“Oh, I don’t think I’ll need to wait that long.”

***

Farraday sat up. He saw an approaching vehicle pull over and stop in front of the old motel office. It was a dark Land Rover and two men hopped out from the front.

“Get pictures of their faces,” he told Walker, who obliged and didn’t stop shooting until the men went inside the building.

“Who are they?”

“I don’t know. But a witness in the Garrett case stated Garrett got into that vehicle a few hours before his death.”

“Are you sure it’s the same vehicle?”

Farraday nodded. “A second witness remembered the personalized license plates. Now I can take these photos back to the witnesses and see if those were the men who were driving it that night.”

“I thought the connection had something to do with the mayor’s office.”

“That vehicle is registered to the mayor. I’ve been waiting on more information to bring him in.”

“Now you’ve got it, but what does the mayor have to do with the Doe Lake Motel?”

“Maybe more than any of us ever suspected,” Farraday said. “I thought this place was closed.”

They watched for another hour. Nobody else came or went, until the men who’d been driving the vehicle registered to the mayor came back out, this time with a girl.

The same wide-eyed, wild girl Farraday remembered from the fire scene.

He listened to the click of the shutter over and over again, until the sound of whirring indicated another film was full. Walker lowered the camera and popped the back open, removing the film as Farraday waited until the Land Rover was a comfortable distance away, and then started the car.

They followed the vehicle, staying far back because of the lack of traffic on the road. As they got further into the city, it didn't take long for them to lose the Land Rover, especially when they got caught at a red light and then the vehicle in front of them stalled.

For a while they drove up and down side streets, looking for signs of the vehicle, but eventually Farraday admitted defeat. "I'll drop you off at your car," he told Walker.

***

They heard a noise on the porch. Collins stood and went to the hallway, his hand on his gun.

He relaxed and dropped his hand.

Farraday's step faltered when he saw Lara. He didn't speak as he disappeared again, returning with ice packs.

Collins looked at his notebook. "You guess five foot ten, 180 pounds or more. Stocky build, dark hair, blue eyes. Anything else?"

Her smile turned into a wince. "I cut his arm with the poker."

"I already got a sample when you were passing in and out of consciousness. You need to be woken up every few hours to make sure you don't have a serious concussion."

"You aren't filing an official report?" Farraday asked, looking from Lara to Collins.

Collins shook his head. "I don't think it's a good idea. Not if one of my men could be involved."

Lara nodded, wincing again from the motion. "I agree."

Collins left and they listened to the door clicking shut behind him.

"Is this because of the Hare case?" Farraday asked.

Lara smiled ruefully. "It has something to do with the hotel story."

Farraday sat back. "That wasn't what I expected."

"That makes two of us."

Chapter 15

Farraday stoked the fire and secured all the windows and doors, returning to the living room, sinking down on the sofa. He could hear the bath water running upstairs.

There were a lot of obvious differences between Trin and Lara, but there were a lot of similarities too. He didn't know exactly how long he sat there thinking about them, but it was long enough to hear the bath water drain and footsteps in Lara's bedroom.

He walked up the stairs quietly. The bathroom door was shut but Lara's door was ajar.

Farraday reached his hand up to knock but he could see inside the room. Lara was standing by the window, trying to brush her hair without lifting her arm too high, wearing nothing but a long shirt. He was about to retreat when she turned.

"Are you okay?" he asked.

Her hand froze mid-stroke as she stiffened and stared at him for a moment. "I'll be fine."

Farraday crossed the room and reached for her shoulder, turning her to face him. He lifted Lara's chin up with his fingertips and looked her in the eye. "Are you sure?"

They stood staring at each other for a moment, until she blinked. He lowered his hand and turned, walking to the door. He was almost in the hallway before he paused and looked over his shoulder. "See you downstairs?"

Lara nodded.

Once he left, Lara had no sense of how much time passed while she stood rooted to the floor. Part of the reason she liked Farraday was that he wasn't so obvious, wasn't such a relentless flirt, like Jimmy. There was something comfortable about Jimmy's predictability, but she could never take him seriously. Farraday didn't seem to act on impulses, proven the day in the hot tub, and he didn't seem interested in casual flings either

With Farraday, a tenuous truce had eventually been transformed into a deeper trust, and ever since she'd learned Trin's real identity it had been hard not to think about where this might lead but she was also struggling with the fear of losing a friend, the fear of stepping outside the boundaries she'd been comfortable with, the fear of falling into a bad relationship like her mother had so many times before.

The fear that the part of her that was convinced no guy could be as decent as Farraday seemed would be proven right.

***

When she got downstairs she could feel the heat of the fire from across the room and there were mugs of hot chocolate on the coffee table, as well as a platter of cookies.

An awareness of her own fatigue struck her as she studied the wrinkles on his brow, the hint of a shadow under his eyes. Suddenly she was aware of how much she just wanted to lie in her bed and close her eyes. Everything that had happened since the day Duane brought her the tape was like a storm that was moving beyond her control. This time, she couldn't understand the reason for the attack. She had no sense of what she had written that had drawn unwanted attention, rattling someone who felt threatened enough to assault her.

What had it been now? More than a month since Farraday had walked through her office door? Some story this had turned out to be. On TV cases got wrapped up in an hour, two at the most. Even crime fiction novels had cases wrapped up within hours or days, yet here she was, still living with a cop under her roof, being assaulted and not even knowing why.

Susan's murder still wasn't officially closed, they hadn't found her baby, and now there was all this other stuff...

She hadn't thought about the risks much at the beginning, but it was getting harder to rationalize how much danger she might be in. It made it harder to convince herself that everything would be okay, and harder to argue when Farraday wanted to keep her off the streets.

"When's the lecture scheduled for?"

"Very funny. This story was cut and dried. You didn't even do interviews. If anything, it proves that even when you stay off the street you can be at risk. I should have had you with me on surveillance."

"Then we wouldn't have known there was more to the robbery story than we suspected. I'm going to have to follow up with..."

"Lara, you are finished with that story." His voice was firm, his face governed by a no-nonsense look that told her not to argue, just this once. "You have another big story unfolding. You have a choice: To stay at the office, under Jimmy's watchful eye, or to work with me."

"You're going to let me work the case with you?"

"It seems to be the only way I can keep you out of trouble."

Lara smiled. Farraday met her gaze and shook his head, smiling back. "You should go upstairs and get some sleep."

"And leave this great fire for you? I don't think so." Lara went to the closet under the staircase and pulled out some blankets and pillows.

They'd moved a smaller sofa downstairs from the spare room Trin was using. It was just long enough for Lara if she curled her legs up. She lay down and stretched out as much as she could as she looked over at Farraday. "What's so funny?"

"I've missed this."

"People breaking into my house?"

"Don't be ridiculous. Do I have to spell it out for you?"

"I wouldn't want to be accused of jumping to conclusions."

"I've missed you."

She was glad she wasn't looking at him. "You've seen me every day."

"It isn't the same. We haven't been able to discuss cases, share theories, chat without Trin walking in."

"Yeah, well, it hurts for me to talk right now."

"A reporter who needs to have their mouth..."

"Don't go there," she said, glaring at him.

Farraday grinned as he passed her an ice pack.

***

The next morning, after an explanation about what had happened, Trin decided not to wait for her meeting with Dan. She was tired of sitting on the sidelines. From what Lara said, something she'd written recently, something that connected to the hotel robbery, had prompted the latest assault. If Farraday had a theory about how it connected to this case he wasn't sharing, so she took matters into her own hands.

In her shock over the attack, Trin had forgotten to mention what Dan Van Biers had told her. About the information he'd given to Vern Fletcher. About his own leads.

There had been a pensive look on Dan's face that told her he was starting to worry.

Dan had promised to meet her at the library but she went early, so that she could start checking stories online. She'd already familiarized herself with the building, but this time it wasn't as crowded. The librarian came over and introduced herself as Nancy, asking if she needed any help.

"Thanks, I'm fine."

"New in town?"

She shook her head. "Just visiting. I'm staying with Lara Kelly."

"Oh, really? Any friend of Lara's is welcome here, even that detective she's spending so much time with. He's a little hard to talk to." Nancy leaned closer, lowering her voice. "But very handsome."

Trin smiled, but didn't comment. Nancy moved away, replacing returned books on shelves, and she resumed skimming through back issues of The Ledger, reading all of Lara's recent work, as well as all of the coverage about the Lakeview Hotel robbery.

***

Farraday drove Lara's jeep to Fulton Ave. and parked in front of Peter Ainesworth's home. He pulled out the keys and started out the door before he realized Lara hadn't moved. She was staring past him, to the house that was now for sale across the street.

"Are you okay?"

She nodded and turned to get out of the vehicle, then followed Farraday up the walk silently. He knocked at the front door, which was soon opened, a time-wrinkled face peering out suspiciously.

"You again? I thought you were those damn kids with the cookies. If they want to make money here they should be selling denture cream."

From the corner of his eye, Farraday saw Lara cover her mouth, pretending to cough. Peter Ainesworth opened the door and invited them in.

"Lara Kelly," she said, offering her hand.

"Call me Peter," he said, holding her hand for a moment and studying her openly.

Lara glanced at Farraday, who arched his eyebrows and shook his head. "I should keep you or Trin handy at all times," he whispered to her as Peter disappeared into the kitchen for refreshments. "He's far more agreeable."

She felt the color in her cheeks. Peter returned with a platter of cookies, evidently not as opposed to buying treats from kids as he'd first asserted. He set the tray down and made small talk with Farraday about all the fuss over the house listed across the street and the steady parade of alleged clients coming and going from the property.

"No way in the world that all those folks are looking to buy. Showing up with cameras and video machines and all that crap. Sensationalists. They just have to take a look into the house where a monster lived. Damn sick world we live in, where everyone is fascinated by perversion and sin."

The doorbell rang then and Peter sprang out of his chair. Soon a woman's voice could be heard and then Peter returned with his guest.

"Mrs. Halliston. How nice to see you again," Farraday said, standing up to greet her. "This is Lara Kelly, a reporter with The Ledger."

"Huh. You didn't tell me that." Peter's eyes narrowed as he scrutinized Lara. "Aren't you the one I was reading about in the paper last week? You had the story about the Douglas woman and then you were attacked by Garrett before he was arrested."

Lara nodded. "You're right. I worked on the Douglas murder with Detective Farraday."

"Oh, Detective Farraday is it? Don't think I'm so old that I can't recognize sexual tension when I see it, Missy. I may be past my prime, but some things never change between men and women." He turned and winked at Deb Halliston slyly. "And thank God for that."

Farraday coughed. "He who is without sin..."

"Is dull and boring," Peter replied with a quick grin. "As long as those sins are against yourself and not others you'll get no trouble from me."

Farraday pulled out the folder he had in his brief case and handed the photos to Peter.

"Recognize anybody?" Farraday asked.

"Him," Deb said as Peter passed the pictures to her. She pointed at one of the men in the second photo. "I've seen him across the street before."

"Can you recall when?"

"Well, several times. The other man isn't familiar to me, but this one was here the night that fellow died. He was driving so I got a better look at him than the other one."

"Are you sure?" Farraday asked.

She nodded.

Farraday stood. He shook hands with both of them and thanked them for their help.

"If you think of anything else, no matter how small, please call me," he said. After being assured by both of them that they would, Peter closed the door behind Farraday, who caught up with Lara on the walk.

"You know, for a moment your cheeks matched your hair."

Her eyes narrowed every so slightly. "Be thankful my foot is still sore or your backside would be."

Farraday smiled as he followed her to the jeep.

***

Walker was sitting outside the principal's office at St. Christopher Secondary School. He felt like he was checking his watch every thirty seconds, his backside numb from sitting on the wooden bench.

The door opened and the principal stepped forward. Mr. Vincent had the austere look Walker assumed a Catholic school principal should have, dark hair peppered with gray slicked back neatly, a physically imposing demeanor that generated respect by intimidation and narrow, piercing eyes that reminded Walker of a vulture.

Mr. Vincent introduced himself, his voice as cold as his hand.

"I appreciate you taking the time to see me."

The principal led the way back into his office, not even engaging in pleasantries or indulging the polite pretense that he had volunteered his time.

Vincent's office contained only the essentials. There was a single wooden bookshelf in the corner, filled with an assortment of bound books. The desk was adequate but not enormous, and there were two straight-backed chairs for those summoned to his office. Mr. Vincent's own chair looked more comfortable, and there was another long bench against the wall by the door.

"Of course, student records are confidential, and without a subpoena I have no intention of answering questions pertaining to them or any extra-curricular activities they may engage in."

"There's been some confusion, Mr. Vincent. I'm not here about one of your students."

Mr. Vincent arched a stiff black eyebrow. "Certainly this isn't about one of my staff."

"No. I am actually following up on some vandalism charges that were filed at the beginning of the school year."

"Oh." Walker had the sense from the way the principal waved his hand and scowled that he now felt this was a profound waste of his time instead of just an inconvenience. "I do believe the matter was handled, but we appreciate your thorough attention to this matter."

"It isn't the charges I'm following up on. It's the boy who was arrested, Allan Hare."

"He's not a student of this school." The cold eyes seemed to be attempting to bore a hole in the center of Walker's forehead.

"Are you not aware that Allan Hare was recently found murdered?"

Both eyebrows rose but Mr. Vincent didn't speak.

"I'd like to know why you dropped the charges against Hare."

The principal avoided Walker's gaze, but there was a subtle change in the tension of his skin, the bite of the jaw. "It was... felt to be a prudent choice."

"By whom?"

"Our school board. They felt unnecessary charges against a wayward teen would attract negative publicity."

"I see. Who serves on your school board?"

"There's a staff representative, Mrs. Pratt. Three parents. Frank Jensen, John Forbes, Steve Bisley. Michael McClure is on the board this year. He's related to one of our students and is the legal advisor to the school and the board. Cathy Perkins is the church representative and Bruce Parks, a major financial contributor. His daughter is a student here."

"Would it be possible for me to get a copy of the minutes from the board meeting where this matter was discussed?"

"It was an informal meeting and not recorded in an official manner."

"I see. Do you have a report on the vandalism?"

"Officer, I fail to see what this has to do with your investigation."

Walker forced a smile. "In a murder investigation, all leads, no matter how insignificant they seem, must be considered."

"Of course. But I have no record."

"Really? When I was in school, a written report was kept of any damage requiring physical repair, paint or parental involvement. And a record was certainly kept if it involved calling the police."

"Clearly, we were lax in our efficiency." The look the principal was giving him appeared to be one of profound annoyance. Something more elusive lingered beneath the surface, some emotion Walker couldn't be certain of. "Is there any further way in which I can assist you?"

"I'll be in touch if there is." Walker stood to leave, and turned back at the door. "If you think of anything, please call the station and leave a message for me." He dropped one of his new cards on the desk, the ones that said Detective Walker.

He closed the door behind him and marched out of the office without another word, rushing down the steps and almost running into a man coming in. The man was swarthy, a little taller and stockier than Walker, with a scar on his cheek. He grunted as Walker apologized. Walker paused, thinking the face seemed familiar, but the man continued marching down the hall and disappeared into the principal's office.

***

Walker sat down at Farraday's desk. He was checking his list when he heard someone walking toward him and looked up to see Oslind sneering at him.

"What's this? Walker without a uniform? You pretending to work for a living instead of just shacking up with a rich chick?"

"Well well. If it isn't Oslind without a brain. Oh, wait. That's just the normal Oslind."

"You're almost as bitchy as a woman, Walker."

"What happened to your arm? Cut yourself shaving?" There was a bit of dried blood on the sleeve.

There were laughs all around at that jab. Oslind had long been called 'Monkey Man' behind his back and everyone but Oslind knew it.

A swarthy scowl had surfaced on the detective's face, his eyes cold. Just then, Becker and Jones walked in.

"What do you think you're doing?" Becker demanded.

Oslind stood up. "What're you going to do, give me a parking ticket?"

"With your fat ass I'd have to give you three. Is he giving you a hard time?" Becker asked Walker.

"I'm fine," Walker said.

Becker sat at his desk and picked up the phone.

Jones sat down on the edge of Farraday's desk and glanced down at Walker's notes. "What's Farraday got you working on?"

"Oh, just piecing together background on that kid that died," Walker said, looking up at Jones. “What can I do for you?”

“Nothing,” Jones said. He got up and walked away.

***

Farraday strolled into the station and was almost run over. “You,” Oslind sneered, stomping past him.

The force of Oslind’s arm pushing him turned Farraday halfway around and he watched Oslind slam the door shut. “Was it something I said?” Farraday muttered sarcastically as he walked to his desk.

“Try your sidekick.” Becker nodded to where Walker sat, reviewing his notes.

Walker looked up and started to stand. Farraday waved at him to sit back down and grabbed another chair and sat across from him. “Was he making you feel welcome?”

“As I’m hoping only Oslind can. Did you find anything helpful?”

Farraday nodded. “An ID on one of the men we saw. What about you?”

“An evasive principal who didn’t keep a record of the vandalism, press charges or want to cooperate with the police.”

“Odd for a principal, isn’t it?”

Walker shrugged. “But there was one interesting piece of the puzzle,” he said, looking up. “I’ll tell you while we drive. I forgot we have an appointment.”

He grabbed his files and sprinted out the door, Farraday following him.

“Where are we going?” Farraday asked once they were out the door.

“The motel where Garrett’s stuff is. Becker was watching us like a hawk. I don’t think we should talk about our investigation in the office.”

After a few hours of going through Garrett’s CDs, Walker reached forward and shut the screen off.

“It’s enough to make you sick,” he said.

Fifteen. Fifteen years old. That’s what kept going through Farraday’s mind as he rubbed his temples, shutting his eyes to block out the faded curtains and lackluster paint of the cheap motel room.

It hadn't been hard to start identifying some of the faces on the porn videos. Allan Hare was in almost every one they'd watched so far, a fifteen-year-old kid who seemed to be a willing participant in some pretty seamy stuff.

He wondered what it was with kids these days. Had they been doing stuff like this when he was a teenager? Farraday thought about Lara's stories, but she'd abandoned her efforts to fit in at an early age, as far as he could tell. How far did you have to go now? Were kids so bored with life they'd try almost anything, especially if it meant approval from older boys or adults or just a chance to do things that made them feel more grown up? How did kids, how did anyone, get into stuff like this?

There were other familiar faces, too. Faces that looked like the kids he'd seen at the crime scene, when they'd found Allan's body, that he didn't have names for yet.

And on the older files, dated as much as seven years earlier, women he'd seen pictures of in the newspapers recently.

Prostitutes who'd died of drug overdoses in the county.

Cases Dan Van Biers had been kicking up a lot of controversy over. Accusations of mishandling of evidence, shoddy police work and arguments over why Oakridge detectives had taken the cases yet left the county ME's office in charge of the autopsies.

And one face he definitely had a name for.

Kaitlin Parks.

He was vaguely aware of Walker talking on the phone, telling Collins that they'd made some progress on the Garrett case. The clips Garrett had weren't standard back-room-purchased porn.

They were editing clips.

Which meant Garrett was either involved in producing these tapes, or he knew who was.

And somehow, one investigation had led to another. Ever since his arrest for statutory rape, Douglas had been keeping a low profile. They'd sent a crew in to search the grounds of the old estate but hadn't found Susan's baby.

The murders of Vern Fletcher and Graeme Garrett were still unsolved, with no suspects even under active investigation.

Now, Allan Hare's murder had formed a tenuous connection to Garrett. It might mean something, or it might just be a coincidence.

He leaned back and blew out a deep breath. There had been a lot of coincidences in these cases, but he didn't want more conjecture.

He wanted answers.

CHAPTER 16

When Farraday and Walker arrived at Lara's, Collins and Trin were waiting.

"Fill us in on what happened with Allan Hare's family," Collins said.

Lara frowned. "Isn't it strange for parents to wait so long to speak to the police? Don't they usually want to find out right away what's going on with the investigation?"

"That isn't even the best part," Farraday said as he sat down on the couch. "The family lawyer handled the meeting."

"Their lawyer?" Lara's eyes were wide with disbelief.

"Michael McClure." He put his hand up as she started to ask. "The one and the same. We learned absolutely nothing about Allan. His parents weren't concerned with our lack of progress and they didn't ask if we had any suspects."

"That's almost unbelievable."

"It gets better. Those charges that were dropped? I looked into it," Farraday told them. "McClure has been representing Allan Hare. He filed a motion to have Hare's records sealed. If that had gone through before Hare died, we wouldn't know about any of that stuff."

Farraday let Walker fill them in about Garrett's porn, and how it connected to Allan Hare and Kaitlin Parks.

Then Trin started to tell them what Dan had said, about Vern Fletcher. "He received a package with a micro cassette in it today, something Vern sent him before he was murdered."

She passed each of them a copy of the transcript.

"Look, I'm not saying that you have to like it, but it had to be done," the first male voice said. "There's no point causing a fuss about it now."

"You're saying I don't have a choice?" the second male voice answered. "I've done my share of looking the other way, but this..."

"This is necessary."

"It's a kid, damn it."

"A kid that can be linked to someone who has been a good friend to us over the years."

"Maybe it's time to think about who we call a friend when he wants us to burn a body to cover his crimes. Exactly what do we wear a badge for?"

"To keep a lid on things. This kid was trouble. He got what was coming to him. You know what his sheet looks like. It's not like he was innocent."

"Maybe I'm just having trouble with what you're making me guilty of."

"Then get over it, or you'll have a different kind of trouble, a permanent kind of trouble. This isn't a debate. He has your DNA, your fingerprints, and can have your name implicated in any crime with enough physical evidence to send you away. You think about that and then tell me you've got issues with this."

"The captain thinks there was a body..."

Once they were finished reading, Trin continued.

"The person who attacked you last night," she said, looking at Lara, "said something about the hotel story. I went to the library and checked. You didn't just write about the robberies, but you also had a filler piece, about a report of a body that turned out to be a vagrant who'd passed out cold."

Lara's eyes narrowed. "What does that have to do with this?"

"A guy with no physical injuries was found passed out cold on a piece of plastic coated with blood. The same day Allan Hare's body is found in a burned-out cabin at Doe Lake Motel. A body that was moved, wrapped up somehow, so that almost no blood marked the trail from the house to whatever vehicle the killers used."

"Isn't it a bit of a leap to assume that one thing connects to the other?"

"One way to find out," Farraday said.

He picked up the phone and called Lessard. After a few minutes of giving nothing more than one-word responses to whatever Lessard was saying, he hung up. "Trin's theory holds water. They still have to run more extensive tests, but it's the right blood type, with some other common factors. HIV positive, for one thing."

He turned and gave Lara a serious look. "He also said that he received a phone call from Dr. Eaton. Apparently, you asked Dr. Eaton to run some tests on a blood sample and compare it to what we collected from the rocks where Susan died."

Lara's cheeks filled with color as she nodded.

"It was a match. Where did it come from?"

"That day in the library, when I cut Graeme Garrett? It wasn't an accident." She told them what she'd heard about his parentage, that he was rumored to be David Douglas' son.

"But you didn't tell Ty so that he couldn't get in trouble over how you got the DNA sample," Trin said. "Clever."

"Unbelievable," Walker said. "What am I supposed to tell Megan?"

"For now," Collins responded, "nothing. We won't officially close the case until we get the results back from the blood work they did for Garrett's autopsy. That way, Lara never has to go on the record and it gives us some time. We'll have to run his DNA against the first child's. Douglas might be innocent."

"Of that crime, maybe." Farraday frowned. "But he's not innocent."

"What about the blood from the break-in here? Garrett confessed."

"That's another thing," Farraday said. "The investigation into the break-in at Betty's was a dead-end, but I assumed whoever broke in here broke in there. What do we tell Betty Zimmerman?"

"I doubt she'd ever coming back," Lara said. "Too much of a coward to even go on the record when her daughter gets murdered."

"Daughter?" Walker stared at Lara. "What are you talking about?"

There was silence in the room for a moment. Collins rubbed his forehead.

"I made a call, not to disclose this, and then, with everything else going on..." He shook his head. "I forgot you didn't know. Betty is Megan's biological mother."

Rob went a chalky white as Collins gave him the abbreviated version of what Betty had said and what they'd established from external evidence.

"And I can't tell Megan, right?" he asked.

Collins shook his head. "Not yet. When the time comes, I'll talk to her."

"You know," Walker said slowly, "her dad's been arrested, her sister murdered and her sister's baby is missing. I mean, we all know the baby is dead, but we can't even have a proper burial. Now this?"

They lapsed into an awkward silence. After a few minutes, Farraday finally spoke.

"There is some progress. Lessard just told me. Tests confirmed gunshot residue on Garrett's hands, but there was much GSR on Vern's. Abrasions on Vern's arms indicated he'd been bound, but he wasn't tied up when we found him. I'm sure Vern didn't kill Garrett, and whoever did was careless. Tire marks, no way for Garrett and Vern to get out there, one gun wiped clean, casings removed from the scene."

"Sloppy." Lara shook her head. "Assuming this is the cops, Douglas, Morrow and whoever else is involved, how did they go all this time without drawing suspicion and then start making stupid mistakes?"

"Maybe it's just as simple as Susan's death rattling them a bit," Trin said. "And a lot of overconfidence. Who's really taken a good, hard look at them before? Nobody. With everything going on, they've suddenly attracted a lot of attention. Between your stories and Dan's-"

"Whoa. What do Dan's stories have to do with Douglas and Morrow?" Farraday asked.

"I... Look, I think Lara should talk to Dan. Ask for background on his drug overdose victims and the investigation, nothing more."

"Hatcher won't let me near that."

"When did you start listening to your boss?" Trin asked.

"Fine," Lara said. "As Rob already pointed out, we still don't have the other baby."

"I don't know where else to look," Farraday said. "Unless David Douglas had the child buried at his house with Susan..." He held his hands up in defeat. "And we won't get a search warrant without something to go on. We can't even prove he knew about the baby, never mind that he was involved. The evidence points to Garrett acting alone."

"Meanwhile, we need to find out more about Michael McClure, and what's going on at the Lakeview Hotel and Doe Lake Motel," Collins said. "And with help from Lara and Trin, we might be able to tie this up soon." He gave them a quick rundown of what he wanted them to do.

***

"Now this is how I like to start my morning," Jimmy said as Lara walked into his office. "My favorite girl comes to ask a favor that will likely bring the wrath of Hurricane Hatcher my way. What more could I ask for?"

"Don't quit your day job for the comedy routine."

He gave her a sarcastic grin. "So where's the ball and chain? He's letting you out of his sight for more than five minutes?"

"Making an appearance at the office. Every now and again we need to look like we actually go to work."

Jimmy leaned back in his chair, propping his feet up on the desk. "Don't let Hatcher hear you say that. What can I do for you?"

"Have I told you you're an angel?" Lara smiled as she pulled a folder out of her bag.

"I was hoping for the love of your life, but I guess angel will have to do." Jimmy reached for the file. "Fill me in."

He sat in complete silence, listening to her, and then shook his head.

"You couldn't just write about a school play?"

"Next time." Lara grinned. "I suppose if some people had anything to say about it, I'd be covering kids sports."

Jimmy laughed. "That's still too violent. Have you seen some of those hockey moms? They're deadly. I'll put this on top of my list."

Lara hopped off the desk and paused to kiss him on the cheek. "You're the best, Jimmy."

"Yeah, yeah. That's what they all say on their way out the door," Jimmy mumbled, watching her disappear, the door shutting softly behind her.

***

Walker was sitting at Farraday's desk, trying to suppress the smile he felt pushing against the corners of his mouth. Farraday was making a legitimate effort to talk to Detective Smith casually at the water cooler. Walker couldn't help thinking that if their colleagues saw Farraday at Lara's house, shirt half pulled out, leaning back against the couch, bantering with Lara or his sister they'd think his straight-laced exterior was nothing more than a facade. Walker knew the truth was somewhere in the middle, that Farraday had personas he adopted in different situations because it suited him. Ultimately, Farraday was pretty casual with people he trusted. There just weren't too many people who fell into that category.

"Well, look who came crawling back to the office." Walker looked up. Oslind was glaring at him.

"Why don't you slither back under your rock? Or did you run out of donuts?"

Walker turned back to the paper he was reading, ignoring the snickers around him.

"You know, most guys around here know enough to make friends when they want to move up the ladder." Walker was engulfed in a shadow and looked up to see Jones leering at him.

"Some people aren't my kind of friends, no matter what it costs me," Walker said coldly, looking Jones in the eye.

"Just because you're worming your way into the Douglas clan doesn't mean the big man will go to the mat for you," Jones said. "And pretty boy Farraday can't win you the favor he doesn't have himself."

"You know, Arnie," Walker said, deliberately choosing the variation on his first name he knew Arnold Jones liked the least, "when I used to come in for a shift, I could always tell something smelled rotten down here. Now I know what it was."

Arnold Jones slid off the desk, knocking half of Farraday's files down in the process. Out of the corner of his eye Walker could see Farraday was about to march over, but Smith put his hand on his arm and shook his head. Walker remained sitting.

Jones grabbed Walker's shirt and dragged him to his feet, but he was ready. Walker blocked the punch and stepped into his swing, hitting

Jones right in the forehead, knocking him to the floor with one shot.

Even the faint hum of the photocopier stopped, leaving the room in complete silence.

Captain Collins stepped out of his office and looked at Becker. "Get him in here."

Becker did as he was told. Collins glanced around the room before focusing on Walker. "You have things to do, don't you?" Collins shut his office door behind him without another word.

***

"What the hell were you thinking?" Collins tried to keep from shouting, unsuccessfully.

"Me? I expect you to bring that punk up on charges."

"The only charges that might be filed will be against you, Jones." Collins stared at him from across his desk. "I saw the whole thing. I know how you like to strong-arm the rookies. As of now, that's over. You're suspended."

Jones clenched his fists and turned purple before he pulled the door open. He marched out of the office and straight toward Farraday, who was just finishing picking up the files Jones had knocked off his desk. Smith stepped into his path.

"Let it go, Jones. Don't make things any worse."

Jones opened his mouth to speak, turned and saw Collins watching, and marched out of the building without saying another word.

***

Farraday and Walker entered Lessard's examination room, greeted by the overwhelming smell of chemicals.

"Where's the pretty one?" the ME asked.

Farraday ignored that. "What do you have for us?"

Lessard summed up all the information he had available about Allan

Hare, most of which they already knew. Then he described the damage to the tattoo on the boy's body.

"Somebody removed part of the mark with a knife, possibly as he was circling the drain. Beyond that, all I can tell you is that the markings appear identical. I did manage to identify the initials J and C."

"I doubt JC stands for his religious persuasion," Walker muttered.

"And it isn't Allan's initials," Farraday said.

"What about a girlfriend?"

"The letters don't fit. At least, they don't fit what we have now." Farraday glanced at Walker. "I guess we've got our work cut out for us."

"Literally," Walker said, glancing at the covered body on Dr. Lessard's table. Lessard passed him a report. "His last meal had been chicken penne in a white wine sauce and some concoction made of bourbon and chocolate. There are only about three restaurants in town that serve either of those items and none of them are cheap."

"And there's only one that serves both," Farraday said.

Lessard's brow puckered. "You memorizing the local menus?"

"Chicken penne is my sister's favorite," Farraday said. "So our victim was killed at home, time undetermined, but an expensive dinner in his belly."

"Small intestine, actually."

"Putting his death around six hours after his last meal?"

"Approximately. It could have been longer, but likely within twelve hours."

"You can't narrow it down further?" Farraday asked.

"Sorry. In order to pay for all the new staff, they cut the budget for my crystal ball."

Walker smiled. "Is that why you're sleeping down here these days?"

"No, Detective Walker. That's so if I die in the night my body is ready for dissection." Lessard scowled. "Maybe if you two stopped bringing me bodies, I'd find some time to rejoin the land of the living."

Farraday laughed. "We'll see what we can do."

Chapter 17

Trin had worn her shortest skirt and a tight blouse. She'd met up with Dan Van Biers earlier, and he'd given her a copy of the micro cassette tape Vern had mailed. She'd listened to it in the car, but the voices weren't familiar to her. She hoped Collins could ID them.

After she called her brother and told him what she was doing, she'd claimed the reservation under the lawyer's name and asked for a table near the back, being seated at the chair closest to the opening to the hallway for the restrooms and payphones.

It wasn't long before the imposing figure of Mike McClure was led her way, his eyes pinched. She stood and extended her hand and he let his gaze linger as he looked her up and down.

"Glad you persuaded me to meet you," McClure said appreciatively. "I'll order for us, doll."

"I've already taken care of that." She was convinced that this was the best way to get a read on the man. Her research had hinted at theories she wanted to test.

"That's not the usual arrangement," McClure said, his eyes narrowing.

Trin shrugged. "I make my own arrangements."

"Ambitious." His expression hadn't relaxed so she wasn't sure he approved.

"Well," Trin said slyly, twirling the straw in her drink, glancing up at him coyly, "I heard you were a man with unique interests."

"This isn't usually how I operate." He looked her over, scrutinizing every inch of her body again. "How much are we talking about?"

"It depends on what you're asking for." She felt his hand on her bare knee.

"The whole deal, sweetie. I don't sell what I don't sample."

Trin averted her eyes as she picked up his hand and pushed it back to his side of the table.

"Then maybe you should level with your terms," she suggested.

He leaned back against his chair. "All in good time. I plan to enjoy this."

***

"Ian Vincent won't be happy to see us," Farraday said as he parked across the street from Callandre's.

"Hold on," Walker said, grabbing Farraday's arm before he opened the door. "Look."

He turned to see what Walker was pointing at. Three men were having an argument as they approached the restaurant. One was Detective Jones.

"The younger one is Ian Vincent, the manager of Callandre's," Farraday said. "I don't know who the other man is."

"I can tell you that. The principal from St. Christopher's."

Jones brushed Principal Vincent's hand off his arm as he yanked the door open and went into the restaurant. A third man sprinted across the street from the far end of the road and made his way toward the two men still standing there.

"Well, well, would you look at who it is," Walker muttered. "The driver."

Farraday pulled open his cell.

"What are you doing?" Walker asked.

"I'm going to get Collins to put surveillance on the guy driving."

***

"I really appreciate this, Dan," Lara repeated.

"Don't thank me yet. I don't know that I can help you at all." Dan Van Biers was studying her with his dark eyes.

He was a handsome guy in his own way, a few years older than Lara and as aloof as Farraday with newcomers. For all she knew, Hatcher had told him she tried to scoop the drug story from him, and that's why he wouldn't let her collaborate with him.

Trin had vouched for Dan, and that was enough for her to trust him. He'd come through with information already, and considering what had happened to Vern that wasn't a small thing.

"I'm not trying to steal your story," she told him. His dark eyes didn't flicker with any acknowledgement or indication that he believed her. She took a deep breath. "But the Hare boy had heroin in his system, and there was heroin in Susan Douglas' possession at the time of her murder."

Farraday had confirmed that when he called earlier. She hoped Dan would be interested, even if it bought her nothing more than an information exchange.

"You do have your sources, don't you?"

Lara felt her face getting hot. "This is all confidential. But it might interest you to know that it was a high-grade cut, the same stuff that was in your three OD victims linked to the prostitution ring."

Dan's face froze, as though he was trying not to show how surprised he was. "How do you know about the prostitution ring?"

"I do have my sources," she said, throwing the statement back at him. "Look, I have no intention of going after your story. But I have something that might be of interest to you."

"What do you want for it?"

"Information about the prostitution ring. Just information."

Dan sat stiffly, tapping his fingers on his desk.

"I'll think about it," he said finally. "What have you got for me?"

"My victims were part of a porn ring that Graeme Garrett was involved in."

Dan leaned forward. "Tell me more," he said.

***

A man stomped through the restaurant and grabbed McClure's arm.

McClure didn't bother to excuse himself as he shook himself loose from the man's grip and walked off, down a hallway at the back of the restaurant.

To the left there were bathrooms. Straight ahead, a door marked Staff Only, and to the right there was an emergency exit. It was as private as they could get.

"Not here. What the hell are you thinking?"

"We have to talk. Who's the skirt?"

"Just a prospect."

"She's a little old for you, isn't she?" There was a sneer in that voice that was familiar to Trin, from the tape Vern had made before he died.

***

When Farraday and Walker entered the restaurant they could hear raised voices from the back. Michael McClure had grabbed Trin's arm, and she'd yanked it away. Even from across the room he could see the flash of anger in his sister's eyes.

"Just who the hell-"

Trin stood up but McClure grabbed her arm to stop her.

His jaw was clenched, the look in his eyes making Farraday quicken his pace as he wove between the other tables. The room had grown silent, only the odd clink of cutlery against a plate to detract from the heated exchange.

"Let me go," Trin demanded as she straightened, a move that emphasized her height.

"I suggest you do that, Mr. McClure."

Mike McClure turned his seething glare from Trin to the Farraday. He let go of Trin's arm and straightened his tie.

Farraday saw Trin start to walk away from the corner of his eye. Then Walker moved beside him and gave an almost imperceptible nod, which was followed by the chime of the restaurant door as it closed.

From the back of the room, McClure's words were clipped but audible in the silence that lingered in the restaurant. "What do you want now? I've answered your questions."

"You could tell me why you lied."

"If you want to talk to me, call my lawyer."

He turned to walk away, but Walker stepped forward to block him. The move knocked McClure's look of pure rage off his face for a moment, replacing it with surprise. Then he scowled, using his shoulder to bump Walker out of his way before he stomped through the tables, only to be stopped by a staff member with his bill.

***

Trin had looked over every piece of information about Mike McClure that she'd found. If it was regular lawyer bio it would be impressive, but with what she suspected about McClure it was sickening.

He'd represented half a dozen local teens on an assortment of charges that showed increasing violence, managing each time to get them off. She'd started making a list of names and then put the pen down. *Where have I heard those names from?* She sank to the floor and dug through a pile of newspapers until she found the issue of The Ledger she was looking for.

Dan had written a piece about the recent overdose of a twenty-year-old woman named Terri Kwan. On the surface, her name didn't ring any bells, until Trin sat up and double-checked the list of solicitation charges McClure had covered. She turned back to the article and looked at the last paragraph, wondering if Dan had connected any more dots without even knowing it.

He had. Shannon Chow and Connie Chen were also named as recent overdose deaths. They were both on McClure's list. He only had four solicitation charges he'd handled this year and Karen Li was the only defendant who hadn't died since McClure had gotten her off.

***

The minute Farraday walked into the library, Nancy put up her hands in declared innocence. "Neither of them are here," she said.

Farraday smiled. "It's okay. I'm actually looking for something else. Lara told me you have old yearbooks here."

Nancy led him to the far corner. "There have been a few times they've helped ID kids who've gotten into trouble. The schools aren't always cooperative."

Farraday pulled out ten years worth of issues, starting with St. Christopher, hoping the information he'd been given about Ian Vincent had narrowed it down to the right time frame.

***

Lara was pacing in her office. She checked her watch. It had been three hours.

She looked up to see Dan Van Biers standing in the doorway. He waved a file.

"Come in," she said, sitting down on her desk.

"So this is how the other half lives," Dan said, glancing around her office.

"Hey, I didn't ask for it."

Dan actually smiled. "Of course not. Hatcher does this to every female reporter. Most newsrooms aren't like this, no private offices. But with The Ledger being in an old, converted dorm we all get our space. Except the women get a bit more. Hatcher believes the best way to rule the chicken coop is to keep the hens happy." He sat down on one of the chairs, still holding his folder. He turned to look at her, scrutinizing her face. "Hatcher's not used to having successful reporters stick around."

"So I've heard. Which makes me wonder what you're still doing here."

He paused. "Look, I want out. That's what I've been working on these stories for. An award-winning series, a number of front page exclusives..." He shrugged. "I want out."

His initial animosity toward her was beginning to make sense. He'd been well on his way to putting together the headlines he needed to be offered a job elsewhere and get away from Hatcher, and she'd come along and taken the wind out of his sails.

Dan continued. "I called in a favor. Someone I know has a tie to the triple-x smut that fills the back rooms of adult entertainment stores. He says my victims are too old for the brand of entertainment that's coming from purely local sources."

"Aren't your victims all twenty or twenty-one years old?"

Dan nodded.

"Just tell me we aren't talking little kids."

"No. Strictly teens, and that's bad enough. My source figures they start at twelve and go up to sixteen or seventeen."

"When did this start?"

"As far as he knows, seven years. Could be longer, but that's as far as the trail goes."

It didn't take two seconds for her to do the math. "Long enough for your victims to have been part of the original crew."

"That would prove your link, wouldn't it?"

"That, and the drug connection between your victims and mine."

"You know, the Douglas case was a fluke. Some doubted you'd be able to turn up something as impressive with old-fashioned investigating. Simmons owes me fifty bucks."

Lara wasn't sure how she should feel about coworkers betting on her failure, but at least she knew that Dan thought she was a good reporter. She glanced up to see her door push open. Her smile widened as Farraday came inside and shut the door behind him.

"Tymen Farraday," he said, offering his hand to Van Biers.

Lara introduced them. As Farraday answered his cell phone, Dan said, "You do have your sources."

She just shrugged as Farraday hung up the phone.

"Dan has some information that might be useful," Lara told him, relaying what Dan had learned. "How did it go with Ian Vincent?"

"Ian Vincent?" Dan interjected, leaning forward. "Any relation to George Vincent?"

Farraday's eyes betrayed the truth, even before he'd looked from Lara to Dan. "Why?"

"He's one of the people I'd call a suspect in my investigation." Dan tapped his folder. "Unfortunately, Detective Oslind was too busy cleaning up these cases quietly, but I found witnesses who had seen a dark-colored SUV in the area around the time each victim was dumped."

"How did his name come up?" Farraday asked, his eyes wide. "He's been hard to track."

"His fingerprints were on money in the last victim's wallet."

"How did you get your hands on that?" Lara asked.

Dan glanced at Farraday, who held up his hands. "I'm not even here."

"The last victim was dumped close to where the first one had been found. I had a witness who'd spoken to me, who wasn't too impressed with how Oslind handled the case. With the second victim she called me instead of calling the police right away. The wallet was scattered along with the contents of her purse. I photographed the area, bagged the wallet hoping for an ID, and got out of there."

Farraday exhaled. "Did you find any other prints?"

Dan shook his head. "But under the circumstances, George Vincent's were enough to interest me."

"You found out about his arrests."

"Dealing, pimping and," Dan paused, "statutory rape."

"Where did that come from?"

"It was cleared off the books almost as soon as it went on. I happened to be monitoring collars I thought were related to the drug and prostitution scene or else I would have missed it."

"It's not possible to clear charges like that off the records without a trial," Farraday said. Dan just raised an eyebrow.

"It is when the arresting officer is Lenny Becker. Isn't he your partner?"

"We're not working together right now." Farraday sat down on the edge of Lara's desk. "I have an ID on the driver of the vehicle from the night Garrett died. George Vincent. Frank Vincent, the principal of St. Christopher Secondary School, is Ian Vincent's brother. George is their cousin."

Dan frowned. "The thing is, I haven't been able to track where the videos are being filmed. My source had nothing on it and he also confirmed that this is special market only. Your name has to be on a list in order to gain access: No over-the-counter purchases. I can't get even get my hands on the videos, never mind view them and start compiling a list of possible venues, which did make me wonder how you'd found out about them."

Lara looked at Farraday and held his gaze for a moment before he nodded.

She turned to Dan. "I think we can help you."

***

Lara and Dan went to her house, where Trin had been rifling through papers in the living room. The minute they walked in, Trin started talking.

"Terri Kwan, Connie Chen and Shannon Chow were all found dead of apparent overdoses. Written up as suspected suicides and ignored by the police, but their bodies were dumped with evidence of sexual trauma, suggesting murder."

Dan nodded. "Nobody has done anything about my insinuations. I'm afraid it was overshadowed by the Douglas case and I still haven't heard that the case is being reopened."

"There's a good chance it will be now."

"What did you find?" Lara asked, pulling her coat off.

Trin pulled a paper from the file on the coffee table and passed it to Lara.

Lara looked over the document. She looked up at Trin as she handed the papers to Dan.

"What am I looking at?" he asked. Then he shut his eyes and shook his head, groaning. "Does anyone know where Karen Li is?"

Trin shook her head. "I've made some calls. People are looking out for her."

"This is unbelievable," Dan said as the front door opened. "Do you think this lawyer is involved in the prostitution?"

Trin pulled out a tape recorder, looking up as Farraday and Walker entered.

Farraday introduced Dan to Rob Walker and they all sat down. Trin pressed play on the tape recorder. Soon, they were all listening to McClure's twisted inferences. The recorder even caught part of the conversation McClure had in the hallway.

"That man he was talking to was one of the men from Vern's tape." She pulled the cassette out and inserted the other one, pressing play.

"That's Detective Jones," Walker said. "Why didn't we see him leave the restaurant?"

"He went in the back, through the Staff Only doors," Trin said as she shut the player off. "I thought you guys were going to talk to Ian Vincent."

"We were told he was in a meeting." Farraday looked at Lara, who shook her head.

"I'm not positive. It could be."

"Could be what?" Dan asked.

"Could be the person who broke into Lara's house and attacked her. The cops Vern was following. Jones and Becker." Farraday's cell rang. "Yes? You're kidding. We'll be right there."

Walker stood up before Farraday cut the call.

"We have to execute a search warrant on Lenny Becker's place."

"Becker's place? Why?" Walker asked, also standing.

"Collins received a tip that he shot Graeme Garrett."

***

As Farraday drove to Lenny's house it started to snow. Fluffy white flakes trickled through the sky, eventually thick enough to force Farraday to turn the wipers on.

"Unbelievable," Walker muttered. "Snow already?"

He pulled into the Becker residence. Collins was already there with a group of men, waiting.

"Where's Lenny now?" Farraday asked.

"He's off duty. And he's not here."

Farraday took the warrant and stepped forward. "Let's do this by the book. Read the warrant before you walk through that door and follow it to the letter. If we're going to accuse a cop, we're going to make sure it's solid and if we're going to acquit him, it needs to be clean. I don't want any doubt left to tarnish Lenny's rep if he's innocent."

It wasn't long before every room was filled, boxes being emptied, drawers rifled, every nook and cranny that were within the scope of the warrant being searched.

Farraday had been supervising, going room to room, when he found an area that looked untouched, compared to the growing mess throughout the rest of the house. He started to check the desk to make sure that it was clean and that nothing had been missed. Pulling out each drawer, he looked under and behind and then scanned the back of the desk, finally concluding they had everything to retrieve from this room. He looked up to see Walker standing in the doorway, holding a gun in an evidence bag.

"Is that the right caliber?" he asked. Walker nodded.

Farraday exhaled. "Make sure it gets dusted for prints."

***

Lara's search for medical information about Kaitlin Parks had only turned up a record of visits to the public health nurse and her family doctor. She decided to take a gamble.

"Yes, my name is Kaitlin Parks. Dr. Dylan was supposed to let me know about the results of my tests."

"You know I can't disclose that over the phone," the tired voice of the receptionist droned automatically.

"I've been in four times in the last month. I need to know if I have HIV."

"You have to make an appointment."

"Can I get in today?" Lara crossed her fingers, hoping the woman wouldn't call her bluff.

"Soonest I have is next Monday."

"But I'll be away." She continued whining and pressuring for an answer, sensing the woman was wearing down. It wasn't exactly reassuring to think that, with enough pressure, medical records might be divulged, but it wasn't unheard of either.

Lara finally got her voice to tremble. "But, it's really important and I need to know. My boyfriend..." She sniffed, hoping she'd said enough.

There was silence on the other end, and then the voice returned, lower than before. "The doctor was supposed to tell you that when you were here last month, on the 22nd. You were supposed to start your treatment this week."

Lara coughed into the phone. "Excuse me," she sputtered, clicking off the untraceable pay-and-talk cell she'd purchased.

"What's the verdict?" Trin asked.

"She knew she was positive on September 22nd, two days before Kaitlin's father charged him with assault."

"That doesn't mean she's guilty."

"It's not that. It's just... Can you imagine? She'd just a kid and her life is practically over. Porn, HIV, a murdered boyfriend."

Trin shook her head. "Even in the circles I grew up in, I knew my share of girls who didn't fare too much better. Not as extreme, but bad enough for our generation."

Lara groaned. "You make us sound so old."

Trin just shrugged. "Ty never told you, did he?"

"Told me what?"

"This girl he knew. She was a ridiculous, flighty thing who was crazy about him and she wouldn't be deterred. She claimed he got her pregnant."

Lara's mouth went dry. Trin's face was clouded, but there was no anger in her words. No judgment.

"As I said, this girl wasn't too bright. Tests proved he wasn't responsible. He denied sleeping with her, but had to have the DNA tests anyway. Ty was seventeen. When he finally talked to me about it, he told me she did him a favor."

"A favor? That's not what I'd call it."

"He'd always had high standards and he'd never been interested in this girl. After that he was impossible. He doesn't make mistakes with relationships."

"I doubt I'd be as forgiving if something like that had happened to me," Lara said.

"My brother's a good guy."

Lara nodded, but didn't say anything. Trin's story explained Farraday's restraint, in part.

But it could just be he wasn't interested.

***

Dan came downstairs and grabbed his coat. Collins had moved the porn CDs and other items from the motel to Lara's, in the hopes that Trin would be able to start matching faces from the porn to the pictures of kids Walker and Farraday had taken on surveillance. He'd agreed to let Dan view the tapes as well, in case he could add any information to their investigation.

"You're leaving?" Trin asked.

"I can't stomach any more of that shit."

"It won't be long before we have dinner," Lara said. "Why don't you wait until you've eaten? It's getting late."

He shook his head. "I've got an idea about where they're filming the porn, and I want to check it out."

"Want me to come with you?" Trin was already getting to her feet but he shook his head.

"I'm not going to do much. Just a quick detour on the way home. I'll see you tomorrow."

After Dan left, Lara told Trin about Jimmy's phone call, the people he'd been able to identify that connected to the case and to the Mayor's office. McClure and George Vincent were quickly making their way to the top of the list, appearing to have "fingers in every pie", as Jimmy had put it. He'd found a piece of information that wouldn't have meant anything to Dan though: Vincent had been arrested for the rape of Kaitlin Parks.

But almost as quickly as the charges were filed, they'd disappeared without a trace. Jimmy was trying to find out where the arrest happened, but so far he hadn't been able to get his own source within the department to talk.

Which had startled Lara. Who did Jimmy know in the department that would talk to him? Then she remembered how she'd instinctively gone to him for information on Farraday when he'd turned up in her office. Jimmy had known a lot, and it had never even occurred to her to ask how.

They continued sorting through papers, looking for any more clues, but hadn't found anything solid.

Eventually, Lara got up and walked to the patio doors.

"The snow's really coming down now," she said. "Roads will be slick. It's early for this kind of weather. I doubt the plows and sanders will be out yet."

She started walking back and forth, rubbing her arms, mulling over all the bits they had, frustrated by the feeling that there were things eluding them.

Still wondering if David Douglas was going to get off. They didn't have much to tie him to this. These guys had been working together for a long time, and they knew how to do business. It amazed her to think that people could be so blatantly corrupt, could be doing such horrid things, and not get caught. But then, when she thought about it, about how much of the police department seemed to be willing to turn their back for a bribe, or even what the one officer had said on the tape, the conversation Vern had heard.

He has your DNA, your fingerprints, and can have your name implicated in any crime with enough physical evidence to send you away.

Once someone had enough power, they didn't need to buy loyalty. They could bully people into cooperating. Cross the line once or twice and think it's innocent enough, but it could catch up to you.

And every time she thought of how unbelievable it was that nobody had been able to expose Douglas, Morrow, Garrett and the cops involved, she thought about everything they knew and how far they were from proving any of it in a court of law. Despite what they'd learned, they were a long way from making charges stick.

"Stop pacing. You aren't making me feel better." Trin glared at her until she stopped.

"I guess this is what they mean by 'hurry up and wait'," Lara said, sinking down onto the sofa.

***

Farraday rubbed his forehead. Walker had taken the gun to rush a ballistics test, leaving him to double-check everything. His insistence on doing this right had turned it into a marathon search, but he didn't regret it.

His cell rang and Walker confirmed the worst. Farraday looked at Collins.

"How do you want me to handle this?"

"You need to bring him in."

"What about this?" Farraday asked, pulling his gloves off but nodding at the crew still combing Lenny's place.

"I'll handle it. We're almost done."

It was slow driving, with the roads being slick, but it still didn't take long for Farraday to find Lenny's car outside one of the bars Lenny frequented.

Lenny was still in control.

"I should buy you a drink," he told Farraday as he walked up beside him. "It might be the last chance I get."

"Do you have your gun, Lenny?"

Lenny glanced at him, not a trace of amusement in his hooded eyes. He pulled the holster from his belt and passed it to Farraday carefully.

"I'm sorry about this."

Lenny smirked. "Not like you weren't expecting it."

Farraday didn't know what to say to that. "Has it been that obvious?"

"It was nothing you did. Just a gut instinct. I knew I could trust you to play it straight."

"Don't say anything, Lenny. You know I can't overlook it."

"Do you want to cuff me?"

"Not until we get to the car." He walked beside Lenny, something in his gut telling him this didn't add up. Farraday had already made a few calls during the search, started checking things out. His mind kept going back to the voices on the tape. *He has your DNA, your fingerprints, and can have your name implicated in any crime with enough physical evidence to send you away.* He'd known the voices. Collins and Walker recognized them too. It was physical evidence they could use, but if anything it cast doubt on this arrest instead of strengthening the case.

Becker had been trying to get out, and he'd been threatened. Now, an anonymous tip had accused him of murder. Whoever was behind the murders of Graeme Garrett and Vern Fletcher was banking that Lenny would stay quiet.

And Farraday was going to have to find a way to get his former partner to go on the record about people who'd shown they'd stop at nothing. Including murder.

Lenny grunted. "I'm almost glad. At least I know you aren't enjoying this."

***

Jimmy spent some time juggling, attempting to catch gumdrops with his mouth and failing, and repeatedly picking up the phone and dropping it down, still thinking about what he'd found out about George Vincent and Mike McClure.

McClure seemed to be less than half a step away from a lot of dirty business. He'd ensured that Vincent walked on every arrest he'd faced so far and he'd also developed a reputation for clearing teenagers of some pretty nasty charges.

He'd met McClure, once. It hadn't been a pleasant exchange. Jimmy was used to lawyers looking smooth and polished, but McClure... McClure was that on the surface, but spend ten minutes around the guy outside the courthouse and he was pure slime.

When he phoned Lara earlier, she'd told him about Karen Li's connection to McClure.

He wished she'd given up on the story, that she'd dropped it before Tymen Farraday had ever turned up. Not because he didn't want her to prove herself, but because he was worried. She was getting in deep.

She'd been emailing him from work, to his home email address. Files, facts, whatever was needed to back herself up on the case, with a promise from him that he wouldn't look at it, just make sure it got into the right hands if anything happened to her and Farraday.

Too stubborn to think that maybe the reason the corruption had never been exposed before was because these guys knew how to deal with threats. Vern Fletcher knew the risks he was taking, and he'd paid for it.

Lara was always putting herself at risk.

Something he hadn't done much of, himself, for a long time. Being content to stick with photos and avoid the bullshit Hatcher dumped on all the others.

Jimmy stood up, grabbed his coat and pulled the file off his desk.

The least he could do was check a few things out.

***

Dan had watched the Doe Lake Motel but it was unusually quiet, even for a closed motel. After more than an hour, he'd almost conceded defeat, but decided to stop at the Lakeview Hotel.

The drive wasn't as bad as he thought it might be. He parked in a spot where they could easily monitor traffic without drawing attention.

Filming here, in a place that was still technically open for business seemed risky, but something about the robberies made him suspicious. It seemed like a legitimate hotel, so it had to be run like one, and they couldn't prevent guests from reporting thefts or incidents.

And the string of robberies fit the pattern of drug fiends, looking for stuff to pawn quickly for cash. How many crooks chanced a break-in for sometimes as little as $50? It wasn't like people carried around a lot of cash anymore, not with debit cards paving the way to a cashless society.

Add in the ineptitude of the local cops, with Becker in charge of a simple case that went nowhere, and it seemed pretty simple. This was where they were dealing the drugs from. It had to be.

Dan phoned Lara, gave her a quick update, and then got out of the car and started walking toward the building.

Outside it was still, quiet, and he walked toward the hotel without stopping to think about the crunching of snow behind him. It didn't register until he felt something strike the back of his head, and the world went dark.

***

Lara hung up the phone. "That was Dan, calling from the Lakeview Hotel. He said the Doe Lake Motel is quiet, he's just checking out the hotel and then he's going home."

"I wish he wasn't alone," Trin said with a frown. "I don't like it."

They made dinner, ate, cleaned up and Trin distracted Lara with another rant about the lack of modern conveniences.

"No internet, no television?"

"Nobody's making you stay, Trin."

"Is that a hint?"

Lara held up her hands as her cell phone rang. "No. It just isn't my fault. TV isn't a priority and I haven't had the time to schedule the internet hook-up. They have to run a cable."

She pulled her cell phone – her real cell phone, not the pay and talk one she'd been using earlier - out of her bag. This time, as soon as Lara identified herself, she fell silent. It wasn't half a minute before she hung up the phone again, this time taking a deep breath before she turned to look at Trin. "Dan was attacked. He's at the hospital."

Trin sprang from the couch. "We have to make sure he's okay."

Lara hesitated. "Shouldn't we wait for the guys?"

"We're together. They're all out. We're going to be at the hospital, a public place. If we aren't safe there, we aren't safe here." She grabbed her coat and bag, and Lara reluctantly followed her out to the jeep.

***

Time had slowed to a crawl while they waited for more evidence. Farraday was aware that it had been hours since he'd left Lara and Trin. He realized then he should have phoned them, just to make sure they were okay, but it was too late.

Farraday followed Walker into the room where Lenny Becker was waiting to be questioned. The same room he'd questioned David Douglas in, when they'd almost come to blows.

"You know your rights, Lenny. What do you want to do?"

"Go back to Vegas and win the jackpot."

"Jokes alone aren't going to get you through this." Farraday sat down at the table across from Becker. "Did you kill Graeme Garrett?"

"No," Becker said. "But what difference does it make? The gun was in my house, and you won't find prints on the weapon."

"How can you be so certain?" Walker asked.

"The people who want to see me go down are good. They've been covering their tracks for longer than either of you have been cops."

"Who wants to see you go down?" Farraday asked.

Becker laughed. "Don't you get it? If I name anyone, I end up like Graeme Garrett. The only chance I've got is to say nothing and hope I keep breathing. And I've been drinking, so none of this is admissible."

He sat back, a hard look settling on his face. Farraday stood up.

"Is there anything I can get you? Anyone I can call?"

Becker shook his head, turning in his chair to look away.

***

Farraday shook his head. "I don't think he's guilty, but he knows who is."

"He's in this neck-deep and he knows more about Garrett's death than he's told us," Walker said.

"Look, I'm not saying he isn't involved, just that he's been set up to take the fall on this. I don't want Lenny ending up on the other side of an investigation like Garrett did."

"Any suggestions?" Collins asked. A uniformed officer hesitantly knocked on the open office door. Collins waved him in, and the officer cast an apologetic glance at the captain before looking at Walker.

"Your fiancé called and asked if you were still alive. It's the fifth time."

Walker groaned. "I'm sorry..."

Collins shook his head. "Go ahead. Call her. I haven't forgotten I have to talk to her about Garrett and Betty either." Collins sighed, rubbing his forehead as Walker left. "What a mess."

Farraday glanced at his own watch. "I should call Lara and Trin, see if there's any news."

***

Just as Trin approached the main door to the hospital Lara's cell phone rang.

"It's Ty," Lara said.

"Go ahead." Trin's pace didn't falter. "Room 139." She'd phoned on the drive over to find out.

Lara nodded. It was a crisp night, not yet too cold to enjoy the fresh air and the dark sky was, finally, clear. The world was sparkling white, colored leaves still clinging to the branches now weighed down with a blanket of snow.

"What happened?"

Farraday filled her in. Once he'd finished telling her about Becker's arrest he asked, "Where are you? I tried the house."

"I'm at the hospital."

"What's happened?" There was a note of panic in his voice.

"Whoa, calm down. Nothing, at least not to us, but Dan's been beaten up pretty bad."

***

Trin marched down the hall, hoping to avoid attention from anyone who'd insist she come back during visiting hours.

Once inside the room she gasped, and then drew a deep breath. Dan's face was covered in bruises. He had a split lip and a broken arm. Her gaze met his and she tried to smile reassuringly, but all she saw back was fear.

"Go," he sputtered.

Her smile faded. "Hey, I'm worried about you. Have you talked to the police yet?"

Dan tried to sit up but he fell back against the mattress. "Just get out." He tried to lift himself up again and wave his arm, but collapsed as she felt strong arms grab her from behind, pulling her back.

The first hand went over her mouth, the second pinning her left arm. She reached back with her right hand, clawing at her assailant's head, digging her nails into his flesh. He swore, releasing his hand off of her mouth as he dragged her into the hallway, smacking her arm down, partially pinning it. She started to scream and choked on her words as something fabric was stuffed in her mouth.

Trin kicked out with her legs, trying to hold on to the doorframe, anything to slow this guy down, but he yanked her out into the hall.

Her purse was still over her shoulder, dangling on her right hip, her hand pressed up against it. She undid the clasp and pulled out the contents, creating a trail down the hall, toward an emergency exit.

***

Collins hung up the phone and opened his office door. He could see Farraday, sitting at his desk, still on the phone. He walked over.

"I need you," Collins said.

Farraday ended the call and hung up.

"What now?" Farraday asked, rubbing his eyes.

"Surveillance just phoned in," Collins told him.

"Surveillance?"

"On George Vincent. You know, you phoned me earlier. The driver of the Land Rover."

"Right, sorry. Have they found the vehicle?"

"No. But something else happened. Vincent met McClure at a cabin just south of the old marina. One of the one's Garrett owned. McClure gave George Vincent a key and he took a van into the city. He dumped a body in an alley near the hospital."

"That's a little careless for him, isn't it? When did this happen?"

"About half an hour ago. They called in another patrol car so that they could stay on Vincent and the uniforms reported that the victim has been taken to the hospital. Dan-"

"Van Biers. Lara said they were on their way to see him now."

"I don't like this. Maybe I should send someone over there to watch them," Collins said slowly.

Farraday nodded. "That might not be a bad idea."

Chapter 18

Lara was walking briskly down the hall. A trail of items trickled down the corridor toward an emergency exit. She pushed the door to Dan's room open and went inside.

The dim lamplight from the bedside table was obscured, the form of a large man leaning over the bed and she could hear someone choking, fighting for air.

A trolley was sitting by the wall. Lara didn't even think, she just grabbed a metal bedpan and smashed the man on the head.

He staggered sideways, the wheezing and coughing increasing as Dan gasped for air.

"Son of a..." Dan's attacker spun around, holding his head. His steel blue eyes met hers and narrowed.

Lara felt as though her heart had turned into a jackhammer as she backed away from the approaching figure.

A nurse burst into the room. "Miss? Oh my... I'm calling security." The woman stopped when she saw the large man wearing black clothes and a matching balaclava. She started backing out into the hallway and then yelled for help.

The man hesitated. Lara pushed the trolley into him, and he groaned and then shoved it away. He rushed straight at Lara and slammed her into the wall before he ran out, knocking the screaming nurse over.

It could have been a split second or half an hour before Lara had the strength to pull herself up off the floor. All she could think about was the pain, but as soon as she managed to get to her feet she stumbled to the bed.

Dan was still coughing and gasping, but he pointed at the door and forced out the words. "They took her."

Lara sprinted out the door. "Phone the police! Get Captain Collins here right away," she yelled at the nurse and group of security officers who were running down the hall toward her. "A woman's been kidnapped."

She ran to the exit and pushed the door open. Trin's purse was lying in the snow, beside fresh tracks of a large vehicle that had already pulled away.

***

Trin had known fear before but it was the kind of fear that comes with adrenaline as you approach what you know is a dangerous situation. This was different.

After they got her outside her eyes were covered. The cloth stuck in her mouth was removed and replaced by a gag that was tied tightly around her head. Her hands and feet were bound. Trin felt her body tense as an extra cord was tethered between the ropes binding her hands and feet, keeping her body arched and rigid. Her muscles ached.

She suspected that was part of the strategy. Even if she managed to loosen her binds, her limbs hurt so much she wouldn't be able to run fast. Without sight, the swaying and bumping of the van beneath her told her they were still moving.

They had gone after Dan to get to her. That was obvious. She wondered if he was still alive. As soon as she was in the vehicle they'd pulled away, so she didn't think they had Lara.

Lara was her only real hope. If she didn't get help in time…

Trin pushed that thought out of her head and told herself not to think the worst. She needed to stay focused.

***

Lara stood outside Dan's room. He was being sedated. When she looked up she saw Collins and Farraday coming down the hall.

"Are you okay?" Collins asked. "Your head is bleeding."

"I'll live," she said as she absently lifted her hand to her head, her fingers feeling the blood.

"Where's Trin?" Farraday asked.

Her eyes were filled with unshed tears. "They went after Dan to get to her. Her purse was dumped. I told them not to touch it," Lara said, swallowing as she nodded at two officers were already cataloging the items. "They got here before you did."

Collins nodded. "I sent them to check on you and Trin."

"Why?" she asked. They'd followed her down the hall and outside, to the place where Trin's purse had been found.

"We know Vincent was responsible for dumping Van Biers in the alley, and McClure had him before that."

"How...?"

"We've had Vincent under surveillance since lunchtime," Farraday told her. "Walker's old partner is handling it."

"So McClure grabbed Dan to get to Trin. Why?" Collins asked.

"Does it matter? It's almost a certainty that he has her."

"Doesn't the surveillance know where Vincent is?" Lara asked. "Can't they just pick him up?"

"That's the thing," Collins said, shaking his head. "Vincent wasn't here. We already know that. He's at the Lakeview Motel."

"That's where Dan was," Lara said. "At least, that's the last I heard from him."

"When was that?" Collins asked.

She looked at her watch. "Hours ago." Lara blinked. "I didn't realize it had gotten so late."

"Then who was here?" Farraday asked. "Would McClure be brazen enough to do this himself?"

Lara shook her head. "Whoever it was, there were two of them. And the one I saw trying to strangle Dan was the same man who attacked me at my house."

"You're sure?" Farraday asked. She nodded.

"I'm positive. The eyes."

"Alright. Lara, you're seeing a doctor. No arguments," Collins said. "I'll call for two officers to stand guard on Dan's room. They tried to kill him after they grabbed Trin, so he might be able to identify them. They could be back."

"Maybe they'll think Trin knows something. Maybe...." Lara's voice trailed off.

While Collins went to call Walker, Lara faced Farraday alone, something she'd been dreading since she realized Trin was gone. "D-do you think I should call your parents?" she asked, almost choking on the words.

Farraday shook his head. "They're out of the country. Dad called the other day to tell me they were going away."

"I guess I understand now how you must have felt when Garrett was after me."

Farraday bit his lip and then shook his head. "I'm not sure you really can." He paused, looking at her with a solemn expression, still no anger in his words. No blame. "How did you find out about the attack on Dan?"

"I received a phone call on my cell phone, from the hospital. Why?"

There was a flash of light in Farraday's eyes and he asked her for her phone. She gave it to him. He looked like he was about to explain, but Collins returned. "Lara, Officer Barrows is going to keep an eye on you while the doctor checks you over." He gave her a firm look. "I don't want you to do anything. Just stay here, wait for us. Do you understand?"

Lara swallowed and nodded, and followed the doctor down the hall.

***

"I'm going to see if we can get enough for probable cause on McClure's place," Collins told Farraday as they walked out into the parking lot. Walker pulled up.

"We have enough reason to knock on his door, but I'd like more in case he's not answering." Collins reached for the file Walker handed him. "No fingerprints."

Walker shook his head. "Lenny did say as much. What about the cabin you said they were at earlier?"

Collins shook his head. "I sent a patrol car there already, just to see if it was in use. No vehicles, no lights, no signs of activity. McClure isn't there."

"I have an idea about how to find him," Farraday said.

He explained as he got into Walker's car.

"I'll check as soon as I get to the office," Collins said just before Farraday shut the door. He ran to his car.

***

Trin heard the doors close and the key slide into the ignition just before the van started moving again. It was funny how not being able to see had already heightened her sense of hearing, but the one thing she wanted to hear eluded her. The muffled sound of voices was too low and distorted and she couldn't make sense of what they were saying.

She'd known Jones' voice as soon as he'd come to the van, only minutes after she'd been grabbed. The other voice had seemed familiar, but it wasn't Becker and it wasn't McClure. It was like the trace of familiarity, something you know in passing but not because it was someone you paid much attention to.

It was nagging at her, but not coming into focus, which was almost as infuriating as the powerlessness that she felt. Her lower limbs tingled from the pressure of her body pushing them against the cold van floor.

***

Farraday pulled his coat over his Kevlar vest as a figure approached from his right.

"Hey," Walker said, holding up his badge and reaching for his gun. "Police."

The figure stopped short and held up his hands. "It's just me. Jimmy."

"What the hell are you doing here?" Farraday asked.

"I've been trying to track down the only living woman McClure cleared on prostitution charges, before she gets murdered and dumped like the others."

"You think he keeps them at his house?"

"No. This is her registered mailing address."

Farraday's jaw dropped. "Are you serious?"

Jimmy nodded. "Same for the other three." He introduced himself to Walker. "Whatever you're doing here, McClure isn't home."

"Damn," Farraday punched the top of Walker's car. "We have to find him."

"Where's Lara?"

"At the hospital."

"Is she...?"

Farraday held up his hand. "She's okay. Somebody kidnapped my sister and beat Dan Van Biers to a pulp. Lara got in the way."

"What else is new? What can I do?"

"Did you come up with any other leads for McClure?"

Jimmy nodded. "He owns three cottages on the lake, two of which are quite close to the old marina."

"Three?" Walker asked.

"He inherited them from Graeme Garrett."

"What the hell?"

Jimmy held up his hands. "Hey, I checked the title transfers. Two in Garrett's name, one in his mother's name. McClure took possession yesterday. He made a stealthy application to get the titles transferred. I was looking for something else in his name, not Garrett's, which is the only reason I found them. McClure already owned a cabin, so what he wants with these..." Jimmy shrugged.

"Where are they?" Farraday followed Jimmy to his car. Jimmy pulled out a map, showing the locations he'd circled.

"Right. We'll check the one closest to the marina. You check this other one. Here's my card," Farraday passed him a card quickly. "Call on my cell if you find anything. If anyone's there..."

Jimmy nodded. "I won't approach, I'll call."

"I mean it. Don't take any chances. If anyone's there, phone it in right away."

He didn't give Jimmy a chance to respond, sprinting back to the other car with Walker right behind him.

***

"Damn! That son of a bitch!" McClure slammed the phone down. He glared down at a small table and then kicked it over.

He spun on his heel, looking at Jones, who stood across from him in the hotel room. "Farraday arrested Becker."

"On what charge?" Jones said, shaking his head and holding both hands up. "I knew nothing about this."

"No, of course not. Because you had to get yourself suspended. You get paid well to be a thorn in your captain's side. What the hell good are you to me if you're not working?"

"It does give you a chance to send me after journalists and pretty girls," Jones sneered. "I put that reporter where you wanted him and I got you your skirt."

"Not exactly. I told you to put Van Biers six feet under, not in intensive care."

"Hey, you're the one who said you needed him in the hospital to draw her there. I couldn't kill him before George dumped him."

"Damn it, this is all going to hell now, isn't it? We can't just kill this one. We have to find out what she knows, how she's involved."

"What makes you think she's involved? I've never even seen her before today."

"But she just happens to be staying with Larimer Kelly? You beat the information out of Van Biers and the number he gives you for her is that damn reporter's home number? You really are all brawn and no brains, aren't you?"

"Too bad Garrett didn't finish Kelly off when he had the chance."

"No point commiserating. We're a man short on this. What about…?"

"He's too close to this. Still trying to keep his head clear. Damn Lenny."

"It's just as well. Lenny was getting squeamish. He didn't want to go through with moving Hare's body. Christ, the timing was absolute shit. One kid finds out about the HIV and suddenly starts talking. Bad enough, but with Garrett and that other reporter, Vern, snooping around... What a mess."

"I thought you were sure Lenny was solid when you started pushing on him."

"Maybe his anal partner's self-righteousness started rubbing off. It was one thing when it was turning a blind on a case or fudging a report to get somebody off. Lenny didn't have what it took to handle a body."

McClure reached into a drawer and pulled out a gun. Checking the clip to make sure it was fully loaded, he passed the gun to Arnold Jones.

"I trust you don't have that problem."

Jones shook his head.

***

Trin felt her body scraping against the van floor after she heard the door open.

There was a sense of urgency as she was yanked out. It was the first time the back door had opened since they stopped briefly, when something had been stuffed in the back.

Trin was being lifted into a sitting position by her arms, the tether between her feet and hands removed, allowing her to uncurl her legs. Her blindfold was pulled away and she turned to see the writhing form of another woman in the back of the van. The woman heaved, forcing vomit past the gag and onto the van floor.

"Shit," one man said, the man not holding Trin. "I supposed I have to clean that up."

"We aren't in a rush," the other man said. He had a distinguished bearing, like a man accustomed to business suits and dealing with matters of the mind instead of muscle. Even now, he held Trin gently but firmly.

He picked her up and carried her into the cabin and set her down on a chair before he removed her gag.

"Thank you," she said, licking her lips. She was looking around the stark room, searching for any hint of what was to come, for what she could possibly do to save herself. The only clue was a stack of videotapes on the counter.

"What did you do with the other one?" the older man demanded when the younger, muscular man came inside, tossing a pile of smelly rags into a garbage can.

"Sitting on the step. She isn't going anywhere."

"How much did you shoot into her?"

"Enough to send her into the sweet bye and bye."

Trin stifled a gasp. Karen Li. The other woman was Karen Li.

She swallowed. It was a safe bet the only reason she was alive was because they thought she knew something. If she wanted to keep breathing, she needed to figure out what that was.

***

"Thanks," Collins said, he pressed down the receiver and then released it and dialed Farraday's number.

"What do you have?" Farraday asked.

"I traced the call to Lara's cell. It came from a cabin on the lake owned by Michael McClure."

"Those cabins didn't have phones when I searched them."

"Put in yesterday. I checked."

"Damn, he's fast. I just pulled up outside one of them. Nobody here."

"It's the one that's farthest from the marina." Collins was studying a map behind his desk. "Off the old boat launch road people used before they built the public docks."

"The one that was in Garrett's mother's name, that I never searched." Farraday groaned. "We're on our way."

"Wouldn't you know it?" he said to Walker as they ran back to the car. "The last one we planned to check."

***

Jimmy saw no evidence of vehicles or footprints in the snow outside the cabin he was sent to, so he called Farraday's cell, but it was busy. He started driving to the other cabin.

He blinked as he shifted his rearview mirror. A van was tailgating him. Jimmy made the turn down the old boat launch road, certain he wouldn't be followed, but he was wrong. As he braked to go over the large pothole in front of him, the van accelerated, ramming into the back of his car.

He stopped and jumped out. "What the hell are you…?" He stopped talking when he saw the gun.

***

Trin was doing her best to relax her muscles as she waited, but she still felt stiff.

Her captors weren't in a hurry. The older one went outside to check on Karen while the other one sat in a chair drinking a pop, whistling.

"She still kicking?" he asked when the older man returned.

He nodded.

They were both wearing balaclavas and black clothing. It seemed misplaced on the older man, but the younger one seemed completely at ease.

Trin heard the whine of an engine and then silence, followed by slamming doors.

The younger man sprang to his feet. Soon, the small cabin was crowded. Trin needed no introduction to McClure or Jones, which meant the younger man who'd brought her here was probably Oslind. Jones pushed another man, hard. The man fell on the floor in front of her.

"What's she doing outside?" Jones snapped.

"She already puked all over the van. I'm not cleaning up another mess in here. Besides, Frank just checked on her. She isn't going anywhere."

"Who's this?" Frank asked, nodding at the figure on the floor.

"Jimmy Wilkes. Well, well," McClure said as he pulled open Jimmy's wallet. "Jimmy just happens to work for The Ledger."

"Likely working with Larimer," Oslind sneered. "Damn reporters." He kicked Jimmy in the stomach. Jimmy groaned, curling to shield himself too late.

Trin instinctively moved to try to help Jimmy, but didn't succeed in doing more than attracting McClure's attention. He pushed her back in the chair.

"And you. You looked better at lunch."

They'd taken her gag off, which meant she was probably in the middle of nowhere. Screaming wasn't going to help.

"I've been treated better, too."

"Oh, I'll bet you have sweetie. Katarina Collins. At first, I couldn't place the name, but you just happen to be friends with Dan Van Biers and when he decides, with a little prompting, to give me your phone number, I run it through the reverse directory. Larimer Kelly's phone number. Thought it was best to call her cell with the sad news about Dan, though." He winked. "I've got a friend who had the number and I didn't want to miss you if you were out."

McClure had swung the other chair around backward, straddling it and leaning his arm against the back of the chair, studying her carefully. "I'm going to give you a chance to tell me what you're doing here."

"You know who I am. As for what I'm doing here, since I don't even know where here is, I can't say. Maybe you could tell me."

McClure stared at her silently, ignoring the snickers from the men behind him. "Wrong answer."

Jones pulled out a gun. He pointed it at Jimmy and shot him in the lower leg. Jimmy screamed, his blood spattering against Trin and the floor.

"Now perhaps you would like to try again, before Detective Jones or Detective Oslind here decide they need more target practice."

"You might not believe me," Trin said.

"Try me." McClure sneered at her, watching her face intently.

"I was working in New Haven for the Mayor's office, but I left. I was having some family problems and I wanted a career change."

"How do you know Larimer Kelly?"

Trin winced. Jimmy was writhing on the floor in pain, blood oozing from his leg.

"My brother knows her." Trin looked at Jimmy. She could see the connection register in his eyes. He tried to shake his head but she looked away.

"Your brother?" McClure stroked his chin for a moment. "You see, Katarina Collins was a name I could look up. You wrote a story that involved Farraday, and suddenly he's getting transferred here. To work with Captain Collins." He stared at her, a cold smile spreading across his face. "Once we had a few pieces it wasn't hard to connect the dots. So Farraday's screwing a reporter."

"I guess now you know how the Lakeview story got leaked," Oslind said, nodding at Jones.

There was a groan from Jimmy as he pushed himself up and vaulted himself head first into Oslind. Oslind kicked his injured leg, sending him back to the floor screaming at the top of his lungs.

"Shut up, or I'll shut you up," Oslind sneered. Jimmy turned his face to the floor, which muffled the sound of his screams.

Jones stared at Trin, then crossed the room and grabbed her chin, twisting her jaw as she tried to pull back, but he also kept moving his face closer. "Did you really think your brother and your uncle and some little reporter were going to get in our way? I'd almost like to keep you around so you can see for yourself how we're going to handle your uncle and your brother."

"We'll deal with Farraday and Collins later. Right now, we have things to take care of." McClure stood up, nodding at Frank.

"Make yourself scarce, Frank. I know you can't stomach this."

Trin heard the door open, heavy footsteps moving further away and then the door closed.

"Shame. I don't really think she's of any use to us," McClure said as he grabbed Trin. He nodded at Jones. "Get the other one."

Oslind pulled Jimmy up. McClure opened the patio door and started pulling Trin down the trail to the water.

***

"It's Jimmy's car," Farraday said as Walker slowed down. "Just keep driving. It's empty."

"Damn these old roads," Walker said as they bumped along.

"Fresh tracks in the snow. Collins is sending backup," Farraday said. He was tapping his knee incessantly.

His cell rang and he pulled it open.

"We just passed a blue Ford with the keys in it and the door wide open," Collins said.

"That's Jimmy's car."

"Jimmy? The one that works with Lara?"

"The same."

It wasn't long until they saw the cabin through the trees. Two vans were parked outside a cabin and a man stood next to the closest one.

Walker slowed down. Farraday jumped out, cutting through the woods and surveying the perimeter. At first he didn't see anyone, until he circled around the van. As he heard Walker pull into the driveway and stop the man he was approaching stiffened and turned.

"Police. Put your hands up and turn around slowly," Farraday said. The man did what he was told.

"Well, well. Principal Vincent. You're a long way from school," Walker said shaking his head, as he approached from the other side.

"Where are they?" Farraday demanded.

"I have the right to remain silent," Vincent said as Farraday finished frisking him. He shook his head at Walker. "He's clean."

Farraday pulled out a set of cuffs and clamped one around Vincent's left hand. The sound of a gunshot exploded in the pre-dawn quiet. Farraday pulled the cuff through the handle on the van door and clamped it securely on Vincent's other hand. He raced down the path after Walker.

***

There was a trail of blood in the snow and a body was already in the water. Walker could see Oslind and Jones. McClure was standing to one side, holding a woman. Jimmy was kneeling on the ground by the water.

There was no time to wait. Jones lifted the gun and pointed it at Jimmy, who was having trouble standing straight, what looked like blood gushing from his leg.

"Stop! Police!" Walker raised his gun but the man didn't even flinch. Walker could see the finger starting to squeeze the trigger, and he fired.

Jones fell into the water. Oslind turned, obscuring Walker's view of Jimmy. He couldn't tell if he'd been quick enough.

"Put it down, Oslind." Walker stepped toward him slowly.

"No way in hell I'm going down," Oslind said as his fingers grasped the cold metal of his revolver, raising it.

Walker didn't flinch. He fired again. When Oslind fell he focused on Mike McClure, who turned, revealing the gun he had pointed at the woman he was still holding.

"You're already in this over your head. You don't want to make it any worse," Walker said. "We have Vincent."

McClure laughed, a long, slow, steady, heartless laugh. "You've got nothing. Not even the tip of the iceberg."

"Becker's in jail. Douglas is facing charges. You were sloppy, overconfident."

"And you're delusional. You haven't got enough to make the charges stick on Douglas. Becker won't talk. Like I said, you've got nothing."

"You should be thinking about what you've got, about what you're willing to lose. Are you going to end up in the water with your partners or are you walking away from this?"

McClure actually seemed to consider that, but then a dark shadow settled in his eyes. "You and I both know I'm not walking away."

"You can walk right out of here. Not literally. But you know every trick in the book. Jones could have blackmailed you. He was a snake. I could believe it. A lawyer bound by client confidentiality, then one day he hears or sees something he shouldn't have. Not because he wanted to, but because his clients tricked him. Suddenly, he's complicit. He's got to shield them, or they'll bring him down with them."

"You know Walker," McClure sneered, "I've heard all about you. You know this won't end. There are bigger fish in the pond than me. You take me in and I'm done."

"So what? You're going to let them win without a fight?"

"You think I want to live waiting for it to happen? With a shiv in the gut in jail or the way it was for Garrett?"

"Why don't you tell me about Garrett? And Vern? It might feel good to get it off your chest."

McClure laughed. "Nice try. What, Walker? You don't get it? You got anyone you care about that they could still hurt? It isn't just about me." He pushed Trin down and raised his gun. She lunged to one side just as the shots rang out.

A bullet imploded on the center of McClure's head as the water turned red.

***

"You can't go in..."

Lara heard one of the officers arguing with someone. After she'd seen the doctor she'd come to Dan's room to check on him. He was still asleep.

An officer knocked on the door, pushing it open, telling Lara to come with her. Reports were coming in. Three dead, three injured. Lara followed, dazed, not even wanting to think about what had happened, about the possibility that Farraday or Trin had been wounded.

Or worse.

At last they heard the sound of sirens, faint at first, drawing closer and then lingering outside the door, every second feeling like an eternity. Finally, the door burst open.

The grim, grey face of Detective Jones went whizzing by, a team of nurses and doctors already descending on him and two uniformed officers following closely behind. The door swung shut for a second, and then flew open again as another stretcher was brought through.

Detective Oslind. Lara swallowed.

The last stretcher came in, this one shrouded by Farraday, Walker and Collins. Trin wasn't conscious.

"Is she...? Are they...?" Lara stopped. "What happened?"

Walker stopped to fill them in.

They'd heard gunfire from the beach. Farraday had circled around but wasn't in position before McClure had shoved Trin into the water and raised his gun, forcing Walker to shoot.

But McClure hadn't gone down before he'd squeezed the trigger, hitting Trin with the bullet.

"McClure and Karen Li didn't make it," Collins said as he slumped against the wall. Lara tried to process that. What had they said? Three injured. Jones, Oslind, Trin.

Three dead. McClure, Karen. Who else?

The question must have been in her eyes, because when Farraday looked at Lara, he reached for her hand. "I'm sorry."

"You're sorry? Why?"

"Jimmy got there before we did."

CHAPTER 19

Hours later, Farraday, Walker and Collins went to the station to tie up some loose ends while Lara went to The Ledger. When Lara finally got home, Farraday was in the living room.

He was sitting on the couch, in the dark, no fire in the fireplace. Just staring vacuously at the wall with no glance or indication that he'd even heard her come in. The look on his face was harsher, angrier than she'd ever seen and one thing flashed through her mind.

Her hand went to her stomach. She felt like she'd been punched in the gut, the wind knocked out of her.

That's when his eyes turned and she saw the hard angles melt.

"She's going to be fine. Dan too."

"And you?"

His eyes widened and then he shrugged. "What about you, Lara? Are you okay?"

She choked back the sob rising in her throat and nodded as she sank down on the chair. After a minute she managed to speak. "I shouldn't have asked Jimmy to get involved."

"And I shouldn't have let him go out there."

They lapsed into silence, neither one ready to process their guilt just yet. It was too fresh.

***

Farraday sank down in the chair behind his desk after a late lunch. He began checking messages, finding nothing important except for a curious note to call Deb Halliston.

He dialed the number, hearing her warm voice answer.

"Mrs. Halliston? This is Detective Tymen Farraday. I just got your message."

"Oh, yes, of course. Well, you said to call if I thought of anything at all," she explained.

"Did you remember something else about Mr. Garrett?"

"Well, not exactly. Just that night, you know, the men in the truck. I saw one of them in the paper. Now let me see..." Farraday could hear the pages flipping as she looked for the picture.

"Michael McClure?" he asked, knowing there was a write-up on what had happened on the front page.

"No, inside the paper. Yes, that's the fellow. Ted Hatcher. The newspaper man."

"Are you sure? You said you didn't see him very well."

"Yes, yes, I'm sure. I saw the other man better, but this man, he was here again, on the weekend. Different vehicle, but he moved the same. He's very tall and broad-shouldered and when I saw him in the paper, I had a name. I'd seen him before, I just couldn't place it. It's him."

He thanked her, hung up and went to Collins' office.

"It's quiet," Farraday said. "It's going to take a while to get used to this."

The three detectives' desks closest to his own were now vacant, with Jones and Oslind in the hospital and Becker under arrest.

Walker was taking time off. Collins had talked to Megan, told her everything they'd learned. At this point, they didn't know what might come out in a court case, or in the press, but he felt she deserved to know. A different person might have been angry, might have even been consumed by rage and resentment, but she seemed to be handling it okay. Megan was still seeing a counselor, with Walker, and she refused to see her father. The only thing she wanted to know about was whether they'd found Susan's baby.

"I could talk to him, you know. Make him tell me where the child was buried."

Collins had been startled when Megan had said that, in a rather calm, detached manner, but there was a resolve to her. It seemed to Collins that it was her way of making amends to her sister, for the first child, for all the things she hadn't known about or hadn't been willing or able to see over the years.

Megan was strong now, but Collins suspected she'd be struggling with the blame for a long time to come.

With Walker on leave, Farraday would be working on his own, wrapping up the last few details of the cases.

"What do you have scheduled for the rest of the day?"

Farraday sighed. "I'm waiting for a warrant to search the last cabin, the one Jimmy went to first. It's the only one we haven't checked out yet, but something just came up, something that should expedite another warrant. Deb Halliston just identified the other man in the vehicle from the night Garrett died."

"McClure?"

Farraday shook his head. "Try Ted Hatcher."

"Hatcher? Why would-"

"Why would he try to discredit you every time he got a chance? Why would he try to stop Lara from pursuing the angle on the drug story? Why would he be so willing to push Dan's articles on the prostitutes off the front page? How did he know I was working with her before I ever set eyes on him?"

Collins' eyes narrowed. "You know, I was reviewing statements. Garrett told Lara he only went into her house the one time. So who broke in the first time?"

Farraday stood up. "I'm going to get a warrant for his office."

***

Jimmy's absence brought home the reality of his death. Lara's throat constricted every time she walked past his door, pausing instinctively to go in, then remembering that he was gone.

She'd already intercepted Kaitlin Parks on her way to school.

"I have to go," Kaitlin had said as soon as she saw Lara.

"Kaitlin, you can't poke a hornets nest without getting stung."

"What do you know about my life? Nothing. But you went to my Dad and you went to the police."

"You asked me to look for your friend. I never agreed to a list of conditions when I said I'd help you."

Kaitlin had turned to walk away, and Lara had grabbed her arm. "I know Kaitlin. I know about the porn, I know about the HIV. You're involved with some dangerous people. You need to think about whether you want to end up like Allan."

"Or what? Grow up, get married and play Mom? Get real." Kaitlin had scoffed at her. She'd wrenched her arm free and walked away.

Once Lara was in the office she had trouble settling in, trying to remember what she did when she actually worked there. She finally polished a few feature articles she'd left languishing during the craziness of the previous few weeks, and filled enough time to call it a day. All she could think about was getting home, getting away from the reminders that Jimmy was gone forever, and catching up with Farraday.

"Just the person I'm looking for," a voice said. She looked up to see Ted Hatcher waiting as she approached her jeep, which was on the far side of the back parking lot, embraced by trees. "You should have quit while you were ahead."

She wasn't sure what he meant by that, but decided to play it safe. "I didn't hear you complaining about the coverage on Susan's death."

"You were supposed to play that into a corruption piece."

"At the expense of the truth?"

"Truth is relative. Like the truth about Susan's first baby, or the first time someone broke into your home, stole a file..."

Lara swallowed and shook her head. "So you were trying to scare me. But what does that have to do with Susan's first child?"

Hatcher leered at her. "There are some questions you'll never have answers for."

"Like what made Garrett so sick."

"Garrett was gullible. He had a weakness for Susan, going back years. You know he actually thought he might clean up, marry her and have a happy little family? Of course, David didn't know how to tell him that could never happen, so he told Garrett Susan was going to take the baby and leave." He shrugged. "David underestimated Graeme."

"And I underestimated you."

Hatcher smiled. "Shall we?"

"I think I'll stay here."

"You didn't think I could just let this go."

"You don't have the guts."

"Then you didn't figure it out?"

"Oh, I knew you were involved. The stolen file, the evidence tampering, the first time someone broke into my house, the fact that somebody gave McClure my cell phone number. You knew things, things Jimmy wouldn't have told you. You knew I was working with a police officer and you weren't surprised when I was assaulted. And you've had a long feud with the captain of the 14th Precinct, a precinct filled with dirty cops and a history of corruption. But it was the captain you had a problem with. A captain who was clean."

"You've got it all worked out."

She shook her head. "Not all of it. I don't know why."

"Why? That should be easy enough. Money."

"Money?"

Hatcher shrugged. "You were expecting something noble, like family loyalty or an obsession with a woman? That was Garrett's territory, not mine. Morrow tried to get Garrett to take a job in another town. David Douglas never wanted Garrett involved. Thought he was a liability."

"I'm surprised he didn't know she was his half sister."

A shadow crossed Hatcher's face. "I didn't. I don't know about him."

"Still leaves a lot of unanswered questions, like what really happened to Angela Douglas and Cynthia Garrett. Who killed Susan's first baby. If Garrett wanted this child so badly, why did he kill it?"

Hatcher shrugged. "Life's a bitch. Let's go."

She stared at him, unmoving. "You can't really think you'll get away with this? There are actually real cops working at the police station now. Ones Douglas doesn't have on his payroll."

"You know, for a while you kept Jimmy out of things. When I heard he'd gone out looking for Karen Li, that's when I knew he must have been more involved than I realized. Wasn't hard to crack the password for your computer. You always were smart, backing yourself up by making sure someone else had all your evidence copied and storied. Thing was," he grabbed her arm, "you didn't have any evidence on me. Not even a hint of suspicion. With Douglas out of jail and Morrow still walking the streets, there isn't even a reason for someone to suspect me. Don't cause any trouble."

Lara dug her heels into the ground, pulling back hard. He let go of her arm long enough and swung his hand back, like he was about to slap her, just as a door opened behind her and hurried footsteps crunched over the ground, getting louder.

"Let her go."

She turned to see Farraday briskly walking across the parking lot, Collins right behind him.

"It's over, Hatcher," Collins said.

Hatcher's face turned a purplish-red as he swore. Collins stepped forward to cuff him, reading him his rights.

Once Collins had taken Hatcher away she looked at Farraday. "I don't think I've ever seen your uncle look so happy."

"He's been waiting for this day for a long time."

Lara rubbed her arm, feeling the skin begin to bruise already from the force of Hatcher's hold. "How did you know?"

"A tip that was enough to get a search warrant for his office. I'm going out to the other cabin Garrett owned, the one Jimmy went to. It's the only one that still hasn't been checked." Farraday handed her a folder. "We found this in Hatcher's office.

Lara's mind drifted while he talked on the phone, checking on the status of the warrant he needed. She looked through the documents that Vern had wanted her to have, documents that might have helped them save Karen Li's life. Photos, of Graeme Garrett talking to the mayor and David Douglas. Data about girls taken from one of the factories, four of whom he was eventually able to confirm had taken jobs with the mayor, although nobody would say what the jobs were and the women had since disappeared. She was aware of the murmur of Farraday's voice but not the substance of his words.

Jimmy, Vern, Susan, Allan...

The four women who'd been recruited from the factory, forced into porn and then prostitution.

Kaitlin Parks, older than her years.

"I have to go to the station to get the warrant," Farraday said, touching her arm to get her attention. "Want to tag along?"

***

"We have a problem," Collins said, looking Farraday right in the eye. "Lenny Becker has an airtight alibi for each murder."

"That's not surprising," Farraday said, sinking into a chair.

"Oslind's heart gave out."

Farraday sighed. This might be the end of the trail, for now. "Is Lenny talking?"

"He wants to talk to you. He's waiting."

Farraday went straight to the interrogation room, aware that Collins was behind him.

"I'm not even interesting enough to keep you around the station," Lenny muttered when he saw Farraday. "What gives?"

"You haven't heard?" Farraday asked.

"That I have a solid alibi for all the charges against me? Yes."

"Then what do you want to talk to me for? You can be released."

Lenny shook his head, his face grim. Stubble shadowed his jaw. There were bags under his lifeless eyes and his skin was pale.

"You can't release me. Don't you get it? McClure would rather die than take his chances in court? Look what happened to Graeme Garrett." He shook his head. "And I bet you think *I'm* stupid."

"Then tell me who you're scared of. We can protect you." Farraday sat down across from Becker. "There must be some way I can help you."

Becker laughed. It was a slow, riveting laugh without heart or feeling. "You can't. There's nothing you can do except keep me in jail."

"McClure and Jones are dead," Farraday said. "Oslind is dead too. Hatcher's been arrested. They can't touch you."

Lenny Becker drew a slow breath and his eyes crinkled sadly as he looked at Farraday. "You have a nice start. But you aren't done yet."

"Then tell me who else is involved."

Becker shook his head firmly. "I can't."

"David Douglas is facing charges."

"And he's got a hell of a story to peddle. You don't actually think you'll win?"

Farraday stood up. "Then you know there's nothing more I can do. The captain will release you."

"Not if I do this," Becker said. He sprung to his feet and hit Farraday squarely on the jaw.

The door flew open behind them.

Farraday felt blood trickle inside his mouth.

"I just assaulted a police officer. You have to arrest me."

"It's not enough to hold you here indefinitely, Becker," Collins said.

"It is if I refuse legal counsel. I fired the other lawyer."

Collins shook his head and ordered another officer to take Becker away and book him on new charges.

***

"What happened?" Lara asked when Farraday finally emerged from Collins' office, an ice pack pressed against his jaw.

Farraday tried to smile and winced. "Isn't this what they call a face lift?"

Lara shook her head, suppressing a smile. "More like a knuckle sandwich. Who hit you?"

"Lenny really didn't want to be released."

"The food's that good?"

"More like the fear's that strong."

She felt her mouth twist, losing the battle against her amusement. "At least the bruises are on your face this time."

He made a face at her, feigning irritation. "We have the warrant."

It wasn't long before they followed the windy, familiar road past the turn-off to the old marina, and stopped outside a small cabin. They could see lights on inside.

Lara frowned. "Did he rent this out?"

Farraday shrugged. "Jimmy was the first one who told us about these cabins." His voice trailed off when he saw the look on her face. His own relief that his sister would be okay had overshadowed his ability to understand how it must feel for Lara, to lose a close colleague.

"You okay?" he asked her.

She nodded and followed him to the front door, standing back while he knocked. From where she stood on the deck she could see the veiled window, covered with thick, dark curtains on the inside. Outside, the windows were covered by thick metal bars. They could hear movement from inside but nobody came to open the door. Farraday knocked again.

A face came to the window, peering out from the far corner of the drapes.

Lara gasped. "It's her."

"Who?" Farraday turned.

"Choy Kim. The woman from Vern's files."

The woman was banging on the window pulling at the latch uselessly. Farraday glanced at Lara quizzically. "What do you think she wants?"

"Out," Lara said with conviction. "She's locked in."

***

Lara felt the warmth of his touch as Mr. Chan clasped her hand. "Thank you," he said, tears streaming down his face. He smiled and went to the ambulance, getting in the back, where a paramedic was wrapping a blanket around his niece. The last thing Lara saw before the door shut was Choy leaning against her uncle as he hugged her.

Her body shuddered. She hadn't realized she was so cold. Opening the cabin door had taken longer than they expected, and it hadn't been easy to calm Choy Kim down. She'd been a prisoner in this cabin for weeks.

Farraday smiled, despite the dark lines under his eyes. "We started out looking for a woman who appeared to have committed suicide. I don't even want to think about what would have happened if I'd given up on this week one."

"David Douglas and Graeme Garrett would have been a lot happier."

"Nice to see you still have a sense of humor."

"It's too bad the lights weren't on when Jimmy..." she swallowed. "Too bad it was the middle of the night."

Farraday nodded but didn't say anything.

"What's going to happen to her?" she asked as she looked down at the tiny bundle in her arms.

Choy Kim had been scared, but diligent. Garrett had provided everything she needed to sterilize the bottles, an ample supply of formula, microwave.

Just nothing she could use to break out of the cabin with. Not a cabin with bars on the windows and multiple deadlocks on all the doors. With Garrett dead, if they hadn't come to search the property... Lara shivered at the thought.

Farraday shook his head as he reached for the baby, gently rocking her for a moment as he smiled. "I already called Megan. She's going to meet them at the hospital."

He passed Susan's child to the paramedic that was waiting. Once that ambulance pulled away Farraday and Lara started walking back to his car. He put his hand on her arm to stop her.

"We need to talk," he said.

"I know. You need to take my statement."

"That's not what I mean."

She sighed and smiled, looking up into his eyes. "I never imagined this would end here."

"This?"

"The case."

For a moment they stood looking at each other, the hum of activity around them enough to remind her that they weren't alone and she had no intention of making this easy for him.

"So what happens now?" he asked her.

"Maybe I should start charging you rent."

He wrapped his arms around her and smiled. "Maybe you should."

ACKNOWLEDGEMENTS

Between the lines are the influence, advice, encouragement and support of many, without whom this book wouldn't be in your hands. I would like to thank:

Brett Battles, JT Ellison, Jason Pinter, Robert Gregory Browne, Bill Cameron, Toni McGee Causey, Sean Chercover, Patry Francis, Philip Hawley JR, Marc Lecard, CJ Lyons, Derek Nikitas, Gregg Olsen, Marcus Sakey and David White, all of whom have made being part of Killer Year a wonderful experience.

All who have helped make Spinetingler what it is: K. Robert Einarson, Marsha Garelick, Kate Charlton, Tracy Sharp, Chris High, Martin Edwards, Wayne Cunningham, Andrea Maloney, M.G. Tarquini, Angela Johnson-Schmidt... I am in your debt.

Mr. Denomy. I feel certain every writer has the English teacher who made a difference to them along the way, and for me it was Mr. Denomy. He was the first to tell me everything I did wasn't wonderful, which was a hard thing to take, but he made me work for what I could achieve. He made me a better writer.

Deric Ruttan, who taught me not to quit.

James Oswald, who is still kicking my backside, but in the nicest possible way.

The critics: Patricia Abbott, Steve Allan, Stephen Blackmoore, Daniel Hatadi, Russel D. McLean, Christa M. Miller, John Stickney, Steven Torres, Tribe.

All who've become part of my virtual life: Patrick Shawn Bagley, E. Ann Bardawill, Bill Blume, Jan Burke, Bonnie Calhoun, Sela Carsen, Lisa Chase, Eileen Cook, Crabby Cows, DesLily, Barry Eisler, Jason Evans, Flood, Forrest, Lynne Fraser, Gabriele, James Goodman, John Gooley, Vincent Holland-Keen, Lisa Hunter, Erik Ivan James, JA Konrath, Dana Y.T. Lin, Jayne Massey, Norby, Amra Pajalic, Graham Powell, The Rentable Writer, JD Rhoades, Linda L. Richards, Stephen D. Rogers, Jack Ruttan, Tanginika Simone, Miss Snark & Killer Yapp, Duane Swierczynski, Tania of I Love A Good Mystery, David Terrenoire, Rob Tiffey, SW Vaughn,

Mai Wen… I am certain I have missed someone and will feel horrid for it, but hope you'll forgive me and remind me to put you in the next book.

Those who found merit - The Cynic, Demolition, Crimespree, Opening Pages.

Cornelia Read. JB Thompson. Anne Frasier. Julia Buckley. Mark Billingham. Simon Kernick. Steve Mosby. John Rickards, Allan Guthrie. For reasons you either know, or can guess at.

To those who were there before: Alison and Steve Pakulak, Milt and Becky Schmidt, Chuck and Mona Pinches, Deletta Dodds, Patti Phipps, Kerry Irion, Hans and Martha Muntz.

Boy Kim. A million things I could say, but I'll have to settle for thanks. The rest isn't printable.

Marsha (again) who had faith in the early days and kept my head on straight.

Waldo Scmidtlap for faith, and Kat Campbell for being persuaded and walking me through this.

Norma Einarson and Robert Einarson.

Charlie, Jacinthe, Christina and Melissa, of the Lessard, Greaves and Lessard-Greaves clan.

Martin, Darlene, Arriel, Athaniel and Dashiell Edwards.

And Stuart MacBride. There aren't words to thank you enough for the footprints on my backside.

About the Author

Raised in Gravenhurst, Ontario, **Sandra Ruttan** had her first newspaper column at the age of thirteen. She studied journalism at Loyalist College and later did studies in communication theory before focusing on special education. Sandra spent several years working with children with learning disabilities while completing a creative writing diploma and she has also worked as a photographer, a receptionist and website designer.

Sandra is co-founder and submissions director for Spinetingler Magazine. In 2007 she has a story scheduled to appear in *Out of the Gutter*, an anthology of extreme crime fiction. To date, her short fiction has appeared in Crimespree Magazine, Demolition, The Cynic, Spinetingler and Flashing in the Gutters.

Sandra has traveled to 25 countries spread across four continents. She lives in western Canada with her husband, two dogs and too many cats. Sandra has a personal blog, and also participates with an industry blog reporting primarily on small press news at www.inforquestioning.com.

Her website is www.sandraruttan.com.

Printed in the United States
97026LV00005B/8/A

9 780977 768899